LATENT HAZARD - *on the edge*

LATENT HAZARD - *on the edge* is a revised version of Piers Venmore-Rowland's debut novel **Latent Hazard**. The author is most grateful to all those who gave him helpful feedback and encouraged him to write this amended version, in which those parts of the original book relating to matters financial have been simplified and shortened.

LATENT HAZARD - *on the edge* retains the compelling plot of conspiracy, suspense and political intrigue.

About the Author

Piers Venmore-Rowland grew up in Hertfordshire. He read Estate Management and Contemporary European Studies at Reading University, and Finance at City University Business School. He worked in London, first as a chartered surveyor and then as an investment analyst. He spent fifteen years at City University, London, where he was a professor and a member of City University Senate. He was also a visiting professor at the Faculty of Art, Design & Architecture, Kingston University, London. Piers is now a full-time writer, is married, with three daughters, and lives in Suffolk, England.

GW00725473

Praise for LATENT HAZARD

City types fleeing their own woes by perusing even bigger ones will love new financial-market thriller Latent Hazard. *Mail on Sunday*

This spooks-meets-financial-markets story comes with a dash of real estate. Our verdict:- Unmissable. *Estates Gazette*

Across the globe, governments wrestle with unparalleled financial collapse. Meanwhile, the terror threat is ever present. Sound familiar? These are the foothills of a novel by Piers Venmore-Rowland. Two years in the writing, the former City man would appear to be as much soothsayer as author... Piers has put to good use the knowledge gleaned from keeping a weather eye on the financial sector from his various perches down the years. *The Sentinel*

Latent Hazard is set against the background of a banking crisis and market turmoil. Venmore-Rowland uses his knowledge of the City to weave a tale of "conspiracy, suspense and political intrigue". *Express*

A terrifying world where terrorism and the credit crunch come together... It is a thinking person's thriller. The book is packed full of action and suspense, but it also gives you something to think about and has a plot that keeps you guessing. *Mercury*

An extremely modern and topical thriller made all the more interesting by the current ongoing economic crisis... Fast paced, informative and action packed. *Assistant Manager, Waterstone's, Newton Abbot*

Scarily convincing! This book is a mesmerising read! An innocent man is whisked from a brutal MI5 interrogation into the heart of the biggest terrorist conspiracy to hit the Western world... the sheer detail, breakneck pace and terrifying accuracy of the story make this book an absolute must-read for all! If any politicians read this, please take this thankfully fictional story to heart and make sure it never happens here. *The Fiction Guru - Amazon Customer Review*

PIERS VENMORE-ROWLAND

To Robyn
With fondest love
Daddy
xxxxx

LATENT HAZARD

- on the edge

Galleons Green

This paperback edition published in 2010 by Galleons Green.

1

English (UK) Edition

Galleons Green Ltd

PO Box 278, Woodbridge,

Suffolk, England IP12 9BS

www.galleonsgreen.com

A CIP catalogue record for this book is available from the British Library.

ISBN-13 978-1-906960-16-2

Typeset in Bembo Book by Belinger Blue Ltd.

Cover David Freeland Design. Image © BigStockPhoto

Printed and bound in England by CPI Antony Rowe

Dedication

To the memory of my father, Owain Venmore-Rowland.
His love, encouragement and all the happy times
he bestowed upon me will long be
remembered and cherished.

Acknowledgements

I would like to thank Lorna for all her help, attention to detail, and assistance with the changes.

My love and thanks go to my family: Lorna, Nina, Robyn and Sasha for their understanding, patience and ability to laugh; to my mother who has unfalteringly continued to be there for her children and grandchildren, and to Mark and Henry for their input.

My thanks also go to Tom, Bruce, Alex and Stewart for their help and suggestions relating to the revisions.

Chapter 1

The splintering crash of the front door hitting the floor woke Rafi Khan with a jolt. Terrified, he sat bolt upright, but was too slow; before he could get out of bed, a harsh voice barked, 'Don't move, or we shoot.' There was no escaping the bright red dots dancing on his chest.

'Move your hands to where we can see them.' Rafi slowly lifted up his arms, but at that second the wind was knocked out of him. Under the weight of his assailant, he fought for breath. His hands were pulled behind his back in a vice-like grip, and in a matter of seconds he was expertly trussed up, blindfolded, gagged, dragged off the bed with a bump and left lying on the floor.

'Suspect apprehended and in our custody. Flat secure. You can come up,' the same stern voice called out.

Rafi was bewildered and scared of what might happen next. He couldn't move and the blindfold across his eyes was painfully tight. It took a full minute for his mind to catch up with everything that had just happened.

'He didn't give any trouble,' said the curt voice. 'His front door was a piece of cake; when will people learn?'

'Thank you, sergeant,' said the man in charge. 'What have we got here? Cases packed; ready to leave. It's lucky we got here when we did.'

The tone of his voice changed. 'Rafi Khan, I'm arresting you under the powers conferred under section 41 of the Terrorism Act. You will be held in detention and informed of the charges against you within the prescribed period.'

The man paused. Rafi sensed he was standing very close to him. 'Put those guns away and take him down to the van, then search this flat from top to bottom. Let's see what's hidden here.'

'Yes, sir.'

A pair of strong hands grabbed Rafi and, forcefully dragged him across the floor, like a sack of potatoes.

What the hell was happening? Everything had taken place so fast. Three flights of stairs later, Rafi felt like damaged goods. He was manhandled out of the building into the cold February air, where, from his blindfolded world, he could hear the sound of an idling diesel engine.

The man pulling him shouted, 'Help me lift him into the back.'

Rafi landed with a thud onto the metal floor. His expletives were muffled by the gag and came out as little more than irate grunts. The tape across his mouth held firm. He was dragged on to the side bench. The doors slammed shut. A bang on the side of the van signalled it was time to go and it lurched forward. In his dark world he heard the police sirens blaring. The van was travelling fast through the deserted streets of London. And then, just as he was becoming accustomed to his environment, it came to a sudden halt.

Rafi was untied and hauled out. Fresh air washed across his face. He was now sandwiched between two men.

'Start walking.'

Rafi moved forward. His shin bumped into a solid object. Sharp pain shot up his leg. He stopped.

'Oi! Keep moving!' bellowed one of the men next to him. 'Keep moving!' he repeated.

Rafi tried to proceed in a straight line, but his sense of balance had deserted him. He staggered along in an ungainly manner.

'Stop! Stand still!' came the stern order.

To the best of his ability Rafi tried to obey. There was no warning of the ripping sound that came next. Pain seared across his eyes as the sticky tape removed chunks of his eyebrows and eyelashes. He'd hardly drawn breath when the gag was ripped from his mouth. 'That hurt!' he yelped.

Rafi screwed up his eyes in the bright fluorescent light. Either side of him were two muscular policemen in full protective clothing.

In front of him, behind a tall wooden desk, was the duty officer, a pen in his hand. 'Name?' he inquired in a no-nonsense manner.

'Rafi Khan.'

A series of quick-fire questions followed. 'Address…? Date of birth…? Nationality…? Personal effects: pyjamas, watch… Yes, sign for them 'ere… Stand 'ere. Height: 175 centimetres.' The duty sergeant read off the measure on the wall. 'Turn to face me.' The flash of the camera surprised Rafi. 'Turn sideways.' Another flash. 'Hands out.'

In a whisk he was fingerprinted. The whole process was like a moving along a production line.

'Come over 'ere! Remove your pyjamas! Bend over!' Unceremoniously, Rafi was strip-searched. His dark-skinned legs showed a selection of new purple bruises. The one on his left shin looked particularly spectacular.

'Been clumsy, 'ave we?' enquired the duty sergeant. No reply was sought. 'Get dressed in these.'

Rafi awkwardly put on the drab clothing. It swamped his slight frame.

'Take 'im away.'

He was led to a claustrophobic and dingy basement cell. Its desolate overhead light shone starkly. The door closed behind him with a heavy thud.

Rafi hardly had time to take in his surroundings before the metal door swung open.

'Follow me,' said a guard. 'Don't get any ideas! This way!'

Rafi was led down a bare corridor to an interrogation room; like everything else in the police station, the room was devoid of character, bleak and utilitarian.

Two interrogators sat on the other side of a narrow desk in a steely silence. Their manner made him uncomfortable: one smirked, the other scowled.

The guard pointed to the chair opposite them. Rafi looked carefully at the two men, his stomach knotted with apprehension. They looked truly intimidating and as hard as nails.

'Sit down!' ordered the dark haired man. Rafi recognised his cockney accent. It was a sound he had grown up with.

The blond haired man turned on the recording device and stared at Rafi with his steely blue eyes. 'We have a number of questions to which we would like truthful answers.' His voice was business-like and lacked any emotion.

'Who are you?' enquired Rafi cautiously.

The dark haired man frowned. 'Cheeky little sod isn't he?' his penetrating eyes stared at Rafi. 'I'm Mike and he's Andy. And for now, that's more than enough information.'

Andy studied Rafi carefully. His craggy face was framed by slightly over-length wavy hair. 'Let's get started.'

'Aren't I entitled to a solicitor?' asked Rafi.

'Sod it! No!' said Mike firmly. He looked like a jackal sizing up his prey. 'You are a terrorist suspect. You don't even get a telephone call and no one gets to see you.'

'Me a terrorist suspect? How the hell... no way! How have I broken the law?' asked a bewildered Rafi. 'I've done nothing wrong... And what about my human rights?'

'The rules are different. You have absolutely no rights. No calls, no visits, nothing,' replied Andy.

'Surely I should at least be told why I have been locked up?'

Mike leant forward. 'No! You'll get nothing from us.' In contrast to his colleague, he had black crew cut hair and a scar running across his left temple into his hairline.

'The law makes it very clear. Terrorist suspects can be detained without charge,' said Andy, 'For rather a long while, as it happens. So don't get your hopes up. You're going to be cooped up here for weeks or until such time as you tell us what we want to know!'

'Mr Khan,' said Mike, with menace. 'You can either help us and make this painless - or you can be difficult, which would be very unwise,' his scowl deepened. 'Being uncooperative isn't your best option. We have evidence that puts you in the middle of a major terrorist conspiracy.'

Rafi couldn't believe his ears. He opened his mouth to say, 'You what?' but nothing came out.

Their questions rained down and became increasingly intrusive. Rafi tried to answer Andy and Mike as they interrogated him on his religion, contacts, reading habits and favourite websites, but they were seemingly dismissive of all of his answers. Their fierce questioning was frightening him.

'I'm a law-abiding British citizen. I'm innocent! Tell me what you think I have done and I will prove my innocence,' said Rafi in desperation.

'That's not the way it works. Sod off back to your cell and think about the dangers of not cooperating fully,' barked Mike.

Rafi was frog marched back to his cell, where he sat on the corner of his bed, shaking. He was cold and his nose was running, but he had nothing with which to blow it. His mind was in turmoil – he'd been accused of being a terrorist. It was all incomprehensible. He was scared. What the hell did they think he had done?

*

Andy and Mike stayed in the interview room. They were frustrated. They agreed that they had got nothing out of their suspect. It was as if he had been expertly tutored in the art of interrogation. He gave answers, but they revealed nothing relevant to his crime. And yet the evidence they had against him was substantial.

'He's a slimy bugger,' said Andy, 'And a first class actor.'

'Gives the impression that he ain't got a clue why he's here,' replied Mike. 'Obviously he's been well trained.'

'He is going to be a hard nut to crack,' said Andy. 'When do you reckon we move on to the Bishopsgate police station bombing?'

'As I see it he knows damn well why he's here, so I reckon we don't need to tell him,' replied Mike. 'Anyway, we've got weeks before we have to charge him – my instinct is to use the time to break him.'

'But time isn't on our side,' argued Andy. 'Our intelligence suggests there could be a follow-up bombing. We have got to get information out of him, or more lives could be lost.'

'If he isn't going to crack soon, what's the hurry? Shouldn't we go for a confession, add it to all the evidence we have and secure a conviction?' countered Mike.

Andy looked concerned. 'But we need information, now!'

'He'll break given time. Who wouldn't in these surroundings? Just think of the praise we'd get,' said Mike.

'So you let another bomb go off just to prove a point and suck up to our political masters?' replied Andy uncertainly.

Mike relented. 'It's an option, but… bugger it! You're right! We've got to bring things to a close as quickly as possible.'

'OK, let's see if we can't tie this up in record time.'

*

Rafi was sitting in his cell. He'd asked for a blanket, but did not get one. He was reflecting on his helpless predicament and his utter lack of rights, when his cell door suddenly swung open.

5

'You're wanted. Now! Get a shift on!' bellowed the guard.

Moments later, Rafi sat down opposite his two interrogators. He sensed they were impatient and keen to start.

'We have evidence that puts you in the frame for the Bishopsgate police station bombing. We've got you on CCTV talking to the bomber next to the cashpoints in South Place, on Thursday lunchtime, the day before the bomb blast,' said Andy.

Rafi was dumbfounded. He couldn't recall speaking to anyone. He'd been in a hurry.

'Watch the tape,' demanded Andy.

A grainy but unmistakable picture appeared on the wall-mounted screen opposite the one-way glass window.

'The City of London has cameras everywhere now. The camera on the corner of Moorgate and South Place picked you up.'

The screen showed a row of five cashpoint machines on the return frontage of the nearby Barclays bank. Moments later, there he was, joining the back of a queue in a smart suit with his neatly cut black hair. His turn came; he withdrew his money and turned. Behind him, to one side, was a man dressed in nondescript clothes with a hoodie largely obscuring his face. They talked for a minute and then the man gave him a hug. His hoodie slipped back off his head, revealing a tanned, ordinary-looking face. The CCTV footage stopped, framing the man standing right in front of him. Rafi was passing something to him, but it was largely obscured from view by the other man's body.

Rafi's mind raced. He tried to recall what he had handed over. Slowly it came back to him. The man had passed him an A to Z map book and asked to be shown which underground station he should use to get to Finsbury Park. Rafi had not needed the map, and explained that Moorgate station was just round the corner, where he could catch a train straight to where he wanted to go. It had been an utter surprise to Rafi when the stranger had embraced him to show his gratitude.

Rafi looked at the picture on the screen, bewildered.

'Caught red-handed!' beamed Andy. 'Tell us how you know Imaad Wafeeq.'

Rafi thought for a moment. The CCTV footage painted a very misleading picture. It made an innocent conversation look very incriminating.

'I didn't know that was his name and that was the first time I met him,' Rafi replied. 'I was just getting some cash for my boss, Jameel Furud.'

'Cobblers!' burst out Mike, leaning forward. 'You can do better than that. Do you think we're dead from the neck up?'

Rafi saw malice in his dark eyes and sensed that the table would offer little protection.

'That was the first time I'd ever seen him,' he repeated.

'Bullshit! We know that you know Imaad Wafeeq, the Bishopsgate bomber. Lying to us is pointless. Why else did he embrace you as a friend? Look at his body language.'

Rafi was dumbstruck.

The two interrogators fired more questions at him.

'Who else was involved?'

'What's the next target?'

They kept on at him for what seemed like hours.

Rafi kept pleading his innocence. There was little else he could do, but it only further infuriated his interrogators. Eventually their patience ran dry. Bland answers were not what they wanted.

Mike looked straight at Rafi; his eyes were those of a cold-blooded snake. 'Let's get this straight: with the evidence we have against you and the new laws, you've next to no human rights. We can send you to Belmarsh Prison, throw the key away and leave you to rot. No one will give a toss! Foxtrot Oscar back to your cell and do some very careful thinking. When you come back, we want answers, or else…' Mike raised his hand in the direction of the one-way glass wall. The door to the interrogation room swung open and a guard walked in.

'Take him back to his cell.'

'Yes, sir,' replied the guard, under his breath. He was ugly, seriously ugly. His face was pockmarked, his nose was bulbous and bent, and he made the dour interrogator look like a softy. He escorted Rafi to his cell in double quick time and slammed the door shut behind him.

*

Rafi tried to come to terms with what he'd seen. It was absurd. He had never met that man before; he had just wanted directions. The implications shook him. Thoughts flooded through his head.

The horrific bombing had taken place on Friday morning. It was now Saturday. There must be hundreds if not thousands of CCTV cameras in the City of London. How did they pinpoint his meeting with the terrorist so quickly? OK, the camera was only a couple of blocks away from where the bomb had gone off, but still Rafi couldn't help wondering whether the police had managed to retrace the bomber's movements, simply been lucky or been tipped off. It all seemed far-fetched.

As his circumstances and plight struck home, his brain moved into panic mode. He realised that he was staring at the back of his dark brown hands. He was a secular Muslim, not a fanatical extremist. He surmised that his skin colour, religion and the misinterpreted CCTV evidence put him squarely in the frame.

Slowly, Rafi regained control of his thoughts. He was in serious trouble. With the new draconian laws, it would be easy for them to hold him in this hellhole with no charges for weeks on end. He looked around at his surroundings: the bed was solid, the floor and walls were bare and there was a slops bucket in the corner. Superficially, the cell looked fairly clean, but there was an all-pervading smell of stale urine and the feel of grime everywhere.

The stark overhead light gave no warmth and just provided glare. It was getting to him. Its rays penetrated remorselessly into his eyes. He closed them. The illumination did not go away. It was as if the bulb had been doctored to give maximum discomfort. He was tired, but he had to keep his brain working. He had to think carefully. The only logical conclusion he could reach was that somebody had set him up. But what might he have done to make someone go to all that trouble? Nothing in his life, neither private nor professional, sprang to mind as being particularly unusual. At work things had been pretty normal... Except for the research Callum and he had been pursuing. So by process of elimination that had to be at the top of the list.

The thud of the cell door opening caught him by surprise.

'You're wanted again,' growled the guard.

'Jump to it you little oik! Time to be on parade!' he shouted when he noticed that Rafi wasn't in a hurry to follow him.

The guard wore irritability in his brutal face and didn't try to hide his hatred for Rafi.

'Get up you little sod. I bet they want your balls for dinner.'

Rafi winced as he was pulled forcefully to his feet and pushed back down the corridor. He was stuck in a nightmare.

★

'You said that you didn't know the Bishopsgate bomber, Imaad Wafeeq. So why did he have one of your £20 notes in his pocket when he died? Let's see you wriggle your way out of this one!' barked Mike.

'Yes, go on!' said Andy. 'And remember, we have proof that the £20 note was from the sequence you took from the cash-point… Three policemen so far have lost their lives and two others are in intensive care.'

Rafi did not answer.

'Speak up! You knew the bomber, didn't you?'

Rafi remained silent.

'Playing the innocent, are we?' interjected Mike.

'Do you think that we are stupid or something?' asked Andy. 'I am waiting for a reply.'

'Can I have a lawyer?'

'No you frigging well can't!' came the retort from Mike. 'The likes of you forfeit all their rights. You don't get a lawyer until you've been charged, and that could be weeks away.'

The questions rained down… 'Who else? Why? and What are you planning next?' Rafi's lack of helpful answers was seriously annoying Mike and Andy.

'We haven't got all bloody day. Start talking or we will get real mean.' Mike's dark eyes narrowed and stared threateningly, just inches away from Rafi.

Rafi's brain was in turmoil.

'Talk!' ordered Mike threateningly.

'We have two cast-iron pieces of evidence against you. The CCTV footage and the £20 note. Case closed! We keep you here for weeks, break you, get your confession, have the courts lock you up and then throw away the keys,' said Andy.

'With the evidence we've got on you, you've become invisible and the system doesn't give a bloody monkeys!' added Mike.

'But I'm innocent, I tell you. All I can think of is I stumbled on something at work, which upset some people,' said Rafi.

'Like what?' snapped Mike.

'Breaking the City rules on takeovers,' replied Rafi.

'What?' burst out Andy.

'Bullshit!' Mike's manner was becoming increasingly intolerant.

'We want to know about the bomber and what his colleagues are planning next. Not about some poncey City insider dealing scam,' said Andy.

'Be very clear there'll be no respite. We'll hound you night and day. We *will* win and you *will* lose,' jeered Mike.

Rafi felt sick with fear. His stomach churned. What was he caught up in? The evidence against him was impressive and the only explanation he could find was that someone had gone to a significant amount of trouble to implicate him. But why? All he could think of was the research that Callum and he had been working on, but what the hell was the link?

'Are you going to talk?' asked Andy.

'Or do we let you rot forever?' added Mike.

How long would it be before they started getting really rough? Soon, thought Rafi. He sensed their physical aggression bubbling just below the surface.

'Make a start and tell us how you were financing the bomber, Imaad Wafeeq,' said Andy.

'I wasn't.'

'Get real!' shouted Mike.

'I think I've been set up,' replied Rafi. 'At least hear me out.'

There was silence. 'OK,' said Andy finally, 'But it had better be good.'

'I stumbled upon some information that suggested my employers, Prima Terra, and a group of Luxembourg investors were in serious breach of the City takeover code.'

'Go on,' said Andy, looking nonplussed.

'Thursday before last, I received a phone call from, Callum Burns, a financials analyst at Landin Young. He's fantastically good at his job and I've been one of his best clients. He wanted to talk about Renshaw Smithers, a niche finance business in which my company, Prima Terra, is a major investor, but he didn't want to have the discussion over the phone, so we met for a drink at a local bar that evening.'

'And?' asked Mike.

'How much do you know about fund managers?'

'They look after other peoples' money,' replied Andy.

'At Prima Terra we have £30 billion of funds under management, of which I manage £4 billion of equities. It was quite a bit more, but we too got caught by the 2008 stock market crash. Have you heard of the Stock Exchange Blue Book?' asked Rafi.

Both Andy and Mike shook their heads.

'It's the rule book governing company shareholdings and takeovers, by which as fund managers we have to abide.'

'Obviously,' said Mike sarcastically, 'But damn it! Why is this relevant?'

'Callum thought Prima Terra had possibly broken the rules. He said he'd found something very dubious that was being hushed up.'

'I still do not see how this relates to the bombing,' said Mike, thrusting his jaw forward at Rafi. 'If you're taking us for a ride, remember we can make life seriously uncomfortable for you.'

'Callum suspected that Renshaw Smithers and another listed company Dewoodson were being controlled by unknown off-shore investors and thought there might be a connection to Prima Terra – the largest investor in these two companies.'

Mike raised his arms and was about to cut Rafi off.

'Before you throw the keys away, what's the harm in hearing me out?' pleaded Rafi. 'Callum and I couldn't come up with any reasons why these companies might be worth controlling. They are unexciting and hardly takeover candidates,' replied Rafi. 'But there has to be something, otherwise why incriminate me?'

'You're not making any sense and why are you pissing around wasting our time?' Mike thumped his fist on the table centimetres away from Rafi.

'So this is a red herring,' interrupted Andy.

No, I don't think so. These shareholdings when added together break all the rules. And there *has* to be a reason why I was set up.'

'You're taking the piss,' said Mike. 'Sounds to me as if you're just trying to distract us from your links to the bomber. Bullshit isn't what we need.'

Rafi looked at Mike's frustrated eyes. 'Whatever I say,

you are not interested, are you?'

'Sod off back to your cell. We'll deal with you shortly,' growled Mike irritably. 'Your time is running out. We'll break you and you will want to talk to us very soon.'

Their lack of interest in his story and Mike glowering inches away from him made the knots in Rafi's guts clench even tighter.

*

Fifteen or so minutes later, Rafi's cell door swung open. A man in catering uniform entered. 'I've got some food for you. Where d'you want it?'

To Rafi's surprise, the tray fell to the floor. He bent down to help pick it up. With the speed and strength of a black belt, the man let fly a kick. It struck Rafi just below his left shoulder blade and was followed by a punch to the kidneys. Doubled up, Rafi slumped to the floor.

'You effing murderer! Prison's too good for your sort!' He stepped towards Rafi, who tried to shout. He had to get the attention of the guard but only managed to let out a strangled noise. To his relief the guard stuck his head around the door.

'The 'alfwit seems to have slipped on 'is food! 'E should be alright soon, when 'e gets 'is wind back. Shame 'e didn't get to eat it. Still, no doubt it'll do 'im good to go 'ungry.' With that the man left.

The guard looked at the crumpled body on the floor. 'You silly ijut! What a waste!' He turned and pulled the door closed.

Rafi remained where he was: an untidy heap amongst the food. He was too sore to get up.

His thoughts went back to his phone call with Callum on the previous Tuesday morning. Callum had been excited, as he had managed to arrange a trip to Luxembourg.

'A couple of meetings have cropped up. I thought it was too good an opportunity to miss! I fly out early tomorrow from City airport and fly back from Amsterdam on Thursday evening. I'm seeing a local REIT. But it gets better: they've lent me a car for the drive from Luxembourg to Amsterdam. One of their directors works in Luxembourg, but has a home in Amsterdam and he's lending me his Porsche. Isn't that great?' Callum had said enthusiastically.

'So a bit of a detour via Germany?' Rafi asked.

'You got it in one. I've always wanted to take a Porsche through its paces on an Autobahn without the fear of speed cameras or blue flashing lights in the rear view mirror.'

Rafi went cold. How the hell had he managed to forget to tell his interrogators that Callum was dead? In the interrogation room he was like a rabbit caught in the headlights. He had to think carefully. When was he going to tell them that Callum had given him a USB memory stick, with files showing the shareholders' lists and the work that they had done on the two suspect companies?

*

Rafi was jolted back to reality. There, standing in the door frame, was the ugly guard again, staring at Rafi lying in a sea of cold, inedible food.

'You're wanted again.'

Waiting for him were the two familiar faces.

'You look worse every time we see you,' commented Andy. There was no sympathy in his voice.

'At this rate we'll need to get a move on,' added Mike, 'or you'll be in no fit state to talk at all.'

'You're a slimy little bugger,' sneered Andy. 'Explain why you didn't tell us Callum was dead?'

'Bloody good ploy, if you ask me,' commented Mike. 'Stops us checking your story!'

'He was murdered!'

'Bullshit!' exclaimed Mike. 'The local police say that he was driving a Mercedes hire car and hit black ice. Are you going to tell us what's really going on?'

'But, he should have been driving a Porsche.' Rafi hesitated. 'Can I explain what Callum was doing in Luxembourg?'

Andy considered this, and then nodded.

'According to a colleague of his, Callum had five meetings: one with a REIT - real estate investment trust - and then a couple of tax advisers, an FCP investment fund and another meeting in the afternoon. The REIT was picking up the tab for the trip. Callum was due to fly back from Amsterdam on Thursday evening.' Rafi paused. 'The MD at the REIT had agreed to lend Callum his Porsche... He'd planned a detour via the German Autobahns.'

'Bloody bollocks!' burst out Mike. 'The local police have

13

spoken to the REIT director. Callum phoned him to cancel the offer of the Porsche, as he'd be running late.'

'Good try,' added Andy, 'but your story doesn't fool us!'

'There's more,' insisted Rafi with a touch of desperation in his voice. 'The afternoon Callum died, he phoned me. He was excited. He said he'd found some proof. He was about to tell me what it was when he was cut off. I tried calling him back but his phone went straight to voicemail.'

Andy scowled. 'That proves sod all!'

'One of the people he saw was in on the shareholdings' cover up. I'm sure of it,' said Rafi. 'Callum got too close…'

'If you refuse to cooperate and continue to mess us around - we do have other options. We've an, er… understanding with the Americans,' said Mike, in a steely voice. 'We suggest to them that you are holding back information that they might find helpful and, magically, through the rendition process you are whisked away to some godforsaken place.'

The knots in Rafi's stomach tightened another notch. He started to speak. His voice was hoarse from the tension and lack of fluids. 'If Callum had found out who was running the clandestine shareholdings and could prove that Prima Terra was involved, wouldn't this give a motive for his murder?' Rafi was aware that, on the surface, this seemed to have nothing to do with the bombing, but he had to keep talking about it as he could find no other reason for finding himself in this nightmare.

'Bloody hell! Not that old story again,' said an exasperated Mike. 'Tell us about the Bishopsgate bombing first. We can get back to Callum later.'

Rafi slumped in his chair and purposefully looked away from his interrogators.

'Get real, you uncooperative little sod! You have told us the square root of nothing. If you continue to take the piss, remember that no one, I repeat, no one has the ability to come and find you. You have disappeared off the radar screen and there is absolutely nothing anyone can do to help you,' said Andy aggressively.

'You're deluding yourself,' spat out Mike. 'You're trying to convince yourself that you're innocent, but in reality you're guilty – as guilty as hell!' He looked like a pug that had licked a

14

nettle.

'Look at the bloody evidence,' said Andy forcefully. 'The CCTV footage of you conspiring with the bomber and the proof that you gave him money is more than enough… Take this bastard back to his cell while we consider whether Belmarsh is too good for him.'

Rafi started to panic but did his best to fight back his feelings of helplessness.

*

The scene looked more like Gaza than the City of London. In the foreground was the burnt-out shell of the building in which the Bishopsgate police station garage had been. The offices above had also been devastated. On the other side of the narrow street, the windows of the 1950s office building had been blown out and Venetian blinds flapped in the wind.

The stage-managed news conference had all the hallmarks of a major media event. The top political reporters and their cameramen were hemmed into the narrow space behind the police station.

In pole position, with his entourage behind him, the Home Office minister strode towards a prearranged spot in front of the gutted garage. He was a man on a mission. He looked determinedly at the destruction, conscious no doubt that the TV cameras were trained on him. One of the burnt-out police cars had been pulled out of the garage and now conveniently provided the backdrop for the minister's meeting with the commissioner of the City of London police. On the ground next to the car lay a police helmet in a pool of dark liquid. It gave those watching a stark reminder of the tragic loss of life.

The commissioner was looking agitated. He had been expecting the Home Secretary, with whom he very much wanted to talk. But at the last moment he had been advised that his number two would be coming. He had been standing in the cold February air, waiting for over thirty minutes, whilst the minister's PR team got the location ready for the press. Their attention to detail when it came to dealing with TV shoots was legendary.

As the minister approached, the commissioner walked across to the agreed rendezvous point close to the burnt-out car and the forlorn police helmet. The senior political reporters were nearby, ready to ask their questions. The minister, in shirt sleeves and a Metropolitan police flak jacket, shook the commissioner's hand and turned towards the TV cameras.

'You see before you the latest carnage wrought on our society by fundamentalists, who seek to challenge our freedoms. I can assure you that the appalling loss of life here will spur us on in our quest to bring to justice all those who assisted the suicide bomber, Imaad Wafeeq, in this heinous act. As I speak, I can reveal that we are already making good progress in our investigations. We have in custody at Paddington Green police station a man who we believe to be the financier of the terrorist cell responsible for this outrage.'

The minister turned to the commissioner, who unlike him had not had the opportunity for a makeover before facing the cameras. 'I understand that the investigations are progressing well?'

The commissioner paused before making his reply. He had his concerns. The modi operandi of the attack troubled him. The bomber was *not* a suicide bomber and had *not* intended to be a victim of the bombing. It looked as if the timer had set off the bomb sooner than expected. Then there was the rucksack of explosives. It had produced far more damage than would have been expected from home-made C4 explosives, the telltale trademark of bomb attacks orchestrated by an ITS – Islamic Terror Syndicate – to which MI5 seemed convinced Rafi belonged. And how the terrorist had managed to get into the garage unchallenged worried him. He had personally reviewed the security of all his police stations only weeks earlier. The garage should *not* have been unguarded. At least he had been able to secure a copy of the CCTV footage showing the suspect's meeting with the bomber.

'We have a number of ongoing enquiries... Which look promising,' replied the commissioner.

'Excellent. Please let me know if you require any additional resources. I shall be available 24/7. My Government has every confidence in your ability to track down and bring to justice these barbaric criminals.'

Had the cameras not been trained on the minister, they would have spotted a fleeting frown on the commissioner's face. He had asked to interview the suspect, but had been thwarted. 'It

16

is a matter for MI5, given the gravity of the situation,' the commissioner had been told by his political masters. He had lost three of his police officers and had two more on the critical list. He did not like being out of the loop and had gone to the top. A meeting was being scheduled for Monday with his longstanding friend, the head of MI5. He wished it could have been sooner. The commissioner stood there while the minister took questions from the press, anxious to get on with his work.

Suddenly a signal was given and the interview was over. The press officer spoke to the reporters. 'The minister will now be visiting the injured at the Royal London Hospital, in Whitechapel Road, and will be available for further questions there. Those of you with red press passes have been allocated seats in the hospital's press room.'

The commissioner watched as the flak jacket was tossed to an aide.

'Nice touch, that helmet,' said the minister. 'What did you use for the puddle?'

'Coca Cola,' came the aide's reply.

The minister smiled and strode off towards his chauffeur-driven car without so much as a goodbye to the commissioner, who turned and headed back to work.

*

Back in his cell, Rafi sat on the bed, trying to work out what was going on. His thoughts kept drifting back to the previous Thursday. The early morning meeting had been an upbeat affair. His boss, Jameel, had announced that he'd arranged an impromptu lunch to mark the bounce in the stock market.

During the morning Rafi had tried ringing Callum a couple more times, but his mobile had still gone straight to voicemail.

Then just before lunch Jameel had walked over to Rafi's desk. 'I think we should be prepared for some serious celebrations,' he had said. 'I need to go across to *The Bishop of Norwich*, the restaurant, to line up a few things. Could you do me a favour and drop by the cashpoint and draw out, say £500, in case I don't have enough cash for the bar bills and tips?'

'Fine,' Rafi had replied, thinking nothing of it. There was a row of cashpoints between the office and the restaurant, in Moorgate. By the sounds of things, it was definitely going to be a session and a half for his drinking colleagues.

Lunch was booked to start at 12.30 p.m. The whole fund management team was invited. The restaurant welcomed the unexpected request for lunch for twenty-eight and arranged an area for just Prima Terra. No expense was spared; the food was first-class and, judging by his colleagues' remarks, the champagne and wine were excellent. Before, during and after lunch the drinks flowed freely. Rafi's colleagues became increasingly well lubricated and were on great form. Rafi, for his part, did not drink.

Ben, a burly lad from the East End, who looked as if he'd missed the opportunity of being a second row rugby forward, was revving up for a long session. He and a group of his colleagues decided that it was the perfect evening to visit a nightclub. They'd recently returned from a stag night in Warsaw and had coined a new expression: zloty for totty. This was their war cry, which the dealer next to Rafi was chanting. It was going to be a very long and lively celebration. Ben and his friends decided that they'd have a few more drinks and then move on to a cocktail bar in the West End, for some visual entertainment.

Rafi remembered looking down at his watch; it had been nearly six o'clock. Half an hour earlier, Jameel had given his apologies and had left to catch a flight to Paris. Rafi still hadn't spoken to Callum. He rang his mobile without success, and then decided to ring his office and leave a voicemail message, but to his surprise his call was diverted.

A kind-sounding woman from Landin Young's HR team had answered the phone. 'Mr Khan, I have some distressing news...' She stopped and then, after a short pause, added, 'I'm very sorry, but Callum Burns has been killed in a car accident. He was in Luxembourg on his way to Belgium when his Mercedes hit black ice, crashed and caught fire. Can I get one of his colleagues to phone you in the morning?'

Rafi could not reply straight away. He was nearly sick on the spot. Utter disbelief had been his immediate reaction. Then the shock struck home and an overwhelming tiredness swept through him. His hands shook. 'Thank you, that would be helpful,' he said weakly before hanging up.

He had tried to put on a brave face. He wanted to leave and

go home there and then. But he did not want to draw attention to his premature departure. He had bought a couple of bottles of champagne, somehow managed to make some small talk, before quietly slipping outside and heading for home.

*

Sitting on his hard cell bed, his thoughts remained on what had happened to Callum and whether his death might be linked to the bombing. Too many things just didn't make sense: why was he driving a Mercedes and not a Porsche? Why had he been driving straight to Amsterdam via Belgium and not towards Germany and its Autobahns? What had Callum gleaned in Luxembourg? How many people were involved? Or could it all just be a coincidence? Rafi's thoughts went round in circles. Eventually he came to the realisation that he simply didn't have enough information to fully understand what was going on.

His thoughts were interrupted by the cell door swinging open. The ugly guard stood a few feet away, scowling. Moments later Rafi was back in the austere interview room, facing his two interrogators.

Andy started the ball rolling. 'We are concerned that there will be further bombings. We have to stop further carnage and bloodshed. Our patience only goes so far. If you don't cooperate, we have a good mind to lend you to the Yanks.'

'I'm not sure that I've any more information that will help you,' replied Rafi.

Andy erupted like a Roman candle. 'What the bloody hell do you think you're playing at? You drag things out, waste our time and refuse to talk. Lives are at stake!'

The grilling went on for what seemed like hours. Rafi answered the very few questions he could.

*

The interrogators knew they were getting nowhere and their behaviour was becoming ever more intimidating.

Rafi was yo-yoing from the interview room to the cell, never given chance to settle and rest. If he tried to sleep then, as soon as he had dropped off, he would be hauled back in front of his two interrogators. He had lost all sense of time – he guessed he had been questioned for all of Saturday and it was now probably Sunday. He wasn't sure though. He was mentally drained and his

19

recently acquired bruises ached like hell, as did his eyes. His head throbbed from the lack of sleep and the relentless stress. It dawned on him that he would not be able to withstand the verbal assault for much longer.

*

Back in the interview room, Mike glowered at Rafi. 'You're close to your sister, aren't you?' It sounded like an accusation.

'What?'

'We think that she can help us. We've been looking into her research work at the University of Birmingham. She is, we're informed, very bright. We think that she could be involved,' said Mike.

'How about we pull her in?' added Andy

Rafi felt the fury building up inside him. His little sister was the one person in the world he would protect with everything he possessed, even with his life. Shock followed by anger flowed through him.

'My sister is one hundred per cent innocent. She has nothing to do with this,' he pleaded.

'As we are not getting very far here, I think it's time for a two-pronged attack,' said Mike. 'We send him for a stint of solitary at Belmarsh prison. Meanwhile we can put pressure on his sister.'

'Andy grimaced. 'She's bound to crack like an egg under a heavy weight.'

Rafi was visibly shaking. 'I'm not lying. Can't you bloody well see I've been set up? Stuff you! I can't frigging well help – I know sod all about the bomber.'

Mike lent forward. 'Don't worry; your sister will tell us what we need to know!'

Rafi weakly tried to swing a punch at Mike who, despite being inches away, caught his fist and smiled.

'Last chance to come clean or Saara gets the full treatment!' threatened Andy.

Rafi said nothing.

'Bog off back to your cell and think of the fun we'll have with your sister.' Mike stood up to emphasise his height over him. 'You'll talk, you *know* you will.'

*

Back in his cell, Rafi thought long and hard. Time had run out;

20

the case against him viewed from the interrogators' standpoint was overwhelming. They didn't give a shit about what he and Callum had found on the two listed companies. They'd played their trump card: his sister. He sat, shoulders hunched. The knowledge that he'd involved her in this frightening world scared him.

His thoughts drifted back to happier times, living at home with her and their parents. He treasured the time he had spent with her. She was eighteen months younger than him, but at times she had treated him like a little brother. He was an able student; in contrast Saara was exceptionally bright. He watched with admiration as she excelled in everything academic: she had been top at school, achieved the highest mark in her undergraduate year and her PhD dissertation had been deemed exceptional by her professor.

Saara's successes had spurred him on. With a BSc in Business Studies and Accounting and a couple of years' experience working in the accounts department of a bank under his belt, he had set his sights on working in the equities markets. He completed a full-time MBA and found a good corporate finance job. Eighteen months later his and Saara's happy lives had been shattered by their parents' untimely death in a car crash.

The money from his parents' estate and his savings had enabled him to muster the deposit needed to purchase his flat. He had worked on an old adage: 'There are three important things to consider when purchasing property, namely: location, location, location.' So, he had spent the summer evenings four years ago visiting smart residential areas in London. He had added a fourth criteria – access to public open space – and had zeroed in on Hampstead, purchasing a two-bedroom flat in the attic space of a large red-brick house in Well Walk, close to the Heath, and not far from the tube station. The entrance to his flat was off a narrow path in Well Passage.

Rafi came back to reality, put his hands over his eyes and forced his brain to think. They were convinced that he knew the bomber. Why the hell wouldn't they listen to him? It was as if they were not interested in the potential wrongdoing Callum and he had uncovered. The more he thought about it the more certain he became that there *had* to be a connection between his finding out about the dubious shareholdings in the two companies and his being set up. He had to find a way to get Andy and Mike to look at things from his perspective. But how?

*

Rafi sat in his cell thinking jumbled thoughts. It slowly dawned on him that he had one piece of evidence that they might want: a USB memory stick Callum had given him… His thoughts went back to the previous Thursday evening.

The devastating news of Callum's death had shaken him to the core. Once back home after the office party he had slumped in an armchair and done nothing for several hours. It had slowly dawned on him that he was wasting valuable time. He had to plan for the worst; he had to assume that someone had killed Callum. Furthermore, it might not be long before the Financial Services Authority and the fraud squad spotted what Prima Terra were up to. Callum's USB stick might just be his insurance policy or even a valuable bargaining chip if he was confronted by the authorities.

He had decided to hide the USB stick away from prying eyes. And remembered wondering whether he was being paranoid. He had concluded that he was not - after Callum's suspicious death he could not afford to take chances.

He recalled looking at his watch early on Friday morning; it had been 3 a.m. and inky dark outside. Where could he hide it? He considered places in the building and its small garden, but ruled them out as being too obvious or too close to home. So where then? It needed to be within walking distance of his flat and easy to find but, perversely, somewhere people wouldn't look.

An idea had come to him. He had changed into warm, dark-coloured clothes and wrapped a black cashmere scarf around his neck. He looked at himself in the mirror: with his dark skin he would be practically invisible in the shadows – or so he hoped. He picked up his gloves, put them with a number of things into his pockets and slipped quietly out of his front door onto the landing. Slowly, in the pitch black, he went down the three flights of stairs towards the communal front door leading out into the alleyway.

He was about to open the front door, when the seriousness of his predicament sank in. What *were* the chances he was

22

being watched? Could someone be outside waiting for him to make a move? He felt a cold shiver run down his spine. It was preposterous, but he needed to be careful. His friend Callum was dead.

He checked in his left pocket: keys, torch, and gloves – all there. And in his other pocket: USB stick and chewing gum – excellent. Tentatively he opened the front door. The catch clicked back like the bolt of a gun being cocked. He jumped, imagining that everyone could hear him. He recovered his composure. His heart raced, but everything around him remained silent. He pulled the door ajar, stopping for a moment to test his night vision. Quietly, he slipped outside, closing the door behind him. The passage was sheathed in darkness. He turned right and, hugging the wall, walked slowly up the murky passage towards the next street.

At the top of the alley, Rafi was about to take a right turn towards the Heath, when he stopped and looked back towards the bottom of the alley and Well Walk. Across the other side of the road, was the silhouette of a Mercedes car parked sideways-on.

Large Mercedes cars were popular around where he lived. Rafi was about to turn away, when his heart missed a beat. Was he seeing things? Inside the car there was a small orange glow. The glow of a cigarette tip brightening as someone inhaled. He was petrified, his feet glued to the spot. The small blob of light moved. Oh sod it! There *was* someone there, watching. He wished the path would swallow him up. If the person had seen him slip out of the front door, surely he would have followed him? Or perhaps he was waiting to see which way he went? Whether they were on to him or not, Rafi knew he had to keep moving.

Warily he headed towards the Heath, and to The Pryors, an upmarket, Edwardian-style apartment block. He turned left off the pavement and made his way carefully down the path alongside the tall wall of The Pryors. The trees on the edge of the Heath appeared ghostlike, just visible, towering over him. The hairs on the back of his neck stood up. There was stillness, a cloak of silence around him. A rustling in the undergrowth startled him. His senses were on their peak setting. He stood still, utterly terrified. The noise faded and he moved on again, his heart racing.

He put his hand into his pocket, pulled out the packet of chewing gum, quietly unwrapped four pieces and put them into his mouth. Sod it, his mouth was parched. Fear had turned off his saliva glands. 'Think lemons, think lemons,' he said to himself.

Rafi turned right and followed the garden wall around a corner for a short distance. In summer, the deep verge between the wall and the path was overgrown with nettles and brambles. In winter long grass, dead brambles and weeds remained. There, against the wall, was a small, dark object, barely visible in the gloom. He had first spotted it a couple of summers earlier, when he had gone to retrieve a ball for a child; it had intrigued him and he had carefully inspected it. He now approached it tentatively, stopped and turned around to check that there was no one behind him. He breathed a sigh of relief; everything was still. He stepped forward, took off his glove and placed his hand on top of the frost-covered metal, slid his fingers over the curved front and felt for the protruding letters. Yes, this was the marker post. The raised lettering on its front clearly stated: *London County Council Boundary*. There was a small gap between the post and the wall. Unlike the other boundary posts next to the wall, the flat metal back of this one had been broken, leaving a small but hidden hole near its top.

Rafi put his hand back into his pocket and pulled out the USB stick; he raised his hand to his mouth, spat out the blob of chewing gum and pressed it to the side of the USB stick. He put his hand around the back of the cold iron post and with his fingertips felt for the irregular hole. He reached inside and pushed the USB stick firmly up into the top section of the post. He smiled as the chewing gum stuck.

The main part of his job done, Rafi retraced his tracks to Heath Road. He'd been gone probably no more than twenty minutes. His eyes had become accustomed to the darkness and he could clearly pick out the outline of the houses fronting on to the road. He looked up into the sky. The cloud cover, thankfully, remained impenetrable. He glanced across at a small bedroom light in the distance. Early birds, he thought. If it had been a *normal* working day, he would only have another couple of hours in bed; he needed to get back home as quickly as possible. Although it was still dark, he was aware that just one light switched on near his front door would scupper his return, making him clearly visible to the person in the Mercedes.

Rafi slipped across the road and retraced his steps back to the passageway. At the corner he stopped; in front of him was the last straight leading to his front door.

Gingerly, he peeped down the passageway. Was the Mercedes car still there? Oh hell! It was. On the way out he'd initially been oblivious to it. Now the black silhouette was straight in front of him. It looked menacing. He studied the car carefully. There was no sign of a lit cigarette. Either the person had stopped smoking, or he had got out to follow him. Oh damn, he thought, what if he was in the shadows waiting for him? Rafi hesitated and then forced himself to move, lest the light of an early-rising neighbour gave him away.

He moved carefully down the path, hugging the wall on his left, and reached his front door. Everything around him was dark. He slipped his key into the lock and turned it. At that precise moment the light from a nearby flat came on. It was as if he had been caught in the arc of a spotlight. He pushed open the door, slipped inside and closed the door. Had he been spotted? Only time would tell. He was relieved to be back on home territory. Quickly, with a bounce in his step, he climbed the stairs in the dark. As he reached the landing, he froze. Could he smell cigarette smoke? Was the person from the car waiting for him? He peered up the last flight of stairs into the darkness, but could make nothing out. He stood still, listening for anything.

Not eight feet away his neighbour's front door opened, lighting up the landing.

'Oh bejesus!' exclaimed the neighbour. 'What the bleeding hell are you doing here? You scared the holy shit out of me.'

If he knew what he'd done to Rafi's nerves, he would have apologised.

Rafi stuttered, 'Sorry mate, just got back from a night with the girlfriend. I was creeping in trying not to make any noise.'

'You lucky so and so,' he commented, smiling at Rafi, and turned on the stairwell light. He closed his front door and muttered, 'Must get going, I've got the early shift at work today.

See you around,' and went on his way in a cloud of cigarette smoke.

Rafi climbed the last flight of stairs, went into his flat and stood there, shaking. He felt as if he'd aged years.

Was the Mercedes still on guard duty out front? He needed to check, so he climbed the narrow staircase to the top floor bedroom. It was in darkness. He stopped before the window, dropped to his knees and shuffled forward, resting his elbows on the windowsill in order to peer down towards the road. It was still there, its dark shape hauntingly visible, but he couldn't make out if the person was still inside the car. He stayed on his knees, who could it be? Did he really want to find out? His mind was full of questions and precious few answers. He dozed off.

The distant buzz of his alarm clock woke him. Rafi raised his weary head from the windowsill and looked outside; it was still dark. He came back to reality with a bump. The Mercedes was still there. He shuffled backwards, stood up and hurried downstairs.

He was being watched, but by whom? Rafi decided that he had no option but to continue as normal. He slipped into his early-morning routine. Twenty minutes later, he was sitting at the small kitchen table, staring at a bowl of cereal and milk. Normally he ate breakfast quickly. This morning, his appetite had vanished and the coffee tasted bitter. He gathered up his things and left for work.

Rafi carefully opened the front door. Would the Mercedes still be there? If so, would he have the courage to walk by it on his way to the underground station? He stepped out into the shadows of the narrow alleyway and looked left towards the road. The Mercedes was nowhere to be seen.

On the tube, Rafi hid behind Friday's *Financial Times*, staring at the pages but taking in little of its news. His head was in turmoil. Act normally, he kept telling himself. His mind was trying to stay rational, but his body was under a different set of controls. He felt his hands shaking and steadied them.

At last, Moorgate tube station arrived. He got out and made his way to his office round the corner in South Place. At the front desk, Rafi greeted the security guard with a wave and headed upstairs for the coffee machine. He felt like death warmed up.

The office was like a morgue. 'You idiot,' he had thought to himself, as he recalled the celebratory lunch and the previous evening's festivities. His spirits rose a little as he realised that at least he would look much better than most of his colleagues.

The office started to fill up. The open plan floor on which he worked was the quietest he could remember; the telephones were being answered in hushed tones and no one was really in the mood to work. By all accounts, the previous night had been an unreserved success; the bar bills would have been huge and the accounts team would no doubt have to do some creative juggling with the expenses claims.

By 9 a.m. the office had started to regain some of its momentum and the noise level had moved up a notch from deadly quiet to hush. The coffee machines were in demand, but unlike normal days there was little gossiping going on around them. At one of them Rafi bumped into Jameel's secretary.

'Did he make his flight last night?' he enquired.

''Fraid not! He missed it by a mile,' she smiled. 'It was a good session yesterday, though, wasn't it?'

Rafi recalled seeing her perched on the edge of a table, enjoying the adulation of a group of dealers.

To his surprise, she said, 'Didn't you see Jameel first thing this morning? He told me he had a couple of things to sort out before he had to rush off to London City airport to catch his flight to Paris. Luckily, I managed to rearrange all his meetings.'

'Is he still due back next Tuesday?' Rafi asked.

'As far as I know.'

Why had Jameel missed his evening flight? He'd left the party early and had plenty of time. Rafi wondered what he had been up to.

His thoughts were interrupted. Seb Warren, a colleague of Callum's, phoned. 'Judy Ballantyne of HR asked me to give you a call.'

Rafi could vaguely put a face to the young individual. He was of a similar age to Callum, but not in Callum's class.

'Is there any further news?' asked Rafi.

'Not really. All we can glean is that he'd finished his work and was on his way to Amsterdam. The Luxembourg police aren't saying much. Callum's body should be flown home early next week. I understand that his family are arranging the funeral for next Thursday somewhere near Bristol, I think.'

'He was seeing some people for me,' Rafi said, hoping Seb wouldn't pick up his white lie. 'Could you run through who he saw?'

Seb hesitated briefly, but then went on. 'Yes, OK. He had a meeting with a REIT, followed by a couple of meetings with tax lawyers. He had lunch with a local investment fund manager and then went to see a contact in the same building for an afternoon meeting... Rafi, I spoke to Callum as he was leaving the afternoon meeting. He was very upbeat, saying, *I've done some useful research... Rafi will be very interested.* I don't know what he meant. Do you?'

'Not really,' said Rafi disingenuously.

Seb paused and carried on. 'He was in a hurry, said he was late for his rendezvous with the REIT director.'

'I tried ringing him at around 6.30 p.m. but got put through to his voicemail,' said Rafi.

'So did I,' replied the youngster.

'Before you ring off, could you tell me who he had lunch with?'

'I'm not certain if I should, but I know Callum was a good friend of yours so I'll tell you off the record. He met Hubert Vynckt of CPR Investment Funds.'

'Thank you Seb, you've been a great help - I'll miss Callum.'

Rafi made a mental note of the name and was just about to go to the firm's library when the whole building was rocked by a dull thump.

'What the hell was that?' yelled Gavin, a director who sat near to Rafi.

'Oscar has self-imploded,' quipped Dominic, to Gavin's left.

A voice from across the room said, 'That was a bomb blast.'

'Are you sure?' asked Gavin.

All eyes in the open plan office focused on the office junior. He was seen but usually never heard. 'Not close, but definitely in the Square Mile. I reckon it went off somewhere to the east of us.' He paused before adding, and going rather pink, 'I'm in the TA so I am used to explosions.'

'So now what?' asked Gavin.

'There could be a follow-up bomb. People should move away from the windows.'

'Gavin nodded. 'OK, do as the man says and get away from the windows. We'll wait for some news; it'll be all over the screens very soon and then decide what to do.'

Rafi looked at the newsflash on his trading screen. *Bombed – garage at Bishopsgate police station, near Liverpool Street Station.* The newsflash continued. *City of London police are unable to confirm whether there will be any further attacks. The London Stock Exchange and Euronext.liffe have closed.* This was followed by, *London underground and all mainline stations are shut.*

Gavin stood up. 'The office is closed for business. You are free to leave for home whenever you like, or to stay put if you wish.'

Rafi knew that news of the bomb blast would be plastered across the media. He phoned his sister at her university where a colleague answered. 'Is Saara there? It's her brother speaking.'

'Not at the moment, she's nipped out. I'll tell her you rang.'

'Thanks,' he said, 'Could you put a note on her desk to say that I'm fine.'

'Will do,' she reassured him and the line went dead.

Rafi decided it was time to leave. 'See you Monday. Have a good weekend,' he called across to Gavin.

Outside, it was bright February sunshine. In the distance there was the sound of sirens. The streets had an unreal feel. It was the expressions on people's faces that were different. They had a sense of anxious determination. The buses and taxis were still working but the queues at the bus stops and cab ranks were very long.

Rafi had considered his options. He wanted to get home. There was nothing for it but to walk and hope he came across an empty taxi on the way. With a stop for a cup of coffee en route, the six mile walk was not too bad. It gave him the opportunity to think things over. He would take a holiday. If he went abroad and Prima Terra was investigated by the authorities, they might think he was escaping from them, so he decided to find a comfortable hotel in Cornwall. He would leave first thing the following morning and being a Saturday it would be a good time to travel.

Just under three hours later he had opened his front door. It had been a relief to be home. He stripped, showered and with a bath towel around his waist, headed for the dining room table, where he opened up his laptop and went surfing for hotels in Cornwall. Into the search engine he entered: Cornwall +hotel +sea and scanned through the very long list of possibilities. He changed sea to "good food" and looked at the new list. Near the top, the Headland Hotel, Newquay caught his eye. He clicked on the link. Its location looked great and its restaurant had two rosettes. Then he spotted they were doing special deals on stays of over five days – perfect. He opened up another window, pulled up the search engine again and found London to Newquay was a five-hour journey from Paddington and there was a 10.05 a.m. Saturday train.

He picked up the phone and dialled the Headland Hotel. In the space of a couple of minutes he'd booked himself a small suite with an ocean view for ten days, starting the following night.

He would travel light and packed some clothes into his computer rucksack and briefcase. He would look businesslike in the hope of concealing his escape plans. Tired, he turned in for an early night.

A few hours later his living nightmare started, when he was dragged from his bed and taken to the godforsaken police station.

*

Rafi lurched back to the present. From the memories he had managed to piece together, he concluded that Jameel, his boss, with some persons unknown in Luxembourg were involved in something highly illegal and could even be linked to the terrorist attack. Callum *must* have found proof of what was going on.

But why did they want him out of circulation? If Jameel *was* involved and something sinister *was* going on with the two companies, what were they up to? But why was he a danger to them, and why hadn't they killed him, as they'd done with Callum? Perhaps two deaths close to home would raise too many questions, and setting him up as the bad guy achieved the desired effect?

Rafi's head ached from the lack of sleep. The absence of edible food and the limited intake of fluids were also taking their toll. The physical side was unpleasant but didn't overly concern him. It was the mental fatigue that worried him. Without a brain he wouldn't get out of there, he told himself.

His thoughts changed tack. How long would it have taken for the evidence to be fabricated against him and the bombing to be planned and carried out...? His conclusion was that the bombing had already been scheduled and it had simply been a convenience to link him to it.

So, how was Jameel, a finance heavyweight, involved? He was a big picture man: fine print and micro-management were not his strengths. Therefore, he had to be working with, or for someone.

Next question, mused Rafi. How were Jameel and Prima Terra linked with the terrorist plot? It had to be something to do with the City of London - one of the three great financial capitals of the world. His thoughts drifted back to the research that Callum and he had been working on... The clandestine nominee names and the two companies in which Prima Terra and others were large investors. Might they have thought he was on to them and close to unravelling what they were planning?

But in practical terms, he had two obstacles to overcome. First, he had to convince his interrogators that the evidence against him was contrived. Then second, he had to get them to believe that he was on their side and could potentially unlock the larger terrorist plot...

'I've got it!' It came to him, out of the blue. What he needed was someone they trusted who could do the persuading for him. Someone who would want to look carefully at the two companies and who would be willing to investigate what Jameel and Prima Terra were really doing. However, in the eyes of his interrogators he was guilty and he knew they wouldn't be prepared to listen to a word he said as long as he insisted on protesting his innocence. Corporate finance was a blank in their book. Who might they listen to? His mind ached...

It needed to be one of them! Yes, of course that might work. He needed a police officer who could put his case to them. Furthermore, he needed someone who was familiar with the workings of the City and understood corporate finance. His mind raced. Ideally it would need to be someone from the Corporate or Economic Fraud Squad at the City of London police force. Would they be prepared to help him? Bloody hell, it was going to be a tall order. The bomber he was accused of being linked to had killed three – or was it four? – City policemen. He would be seriously unpopular, but it was on their turf and they might be interested in his story if they thought it would hasten the arrest of those who had masterminded the bombing.

Rafi thought through the practicalities… He needed to get someone from City of London police to visit him. He could give them the location of the memory stick, but it would be unwise to tell MI5 as they might then block the police's involvement.

There was a problem, though. He probably only had twelve hours left before it all became too much for him to handle coherently. In particular, the lack of sleep and water were taking their toll. As he wondered how best to get things moving, the cell door swung open.

*

In the interrogation room, Rafi faced his two least favourite people. He had lost track of time and felt desperately tired. He guessed that he hadn't slept for over twenty four hours.

Andy started the talking. 'We passed your laptop to our boffins. They've found *nothing* to do with your two companies.'

Thank goodness he hadn't copied the files from Callum's USB memory stick, thought Rafi.

'Very suspicious if you ask me,' said Mike. 'So where is the information Callum and you put together on the two companies?'

Rafi's stomach tensed up; he would have to play things very carefully. The information on Callum's USB stick might just be his passport out of there.

'It's rather complicated,' said Rafi.

Andy looked down his nose at him. 'Proceed. Do we look thick?'

Rafi allowed himself an inward grin. He hesitated - time for a bit of financial gobbledygook.

'Oi! Wake up and get your arse in gear!' shouted Mike as if every second was urgent. 'You're here to talk to us, not to daydream.'

Rafi drew breath and started: 'Do you understand what I mean by butterfly positions in the forward financial futures markets, when a leveraged investor is speculating on a break out of a trading range, precipitated by new information coming into the market?' He stopped.

The two interrogators looked at each other, dumbfounded. It was bullshit, but not total bullshit.

'OK, I'll go through it slowly. In the futures markets you have two positions: *calls* when you're a buyer and *puts* when you're a seller of the market. With a call position, you make a profit if the market rises more than is anticipated and in a put contract you make a profit if the market falls by more than is anticipated. OK so far?' Rafi carried on before they had had the opportunity to respond. 'Leveraged derivatives are when you've borrowed money to finance your positions in the market, thereby making your profits bigger. Do you follow me?'

'Er... Could you perhaps speak English?' said Andy.

'Where do these butterflies come in?' asked Mike in a bemused manner.

'They're a type of trade where you mix call and put contracts together. It's the information flows that make the derivatives market appealing in highly volatile times.'

The two interrogators obviously didn't have a clue what Rafi was talking about. Their faces showed that as much as they wished to follow his line of thought, it wasn't their area of expertise.

'Perhaps we should have a break whilst you check out what I've said?'

Mike scowled. They chatted between themselves for a couple of minutes. Apparently they'd had enough trouble understanding what an equity was, let alone a futures product.

'By the way,' said Rafi. 'I have a USB memory stick with the data on it, which should back up my assertions.'

'You what?' exploded Mike. 'You are a sodding awful piece of work! Why the hell didn't you tell us earlier? '

'Where is it?' demanded Andy.

Rafi remained silent.

'You devious little bastard,' said Mike. 'Back to your cell while we decide what to do with you.'

*

Rafi was bundled back to his cell. He lay on the bed hoping that they'd make a decision relatively quickly.

The bolts on the cell door clunked loudly and the door swung open. There, standing in the doorway, was his bête noir.

'They want you back, now!' the guard said ominously. 'Come on,' he barked.

Rafi struggled to sit up, but his back had seized up as a result of the blows he'd received from the man who had brought his food. He rolled on to his side, slid off the bed and on to his knees. Yes, he could stand up now, he thought, as he straightened his legs.

Rafi was too slow. Suddenly he felt the vice-like grip of a pair of hands lock around his neck and forcibly haul him upright. He couldn't breathe and started to struggle, which had no effect other than to increase the pressure on his neck. Rafi felt himself starting to black out.

The guard was strong, very strong, and with ease he pulled Rafi up. Then in one movement sent him flying towards the corner of the cell.

Instinctively, Rafi tried to cushion the impact by stretching his right arm out in front of him - it hit the inside rim of the slops bucket. A nauseating pain shot up his arm from his wrist. Then his shoulder hit the wall with a thud. He slid down on to the floor and in to the spilt contents of the slops bucket.

'You messy little git,' said the guard. 'Can't take you anywhere without you making an effing mess of yourself. Phwaaw! You smell like a sewer rat. Better not keep 'em waiting.' With that he hauled Rafi to his feet and frogmarched him down the corridor.

Rafi's wrist was already swelling up and going a deep purple-blue colour. He tried to move his fingers; they hurt like hell, but he found he could partially move them. At least nothing seemed broken.

As he pushed Rafi towards his chair, the guard hissed under his breath, 'You won't be so lucky next time!' His distinctive company's badge - the BlueKnite emblem - was inches away from Rafi's eyes.

'Silly idjut tried to get here in too much of an 'urry, slipped and put his hand down the karzi. A right plonker, in't 'e?' said the guard.

Rafi laid his swollen wrist and reeking wet sleeve on the table. He looked at his two interrogators and tried to give them his best grin.

'Phew, you stink! Before we go any further we need to get you cleaned up.' Andy beckoned to those behind the one-way glass window.

A couple of minutes later there was a knock at the door and a new face appeared. The man was carrying a clean shirt and a plastic first aid box.

'Meet Sergeant Chris Archery. We thought you should be checked over before we continue,' said Andy.

Rafi slowly unbuttoned his shirt and then got stuck.

'Could you help me pull it off?' Rafi sat there, leaning slightly forward in his chair.

As his shirt came off there was an involuntary intake of breath. 'Bloody hell, mate!' exclaimed the sergeant. 'You're looking a bit rough aren't you?'

Rafi's wrist had swelled up to nearly three times its normal size and had turned a deep shade of purple. He couldn't see the bruises on his back, but they ached like hell.

'I can't do much about your back, but I can strap your wrist,' the sergeant turned to the two interrogators. 'Can I give him a couple of painkillers, or are they off the menu?'

'Don't see why not. Don't want him accusing us of treating him badly,' replied Mike sarcastically.

The sergeant carefully lifted Rafi's arm up. 'Looks painful; let's get it washed and strapped.' He opened his first aid box, pulled out a couple of sterilised cleaning cloths and wiped Rafi's forearm, wrist and hand.

'Hold still; this may be a little uncomfortable.' An understatement if ever there was one. The sergeant quickly and efficiently strapped his wrist from the base of his thumb to his elbow, then helped Rafi put on a clean shirt.

The sergeant rummaged again in his box and took out a plastic bottle of a yellow-looking liquid. He opened it, poured some of the contents on to a piece of cotton wool and wiped Rafi's swollen hand. 'Nothing to do with the treatment. I thought it might cover up the smell; it's the best I can do on the deodorant front,' he said grinning at the two interrogators. 'If that's all gentlemen, I'll go now.'

As soon as the door closed, Mike recommenced the inquisition. 'Tell us where you have put the USB memory stick… And what's in the files. If you don't, we'll give you to the Americans.'

Though the threat was probably hollow, the idea of what they *might* do scared Rafi. He remained silent for a moment. 'I suppose a phone call is out of the question?' he asked hopefully.

'Bloody well right!' said Mike.

'What was on the files? Tell us! Then you get a phone call,' added Andy.

At last he had something to go on. Up to then he'd been hitting a brick wall. 'I've a proposal,' Rafi said quietly.

'Yes, what is it?' questioned Mike.

'I'd like to speak to someone, but I'll need your help.'

'No way!' interjected Mike.

'Please hear me out,' pleaded Rafi.

'Make it quick,' replied Andy.

'Find me a detective who's an expert in corporate or economic fraud. The City of London police force has a specialist team. I know they'll be livid with me as a prime suspect, but if you can get one of them to interrogate me, they'll understand what I have to say.'

There was silence; it was definitely not what the two MI5 officers had expected to hear.

'One of our specialists should be able to understand,' said Andy, who looked as if he'd just eaten a lemon.

'*Should be*, isn't enough. I need to speak with someone who *really* knows their stuff. The people at City Police are experts and won't suffer fools gladly. If I'm seen to be wasting their time, they'll no doubt tell you,' countered Rafi.

'Your suggestion is not viable. They are not MI5, nor anti-terrorism, so they are outside the group of people we work with,' said Mike.

'Even though they've got a vested interest in the Bishopsgate bombing?' insisted Rafi.

'Oh hell, you're a little shit, aren't you? We've got enough to bang you up for decades. Your bargaining position is crap and yet you're asking to be interrogated by a plod from the City of London.' Mike looked far from pleased.

'Bloody nutmegs, if you ask me,' cut in Andy.

Mike frowned. 'Yes, I agree. I think he is simply trying to give us the run-around.'

36

'We'll ask the boss, but I reckon the answer will be a categorical *no*,' said Andy.

They left the room, leaving Rafi to wait anxiously. A couple of minutes later they reappeared.

'We've a proposal. You tell us the information and we then pass the tapes to City of London police.'

'Are you sure there's time?' Rafi asked. 'All I'm asking is to meet a detective from the City police; you can record the conversation and hear everything we talk about.'

'I still don't think it's a good idea,' mumbled Andy under his breath.

'Time for you to go back to your cell,' ordered Mike.

Rafi was ushered to his cell by another guard, who had obviously been to the same training school as his ugly colleague.

*

Rafi waited nervously in his cell. He rehearsed in his mind what he was going to say. He waited and waited. Finally they came for him - the walk down the corridor felt like the longest of his life.

As Rafi entered the now familiar room, his heart sank. There were just Andy and Mike waiting for him. His request had fallen on deaf ears. There was no one from the City of London police to interrogate him. He felt thoroughly dejected.

Mike started the conversation. He was looking very pleased with himself. 'Let us recap why you're under arrest. We've got CCTV footage of your meeting with the Bishopsgate bomber; one of the £20 notes you took from the cashpoint was found in the dead bomber's wallet; you've hidden a USB memory stick with crucial data on it *and* you've consistently refused to cooperate.'

'What on earth is your defence?' added Andy.

Rafi's brain was close to calling it a day. He hesitated. A phrase a former hostage had once used in a TV interview came to mind: *It's the belief in there being a future, that pulls you through the ordeal.* Goddamn it, he thought; even if the City Police weren't there, he still had to give it a try.

'Could I have a whiteboard or a flip chart?'

'No, you bloody well can't!' snapped Mike.

'It would speed things up and make things clearer,' Rafi countered weakly.

'The answer's still no,' added Andy.

'How about some paper and a pen?'

Andy pushed his pad and a pen over to Rafi, who picked up the biro in his left hand and transferred it across to his swollen right hand, wincing as he started writing on the sheet of paper... The pain wasn't too bad if he supported his swollen wrist with his left hand. On the the sheet he wrote: *£20 note; CCTV footage; Packed to leave; Callum's car crash; Prima Terra / Jameel;* and *USB Memory Stick.*

His handwriting was awful, but it was legible. Rafi smiled; he had a framework from which to operate. All he had to do now was to ignore the pain and get his exhausted brain to remember everything he had to say and to put it across clearly.

His throat was dry and his voice scratchy. 'Any chance of a cup of coffee, white with sugar and no salt, please?'

Andy nodded and, as if by magic, a cup of hot coffee was brought into the room a few moments later.

It gave Rafi the boost he needed. 'You have me here as your prime suspect. Let me explain why I'm innocent.'

'This better be good,' Mike interjected under his breath.

'I am an innocent bystander, but at the same time I believe I *am* linked to those involved.' He looked at the two interrogators. He had got their attention. 'The CCTV footage showed me taking £500 in £20 notes from the cashpoint, one of which ended up in the dead terrorist's pocket. How did this happen...? Your records will confirm that, after withdrawing the money, I went straight to *The Bishop of Norwich* where my firm was holding a celebratory lunch. Jameel Furud asked if I could sub him £360 towards the restaurant tip. The total tip was £500. If you check with the restaurant, you will find that the denominations of the notes that they received were fifteen of my brand new £20s and four £50s.' Rafi knew this was just a calculated guess, but was prepared to bet he was right. Jameel was a big tipper and liked round numbers. 'In the process, he pocketed three of my £20 notes, and it was one of these notes you found on the dead body.'

Mike and Andy looked at him unenthusiastically.

Rafi wondered whether he was talking sense. He had a splitting headache. 'Let's turn to the CCTV footage. My office in South Place isn't that near to Bishopsgate. I reckon that there must be thousands of CCTV cameras in the Square Mile. Let's assume that there are 4,000 cameras - that's something like 100,000 hours of recordings. Finding the bit showing me handing the money over to the bomber would have been like looking for a needle in a haystack and yet it was found in a matter of hours. I'd make an educated guess that it was found thanks to an anonymous tip-off and not by tracing the movements of the bomber. Where did the tip-off come from? It was the person who arranged for me to bump into the bomber; the person who had asked me to go to the cashpoint before going to the restaurant to get cash for the tip. The same person who knew that there was only one set of cashpoints between my office and the restaurant. The person who set me up is Jameel Furud, *and* he has conveniently left the country.'

Andy and Mike looked straight at Rafi. Their blank faces gave nothing away.

'I would now like to explain the items at the bottom of the sheet of paper.' Rafi dropped his head for a few seconds, partly for effect and partly because he felt like death warmed up. His body was crying out for some rest.

He paused. 'To reinforce my allegation that Callum was murdered, please consider the following. He'd arranged to borrow a Porsche and drive it to Amsterdam via the German Autobahns. He was really excited about this and wouldn't have given up the opportunity of driving it lightly. So why was he found in a rented Mercedes, driving east towards Belgium and not west to Germany? My answer is: his assassins put him there and set fire to the car to cover up any evidence.'

Mike and Andy looked at Rafi as if he was as mad as a box of frogs.

'There is more to this than meets the eye,' continued Rafi. 'You've quizzed me about impending attacks on police stations, railway stations, airports and other public places. You've got this wrong. Jameel is part of a team plotting something far larger. I believe they wanted me out of the way as they thought I'd stumbled onto something that could expose what they were planning.'

Rafi raised his aching head and looked at the interrogators. 'The data on the USB memory stick holds the key to this conspiracy. That's why I want an interview with someone from the City of London police. They're uniquely placed to understand the data and to put them into the context of the workings and intricacies of the financial markets. I implore you to let me be interrogated by one of them. What have you got to lose?'

'So where is the memory stick?' asked Andy.

'Safe,' Rafi replied.

'Do continue,' said Andy.

'Why was I packed to leave? And why was I not going abroad? Quite simply, I feared for my life and wanted to go somewhere safe to mull things over. I booked ten days' at a hotel in Cornwall. If I had been involved with the terrorists, surely I'd have gone to a safe haven overseas?'

Rafi looked at his two interrogators. He reckoned he had at best a 50:50 chance as to whether they believed anything he'd said. They remained silent, their faces unfathomable. He sensed he'd lost. He wasn't going to get out of jail - ever.

Just then the door opened. A smartly dressed police officer stood in the doorway. He paused momentarily to take in the scene in front of him, before striding in, head held up high. He introduced himself as Commissioner Giles Meynell of the City of London police and sat down next to the two interrogators, opposite Rafi.

Rafi was gobsmacked. Oh hell, why did the commissioner have to arrive late? He'd have to do the whole presentation again and realised he physically couldn't – he was just *too* tired.

The commissioner studied the prisoner. 'Mr Khan, I've listened to what you've had to say. It's too early to determine whether there's any truth to your story.' His voice was calm yet forceful, packed with authority, no doubt gleaned over many years of high ranking service.

Rafi's hopes rose and then fell.

'However, even if there's an outside chance that your theory has substance, I'm duty-bound to investigate.'

Rafi could have leant across and hugged him. He felt he had been given a new lease of life.

The commissioner looked at Rafi gravely. 'You are no doubt aware that the Bishopsgate bombing has robbed my force of four excellent police officers. A further two are still in intensive care. My first instinct would be to leave you with these professionals and let them break you. However, my police training and experience tell me that I need more information. I have one question.' He carefully studied Rafi. 'Where exactly is the USB memory stick?'

'Could I use your notebook, please?' replied Rafi.

The commissioner unbuttoned his outside breast pocket and passed a small notebook, open at a blank page, across to Rafi. A biro was attached to the side.

'Thank you.' Rafi carefully removed the biro and put it in his swollen right hand. He rolled his shoulders over, sitting hunched over the pad so that the CCTV cameras couldn't see it, and with a feat of great willpower, started writing. He looked down at his scrawl, closed the pad and handed it back.

The commissioner opened it and glanced at the page as if keeping his cards close to his chest whilst playing bridge, and replaced it into his pocket.

Their eyes met. 'I'd be happy to explain the contents of the memory stick to your analyst,' said Rafi.

The scribbling in the commissioner's notebook had caused a significant amount of consternation amongst the two MI5 officers. Andy and Mike both started to protest.

'Sir,' said Andy, 'May we please see what Mr Khan wrote? As you know it falls under our jurisdiction.'

The commissioner drew himself up to his full height and studied the two MI5 men carefully. 'All in due course, gentlemen. I am conducting a murder enquiry and it is my duty to determine the validity of what Mr Kahn has written. I can assure you that the information is in safe hands. We shall discuss whatever we find as soon as it is appropriate.'

Rafi moved his gaze from Mike, a character as hard as nails, to the commissioner, who gave a totally different impression: middle-aged, smartly dressed and with a thatch of neatly combed white hair. His blue eyes didn't have Mike's ruthlessness; nevertheless Rafi hoped that he never crossed him.

'Mr Khan. Provided you have not sent me on a wild goose chase, you can expect to see one of my team here later today. They will pick your brains, in particular on the contents of the USB stick. And be in no doubt, if they believe you're telling lies

41

or half-truths, Andy and Mike will be more than welcome to do whatever they like to you and then throw away the key. While those who helped the Bishopsgate bomber are at large I shall leave no stone unturned,' with that, the commissioner stood up and left.

The faces of the two MI5 interrogators were as black as thunder. They turned to look at one another and spoke in hushed tones.

*

Rafi was escorted to his cell, a little less roughly this time. He sat down on the edge of the bed, mentally and physically exhausted, and waited. Time passed slowly. A couple of hours later he had started to worry that the commissioner had changed his mind.

The cell door swung open.

'Someone's 'ere to see you,' said the guard.

Rafi was bundled into the interview room. 'Sit! They'll be 'ere shortly.'

There was a knock at the door. Rafi looked up and saw the slightly nervous face of a female police inspector. She rapidly regained her composure and closed the door behind her.

'Good afternoon,' she said. 'I'm Detective Inspector Kate Adams of the City of London police.'

She sat down, as if waiting for someone or something.

Rafi looked carefully at the policewoman opposite him. Her wavy hair was tied back severely. It was a warm rusty brown colour. She had pale skin which was covered with splashes of freckles and her eyes were a deep hazel brown.

Kate meanwhile had been trying to size up the dark, grubby-looking man hunched in front of her. His straight black hair was greasy and bedraggled. He looked in a bad shape.

Their thoughts were interrupted by the guard. 'Someone else 'ere to see you.'

A tall serious man, with strong angular features, walked into the interview room.

'Mr Khan, I'm Chief Superintendent David Pryke, Detective Inspector Adams's boss.'

He sat next to DI Adams and nodded for her to start.

'I've looked at the Excel files on the memory stick. The analysis is detailed… And it may lead to a dead end. But it seems to us that the only explanation of why anyone would want you out of

42

the way is if you *were* on to something,' observed DI Adams.

CS Pryke, beckoned for one of those watching from behind the one-way glass to join him.

Andy and Mike appeared at the door.

'I have a message from the commissioner. Could you ring his mobile? Here's his number,' said CS Pryke.

Andy took the piece of paper and they left.

CS Pryke said in a quiet voice, 'We're moving you to MI5 headquarters, where we will be interviewing you, to see if you really can help us unravel this terrorist plot.'

Rafi could not believe what he'd heard. He suddenly felt light-headed.

Minutes later, Andy and Mike returned; they were unhappy.

'I have made the call,' said Andy. 'And darn it, if I didn't find myself talking directly to the head of MI5.'

'Can you repeat what he had to say?' asked CS Pryke.

'We are to let you have Mr Khan and are to arrange for a van and a driver to be waiting in the rear car park.'

'You lucky little sod,' scowled Mike.

'Suppose you will want a blanket to cover Mr Khan's head?' said Andy as he left the room with Mike.

Moments later, Andy returned with the blanket. Rafi meanwhile had been handcuffed, and with the blanket over his head he was escorted by CS Pryke and Kate to the rear car park.

The chief superintendent turned to Kate. 'Sorry, I could not talk inside as we were being recorded... Time isn't on our side. Transporting Mr Khan in a police car or van will attract too much attention. So Mr Khan, you'll be doing a switch with my driver. He'll be the one making the journey to MI5 headquarters. And you will be travelling to our police station, handcuffed in the boot of my car. Any complaints?'

Rafi shook his head, by now dumbfounded by the rapid change of events.

The chief superintendent turned to DI Adams. 'I will leave with lights flashing and sirens blaring, and go to MI5. I'll stay there for fifteen minutes and then meet you back at Wood Street. A bit of a charade, but we can't let anyone guess what we're up to.'

CS Pryke then hesitated but soon continued, 'Oh, by the way,

I forgot to tell you part of the deal the commissioner struck with the head of MI5 is that we also get Jeremy Welby, an MI5 operative. He will be responsible for making sure that the interrogations, or perhaps I should say the interviews are done properly. Do not be fooled by his boyish looks. His CV is very impressive. He will no doubt turn up at Wood Street in due course. Remember, we must keep Mr Khan off the radar screens. The fact that he's not here or at MI5 must remain our secret. Understood?'

'Yes, sir,' replied DI Adams.

DI Adams opened the boot of CS Pryke's unmarked car. 'Climb in.'

Rafi did as he was told. He hated confined spaces, but this one he welcomed.

Away from prying eyes the blanket was put over CS Pryke's driver and the switch was made.

Chapter 2

Rafi was glad that he was only 5' 9"; as it was a tight squeeze. His initial panic of being bundled into the small space had soon disappeared. The claustrophobic boot was definitely better than facing Mike and Andy.

Their arrival at the City of London police headquarters in Wood Street was low-key. Kate parked in the covered rear car park.

Rafi was motionless when she opened the boot. The rocking of the car had lulled him into a deep sleep. He heard a woman's voice saying, 'Wake up,' and felt his body being shaken and prodded.

'Christ, I thought you were unconscious and for a horrible moment that you'd been asphyxiated. Roll over and let me take your handcuffs off,' said Kate. 'And in case you have any ideas, let me point out that this is a secure compound. You are going to cooperate, aren't you?'

Rafi nodded. 'Sorry to have scared you,' he mumbled. 'I haven't had any sleep for a couple of days. I could have slept in a dustbin and not given it a second thought.'

With the blanket draped over his head, Kate hurried Rafi though the back door. They made their way up the back stairs to a modestly sized office on the fourth floor.

'This is where I work. Let me introduce you to Detective Constable Emma Jessop – my ever-helpful sidekick.'

Rafi looked across the room and saw a beautiful woman sitting behind a computer screen. She had a mop of curly fair hair, light brown eyes and a disarming smile.

Kate surveyed Rafi carefully. 'First we need to get some ground rules sorted out. You are to remain with us until this is all over. You will keep a *low* profile. As far as everyone else is concerned, you're being held by MI5. In the meantime Emma and I will try to make your stay here as comfortable as possible.'

'Thank you,' Rafi replied.

'I think we need to get you cleaned up. A shower and a shave wouldn't go amiss,' said Kate.

Rafi stroked his left hand over his rough stubble and nodded.

'Would you like a coffee and something to eat?' Emma asked.

'Something long and cold to drink would be nice, please,' Rafi replied in a hoarse voice.'

Emma smiled, 'Thirsty, are we?'

Rafi nodded. He was badly dehydrated and hadn't peed for what seemed like ages.

Emma left the room and returned a couple of minutes later with a bottle of chilled water and a can of cold Coke. 'I thought that this might keep you going.'

He was going to like working with Emma. 'What do I call you two?'

The two women looked at each other and smiled.

'Kate and Emma would be fine, Mr Khan,' replied Kate.

'Rafi, please.'

'Done!'

The phone rang. Kate picked it up and listened intently.

'That was the commissioner. It seems Special Branch down-stairs have found an eyewitness who was standing behind you in the queue at the cashpoint. She has confirmed that you put the cash straight into your wallet. It seems she was amazed to see so much money coming out of the machine and didn't believe it would fit! Also, she overheard your conversation with the terrorist, and confirms that you simply gave him directions and handed back his A to Z.'

Kate smiled. 'This substantiates your claim that you were an innocent bystander. The commissioner says that we can treat you as a colleague,' she paused. 'Though he thinks it's best if your presence here remains our secret. Please bear in mind that we lost good friends in the Bishopsgate bombing and our colleagues may not be as welcoming… And I am to ask, if you will cooperate fully with our enquiries?'

Rafi remained silent as he took in the news.

'Will you help us?' asked Kate.

'Yes, I'd be pleased to,' replied Rafi - overcome by a sense of relief. 'I am so sorry about your colleagues. Believe me, I want these bastards caught as much as you do.'

'That's good... And Mr Kahn – sorry – Rafi,' said Kate, ' Just so that there is no misunderstanding - you will use *only* those parts of the police station we tell you to... Is that agreed?'

Rafi nodded.

'Excellent, that's settled then.' Kate left the room, leaving Rafi to enjoy his drink. He looked around his new surroundings and found them to be typical of an older style office building: plain and functional.

Kate returned clutching a pair of dark blue tracksuit trousers, some white jogging shorts, a pair of white socks and a Harlequins rugby shirt with the number 14 on the back.

'Best I could find but at least they're clean. I hope that they fit.' In her other hand was a large white towel and a bottle of shampoo. 'Unfortunately, I couldn't lay my hands on a razor,' she added.

'Don't worry,' replied Rafi, 'my wrist isn't up to shaving.'

'Follow me,' said Kate.

Rafi was taken off to a utilitarian washroom with an adjoining shower cubicle. 'I'll come back and get you in fifteen minutes,' said Kate.

Rafi beckoned her to stay. 'Actually could I possibly have some help, please? I'm having problems getting my shirt off!'

'That's one of the worst chat-up lines I've ever heard,' Kate said with a smile.

Rafi hesitantly finished unbuttoning his shirt with his left hand and she helped him slide it off.

There was silence. She stood there, looking at his back. 'I'm sorry... I didn't realise. How the hell did you cope in the boot of the car? The bottom of your back looks as if it stopped a runaway train... The bruises on your shoulder and arm look awful.'

'You should see my legs.'

'Don't tempt me!' Kate turned to leave. 'Please lock the door when I've gone.'

Rafi stepped slowly into the shower and stood under the flowing water, still holding the cold water bottle in his left hand. The warmth of the shower and the ice cold of the drinking water were pure bliss.

He had no idea how long he'd been there when there was a knock at the door. It was Kate. 'Can I come in?'

'Yes. Give me a moment.' At the third attempt he managed to wrap the towel around his waist with his left hand. He unlocked the door and stepped aside to let Kate in; she was clutching a first aid box.

'I thought this might come in handy. I'm afraid there's not much I can do for your bruises. She started to work on the grubby, wet Elastoplast dressing on his wrist. There was gauze underneath the sticky plaster bandage, which made removing it a fairly straightforward task. She cleaned his arm.

Kate considered the swelling; his wrist was at least twice its normal size. The angry colours of the bruise spread up his arm towards his elbow and down to his fingertips. They matched the bruises on his shoulder, lower back and calf. She glanced at his wet hirsute chest. His physique, for a lightly built man, was surprisingly good, but – my God – he had taken a battering.

'Do you have any water left?'

He nodded.

'You might like to take a couple of these. They'll ease the pain.' Kate carefully re-strapped his wrist. There was no gauze in the first aid kit. She hoped she wouldn't be the one to take the sticky plaster off. 'Would you like a sling?'

Rafi shook his head. 'Thanks, but no thanks; I may have some writing to do.'

Kate raised her eyebrows. 'Forgive me for asking, but how precisely do you propose to hold a pen?'

'With difficulty,' came Rafi's modest reply. 'Could I ask you a favour, please?'

Kate noticed he'd started to blush.

'I'm not very good at bending at the moment and my right hand doesn't like gripping things. If I move over to a dry bit of the floor could you help me pull my shorts and tracksuit trousers up to my knees?'

Kate pointed to a dry area of floor.

Trousers and shorts in hand, Rafi walked slowly to the spot and dropped the two items of clothing on to the floor. It was a close-run thing between his towel unknotting and slipping down, and the shorts and trousers being pulled up.

Kate had to smile to herself. She liked what she saw, despite the bruises all over his body.

48

Minutes later Rafi was fully dressed, hair combed and looking and smelling like a normal human being. He ached all over, but despite his tiredness, he felt equipped to meet the world again.

Back in Kate and Emma's office he was shown to a desk. 'This part of the fourth floor is your home for the foreseeable future,' explained Kate. The Gents across the corridor is for now off bounds to the rest of the force here. That's as far as you can go, understood? If you need to go elsewhere else, please ask.'

'Will do,' said Rafi.

He was given a desk opposite Kate's. Across the room, to his left, was Emma and to his right there was a large whiteboard and a pair of empty desks positioned back-to-back. Scattered around the room were a number of filing cabinets and there was a networked printer next to Emma's desk. The room had a lived-in feel. Paperwork was everywhere.

Kate looked across at Emma. 'I think we need to tidy up. Any empty filing cabinet drawers?'

Emma nodded. 'OK, let's collect all the paperwork that does not relate to this case and for the time being put it in the empty drawers.'

Fifteen minutes later the room had taken on a minimalist look.

'Nice work,' said Rafi to them both.

'Thank you... Now we can make a start and have a proper look at your USB memory stick. But first let me tell you more about the team you'll be working with. Emma, who you have already met, has a first in something or other highly numerical from University College London and is great at finding things out. Point her in the right direction and wait to see what she uncovers. She's our little Exocet missile. Before she joined us, she qualified as an accountant, so knows her way around things financial. We will shortly be joined by Jeremy Welby, who is being seconded here from MI5 to keep an eye on you and, no doubt, us, and to help where he can, but otherwise I know very little about his previous experience.'

'It depends what you mean by *experience*,' said a masculine voice from the doorway. 'Mine is OK but I have recently spent far too much time undercover. My section commander Neil Gunton thought I might like a change of scene.' He paused, then continued, 'It seems that your commissioner pulled an impressive flanker on us to get our friend here sprung from Paddington Green.' Jeremy grinned and went on, 'A good move, no doubt. My instructions are simple: "Help them get whoever is behind the Bishopsgate bombing. Find out what the terrorists are up to next and please make certain that Mr Khan doesn't go missing." Neil has offered us whatever support we require because, in his words, "This is a joint venture". Basically, I'm here to help you get to the bottom of what's going on.'

Kate looked at Jeremy. He was in his early thirties and in great shape; his handsome tanned face and his boyish good looks were emphasised by a strong jawline. She introduced Emma and herself. 'We're part of a specialist team that looks into major corporate and financial fraud. We tend to do the research side of things and from time to time are allowed out! We report to Detective Chief Superintendent David Pryke who's on his way back from MI5 headquarters, having given the press and anyone else interested in Mr Khan the runaround.'

'I had hoped to get here sooner,' Jeremy hesitated as he decided on how much to tell his new colleagues. 'I'd a couple of matters to deal with after this morning's Joint Counter-Terrorism meeting. They think that you are part of an ITS, and are at Paddington Green.'

'What do you mean by ITS?' enquired Rafi.

'Islamic Terrorist Syndicate – it's our catch-all phrase for Islamic groups hell-bent on terrorist activities in the pursuance of their fundamentalist ideals.'

Rafi nodded, 'Thank you.'

'As I was saying,' continued Jeremy, 'My boss Neil and I have been told by the head of MI5 to run with Mr Khan's line of thinking. The head of Five reckons there are inconsistencies which need investigating – quietly – off other people's radar screens. Neil's section and I have stuck our necks out on this one, so Mr Khan I look forward to you proving your doubters wrong!'

Jeremy stopped talking and looked around the room. 'How many people know that Mr Khan is here?'

'The three of us plus David, our boss, and Commissioner Giles Meynell,' replied Kate.

'Good. Let's keep it that way. My section is briefed and will be able to provide you with back-up.' Jeremy turned to Rafi. 'I look forward to hearing what you suspect is going on. By the way, you really pissed off my colleagues who interviewed you. It seems that you managed to evade their questioning for over sixty hours without any sleep and practically no food or water. I dropped by to see them before I got here. They looked absolutely knackered! They thought that they'd got you hook, line and sinker, and are now – how can I put it? – in the doghouse! They'd never seen so much evidence stacked against a terrorist suspect and have the bugger slip through their fingers. I'm sorry for the harsh treatment the guards gave you.' Jeremy paused. 'It seems that you were set up good and proper.' Jeremy looked at Rafi. 'Mr Khan I hope we can forget Paddington Green and focus on unravelling what the hell is going on.

'Fine by me, but do call me Rafi – please.'

'Good; thank you,' said Jeremy. 'And by the way we have arranged for Jameel Furud to be put under surveillance in Morocco…

Rafi suddenly remembered Mike and Andy's comments about his sister, and looked across at Jeremy 'On the basis of me being innocent, could you check that MI5 haven't arrested my sister, and if they have, arrange for her release, please?'

'A reasonable request… Leave it with me,' replied Jeremy.

Rafi smiled - a weight had been lifted from his shoulders.

'Kate what have you got planned for us?' enquired Jeremy.

'David should be back shortly. I suggest we then have a council of war to sort out our strategy. In the meantime I've asked Greg Thompson, our IT specialist, to pay us a visit to set up some more computers. He should be with us any time now.'

As if on cue, Greg, a thin, bespectacled man of indeterminate age, walked into the room. 'How can I help? I have arranged for two more networked desktops to be set up. Do you need anything else?'

'When you have a spare minute could you ring Ray Isles, our IT gatekeeper?' said Jeremy. 'And Kate, who would you like to have in the loop with my section at MI5?'

'Emma and me, please.'

'Greg, please ask Ray to sort out the necessary encryption software so that MI5 emails and texts can be read. Also, please give him Kate's and Emma's mobile numbers.' Jeremy turned to Kate. 'I'll run you through the text message codes which will alert you when an important email has been sent.' He turned to Greg. 'Ray is a bit sensitive when it comes to his security software. If he stalls you, tell him you have clearance from the top,' Jeremy smiled. 'You know how it is?'

Greg nodded. 'If that's all, I'll be off.'

As he was leaving the room, Kate turned to her team. 'Let's get started. First how about we get Rafi to tell us what he really believes is going on. How long will you need to pull your thoughts together?'

'A few minutes should do,' came Rafi's hesitant reply.

'Excellent,' said Jeremy. 'That will give me time to visit *Luigi's*, a small restaurant round the corner. Is it any good?'

'Yes, but we tend to use the canteen downstairs,' replied Kate.

'I've been living off cruddy food for the past eight weeks,' explained Jeremy, 'I could do with something to perk me up; if it's alright with you lot I'll nip out to see what they do. How about I put the first lot on my card and after that someone else can have a go?'

Everyone looked sheepish.

Rafi guessed that expenses for food weren't reclaimable. 'Does anyone know where my personal effects and wallet ended up?' he asked.

Kate looked at Rafi. 'We got you out of Paddington Green in a bit of a hurry. Sorry, I've no idea.'

'I've a suggestion,' Rafi continued. 'Could you get *Luigi's* to run a tab, and as soon as I've got my wallet back, I'll pay the bill?'

'Great plan Rafi. I'm going to enjoy working here.' Jeremy looked delighted and was off out the door.

Kate and Emma looked a little surprised and uncomfortable.

'I'm uncertain how to say this Rafi, but that doesn't seem fair,' said Kate.

'I could do with some good quality food, and I owe you for getting me out of that hellhole. Don't worry; I'm good for the money regardless. We're in the City, remember? *My word is my bond*, and all that.'

Emma smiled. 'Most unusual, but thank you.'

*

52

The door swung open and Jeremy entered, acting like a conjuror who was about to pull a rabbit out of a hat. He was clutching three bags with *Luigi's* restaurant logos.

'Here we are! Sorry for the delay. Luigi is a great chap. I've lined up a tab and have put it in your name, Kate. I hope that's in order. Seems the guys downstairs were helpful when someone tried to break into his restaurant several months back. He's very pleased to help in any way, any time of day. Who's for coffee? And I've got orange juice, cappuccinos and some pizza... Help yourselves!'

The two women looked at the pizza and hesitated, thinking of the calories, then grinned at each other.

'I should tuck in, you don't know when we'll next have time for a break,' said Jeremy. He looked at his watch with a smile, 'Or even time for a meal!'

Rafi sat savouring the food and drink.

'Now that Jeremy's back and Rafi has done his thinking, let's get started,' said Kate. 'First question: how does the Bishopsgate bombing fit in with your theory of what is going on?'

'I'm not entirely certain,' replied Rafi, 'but my gut feeling is that Callum Burns was on to something in Luxembourg and his crash was no accident. It also suggests that Prima Terra and others were up to no good.'

He paused. 'Do we know what Jameel Furud is doing in Morocco?' asked Rafi. 'I thought he had work to do in Paris.'

Jeremy flipped open his mobile and spoke to a colleague. He listened intently and hung up. 'My colleagues tell me that Jameel's on his way to Marrakech. If I wanted to go somewhere safe as a Muslim, Morocco would be an excellent choice. He has booked a two week stay at a luxury five-star golf hotel on the edge of the city where he is scheduled to arrive later this morning. We've a colleague keeping an eye on him.'

'I thought he'd do a runner,' said Rafi smiling.

'Can we please move on to the spreadsheets,' asked Emma. 'I see that Callum identified two public quoted companies with dubious shareholders: Dewoodson plc, a property services business and Renshaw Smithers plc, a small finance house focusing on public sector projects and outsourcing companies.'

'Yes that's correct,' replied Rafi.

'Let's start at the beginning - exactly when did Prima Terra buy into these two companies?' enquired Kate.

Rafi thought for a moment. 'About two years ago. We took a large stake in Dewoodson plc when it came to the market.'

Jeremy grimaced.

'What's wrong?' asked Kate.

'That's bad news. If you plan something for a couple of years you are *definitely* up to no good! We're likely to be up against a very well-planned plot, whatever it might be.'

Rafi sat there, thinking about what Jeremy had just said. Then, as if from nowhere, an associated thought flashed through his mind. He was wasn't sure, but *what if*...

'Are you feeling ill?' asked Emma.

'Er... No, I just remembered a company presentation I attended a few weeks ago and an incident that completely slipped my mind. Please bear with me for a moment,' Rafi began hesitantly. 'Let me try and recall it. It may seem like a shaggy-dog story, but it's relevant, I'm sure.'

Rafi closed his bloodshot eyes and took his mind back to a bright January morning a few weeks earlier... 'Yes, I recall it was a Wednesday, three weeks ago. I'd had a hectic morning. The market was buoyant. I had lunch scheduled with a bank and some brokers who were launching an IPO. It was a normal sell-side promote. I was running late and took a taxi. It dropped me a couple of minutes' walk away from their smart new office building on the South Bank; a stunning development scheme. Great attention to detail: black granite walkways, fountains for children to play in and even a small *Pooh sticks* stream which flows down the middle of the walkway to Tooley Street, almost 400 yards away... Sorry; I digress.'

Rafi paused to collect his thoughts... 'After the short presentations, the cheeky buggers pushed through lunch at a cracking pace - they were running two sittings. At 1.15 p.m. I was politely offered my coat and a couple of minutes later I was standing in front of the building feeling rather pissed off. My nice lunch had turned into a fast food experience. I stood there, taking in the view across the Thames. It was a lovely afternoon; the winter sun was out and London looked great, so as I wasn't expected back in the office before 2.30, I decided to stretch my legs and walk back to the office rather than take a taxi.'

Rafi smiled. 'I set off towards Tower Bridge, along the river walkway past the London Assembly Building.'

'Is that the one with the unfortunate nickname relating to a part of the male anatomy?' enquired Jeremy.

'Yes,' Rafi smiled, 'a singularly imposing building,' he paused. 'I then made my way up the steps of Tower Bridge. By the time I reached the far side, the cold wind had got to me. I considered being a wimp and taking a taxi back to the office, but opted for the exercise and turned down the steps that cut under the bridge, went past Dead Man's Gate and headed out into the sunshine past the Tower of London. Whoops, sorry I'm rambling again.'

'Don't worry. As long as you remember something useful we don't mind if you ramble on a bit,' said Kate reassuringly.

'I continued my stroll and headed along Lower Thames Street. I crossed the road and walked up St Mary at Hill, then turned into a narrow cobbled street - St Dunstan's Lane. What prompted me to go that way, I don't know. Perhaps it was because I was enjoying my amble and the lane, with its cobbled surface, looked quaint. It was an impulse. On the corner where St Dunstan's Lane turns into Idol Lane there was a delivery van blocking the single carriageway.' Rafi paused again. 'And fifty metres up Idol Lane, was a chauffeur-driven Mercedes, with its door open waiting for someone to come out of a building.'

Rafi stopped; time seemed to stand still. He stared towards the printer to the right of Emma's desk. It all came flooding back as if it were an action replay. He continued with his story. 'I walked around the corner behind the parked lorry and reappeared just in time to see someone getting into the car. At that precise moment the lorry driver leant out of his window and called to me. I turned and walked back towards him. He wanted to know where the nearest McDonald's was. I apologised, saying that I didn't know, but thought that there was one in Cannon Street and pointed to the end of the road. He thanked me and drove off.'

Rafi's eyes widened. 'As the lorry left, it was followed by the Mercedes; no wonder the person in the car had looked familiar: it was Jameel! I looked at him and, fleetingly, our eyes met – but he didn't acknowledge me. At the time I assumed that he was engrossed in his work. Thinking about it though, *what must it have looked like to my boss*? One moment I was there, the next I was hiding behind a lorry. He couldn't have known I was speaking to the driver.'

'It would have looked suspicious,' said Emma, 'Like you didn't want to be seen.'

'So what did you do next?' asked Kate.

'I walked to the top of the lane and passed by the building Jameel had come out of. It was nondescript, with the numbers 2 - 4 on a plain dark blue front door. There was nothing to give away who or what was based there. At the time I wondered who Jameel had been seeing but, as I didn't think it was important, I dismissed the thought and carried on back to the office,' said Rafi.

'Anything else?' asked Kate.

'That's it!' Rafi, looked at his audience. 'Sorry it took a while to get to the punchline. Could I have spotted Jameel doing something he wanted to keep secret… And that is what triggered his interest in me, particularly if he thought I was spying on him? What do you think?'

Emma looked up. 'Rafi, did he look sheepish when he left the building in Idol Lane?'

'No - just businesslike.'

'I think I should get a list of all the occupiers,' said Emma. 'You can then see if any ring a bell. I'll nip downstairs and raid our database.'

'Good idea,' said Kate.

A short while later Emma returned looking rather pleased with herself; she walked confidently up to Rafi's desk and handed him three sheets of paper.

'Here is the list of occupiers for Idol Lane. Bit of a rabbit warren down there. In case your boss was visiting someone nearby, I took the liberty of checking the adjoining streets as well,' said Emma.

Rafi ran his eyes down the list.

'Emma, could you find out what AGVC does, please? And could you get me a large-scale map which shows exactly where their offices are?' asked Rafi.

Only a few minutes later she had the requested information up on her screen. 'Right, here goes. AGVC – business type: venture capital company and financiers. Any good?'

'Yes!' said Rafi. 'That is what I was hoping for.'

'They are located halfway down on the left-hand side of St Mary at Hill.'

'Hold on a moment,' said Kate, 'I thought you said you saw Jameel in Idol Lane?'

Rafi looked at her slightly crestfallen. 'Good memory,' he said looking at Kate approvingly. 'Yes, you're right.'

Emma smiled. 'No problem, the two properties back on to each other.'

'That's interesting. Who are the occupiers of 2–4 Idol Lane?'

'Rainer Spencer and Mitchell,' answered Emma. 'Says here that they're chartered accountants and company registrars.'

'What's the link?' asked Kate.

'Link?' said Emma. 'What if the buildings were physically linked or interconnected, this would allow Jameel to keep his visits to AGVC's offices secret. Shall we see if the two buildings are in the same ownership?' Emma's fingers worked quickly over her keyboard. 'Right, I'm into the Land Registry website; let's take a look at AGVC's offices first. The address and postcode?' Before anyone could answer, Emma had cut and pasted the information into the Land Registry boxes. 'Oh dear, not much help: the freehold is owned by British & Scottish Property Company.'

'A major London listed property company,' Rafi chipped in.

'Hold on a minute,' said Emma. 'I shouldn't have been too hasty. There seems to be a long leasehold interest in the property owned by a company called PREH.'

'OK, what about the building next to it in Idol Lane?' said Kate.

'Would you believe it; it's owned by PREH as well.'

'That's fantastic, so they *are* connected.' Kate was standing behind Emma, and gave her a friendly pat on the back and then did the same to Rafi.

He almost jumped out of his skin. 'Ooouch!' he exclaimed.

'Whoops, sorry, I've done it again!,' said Kate. 'I forgot about your bumps and bruises.' Her look turned pensive. 'So what have we got? A venture capital business, a property company, plus a firm of chartered accountants and company secretaries. Jeremy could you ask your teams to get chapter and verse on these three businesses, and see if there are any links to Jameel Furud or Prima Terra.'

'Will do… By the way, Rafi what precisely does Prima Terra do?' asked Jeremy.

'They're fund managers, with about £30 billion of funds under management,' replied Rafi.

'It's not your money, is it?' added Jeremy.

Rafi looked at him. 'No.'

'So what's to stop you flushing it down the pan?' continued Jeremy.

'Our reputations. Plus we do get bonuses if we outperform,' replied Rafi.

Jeremy smiled. 'Just a thought - but in my book, bad guys don't go around improving things, they trash them…' He was stopped mid-sentence by his phone. He glanced at its small screen. 'Sorry, I need to take this…'

*

Several hours later, Commissioner Giles Meynell and Chief Superintendent David Pryke walked into Kate's office, which had paper everywhere.

Giles looked around the room. 'Hell's bells. Last time I came in here it looked sort of tidy!'

'Sorry, sir… Things have sort of mushroomed. We found a link between Jameel and a venture capital business,' replied Kate. 'The link has taken us all over the place. They have a wide range of business interests. They're into security, fish processing, have a large property investment company… And one of their businesses runs various public sector services - hospitals, prisons, schools, government buildings…'

The door swung open and Jeremy walked in, looking pleased. 'Sorry to interrupt - MI5 have found that Jameel and Basel both did their PhDs at the London College of Finance.'

Kate glanced across to Giles and David. 'Would there be any chance of borrowing DCI John Dowsing to visit the London College of Finance with Jeremy?'

'Good idea. As the officer in charge of the Bishopsgate bombing, it would be sensible to have him involved with your enquiries,' said Giles. 'Do please keep me informed of your progress. We have to leave you now, David and I are late for another meeting.'

'My MI5 colleagues,' said Jeremy, as the door closed behind Giles and David, 'Tell me they're expecting another series of bombings. The consensus of opinion is that the target will be a transport hub. Security levels have been increased and leave has been cancelled. Rafi, they now think you're a bit of a red herring. Talking of food,' said Jeremy, 'Would you like a cake?' The food had arrived fifteen minutes earlier and been put on the top of a couple of filing cabinets next to Kate where it had been forgotten.

Jeremy tucked in. 'Yum, I must give Luigi a ring and thank him.'

Emma looked across at Kate and smiled. She was about to add something when Jeremy caught her look. 'If you'd spent two months living off Pot Noodles and black coffee...'

'Sorry, I forgot. It's just that we are not used to this,' apologised Emma.

'Now that I've topped up the food levels, where's this London College of Finance and what's the low down on John?'

Emma, on the ball as ever, had found the vice chancellor's address and that of the administration department. She walked over to the printer, collected the sheet and passed it to Jeremy.

Kate picked up the phone. 'Hi John,' she said in a friendly tone, 'Would you have a spare moment? I need some help, please. We've unearthed something that has a direct bearing on the Bishopsgate bombing. I could do with a seasoned brain to give Jeremy Welby, our MI5 friend, a hand. Yes... Yes, I know you're very busy and dislike spooks.'

She paused and listened. 'Yes, I appreciate everyone thinks it's going to hit the fan. But we've come up with an angle which opens up a whole new dimension. I need *your* input and not that of a sidekick, please... Fantastic, thanks. Jeremy's on his way down to your car. He will brief you on the way. I owe you.'

Kate looked across to Jeremy. 'John will meet you downstairs. Don't be put off by his manner. He can be a bit of a gruff old codger, but he's got a great nose for information and has a good sense of humour once you get to know him.' She smiled. 'One other thing, Jeremy, time may well be of the essence... So be as quick as you can, please. And good luck'

Jeremy nodded and left.

'Let's see what we can dig up and reconvene at, say, 5 p.m.,' said Kate.

*

John and Jeremy had an uneventful drive to the London College of Finance. Initially, though, John had been somewhat taciturn. Jeremy had decided that it was best to take the bull by the horns. 'What in particular do you dislike about spooks?' he enquired.

'Basically too bloody secretive by half and treat the rest of us as if we couldn't run a frigging whelk stall.'

'Fair point,' said Jeremy. 'Do me a favour; if you think I'm freezing you out then tell me... No excuses, but from time to time we have to watch our backs. Cock-ups put people like me in danger, so we can get a bit obsessive.'

John's frostiness thawed as Jeremy brought him up to speed on Rafi and the leads that Kate's team had uncovered.

They drew up in front of a smart, white, Georgian terrace and made for the vice chancellor's office. The reception hall could have graced any palace. No expense had been spared - the crystal chandeliers, ornate ceiling cornices, the large, period, gilt-framed mirror, the old grandfather clock and an array of oil paintings gave an air of refinement.

John walked over to the reception desk. 'The vice chancellor, please. He *is* expecting us.'

'And you are?'

'Detective Chief Inspector John Dowsing, Special Branch, City of London police.'

The smartly dressed, forty-something receptionist looked uncomfortably at John and imperceptibly squirmed in her seat. 'Sir Gerald Staniland is rather busy at the moment. If you could please sit over there, I'll find out when he can see you. Would you like a cup of tea or coffee while you wait?'

'He is expecting us. How long do you think he might be?' John looked displeased. He didn't like to be given the runaround.

'I really can't say. Unfortunately, he's left strict instructions not to be disturbed and his meeting could go on for quite some time.'

'Tell the vice chancellor we're here and it's not in his best interests to mess us around.'

The receptionist picked up the phone. 'Margery, I've two

policemen to see the VC. They don't like being kept waiting. Can you help? Thank you. Gentlemen, if you could go upstairs Sir Gerald's PA will look after you.'

Margery looked a formidable gatekeeper. Her anteroom dripped with antiques. John guessed that few students made it this far. He approached the ample, well-manicured PA.

'Sir Gerald is expecting us,' he announced waving his warrant card under Margery's nose.

'There may be a bit of a problem...' she started.

'Too bloody right! If he doesn't see us here and now, he'll spend the rest of the sodding afternoon in an interview room and he won't be offered flaming tea and biscuits!' exclaimed John.

Jeremy had moved in front of a pair of tall double doors. 'This his office?'

'You can't go in.'

'Thank you,' said Jeremy as he opened the doors and beckoned John to follow him.

The vice chancellor's office was huge. He was sitting behind an antique desk at one end of the room; in between him and the door was a set of comfortable-looking armchairs in front of an ornate fireplace to one side and, on the other side, a boardroom table which would not have looked out of place in the dining room of a stately home.

The VC looked up from his paperwork. 'I'm busy, go away.'

Undeterred, John and Jeremy entered, closed the doors and walked towards him.

'If you cooperate this won't take long, or would you perhaps like to see where *we* work?' said John.

Jeremy took up the running. 'We're here to get information on two of your former PhD students: Jameel Furud and Basel Talal. What can you tell us about them?'

The VC stalled. 'When did they study here?'

'About ten to fifteen years ago.'

'Ah! We've a problem there – we archive most of our old student records; data protection and all that, you know. It doesn't pay to get on the wrong side of the law.' He looked at John over his half-moon glasses as if he were a student who had just had an appeal turned down.

'We'll come back to your former students in a moment. Tell

us about the college's PhD programme,' said John.

'We offer one of the largest PhD programmes in the field of Finance. The college takes on between fifteen and twenty-five new applicants each year. We have over 100 PhD students coming from more than fifteen countries.'

'And how many non-EU students are there here?' asked John.

'Nearly 500 out of almost 850,' came the reply.

'So, roughly speaking, I guess your college earns, say, £10 million a year from its overseas students… And without them would it be fair to say that you wouldn't have a business?' enquired John.

'Er… Yes, I suppose so, but that's not relevant,' snapped the VC.

Jeremy stepped forward. 'It is, as I can arrange for the visas of all your non-EU students to be rescinded. It would take just one phone call.'

'Who the ruddy hell do you think you are – barging in here, threatening me with something outside your powers? The City Police can't take away visas.'

'Correct,' said Jeremy, 'But MI5 can! Here's my identification.' Jeremy flashed his warrant card under the VC's nose.

'Now let's start again,' said John.

'What do you know about Drs. Furud and Talal?'

'Nothing! Why do you ask me this banal question?'

'OK your time is up,' said John. 'Gerald Staniland, I'm arresting you in connection with knowingly hindering police investigations into a terrorist activity. I must advise you that under the new anti-terrorism laws, you do not have the right to legal representation.'

A deep scowl came over the VC's face. 'It is Sir Gerald to you. And you have no right to accuse me of some trumped up charge. Get out of my office and don't forget to close the doors behind you.'

'You just don't get it, do you? You're implicated and in the proverbial shit.'

'You can't talk to me like that! Get out of here or I'll call security and have you thrown out.'

'Gerald Staniland, I have reason to believe your college is being used as a recruiting ground for terrorists and, should you be convicted, you will formally and publicly be stripped of your title by the Palace,' said Jeremy. 'John, pass me your handcuffs. If the bastard wants to play hardball, so be it; read him his rights and take him away.'

The VC's confidence crumpled. His face turned ashen grey.

'Alright, alright, I'll help. Their files are in the registry building – next door. Margery knows where to find them.' He picked up the phone.

Moments later Margery appeared at the door. 'Vice chancellor?'

'Please show these two gentlemen to the registry where the student files are kept.'

*

It was 7.20 p.m. on Wednesday evening, and it was all hands to the paperwork at Wood Street. Emma was busy printing out and collating all the documents coming in from MI5.

The door swung open. 'My goodness, you've been busy,' said Jeremy as he entered the room. 'Where on earth did all this paper come from?'

He was followed by John, who looked equally surprised and impressed.

'Had a useful time?' asked Emma, trying to sound upbeat.

'Too right,' replied Jeremy beaming from ear to ear. 'I reckon that the vice chancellor just aged a year or so, don't you John?'

'Well, he was being rather obstructive.'

'OK, the suspense is killing us,' said Emma, 'what did you find out?'

'We have three more names for you,' replied John. 'Jeremy has his colleagues at MI5 digging up as much as they can on them. Before we start briefing you, we've got a few things in our notes to sort out,' John shot a momentary look at Jeremy, who nodded. 'Perhaps we could chat over a bite to eat in a few minutes?'

'Pardon?' said Kate.

'Oh, we stopped off at *Luigi's* and ordered a selection of things to keep us going - a sort of buffet supper. It should be here shortly,' said Jeremy with a grin.

Minutes later the food arrived in reception. Jeremy and John deep in conversation, went off to collect it.

'I've no idea what we've got here,' remarked Jeremy as he came back in. 'I hope you find something you like. Help yourselves. We've organised our notes. John, do you want to start or shall I?'

'OK, I'll go first. The vice chancellor we visited is living the life of Riley. He's on a different planet,' said John.

'Lord Muck was well out of order. He tried to pretend he knew nothing. Didn't take John seriously, refused to help. We sort of leant on him, didn't we John?' interjected Jeremy with a cheeky grin.

John quickly finished a mouthful of food. 'Our two original suspects, Jameel Furud and Basel Talal were part of a clique of five students, who all frequented the same mosque. Sheikh Akram Tufayl and Miti Lakhani, an Asian-African were fellow PhD students and close friends. The fifth member was Maryam Vynckt, Basel Talal's younger sister, who studied for a Masters in Law nearby.'

'Bloody hell! I think she could be related to the Luxembourg financier that Callum visited just before he died,' interrupted Rafi. 'Sorry – do go on.'

'We tracked down one of their contemporaries, Dr Mario Lutchins, who is now a senior lecturer at a business school in London. We dropped in to see him on our way back,' said Jeremy, reaching over to help himself to more food, whilst John took up the running.

'To cut a long story short, the VC is caught between a rock and a hard place. His problem is that Sheikh Tufayl makes a hefty donation of half a million pounds a year to the College, but there is a non-disclosure clause… The money stops if the sheikh's name is made public. And without the money the VC's lifestyle would go down the pan.'

It was now Jeremy's turn. 'These five individuals certainly made an impression on our Dr Lutchins, who at the time was going out with a secretary in the Faculty Office. Unfortunately for him, Jameel turned on the charm, had his way with her and then dumped her. Mario has never forgiven him and has since then taken a sinister interest in Jameel and his colleagues' activities. He has been particularly helpful in filling in some of the gaps.'

Jeremy looked down at his notes. 'Sheikh Tufayl was the man with the money. He had a lovely duplex flat in NW8 overlooking

Regent's Park. He led the high life.'

John continued while Jeremy took a mouthful of food. 'The sheikh was outwardly religious, a driven man, always on the go. He was seriously wealthy, enjoyed a luxurious Western lifestyle, and thought studying for a PhD was a great way to live, particularly as it kept his father off his back. He liked to hypothesise and seemed to be more interested in the big picture side of things.'

John looked down at his notebook. 'To quote Mario: *The sheikh despised us for Iraq, disliked our meddling foreign policies*. He thought the UK had become too soft and trusting and forgotten one of the key rules of economic and personal survival - *when the chips are down, the oil-rich countries look after themselves*. Or put another way - *if a country runs out of energy, it is stuffed*,' John took another mouthful and nodded towards Jeremy.

'The sheikh completed the last eighteen months of his PhD from his home in the Gulf, following his father's death in a freak skiing accident,' continued Jeremy. 'A MI5 source tells me that he fell into a small ravine. The fall didn't kill him, but he was injured sufficiently badly that he wasn't able to climb out, and died from hypothermia… Sadly for him, his mobile phone's battery was knackered. Sheikh Tufayl was on holiday with his father at the time.'

Jeremy looked at his notes. 'Sheikh Tufayl took over the family business – or should I say, the oil wells. When the sheikh received his PhD two years later, the VC talked him into funding a high profile annual lecture… and the sheikh's money started rolling into the College. The great and the good are invited to the lectures and to a sumptuous dinner afterwards at one of the finest City of London livery companies. The vice chancellor plans the lectures and dinners with military precision.'

'Now let's turn to the number two in the clique: Basel Talal,' continued John. 'According to Mario he was moderately wealthy by Arab standards – bloody rich by yours or mine - and lived within walking distance of the sheikh. He had an incisive but practical brain, and paid great attention to detail. He was an excellent manager and manipulator. According to Mario, Basel has been successful in the venture capital business, but keeps a surprisingly low profile. And Mario believes that Basel has a wealthy offshore backer... His guess is that the money comes from the sheikh.'

'Oh, did we mention that Basel was the sheikh's cousin?' interjected Jeremy.

'And now on to number three in the clique: your erstwhile boss Jameel Furud,' continued John. 'He was a close friend of the sheikh and his cousin, but lacked their money. He shared their interests in discussing economic strategies and how markets worked, and whether they could be manipulated. He loved the high life and his particular talent was his ability to charm the ladies. This talent went down especially well with the sheikh, who loved to party and to have a beautiful woman on his arm. After his PhD, Jameel spent time setting up and running a fund management business in the Gulf and looked after the sheikh's newfound wealth. The business grew and moved to Zurich for a short while, before moving to London where it was rebranded as *Prima Terra*. Mario finds it strange that since his return to the UK, Jameel rarely promotes the fact that he has a PhD...'

'I suppose he likes his wheeler-dealer image,' said Rafi.

'According to Mario the fourth member of the group was Maryam Talal, now Mrs Maryam Vynckt. She's the younger sister of Basel and of course cousin to the sheikh,' said John. 'She read Law at Cambridge, followed by a two-year Master's in Law in London. Her masters dissertation was on: *Cross border investment vehicles and cross border taxation*. According to Mario, she an Eastern beauty and a fantastic linguist – she speaks most of the main European languages as if they were her native tongue.'

John looked at his notes. 'Maryam worked for the international legal firm Tollemarsh Ruddock and Leveritt in the City where she specialised in corporate acquisitions. There she renewed her acquaintance with Mr Hubert Vynckt - he'd read Business Administration at the Judge Institute and had been in the same Cambridge University college as her. Hubert's family investment business, CPR Investment Funds, became a big client of hers.'

'John, you're losing out on the food,' commented Jeremy. 'Let me do the next bit. Maryam, visited Hubert frequently and then Hubert made Maryam an offer she couldn't refuse: to head up his private clients division *and* a wedding ring. They married and she moved to Luxembourg. Then, out of the blue, her division was bought by the Gulf Trade Bank. Maryam, is CEO, of the merged private clients departments and now works from the Bank's headquarters in the Gulf and from its offices in Luxembourg, which are in the same building as Hubert's CPR Investment Funds.'

Rafi sat bolt upright. 'Oh yes! I really do bet Callum met her.'

'OK, I'll get that checked out,' said Jeremy.

'According to Mario,' said John, 'the Gulf Trade Bank is part of the sheikh's business empire and that the bank's acquisition of Hubert's private clients division was the sheikh's way of ensuring that Maryam was close by... Ah yes, I nearly forgot. Mario says that Maryam is the most driven of the clique.'

'That leaves us with the last member: Miti Lakhani,' said Jeremy. 'He struggled to make ends meet whilst in London. It seems that the money was there but his father wanted his son to work and not play and so kept Miti on a tight financial rein. Unfortunately, after five years he went home to Mogadishu with an MPhil and not the expected PhD. It seems he drew the short straw, in that his supervisor was more interested in his consultancy work than tending to his academic flock... Miti's family owns a thriving import/export business based in Sudan and Somalia. Mario reckons they also own a lot of land there.'

'Now for the scary bit,' said John looking at his notes. 'To quote Mario, *In a crazier world, the PhD dissertations of Tufayl, Talal and Furud, when put together, could be viewed as the instruction kit for building a financial atomic bomb...*'

Kate, who up to this point had been listening quietly and intently, suddenly sat up and took notice. 'Explain, please.'

'Rafi knows more about these things than I do,' said Jeremy. 'If I read out the dissertation titles, perhaps Rafi can explain? Sheikh Tufayl started his on: *Sovereign credit ratings and public sector debt,* but amended it after his mid-stage viva to: *The impact of energy shortages on the financial markets.* Basel Talal's thesis was on: *The identification of business failure and contagion in finance, insurance and banking sectors.* He looked mainly at the reasons why these businesses got into financial trouble and the ripple effects that this could cause.'

Jeremy looked at Rafi. 'Does that make sense?'

Rafi nodded.

'Jameel Furud's thesis,' Jeremy continued hesitantly, reading carefully from his notes, was on: *The risks of financial products in destabilised markets.* His thesis considered whether it was possible for a significant number of small items to go below the risk management radar screen, with the consequence that if the markets took a plunge one or more institutions might become insolvent.'

'I agree with Mario,' said Rafi, 'If one puts the three theses together – energy shortages, with business failure and large losses in the derivative markets – it makes for a very volatile and potentially dangerous cocktail.'

Emma and Kate looked concerned. Emma was about to say something when John carried on. 'Oh… I quite forgot. We spotted that two of the PhDs had dedications. The sheikh's dissertation was dedicated to Yousif and Basel's to Khalid. MI5 are trying to find out who they might be,' said John.

Wisps of ideas were swirling around inside Rafi's head. They did not paint a reassuring picture. The bombing was only a *distraction.* Jameel and his associates were after a *far* larger target.

Sensing Rafi was deep in thought, Kate stepped in. 'Thank you both. That was an extremely useful synopsis! You did well to find Mario. We're fortunate that he took such a keen interest in the group.'

'All thanks to Jameel's fling with his girlfriend!' said Emma.

Kate ignored her comment. 'I reckon you've found us our ringleaders. I'm uncertain where Miti fits in, though. Thank you both. Any questions?'

'I've one,' said Emma. 'Where is the vice chancellor now?'

'I have arranged for him to spend a few days enjoying the hospitality of MI5… As we couldn't trust him to keep his mouth shut,' added Jeremy. 'His PA overheard John and I talking. We let her think that we'd charged him for molesting one of his daughter's underage friends. You should have seen his face when the squad car arrived to take him away. Serves him right!'

'I have a big problem,' said Kate. 'I worry that this is all too circumstantial. Are we going in the right direction, given the starting point of the Bishopsgate bombing? Shouldn't we be looking at other scenarios? Though I'll be damned if I know what they might be.'

John looked at her in a reassuring way. 'Kate, by all means keep an open mind and if another scenario comes along, use my team downstairs to work on it. But for now, you must run with what you've got.'

'Emma and Rafi, keep researching the companies,' instructed Kate. 'John, Jeremy and I will focus on the individuals involved. Let's touch base in an hour's time.'

Emma pushed her chair across to Rafi's desk. 'Can we go back a step? Is Prima Terra valuable?'

'Yep,' replied Rafi. 'Something like £1.5 billion.'

'And the ultimate owner of Prima Terra is the sheikh?'

'Yes, I now believe so.'

'So if the sheikh is willing to jeopardise Prima Terra and as a consequence lose an investment worth many hundreds of millions of pounds… He must be confident of making a great deal of money from whatever he is planning to do.'

'And as I see it,' said Rafi, 'The two dodgy companies that Callum found plus the venture capital business are too small to make the sort of returns they'll need.'

Emma frowned.

Rafi could almost see the cogs going round in her mind.

'If one takes their PhD topics and then add in Jameel Furud and Maryam Vynckt's expertise and financial clout… I'd put my money on the terrorists targeting the derivatives markets,' said Emma.

'I agree… If they could find a way to make the markets crash, they could then walk away with shed loads of money,' added Rafi with a large yawn.

'Precisely,' continued Emma, 'And there must be enough dishonest international bankers out there who – for a fee – would provide a front for dubious derivatives trading. And it would be practically impossible for the authorities to track down where the profits went – let alone get them back again!'

'OK, so the terrorists will want to give the market a fright,' started Rafi. He was about to say something more, but was interrupted by a series of large yawns.

'You look dead on your feet,' said Emma.

Kate looked across at Rafi. 'Time for you to take a nap I reckon.'

Rafi stifled another yawn and nodded.

'Follow me.' She led him down to the basement cells, with a blanket over his head. When they reached their destination, she picked up a second blanket and a pillow and ushered him into a cell.

'Not five-star accommodation, but at least it's quiet. I'll come back and get you in a couple of hours. I'm sorry but I need to lock you in, otherwise the duty policeman might investigate.' The door swung shut behind her.

Rafi climbed onto the hard bed and pulled the blankets over him - a few seconds later he was sound asleep.

*

The next thing Rafi knew, Kate was standing over him.

'Come on sleepyhead, time to get up.'

He followed her back to the office. On his desk was a cup of steaming hot black coffee; next to it was a large pile of papers.

'I thought you might like to get your teeth into the accounts of the companies financed by the venture capital business. Let me know if you spot anything out of the ordinary,' said Kate.

'Will do,' replied Rafi, picking up the first set of accounts.

*

A couple of hours later Rafi was hunched over his desk hard at work - the clock on the wall showed WED 21:15.

'Anyone else found an Estonian connection?' called out Rafi. 'The security business has an activity there. It's in the fine print in their accounts, under currency exchange rates.'

Emma rifled through a stack of papers. 'Hold on a minute... Yup... The fish processing business has the same!'

'Good work, you two.' Kate picked up her phone. 'Let's see if David has any Estonian contacts... Good evening David... How do I find a police or security services contact who we can trust in Estonia? There's some digging that we need done and quickly.'

'That's a good one,' came the reply. The speakerphone went quiet for a moment. 'If you go to my office... You know where the keys to my filing cabinet are, don't you...? Go to the second drawer down; near the back is a folder marked *EU Money Laundering and Illegal Trade Conference*. At the front you'll find a business card stapled to a sheet of paper – Colonel Hendrik Matlik. He is one of their top dogs in their Security Police. Give him a ring and say that you're working with me and that you could do with some help. On first impressions he comes across as very severe, but underneath he's a huge teddy bear. He's a real five-star compatriot, very proud of his country joining the EU and is determined to keep organised crime out. Oh yes, and remember to send my love to his daughter, Kristina. She must be at university now... Also ask him to ring you back on a secure line - he'll appreciate that! Good luck.'

A couple of minutes later, Kate returned with the business card – "Colonel Hendrik Matlik, Kaitsepolitseiamet". On the reverse was the English translation – "Estonian Security Police". 'There's a direct line number. Excellent!'

It was 9.40 p.m. in the UK and 10.40 p.m. in Tallinn. As Kate dialled the number, she wondered whether there would be anyone in the office.

'Halloo, tere õhtust.'

Kate raised her eyebrows. 'Do you speak English?'

'Of course.'

Kate breathed a sigh of relief. 'Could I please speak to Colonel Hendrik Matlik?'

'Do you know what time it is?' came the reply.

'Yes, I must apologise, but it's important that I speak to him.'

'Can I say who is calling?'

'Detective Inspector Kate Adams, I'm a colleague of Chief Superintendent David Pryke, City of London Police.'

'Thank you.'

The phone went silent. The wait seemed to go on for ages. Then a deep voice came on the line.

'Hello, Matlik here.'

'Good evening,' said Kate, 'My boss, David Pryke, suggested I called you as he believes you might be able to help us. Oh, and he sends his kind regards to Kristina.'

'Is it essential that I should help... Now?'

'Yes, please,' replied Kate. 'We're investigating the Bishopsgate police station bombing and a follow-up terrorist attack.'

'I read of that atrocity; please pass my condolences to David,' said the colonel.

'Could you ring me back on a secure line?' requested Kate.

There was a loud chuckle from the other end of the phone,

which turned into a laugh. 'I'm going to like working with you.'

Kate looked blankly at the phone and wondered how David knew her comment would tickle the colonel's sense of humour.

'No need to worry about the phone line. As one of the bosses of the KAPO my line is secure and before you were put through my office traced your call back to Wood Street police station. Isn't technology wonderful? How can I be of assistance?'

Kate told the colonel of her pressing need for information on two UK companies with operations in Tallinn and gave him the name and Tallinn address of a former director, Pinja Koit. 'We sense time is against us. At the moment we've identified a network of companies that seem to be involved.'

'I'll see what I can do to help and get back to you first thing in the morning. If you want to reach me, I'll be on the number you phoned.'

'Thank you,' said Kate, hanging up.

'While you were on the other line, the commissioner phoned,' said Emma. 'John's now formally on our team. He said we could do with his experience and low cunning.'

John smiled and nodded. 'Pleased to help.'

'And we've also co-opted Peter Ashby from Traffic. He's to be our gofer.'

The phone rang – it was reception for Jeremy. 'OK,' he said, 'I'll be down straight away.'

He was soon back, clutching bags filled with steaming cups of coffee and delicious-looking Italian cakes. 'With Luigi's compliments,' he smiled as he passed the coffee around.

Emma looked across at Jeremy. 'But we only had our supper a few hours ago. When will your obsession with food calm down?'

'This is the afters! Who was it that said: *An army marches on its stomach*?'

'Napoleon?' ventured Emma, pleased to have answered before Kate.

'Precisely. I asked Luigi to prepare us something to keep us going, in case we begin to flag. It's going to be a very long night. And you try living off crap for two months and see if you can keep away from good food.'

'Point taken,' said Kate. 'Now we have Rafi back with us, it would be a good moment to pull together all we've been doing over the past four or five hours, so that we can keep an eye on the big picture and make sure we aren't going off on a wild goose chase. OK, who wants to start?'

'I will,' said John. 'My team downstairs has been helping me with the terrorists' public sector services businesses. They are investigating exactly what they do and who they employ. Thankfully, as incorporated limited partnerships, their businesses have to be registered at Companies House.' John paused and looked at his notes. 'The scale of these activities is downright impressive or, from our perspective, very scary! Their empire comprises numerous operations: security for police cells - and includes Paddington Green. They also operate prisons, schools and hospitals. They have a number of *soft* facilities management contracts for the Home Office and the Foreign Office. And through a spider's web of connected limited partnerships they employ over 200,000 people!'

'Wow, that is impressive.' exclaimed Kate. 'What are their finances like?'

'They're sailing very close to the wind. They've got massive debts, and carry unlimited liability if things go wrong,' replied John.

'So if we take Jeremy's line that the terrorists will be in destruction mode, this public sector business of theirs is a house of cards?' asked Kate.

'Precisely,' said John. 'And it wouldn't be difficult to make it collapse.'

'And if it did go bust?' asked Kate.

'It would leave one hell of a mess across the public sector!' John took a slurp of his coffee. 'My team has also come up with another angle. With the help of Companies House we've drawn up a list of all the people who sit on the management boards of these limited liability partnerships. Several of the names are very interesting. There are a couple of politicians *and* some professional advisers to Government departments! I have given Jeremy's colleagues the full list of names to see what they can make of it.'

'Oh, I almost forgot to say,' added John. 'We had a look at where else they operate. One of their businesses provides the guards to the garage at Bishopsgate police station! MI5 has traced their security man, who was away from his post at the time of the bombing. He's now on holiday in Spain and, rumour has it, he's buying a villa out there!

'I've passed our preliminary findings to the commissioner and he's briefing all his opposite numbers that their security may be compromised and that they *have* to keep this under wraps. So far he hasn't spoken to the Government departments, given the number of politicians and special advisers that seem to be on the terrorists' payroll, innocently or otherwise.'

The atmosphere in the room had perceivably cooled. Kate finally broke the silence. 'Who would like to go next?'

'MI5 has found another link between Jameel Furud and Basel Talal,' said Jeremy. They are trustees of a charity, which works with a number of high profile companies, and sponsors students undertaking voluntary work in Africa. It's not a big enterprise. MI5 are looking into how the airline tickets are booked and where the students have worked.'

'My team has also been looking into their fish processing business,' continued John. 'It's a substantial business and a nicely profitable one at that. It operates a fleet of trawlers out of the UK and Estonia, which gives them a base close to the old Soviet Bloc.'

Kate looked thoughtfully at John. 'Their fishing boats could provide a means of moving things and people in and out of the UK... We should locate all of their trawlers...'

'We are already on to it,' said John. 'On the internet there are lists of EU trawlers. The information includes lots of details on each vessel and who owns them – shown by port...'

'Can I make an observation?' interrupted Rafi. 'I'm thinking practicalities. We're talking in terms of trawlers being used to get people in and out of the UK. I agree with their usefulness for getting things in, but I've a problem with using them for an exit... Wouldn't they be too slow?'

'I agree,' said John. 'How about they use them just to get the terrorists out of UK territorial waters? Thereafter, I personally would want something much faster to whisk me away.'

'That's a good point John; make sure that we pick it up when we discuss the terrorists' exit strategy in more detail.' Kate paused. 'Where have we got to on the property front?'

'Emma and I were wondering whether they might use one or more of their properties to support potential terrorist attacks,' said Rafi. 'Just imagine how much easier it would be to attack something from a secure, nearby property over which you have complete control. And if one takes PREH's full name – Prime Real Estate Holdings – literally, their portfolio should comprise property investments of institutional quality. Ergo, the properties should be in prime locations. The list of property addresses from the company's mortgage register runs to three pages and, among those, I've identified four properties which look distinctly out of place...' Rafi studied his scribbled notes. 'A retail park on the outskirts of Peterhead and three industrial estates in: Prestwick, North Walsham and Hartlepool. I've given Emma the addresses. She's seeing whether they're near any potential targets.'

'Why do you think that?' enquired John. 'Surely that's a bit over the top. These days a plain van suffices for most purposes, so who needs properties?'

Emma raised her head from the screen of her PC; her face was sombre. 'What if one of the properties overlooked a nuclear power station – would that change your view?'

'Oh shit, yes!' replied John.

'Well, at a first glance, the Hartlepool property is bang next to the nuclear power station. If you follow the energy theme,' continued Emma, 'The North Walsham property is only a stone's throw away from the huge gas terminal at Bacton. Peterhead is one of the major Scottish fishing ports and it's close to another gas facility at St Fergus... Which is vast. The fourth property is next to Prestwick airport and is not that far from Hunterston nuclear power station.'

A shocked silence fell over the room. It was broken by Jeremy who spoke to John. 'Remember when we chatted to Mario about the PhD dissertations?'

'Bloody hell! Yes. Energy targets would fit.'

'How's about we get a large map, plus several sheets of acetate which can be laid over it with the locations of the properties? We can add the other items as we come across them. For example, Emma will soon have the ports that the trawlers are operating out of and the list of key energy installations.'

'We can do better than that,' added Kate. 'Let's borrow the touch screen monitor and the computer with mapping software from downstairs.'

'Great idea,' said Emma, 'I'll sort it.'

*

Rafi felt shattered. It was well after midnight. Sleep deprivation was closing in on him. Slumped over his desk, something nagged at him. On the one hand, his brain told him it needed to turn off; on the other hand, a thought was niggling at him - he felt sure there was something obvious he'd missed. He would reread the property company's accounts and then get some sleep.

He opened up the accounts for the current and previous years; some sections had scanned badly. He found the note on properties in both sets of accounts. They were not very clear. Rafi took out a blank sheet of paper and started to decipher what was written there. He picked out the word *external* and a word beginning with *valu*.... It was as if someone had let off a firecracker behind him. He sat bolt upright. His tiredness evaporated. Of course, how bloody stupid of him! The accounting standards required property companies to have annual revaluations of their assets.

He called across to Kate. 'There's an external valuer out there with the full details of all the properties in the portfolio. Sorry I've been a right idiot not to have thought of this earlier.' He was annoyed by his elementary slip-up. The nagging feeling had stopped and abject tiredness took over.

'I'm off to get some shut-eye, before I keel over. Kate could you arrange for me to be woken first thing, please?'

'Will do. Sleep well.'

*

Rafi slept soundly. By 6.40 a.m. he was back at his desk with a steaming cup of strong coffee, wondering what Thursday might bring. First, he rechecked the web to see if he had missed anything on PREH, the terrorists' property investment company. There was little there to help him. His next task was to find the elusive property valuers and quickly. He was pleased that PREH used an external and not an independent valuer. The latter would be difficult to track down quickly as it could have no dealings with the company other than undertaking its valuations. In contrast, an external valuer could undertake other work for the company, and their property lettings, buying or selling work would, with any luck, be recorded on one of the specialist property databases. Rafi realised this was where he had to look. The cynic in him surmised that PREH's external valuers would be rewarded with excellent fees for their non-valuation work.

He shouted across to Kate and Emma. 'As a matter of urgency, we need a contact at a commercial property agent who will do a search of their property databases for us. Do you know anyone? Unfortunately, I now can't trust any of my contacts.'

Kate shook her head.

'Would the commissioner be able to help?' asked Rafi.

'More than likely,' said Kate. 'I'll give him a call.'

A couple of minutes later she had the name and mobile number of a Mr Perryman: a director at a major international property agent. Kate smiled. 'The commissioner hopes that this individual will be more cooperative than the vice chancellor!' she said as she dialled the number and was put through to voicemail. She left a message asking whoever picked it up to return the call as quickly as possible.

Kate hung up, then rang back and spoke to the receptionist. It transpired that there was no one in from Mr Perryman's team. The receptionist promised to get the first one who came in to ring her.

Ten minutes later Kate received a call from Mr Perryman's personal assistant: Pam Blake. Kate introduced herself.

'Could I speak to Mr Perryman?'

'I'm afraid not; he's on his way to a property inspection.'

'I have a problem and was wondering whether you might be able to help. What I am about to tell you is in strictest confidence.'

'I understand.'

'We're investigating a serious crime; my commissioner advises me that your boss is the man to help us access your databases. We could do with his help, now, please!'

'Leave it to me; I'll contact Mr Perryman and ask for his permission to help you.'

Only a few minutes later, Pam was back on the phone to Kate.

'I have confirmation that I may help you – within reasonable bounds, of course.'

'Thank you,' said Kate. 'May I email you a list of the addresses? What I need,' she looked down at Rafi's scribbled note, 'Are the printouts from your in-house database, Focus and EGi giving details of which agents have done deals at these addresses in the past four years. Could you do this as a matter of urgency?'

'Of course! I'll get Mr Perryman's colleague, Justin Smith, to run the searches. As luck would have it he's just walked in the door.'

'Will you please advise Mr Smith that this information isn't to be discussed with any of his colleagues. When he's printed it out, I'd be most grateful if you'd ring me so that I can arrange for it to be picked up. If there's going to be a delay, could you please let me know?'

'Will do.'

'Thank you, Pam.'

'My pleasure.'

Kate turned to Rafi. 'This has all happened so fast. Remind me what precisely you are looking for? And what are Focus and EGi?'

'If we can find the external valuer, we can get hold of the property portfolio valuation report. I've a feeling it'll show properties which are *not* on the mortgage register and which *could* be part of the terrorist plans. Focus and EGi are the two huge online databases that property agents use to find information on deals done, amongst other things.'

'Thanks... If it helps us find more properties, it seems like a good call,' said Kate.

*

Kate took a call from Colonel Matlik. 'Good morning colonel. Your timing is perfect; David has just walked into the room. Let me put you on the speakerphone.'

'Hello David,' said the distinctive voice of Colonel Matlik.

'Good to hear you again,' replied David.

'I was so sorry to hear of the deaths of your colleagues; rest assured we are leaving no stone unturned at this end,' said the colonel. 'And we are treating your request on a strictly need-to-know basis, as asked.'

'Thank you.'

'Regarding the security business; initially we were unable to find any link to them, but the name you gave us is very interesting. Mr Koit was well-connected and very wealthy. He had a shadowy past. The FSB – Russian Federal Security Service – had been keeping an eye on him. They tell me that he was killed in a private plane crash several months ago and that he had some very unsavoury connections with people from Chechnya. Through Mr Koit we have traced a local company specialising in executive training in guns and personal security. They are based deep in the countryside, twenty kilometres from Tallinn. I have sent two of my officers undercover to see what is there.'

'Excellent,' said David.

'I have also been looking into their fishing activities. Your terrorists operate two trawlers, and it seems that they have quite a set-up in Tallinn. I have spoken to a tax inspector and asked him to look at their books. He knows nothing of our suspicions. In one hour's time he will be paying their warehouse in the docks a visit. Two of my operatives are tagging along to have a proper look around.' A deep chuckle echoed down the phone line.

The colonel hesitated. 'What worries me is that they aren't showing the telltale signs of an Al Qaeda cell, but those of a very professional organisation which uses experts rather than recently trained recruits.'

There was a pause. 'My team monitors the activities of Russian investors and mafia. This creates tension from time to time with the Russian FSB, but as there is a Chechen connection they're being most cooperative. Oh, by the way, our laws prohibit us from using phone taps unless we have a court order from a judge. A colleague will petition the judge as soon as the court opens this morning. I'll let you know if they produce anything useful.'

'Thank you,' said David. 'By the way, how's Kristina – is she enjoying university?'

'Yes, thank you. When all this is over you must come and visit us. We will talk again soon.'

The speakerphone went silent.

David turned to Kate. 'Kristina is his only daughter; his wife was killed by a car bomb meant for the colonel several years ago. It seems that he upset some people in the Russian mafia who were trying to set up business in Tallinn. He's a driven man, determined to right the wrong of his wife's death. Heaven help any terrorist who crosses his path. We couldn't ask for a better ally.'

*

It was 7.45 a.m. when Giles arrived for his morning briefing. He indicated to Kate that she should make a start.

'Commissioner, we've uncovered a large amount of background material which indicates that the terrorists are thinking big. As the financial markets are involved we believe that the attacks will be sooner than later; probably a matter of days, certainly not weeks.'

'Kate, it does no harm to work to a short timescale, but be very, very careful not to overlook critical pieces of information in your quest for speed.' The commissioner glanced up and looked at the others. 'Is that noted?'

'Yes, sir,' they chorused.

'What investigations are ongoing?' enquired Giles.

'We have a number of balls up in the air, sir,' replied Kate. 'The Estonian Security Service is investigating the terrorists' activities on a firing range outside Tallinn, an Estonian import/export business and their fishing business there. Emma is researching the whereabouts of the terrorists' trawler fleet, as we believe that they may use it as part of their exit strategy.

'Rafi,' continued Kate, 'is working on the property angle to see how many of the properties the terrorists own are close to likely targets. John and his team are working with MI5 to unravel the terrorists' sizeable public sector businesses. This is proving to be an unexpectedly large project. They're working on the list of its public sector contracts and the senior people on their payroll. The list is long and the names include a couple of Members of Parliament and many very well-connected people. This causes MI5 and us major concerns. Our investigations could be set back if one of these people learned of what we are doing and tipped off the terrorist leaders.'

David and Giles nodded. Kate continued, 'Also, Jeremy has received confirmation that Callum's last meeting was with one of the suspected ring leaders: Maryam Vynckt. She's a director at Gulf Trade Bank and is ideally placed to move money around unseen, offshore.'

Giles turned to David. 'We've got a meeting with the London anti-terrorist committee at 12 o'clock. They're still convinced that the next attacks will target public places: airports, underground trains, stations, and the like. We'll have to break cover soon or else we'll be in deep s h one t, if events conspire against us.'

'Kate, how much longer before we have a clearer picture of what they're targeting?' asked the commissioner.

'Sir, one of our lines of thinking is that they could use their property portfolio as the base for attacks on energy installations. Rafi believes their aim is also to crash the financial markets and in the process make a fortune in the derivatives markets. They're thinking big, as they seem willing to throw away Prima Terra which is worth around £1.5 billion, *and* we reckon that they've invested a couple of years in planning these attacks.' Kate paused. 'We also think that they'll pull the rug from under their public sector company and all in all give the Government a particularly bloody nose.'

'Surely you're exaggerating the position, aren't you?' asked David.

'Well, no, I'm afraid not; in fact, as things stand I'd be willing to bet a year's salary on this hunch,' said Rafi.

'Do, please, keep me informed. See where you've got to at 2.00 p.m. David and I will make a decision on who to inform at that point.'

'Could I make a request?' ventured Rafi.

'What is it?' enquired David.

'I think we need an expert to see what Jameel and his colleagues have been up to in the derivatives markets.'

David looked across at Rafi. 'Do you know a suitably qualified person?'

'Yes, sir.'

Jeremy, who had been sitting quietly, spoke up. 'Seems straightforward enough – you name him, I get him, problem solved.'

'Agreed,' said the commissioner. 'Please see to it as soon as we finish this meeting.'

The two senior officers stood up to leave. 'We'll be close at hand should you require any, and I repeat, *any* assistance,' said Giles. 'All this station's resources are at your disposal – just ask.'

'As are all those of my colleagues,' added Jeremy.

The meeting was over.

Chapter 3

'Jeremy, using your diplomatic skills, could you pick up Aidan Gilchrist from Maine Leadbetter's dealing room? Rafi will give you the address,' said Kate. 'Do it quietly and get him here as soon as possible. Tell him some cock and bull story that you're looking into a money laundering scam for MI5 and if he's not convinced reassure him that you've been given his name as a head honcho and a quiet chat would be much appreciated.'

'Oh, you mean, the could-he-give-James-Bond-a-helping-hand story?' said Jeremy with a grin.

Kate looked across at him and returned the smile. 'You read too many comic books!'

'But it isn't half fun! And what if he's too busy and won't come?' asked Jeremy.

'I suggest you take him somewhere quiet and advise him of the powers of MI5, should they wish to flex their muscles,' suggested Kate. 'I think it would be best if you went alone. It'll raise less suspicion. We don't want Gilchrist's colleagues to know what's going on. I'll arrange for a car to take you.'

Jeremy picked up his jacket from the back of his chair and was gone.

'Kate, we're going to need a couple more computers and access to some databases,' said Emma glancing around the room. 'Shall I chat to Greg or do you need to clear it with the boss?'

'No problem. I have his delegated authority on this one. Leave it with me,' replied Kate.

John looked at Rafi thoughtfully. 'Could you explain in layman's terms why the derivatives market is potentially so dangerous... And so lucrative?'

Rafi smiled. 'Put simply, derivatives are a way of betting whether a financial asset will go up or down relative to peoples' expectations. In our case, let's say that the terrorists do something which causes the markets to plunge unexpectedly. If they have bought put contracts, the more the market goes down the bigger the profit they'll make. If you speculate correctly you can make big profits of say ten, maybe twenty times your initial outlay. However, derivative markets are a zero-sum-game, thus for every winner there's a loser. They're the rocket science end of things, which is why I could do with Aidan's help.'

'Thanks,' said John. 'So if the sheikh and his associates were to speculate say £1 billion in these markets and they rig things to go their way, they stand to make £10 to £20 billion? Sort of puts all their planning into perspective, doesn't it?'

'I fear so,' replied Rafi.

A look of concern spread across John's face. 'For a payout of £20 billion, heaven only knows what they have planned! Oh, by the way, I've been mulling over something you said about their exit plans. If they are intending to get *that* rich they won't want to hang around. So I would put looking for a fast motor cruiser at the top of my "to do list". Just a thought. Must dash now - I've got a meeting with my team. Let's talk soon.'

★

Jeremy was standing at reception accompanied by a very unhappy individual. 'Give DI Adams a bell and tell her I have Mr Gilchrist with me and that I am heading for the fourth floor interview room.'

Kate, Emma and Rafi arrived at the interview room moments before Jeremy and a very disgruntled Aidan Gilchrist, who looked as if a thunder cloud was hovering directly over his head.

'What do you want from me?' He was annoyed. 'I thought you were taking me somewhere civilised to talk, not to a bloody police station.' He turned and, on seeing Rafi did a double take.

'What the hell are you doing here?'

Suddenly, it dawned on Rafi that his mugshot – as the man behind the Bishopsgate bombing – must have been all over the papers.

Aidan looked uncertainly at Rafi then, like the first class financial dealer that he was, he quickly regained his composure. And acted as if he had known what was going to happen all along.

Kate decided to take charge of the situation and spoke up. 'Let me introduce you to my team: I'm Detective Inspector Kate Adams and this is my assistant, Detective Constable Emma Jessop.

We specialise in financial fraud. You already know our infamous friend, Rafi. We'll shortly be joined by the head of our IT section, Greg Thompson, and you've met Jeremy, from MI5. Please bear in mind that you're here as our guest. I'm sorry that our hospitality doesn't match the standards set by your bank.' Kate smiled with a twinkle in her eyes. 'Rafi has been helping us with our enquiries. He's best placed to explain why we need your help,' she concluded, indicating to Rafi that he could begin.

'Thank you, Kate. Aidan, I'm sorry for the cloak-and-dagger stuff. Basically, I was framed. By accident, I stumbled across pieces of the terrorists' plans. Before we go any further I should explain your position and make it absolutely clear that you're here under no coercion. I asked Jeremy to get you as we need your help – we believe they are targeting the derivatives market.'

'OK, wait a minute. Are you saying that if I think you're talking a load of bullshit, I can walk out of here?'

'Yes,' replied Rafi, 'With one proviso: you can't tell anyone you've seen me. Agreed?'

'Agreed,' said Aidan. 'Please start, I'm all ears.'

Rafi sensed that the other members of the team weren't happy with what he had promised Aidan. No doubt the signing of some formal documentation would be the norm. But this was the City of London, where for Rafi and his work colleagues *one's word was one's bond*.

The phone rang before Rafi could begin. Kate picked it up, listened for a moment and spoke to Jeremy. 'Your delivery from *Luigi's* is here.' He disappeared out of the room and returned a few moments later with coffee and croissants.

Rafi started. 'We've uncovered a network of companies controlled by a terrorist cell. Amongst other things we believe that they will attack energy installations thereby triggering a meltdown of the financial markets and enabling them to reap huge profits from their positions in the derivatives market. As a top, if not *the* top derivatives man, please help us find out what they're up to and help us stop them?'

Aidan had listened intently. 'What help will I have?'

'You'll have Emma to help you,' said Kate.

'That's it? Bloody hell, this isn't going to be easy!' Aidan looked across at Emma. 'Tell me you've got a degree in rocket science!'

'Afraid not,' replied Emma. 'I studied applied mathematics and I have experience as an accountant…'

Aidan cut her off. 'Well, you can't have everything,' he beamed. 'Emma, you'll do fine. What about IT kit?'

'You'll meet Greg, our IT Manager, after this meeting,' said Kate.

She looked carefully at Aidan. 'Are you willing to promise that everything you see and do here remains *strictly* confidential?'

Aidan nodded. 'I have no doubt that you could make life very difficult for me and my employers if I broke my promise.' He took a sip of his coffee. 'My lips are sealed. Shall we get started?'

His demeanour, which to start with had been a mixture of tension and annoyance, was now relaxed and businesslike.

'What we need to know is whether they are trying to short or manipulate the relevant futures or options contracts.' Rafi paused. 'My educated view is that the action will be in the long gilts and interest-rate contracts.'

Aidan's face was deadly serious. His light blue eyes, sharp as sabres, focused on Rafi. 'It's funny - no, let me rephrase that - it's a great coincidence that you should be talking of these two markets. Up to a fortnight ago, they were trading as might be expected in these volatile times and everyone was comfortable with an interest rate scenario where over the next year they move up by a per cent or so.'

He paused. 'The funding of the Government's debt mountain is on a knife edge. As things stand the big international investors are just about happy with the UK's creditworthiness. Any significant increase in borrowings or a knock to the economy would be *very* unwelcome.' He grimaced. 'Were something to happen which shook investor confidence and caused the Government to issue shed loads of debt, it would become very expensive… recently the volume of deals betting on interest rates rising significantly has grown to the point where someone, or a group of people, out there fervently believes that they are heading towards double digits!'

Rafi raised his eyebrows.

'The view amongst the traders,' continued Aidan, 'Is that a few punters have lost their marbles and instead of playing the roulette tables have decided to place some big bets in these derivative contracts. If they're right they'll make huge profits! My informed guess is you could be on to something. I'd be glad to check it out for you.'

'Excellent - thank you - that'd be perfect,' said Rafi.

There was a quiet knock on the door; Greg, not waiting for a reply, walked in.

'Kind of you to join us,' said Kate. 'Let me introduce you to Aidan Gilchrist of Maine Leadbetter, the international bank. He's a derivatives guru and is here to help us. Aidan, Greg is our IT manager. He has an uncanny knack for getting into online databases and making things work. He'll set you up with whatever you need in terms of hardware and software. His budgets are a tiny proportion of yours, so the kit isn't as smart as what you're used to, but it should do the job.'

Greg had found a plate and was enjoying the last croissant.

'Aidan, please tell Greg what you'll need.' Kate shot a brief smile at Greg.

'First of all,' said Aidan, 'I could do with access to my bank's intranet, in such a way that no one can trace it.' He hesitated. 'No, on second thoughts, that would raise too many suspicions.' Aidan thought for a moment. 'Would it be possible to arrange access from here via my home IP address?'

'Shouldn't be a problem.'

'Second, I could do with access to the central computers of the main UK derivatives markets. Also, if possible, some names of contacts in their settlement teams would be a real bonus.'

Greg nodded.

'Third, I could do with a desktop PC with a bit of grunt and access to a good printer. And fourth,' he turned and looked at Emma, 'Access to a supply of coffee would be much appreciated.'

As if to signal the end of the meeting, Greg slid his empty plate forward and looked up. 'If that's all, I'll get started on your shopping list. If I seem a bit stressed, please bear with me. The commissioner has asked that I give you priority, but why does everything arrive in twos and threes like London buses? We still have a load of unfinished business following the Bishopsgate bombing, which took out their IT servers and means they're using ours. It's all a bit of a bugger's muddle,' Greg added as he left.

'Emma, would you please take Aidan under your wing?' asked Kate, changing the subject.

'Yes, sure. I'd be happy to,' replied Emma.

Kate turned and looked at Rafi. Her eyes twinkled. 'And I'll team up with Rafi.'

She looked pleased, as if she'd got what she wanted. She held Rafi's gaze, gave him a barely perceivable wink and added, 'Which should be interesting.'

Rafi got up to leave as if he'd finished a normal business meeting.

Kate looked a little crestfallen by his lack of interest and right at that moment it dawned on Rafi that he had accidentally ignored her gesture.

He looked at her with new eyes. She was attractive in a gamine sort of way; her hazel eyes were gorgeous... He cut short his thoughts - this definitely wasn't the time for distractions.

Aidan stood up. 'Where's my desk?'

'Follow me, I'll show you where we work,' said Emma.

*

'Where do you want it set up?' asked one of Greg's team, pulling a trolley with a serious-looking PC on it. Emma pointed to the desk to the left of the whiteboard.

Greg popped his head around the door. 'By the way, do you happen to know your home IP address or would you like me to find it out for you?'

Aidan gave Greg his nine-digit IP address. 'Could you also arrange for my home phone line to be routed through to here?'

'No problem.' Greg turned and left.

'Will your colleagues notice your absence?' asked Emma 'You might like to tell them you'll be away from the office for some while.'

'Good idea. I'll be able to tell them I'm working from home as soon as Greg has me set up.'

Minutes later Aidan was up and running.

'The printer is where?' Aidan called across to no one in particular.

Emma pointed to a large, old HP printer next to her desk.

'Bloody hell! I haven't seen one of those for years. Did you get it from the museum up the road?'

'That's a bit too close to the truth to be funny,' interjected

Kate.

Aidan busied himself and in no time the printer was churning out sheets of paper.

Emma glanced at him. 'I didn't know you had your IP address rerouted yet. What are you up to?'

'I thought I'd access some background data from the Web to save some time.'

Fifteen minutes later, the phone on the corner of Aidan's desk rang. He scooped it up without taking his eyes away from his screen, said, 'Thanks' and put it down. He now had access to his bank's intranet.

Rafi went over to Kate. 'I'm sorry I didn't seem enthusiastic about the prospect of working with you earlier. My mind was on other things. Shall we get started?'

Kate looked at him carefully, almost quizzically - she couldn't make him out. 'Where do you suggest we start?'

'Let's work on the property angle. It shouldn't be long before we hear from the agent,' replied Rafi.

Twenty minutes later Justin Smith telephoned. He sounded rather sheepish. He had put the list of properties through the three databases and had expected reams of information to come out, but had obtained only seven pages of data.

Constable Peter Ashby was waiting nearby in a squad car and made the pickup.

Less than twenty minutes later, he was handing over the envelope with the data to Kate.

Rafi looked at the printouts. Six agents showed up. Dewoodson cropped up more than any of the other names. Rafi smiled; so they *were* involved. They would be his starting point. From their website, he located their head office in Manchester, and noted that they also had offices in London, Edinburgh and Bristol. He passed the contact details to Kate.

She rang their head office - she was slightly nervous as this was going to be a difficult phone conversation and she didn't want to tip them off that she was from the police. 'May I please speak to the person dealing with the property company PREH?'

The receptionist hesitated.

'Oliver Stone, our managing director, looks after their agency deals and William Wesson deals with their valuations.'

'I'd like to speak to Mr Wesson then, please.'

There was a short wait before Kate was put through to his secretary. A curt voice said, 'Mr Wesson is out of the office and isn't expected back until after lunch - I suggest you ring back then.' The secretary hung up.

Kate rang back and asked to speak to Oliver Stone, the MD. After another wait she was put through to his personal assistant.

'Mr Stone is in a meeting and can't be disturbed.'

'It *is* important.'

The PA was firm in her reply. 'Mr Stone has left me strict instructions that he mustn't be disturbed,' and hung up.

Kate looked across at Rafi, 'I wonder if it was the mention of the name PREH that made them so unhelpful?'

'Quite possibly.'

Kate picked up the phone again and rang through to the switchboard.

'Could you please put me through to Manchester Central?'

Kate spoke to the duty officer. 'DI Adams here. Could you please put me through to one of your senior colleagues in Special Branch - counter-terrorism?'

A Detective Chief Inspector Rick Feldon picked up the phone.

'Good morning, how can I help you?'

Kate introduced herself and explained what she was working on. 'I have good reason to believe that a firm of surveyors, Dewoodson, who are based in Spring Gardens, have information on a property company, PREH, which is linked to our investigations. They are being uncooperative. As a matter of some urgency, I'm after a copy of the last valuation report, together with any other information available on PREH.'

'Can you email me details of what you want?'

'Will do.'

'Also, Rick, please bear in mind that this needs to be done with diplomacy and very quietly. They can't know we're on to them. I could do with their MD, Oliver Stone, and their valuer, William Wesson, being interviewed and kept totally incommunicado for at least twenty-four hours.'

'Sounds right up our street!'

There was a short silence before Rick said, 'How's about we pull them in on something else? Leave it with me, I'll come up with something which will enable us to search their premises and confiscate their computers. My colleague, Phil Smith, and I will pick them up as soon as we get your email.'

It was nearly 10 a.m. on Thursday morning. Rafi had his fingers crossed that the valuation report would reveal more properties. If they, too, were close to energy targets it would confirm his suspicions and fill in valuable missing pieces of the jigsaw puzzle.

★

Their work was interrupted by a call from Colonel Matlik.

'Hello, Colonel,' said Kate, putting him on speakerphone.

'Sorry for the delay - I had hoped to get back to you sooner. However, your leads have proved most fruitful. Are you sitting down?' There was an ominous tone to his voice.

'Er… Yes.'

'My men have paid a visit to the firearm club which was owned by your former Mr Koit. They tried their hand at shooting on the 1,000-metre range. Behind the firing positions they spotted an area where the winter vegetation was partially scorched - the telltale signs of a missile launcher - and to the side of the targets was what seemed to be a demolished building. After their session they went to have a discrete look. It was not a building, but a concrete wall over two metres thick. Whatever had been fired at it had punched a hole straight through the concrete. It had been hit a couple of times, which explained why it looked such a mess. Beside the rubble, covered by a layer of soil, they found a three-metre by five-metre block of metal. It was made from fifty steel sheets, each two centimetres thick, which had been welded together. It was over one metre thick and it too had two gaping holes in it.'

'Bloody hell!' exclaimed Kate under her breath, but she let the Colonel continue.

'I've been doing some research on what could cause such damage. We believe something like the Kornet E Anti-Tank Armour missile was used. It is an impressive piece of equipment and truly destructive if you are on the receiving end. It can blast a hole through one metre of armour; and not just steel armour, but explosive reactive armour. It's the kit that gives the likes of you or me nightmares. In daylight its range is up to 5.5 kilometres and trained users can fire two missiles per minute. To add spice to its capabilities, it can be fitted with either tank busting or high explosive thermobaric warheads. It gets worse: it is very accurate as it has either thermal or optical sights to detect and track the target. And the launcher comes with a tripod – both are transportable.'

'Would it need trained operatives to use it?' enquired a horrified Kate.

'One professional would do - though it would be like holding a tiger by its tail. One thing is for sure, though: it should not be fired in a confined space unless the operator wishes to have an early cremation.'

'Can these missiles and the launchers be purchased on the black market?'

'What can't these days?' replied the deep voice. 'I reckon €50,000 would suffice.'

'Very helpful and disturbing. Thank you,' said Kate. 'You have done a fantastic job...' she was interrupted.

'There is more. We brought in the warehouse manager earlier this morning on the grounds of committing a serious road traffic offence involving the death of a pedestrian. A tax inspector and two of my officers have been searching the warehouse and offices. Amongst the paperwork they found two interesting invoices: one was for five miscellaneous launchers, and another one for twenty miscellaneous missiles. The name of the purchaser was left blank. It was dated eleven days ago. The import manifest showed dealings with a private Russian company - Restaya - which is known to the Russian FSB and is believed to be involved in the black market arms trade.'

The colonel paused. 'Unfortunately, I have some more bad news. The FSB tell me that several months ago pro-Chechen rebels captured a consignment of Kornet E Anti-Tank missiles - five launchers with optical sights and twenty missiles, to be precise.'

Kate was going to speak, but the colonel carried on.

'I have interviewed the manager. He is pleading ignorance. He insists that he only looks after the day-to-day activities and doesn't ask questions. The real decisions, he says, are made by his boss who he rarely sees. When I interrogated him further, it turned out he did not know to whom the missile launchers and missiles were sold, just that he delivered them to the same rifle range outside Tallinn that my colleagues visited. He described the size of the wooden crates and the lettering on them. Unfortunately, I can now confirm that they are a match for the missing Kornet missiles and launchers. We are keeping the manager in custody, and he will not be allowed to talk to outsiders. His secretary has been told of his driving accident and that he is being held pending a murder charge.'

'How long can you hold him for without him seeing his solicitor?' asked Kate.

'As long as you like,' came the reply, 'now that we know he is involved with a major terrorist plot. Questions will be asked as to why he cannot speak to his solicitor in probably forty-eight hours. My team is currently going through the import/export agency's paperwork with a fine-tooth comb to see whether any other armaments have recently passed through their hands. I will keep you informed of their progress.'

'Thank you,' said Kate.

'That is not all. I have been looking into the fishing company you mentioned. It owns two deep sea trawlers, the *Anu Riina* and the *Anu Maarja*; they both operate out of Tallinn docks. Both are at sea - they left port a week ago. A reasonable assumption is that your Kornets were on board. We understand the vessels are somewhere north of the Faeroes. That is all for the moment. I will get in touch again as soon as we know anything else.'

Kate hesitated and then replied. 'Thank you. You've given us more than enough to get on with. All your help is much appreciated.'

'A pleasure. I must go now. Give me a call if you need anything more. I regret being the bearer of such bad news.'

She switched the speaker phone off and sat there, taking in what the colonel had just told her... Kate broke the silence. 'These Estonian trawlers sailing from the Baltic Sea to the Faeroes would go within a couple of hundred miles of Peterhead. If en route they rendezvoused with one of the Peterhead trawlers, then the missiles could now be in the UK!'

'Things have just got bloody scary, haven't they?' exclaimed Emma. 'When the safety specifications were drawn up for oil and gas depots, or even airports or nuclear power stations, they can't have had any idea that such a monster as the Kornet missile existed?'

'I doubt it,' replied Kate, 'or if they did, it was a masterly cover-up by our political masters.'

'If only we had a better idea of the timescale,' mused Rafi.

'We should work on the basis that the attacks are imminent,' said Kate.

'A thought,' Rafi replied. 'If Aidan and I are right and the financial markets are at the heart of the terrorists' plan, then the attacks won't come today – it's already too late. They'll come first thing in the morning. That way they will get full news coverage and have the whole day to spook the markets. Now whether that's tomorrow or next week, I don't know.'

'We must get information on who the foot soldiers are and what they are targeting. Carry on researching your leads and keep me informed of any developments,' said Kate with a note of urgency in her voice. 'I need to brief the commissioner.'

John returned with Jeremy right behind him.

'Rafi, I've been thinking a bit more about the terrorists and their possible exit routes,' said John. 'I really *would* put good money on them using a fast motor vessel in addition to the trawlers. Especially as they could easily afford something very fast.'

'Where would you start looking for something like that?' Rafi asked.

'Firstly, I'd look at the ringleaders,' replied John, 'And check out whether the sheikh, Basel, Jameel or Maryam own a large powerboat.'

'I've a friend at Lloyd's Shipping Register. Let me give her a ring,' said Emma.

It turned out to be a short conversation. 'She says our task will be difficult. There are many large powerboats scattered all around the smart harbours and marinas of Europe. The difficulty is that most are owned through special purpose companies for tax reasons and this makes it hard to trace their owners.'

Emma thought for a moment, then got up and went to see Aidan, who was sitting behind a large volume of paper.

'Aidan, if you wanted to find out if a business contact owned an expensive motor vessel, where would you start?'

He looked at her thoughtfully. 'Anyone who spends several millions on a yacht will no doubt think it's the best thing since sliced bread. My bet would be to go and look in their offices, where they're bound to have photos of it.'

'Good idea, but we don't have the time,' said Emma.

Rafi lifted his head up from his paperwork. 'Of the four individuals, I doubt whether Jameel has one stashed away. He's never spoken of boats to me and, to my knowledge, he spends most of his holiday time skiing or playing golf. Basel is a workaholic and I don't see him leaving something valuable tucked away in a marina, unused. That leaves Sheikh Tufayl and Maryam.'

'I'd rule out Maryam,' said Emma. 'She also works long hours and spends too much time between her homes in the Gulf, Luxembourg and London. I don't see a large powerboat and outdoor activities going with her lifestyle.'

'What about her hubby?' asked John. 'He is extremely wealthy.'

'Could be,' said Kate, 'But in my book the sheikh seems to be the most likely.'

'I've got an idea,' said John. 'It's a bit off the wall, but how about we chat to someone working for the tabloid press and see if they've any photos of Sheikh Tufayl or Maryam's husband on board a big boat? We must have some good contacts. Should I make a couple of phone calls and get some names?'

Kate nodded. 'But the discussions will have to be in confidence, perhaps in return for a story later?' Ten minutes later, John's phone rang; he scribbled down the information on two contacts: one working for a red top newspaper and the other for a tabloid magazine.

'I could do with a volunteer to pay a journalist a visit,' said Kate.

'Count me in,' offered Jeremy.

'See what you can find,' said Kate.

'Will do.' Jeremy picked up the piece of paper with the names and phone numbers on. 'Which do you reckon I should try first?'

'I'd take the top one - he works down at Canary Wharf when he's at home but, like most tabloid journalists, he could be almost anywhere.'

'Thank you,' said Jeremy, slightly sarcastically. 'It seems a straightforward task.' He dialled the first journalist, Pete Lockyer, and smiled when the mobile was answered almost immediately.

'Hello, I was wondering whether you could help me?'

'Who are you?' a rather high pitched voice enquired.

Jeremy gave a wry smile. 'Someone you don't know. And who probably doesn't exist in any of your files.'

'Are you taking the mick?' snapped Pete Lockyer.

'No,' replied Jeremy. 'I work for a rather special part of the Government and your name has been put forward as someone who could help us.'

'Sorry mate, I'm rather busy at the moment.'

'So be it,' said Jeremy. 'I thought I'd try you first as you come highly recommended, but if you're too busy, not to worry. I've another couple of people to try, including a rather pushy sod at a tabloid magazine.'

There was a silence at the other end of the phone; one could sense Pete considering whether he was about to turn down a potentially lucrative story.

'How much of my time would you need?' inquired Pete.

Jeremy tried hard to conceal a large smile and winked at Emma. 'Not long! Perhaps you might have time for a cup of coffee or a glass of wine?'

'It's a bit early for me. Let's make it a cup of coffee. There's a decent coffee bar around the corner from where I work.'

Jeremy took down the address. 'Could we meet there in, say, twenty-five minutes?'

'Fine,' agreed the journalist. 'How do I recognise you?'

'Oh,' said Jeremy, 'I look fairly nondescript - 6' 2", brown hair and in a grey suit. My name's Jeremy, by the way.'

'See you in half an hour.'

'Twenty-five minutes would be better,' said Jeremy and hung up. He looked across at Kate. 'Any bright ideas on how I get to Canary Wharf and back?'

'No problem. If you go downstairs, I'll arrange for you to be looked after.'

'Thanks.' Jeremy picked up his notepad and hurried off on his errand.

The pressure was on. The team had uncovered a number of crucial leads, but the overall picture was still far from clear. There was tension in the air.

'Emma, how have you been getting on with your maps?' asked Kate.

'Rather well, actually,' replied Emma. 'Before I show you what I've got, though, I think we should consider how many targets there could be.'

'Good point.' Kate nodded for her to continue.

'They have five missile launchers. Of the twenty missiles they started off with, four were used in Estonia, leaving three or four missiles per launcher. This gives each operative probably one or two targets only. The missile launchers and their tripods are bulky. If the terrorists don't want to be captured and are keen for a quick getaway, I'd go for one target per launcher and use the three or four missiles to knock the living daylights out of it. A well-trained operative could fire four missiles in less than two minutes and then leave the area discretely.'

'What if they fire their first couple of missiles at one target and then take their missile launcher with them to some pre-stashed missiles at a property or a vehicle parked near to their next target?' added Rafi.

'So we could have ten targets!' whistled John. 'Flaming heck! And if they had access to the roof of a suitably located property, they'd have a great launching pad!'

'Or if a vehicle is involved, a nearby property would be useful to keep it out of sight prior to an attack,' added Emma.

'OK then... I suggest we look for ten targets and scale the number down only when we have conclusive proof,' said an agitated Kate.

'I have been making progress on the property front,' said Rafi. 'The mortgage register of PREH gave us an interesting set of addresses. Emma has chatted to John's team who have been helping us rule out the true investment properties. We are left with our original four properties as possibles for the terrorists to use: Peterhead, Hartlepool, North Walsham and Prestwick.'

'Now for the clever bit,' said Emma. She was standing next to a large, touch screen monitor which Greg had set up.

'First, let's put up a map of the UK and add on to it the four suspect properties.' Emma tapped the LCD screen, highlighting the four locations with bold blue crosses. 'We can now add an exit port where we know there is one of their trawlers.' As if by magic a little icon depicting a trawler appeared next to Peterhead.

'I'm still working on where the other trawlers are. However, I have done some work on the location of our major energy installations.' She moved back to her PC and, with several clicks of her mouse, a mass of coloured dots appeared on the screen.

Rafi let out an appreciative whistle.

'To make life easier I've colour-coded them,' said Emma. 'The green dots are for major gas and oil plants, red dots for the nuclear powers stations, the large red blob is for the Sellafield reprocessing facility in Cumbria and, lastly, the numerous black dots are the oil, gas and coal fired power stations.'

John swore. 'Bloody hell! I didn't realise that there were so many of them.'

'Absolutely,' replied Emma. 'But I reckon we can safely remove the black dots. The fossil fuel power stations, whilst large, aren't in the same league as the others.'

A couple of clicks later and the black dots disappeared from the screen.

'What precisely are those dots close to the four properties owned by the terrorists' PREH?' asked Kate.

Emma pointed at the screen. 'Peterhead is between the vast gas facility at St Fergus and the main North Sea oil pumping station at Cruden Bay. The Hartlepool property - here,' Emma tapped the map, 'is right on top of a nuclear power station. If we go down a bit, the North Walsham property – here,' Emma tapped again, 'Is next to the huge gas terminal at Bacton and just down the coast is Sizewell nuclear power station. And, over *here*, Prestwick is only twenty miles from Hunterston nuclear power station.'

'Phew!' exclaimed Aidan under his breath. 'What percentage of our gas supply comes through St Fergus and Bacton?'

'I guess around thirty to forty percent,' replied Emma.

'It's highly inelastic,' said Aidan. 'A shortfall of just ten percent would cause problems; thirty would be catastrophic - sections of UK industry would have to shut down. There would be electricity blackouts; the financial markets wouldn't like it at all, sentiment would be hit and the falls could be dramatic. On top of this, crippling the North Sea oil pumping station would shut down the oil refineries it serves, causing considerable knock-on effects.' Aidan looked worried.

John looked thoughtfully at the map. 'If we added this up, what would we have?'

'Potentially six substantial energy targets, of which three are nuclear,' replied Emma frowning. 'The bad news is, if you look at the screen, there are a number of other possible targets.'

'Oh my God! It's like looking for ten bloody needles in a frigging haystack if you ask me,' said John.

'I've got a question.' Kate was looking worried. 'How does the nuclear fuel travel to and from the power stations and the reprocessing units – and how often?'

'By train,' answered Emma, rummaging around for some paper on her desk. 'Ah, yes, here it is. The trains average one round trip a week.'

'Do any of them by any chance go near London?'

'Yes, the Sizewell train does,' answered Emma. She flipped through her notes. 'It uses the North London line from Stratford round to the marshalling yards at Willesden Junction, before going on to Sellafield.'

'Next question,' said Kate. 'How robust are the canisters that carry the nuclear fuel?'

Emma looked through her paperwork. 'It says here that their design and specification have been certified by Government experts.'

'Does this include the ability to withstand state-of-the-art missiles, like the Kornet missile that our terrorists most likely have?' continued Kate.

'Their thickness is…' Emma looked for the figure. 'Yes, 900 mm – about three feet.'

'Could a direct hit penetrate a canister?'

'Yes, I reckon so,' replied Emma slowly, looking at Kate to see if there was yet another question winging her way.

'And a glancing blow would probably ricochet off?' added Kate.

'Probably,' replied Emma, uncertainly. 'However, the experts who determined the safety specifications don't seem to be worried. Somewhere it says that - Ah yes! Here it is - the worst radioactive release following a terrorist attack is calculated to be only 0.0024 of one percent of the nuclear waste escaping as particles capable of being inhaled. Each canister contains three and a half tonnes of spent nuclear fuel.'

Emma paused. 'So by my calculations their figures point to only 0.1 kg of nasties being released, which they think isn't too calamitous. And as I read them, the reports don't consider there to be a remote possibility of a successful missile attack. What scares me,' continued Emma anxiously, 'Is that I reckon the contents of each canister contains about a quarter of the fallout from Chernobyl and spent nuclear fuel is around a million times more radioactive than the uranium initially sent *to* the nuclear power stations. I know they *say* it's as safe as houses, but if a terrorist were to...' her voice trailed off.

The uneasy silence was interrupted by John. 'The question that the terrorist leaders would have to ask themselves is: how easy would it be to hit a moving canister accurately? And are the odds ones that they would be prepared to gamble on? Having said that, a successful attack at Willesden would have a devastating impact on north London.'

'I suggest you put Willesden marshalling yards on your map,' said Kate.

'John's got a good point - nuclear power stations seem more likely targets, don't they?' said Emma sifting through a pile of papers. 'And I've browsed through the reports from the House of Commons and the Mayor of London's office, which have looked at the issue of nuclear waste transport. Neither is best pleased with the nuclear cargo going through London, but they both conclude that the canisters are safe - as advised by their experts.'

'For the time being, let's focus on key oil and gas plants, the nuclear power stations and reprocessing plants,' said Kate. 'Excellent work Emma.'

*

'I have been thinking,' said Aida. 'Hypothetically, let's say Hartlepool nuclear power station was compromised following a terrorist attack and shut down due to radiation leaks. Public

99

opinion could easily swing against all things nuclear. If nuclear power became politically unpalatable and phased out sooner rather than later, the Government would get hit with a bill of, say, £75 billion for the radiation clean-up and decommissioning costs. If at the same time a couple of large gas plants were to go out of action causing power cuts *and* if their public sector out-sourcing business went belly up... A tipping point would be reached and the UK financial markets would be pushed over the edge.'

Aidan paused. He looked deadly serious. 'The financial mar-kets would drop like a lead balloon, enabling the terrorists to make a fortune from their positions in the derivatives markets.'

'I agree with Aidan,' said Rafi. 'Their plan is to attack a number of energy installations and at the same time burden the Government with increased financial liabilities.'

'So, to put it bluntly, they want to crucify our markets and our economy and *then* walk away with billions,' observed Emma.

'It looks as if we have two separate issues to deal with,' said Kate. 'The attacks, and then what they are doing in the financial markets. Aidan, you focus on the financial markets and the rest of the team will concentrate on the attacks.'

'Will do,' replied Aidan.

'Well, who do we think will deploy the missiles?' Emma enquired. 'A student fanatic might be trained to use a semi-automatic gun or explosives, but Kornet missiles are a very sophisticated piece of equipment.'

'I'd go with terrorists with military experience,' said Kate.

'But such people wouldn't be easy to get into the UK, would they? Even on false passports,' Rafi asked.

'Who knows?' replied John. 'As things stand we can not rule anything out.'

'We have to substantiate these suppositions and convince our bosses,' said Kate. 'It won't be an easy task.'

'Oh hell!' The exclamation came from the direction of Emma's desk; she turned to Kate. 'I said that the sides of the steel canisters were 900 mm thick. I was looking at the wrong figures - the ones that are normally used in the UK are only 400 mm, i.e. fifteen inches thick. A thermobaric Kornet missile would literally rip the container apart and spew the contents here, there and bloody everywhere.'

'My God!' said Kate. 'The consequences would be unthinkable.'

There was a stunned silence in the room.

It was broken by Rafi. 'Aidan, we both believe that part of their plan is to make a financial killing in the derivative markets, don't we? What if they have placed bent people into the dealing rooms of a number of UK financial institutions. There must be handfuls of people who are now missing their bonuses who could be bought. And if they were discreetly acting as counter parties to the terrorists' transactions, it would enable the terrorists to build up very big positions, wouldn't it?'

Aidan cursed under his breath before adding, 'The impact would be like walking in front of a speeding Chieftain tank.'

'It doesn't bear contemplating,' Rafi added. 'And it would make it very expensive for the Government or the Bank of England to stop the financial system going into complete meltdown.'

'And they would have to react very fast...' added Aidan.

*

A quiet determination filled the office as they concentrated on the work at hand. Suddenly Emma stopped what she was doing and sat bolt upright. She was looking frustrated.

'What's up?' asked Kate.

'It's just that I can't place something; I'm looking at the cold store and packaging operations of the terrorists' fishing business. Something is bothering me; I just can't recall what it is that I'm trying to remember!'

Aidan looked up from his desk. 'What makes you think that you are missing something?'

'Well,' said Emma, 'I was reading something which mentioned fishing - and I can't remember what it was!'

Aidan smiled and popped his head back down below his parapet of papers.

'It's a wonder you manage to get any work done, sitting there daydreaming,' he muttered, just loud enough for Emma to hear him.

Emma got up and walked determinedly across to his desk. Aidan sensed that he'd gone too far with his banter. Emma, who was shorter than Aidan, looked straight at him and said, 'Stand up, please.'

Aidan looked a little apprehensive; he stood up and Emma moved closer. Rafi had his fingers crossed that the team wasn't going to come apart at the seams. Emma stood there, milking the anticipation and doubt in his mind. She leant forward, raised herself up on to her tiptoes and placed a fleeting kiss on his cheek.

'What was *that* for?' asked Aidan, astonished.

'Oh, you're just brilliant,' Emma said looking at him. 'It's you and your sense of humour. It gets me thinking in strange ways.'

Aidan blushed slightly.

'No, not that way - you mentioned the word *work* and that helped me remember what was niggling me.'

Everyone looked blankly at her as she made a beeline for a filing cabinet and rooted through the contents of a drawer.

'What are you looking for?' asked Kate.

'A briefing note on immigration; we got one a little while back setting out the priority employment sectors and how these might be exploited to gain fast track work permits and entry into the UK. It highlighted certain industry sectors. Found it! Yes! *Fish packers* are on that list and the terrorists have large fishing and fish processing activities. This would give them a legitimate and easy way of getting undesirables into the UK.'

'It's a long shot. Leave it with me and I'll see what I can find.' Kate phoned the switchboard and got the number for their contact at the Immigration Department.

'Oh blast,' said Kate, 'They've got the answerphone on.' She left a message asking for her call to be returned with utmost urgency.

A few minutes later the phone rang. It was a man from the Immigration Office. Kate explained what she needed.

'Here are a couple of names and mobile phone numbers. If they are busy, please ring me back and I'll see whether I can find you someone else who can assist you,' he said helpfully.

'Thank you,' replied Kate. She hung up and dialled the first number - it was switched off. The second was answered with a quiet, 'Hello, Steve Lee here.'

Kate explained her pressing need for information and the importance of confidentiality. 'Can you help?' she asked.

She was greeted with, 'Oh shit! Oh shit not again, why now?'

Kate's face turned very serious; she was about to read the riot act to the person on the other end of the phone when she heard him shout, 'Lucy!' and then louder, 'Lucy, can you rescue me please? The little tyke has done another projectile poo!' There was a brief silence. It seemed that Lucy had arrived in the nick of time and had taken charge of the situation. 'Darling, let me have him; I'll finish off the nappy changing. You can sort out your work.'

Steve was most embarrassed and very apologetic. 'It's meant to be my day off. Oh hell, I need to put the phone down again; he got me all down the side of my trousers as well. Lucy is going to love it; I've just backed into the side of the sofa! Look,' he said, 'The sooner I get out of here, the better for everyone; give me a couple of minutes to change and, say, twenty minutes to get to the office. Ring me on this number in twenty-five minutes and I'll be at my desk where I'll be in a better position to help. I promise that this isn't a brush off.'

'It'd better not be!' said Kate and hung up.

Aidan looked up at Emma, who by coincidence had been looking his way; their eyes met for a brief moment but both thought better of saying anything. A couple of smiles later they were heads down, focused on their paperwork.

*

Kate phoned Steve. 'I'm looking at a couple of companies. I need to know whether they've employed any non-nationals via fast track visas, working as, say, fish packers or filleters over the past three or four years.'

'Fire away,' came the reply. 'Let's see what we can find. Can you give me the company name and its address?'

Kate spoke to Emma, who passed her the information Steve requested.

'Thank you,' replied Steve. 'I must apologise, the system is always slow bringing up information. I suspect it's feeling a little overworked at the moment, though please don't quote me on that. Ah yes, your fish processing company has seen a significant growth in their workforce over the past couple of years. They've put in six - no sorry - seven fast track visa applications for fish packers and filleters. Of these, we were able to process three on the nod as they were for EU citizens from Eastern Europe. The other four were non-EU nationals and their visa requests have been approved too. All in the past sixteen months! I see from a note on the file from my colleague Roger that they're opening up a large new cold store and packaging facility later this year, hence their recent requests.'

'Would you know where?'

'Unfortunately, that's not on the electronic notes. Roger, my assistant who deals with this company, is away on holiday. He'll be back tomorrow morning though. By the way, what's your email address?' asked Steve.

There was a brief silence after Kate provided him with the information and then Steve came back on the line. 'I've emailed you the details we have on each of these individuals. I've tried Roger's mobile but it's switched off, as is his voicemail. I'll send him a text message and put a note on his desk letting him know to get in touch as soon as he's back. Wait a minute! I am a berk - of course he's not answering; he's flying back from his holiday in the States. What's your timescale?'

'Yesterday would be ideal. As soon as possible, please. It's really important,' urged Kate. 'Steve, if you or Roger can't get through to me, here is my fax number. Please mark any faxes as *Urgent*.'

'Will do,' he said, 'I can't promise that Roger will remember where the new cold store is located. He keeps a number of notebooks, but I've never been able to decipher what he puts into them. One of us will be in touch first thing tomorrow.'

'Oh, by the way, while I've got you on the line,' said Kate, 'What other fast track ways into the UK are available?'

'Off the record, news agency journalism is a good one,' Steve replied. 'Interestingly, representatives of overseas newspapers who are employed and paid in the UK don't need a work permit. All they have to show is evidence that they've been engaged by a news organisation outside the UK, that the posting to the UK is a long-term assignment and they have sufficient funds to live here. We don't always have the time to check that the foreign organisation is in business. The process is remarkably straightforward. Like fish processors and filleters, journalists aren't seen as a priority area to scrutinise. The paperwork often gets only a cursory glance. And did you know that after four years they become eligible to apply for residency?'

'No I didn't... Could you look up a few more companies and check if they've made any visa requests that look in any way out of the ordinary?' asked Kate.

When they came to the venture capital business, AGVC, Steve said, 'Yes! They have an individual who fits your description: an overseas journalist who joined them six months ago. He's setting up a weekly newspaper on the venture capital sector. I'll email his details to you.'

They found nothing more.

'Thank you Steve. You've been really helpful,' said Kate. 'Best wishes to Lucy. Tell her from me that you're a star for coming into the office on your day off.'

Kate printed out the details on the eight individuals and bounced the email on to Jeremy who, as luck would have it, returned a couple of minutes later. 'Jeremy, could you help me track down the eight people I've just emailed you? They are employed by the terrorists' businesses and have all taken advantage of the fast track visa application process. It seems that they've been here, acclimatising to the UK way of life, for between four and sixteen months. The likelihood is that they're using false names.'

As an afterthought, Kate forwarded the email to Colonel Matlik in Tallinn, with a short covering note: *These people have come up on our radar screen. Do any of them look familiar to you?*

She then called across to Emma. 'Have you made any progress with the trawlers?'

'Yes; they've got a fleet of eight modern vessels. Four are registered at Peterhead, two at Grimsby and two in Tallinn. I've confirmation that three of the Peterhead trawlers are out in the Atlantic Ocean, somewhere in the vicinity of Iceland, and they're due back next week. The fourth, *Northern Rose*, is in port at Peterhead. The two Estonian trawlers in the Norwegian Sea are due back in Tallinn late Sunday or Monday. Unfortunately, *Highland Belle* and *Rosemarie* from Grimsby are still unaccounted for.' Emma continued, 'And I've been talking to the coastguard. The talk is that *Northern Rose* in Peterhead is due to sail tomorrow around lunchtime.'

'Good work.'

'And, they have a cold store and processing unit in Peterhead,' added Emma, 'From which they supply hotels and restaurants country-wide. I wonder why they don't have a cold store in the South of England. It would make the distribution process simpler?'

'The north side of London would be ideal,' commented Kate. 'Somewhere near Willesden, perhaps?'

'Exactly!' said Emma. 'Anyway, I phoned their sales office in Peterhead, posing as the manager of a fish restaurant in South London. I enquired whether they operated around London. The reply was that their nearest depot was up North. They do deliveries to London, but there was a large minimum order. The person I spoke to believed there might be plans afoot to open a facility outside London, but she hadn't been formally told as yet. She asked me to give her a ring in six months time.'

Kate frowned. 'That ties in with the comment from Steve at Immigration about them looking to expand. So they could well have bought a property in the South of England.'

★

The phone rang. John picked it up. It was one of Jeremy's MI5 colleagues. 'Jeremy asked to be kept informed of the whereabouts of Basel Talal. Sorry for the delay; some information has just come through from the Belgian authorities. Your man, Talal, landed in Paris last Tuesday morning almost two hours before Jameel flew out from there to Marrakech. We don't know if they met.' The MI5 man hesitated. 'As Basel had no onward flight we had assumed that he was staying in Paris. The boss, however, wanted us to be more thorough and we gained access to the French, Belgian and Dutch passenger manifests. It transpires that Basel hopped onto the TGV to Brussels, boarded a flight to Copenhagen and then flew on to Reykjavík. He must have antifreeze in his blood to go there at this time of year! We've sent an operative up to Reykjavík to investigate and another is keeping an eye on Jameel.'

'Thanks,' said John and hung up. 'All of you, our man Basel has done a runner and - would you believe it… Gone to Iceland?'

★

Jeremy's journey across town was straightforward and he arrived at the coffee bar with a couple of minutes to spare, wondering whether he had whetted Pete Lockyer's appetite, or if he would be wasting his time.

Pete was on time. Jeremy watched him saunter into the café. He was of medium build, slightly paunchy with receding mousey-brown hair. His face told a story of too many late nights. Pete was smiling, which was presumably a good sign.

Pete spotted Jeremy, came over and sat down opposite him. Introductions out of the way, the coffees were ordered and they started chatting.

'What have you got that makes it worth my while being here?' asked Pete bluntly.

'I am doing a bit of undercover work on a rather wealthy individual who has his fingers in some interesting pies and I'm not certain what's in it for you yet.' Jeremy watched Pete. He didn't look overly pleased.

'Have you ever met a real spook before? I thought not. Well at least this can be marked down as part of your professional training.'

Pete had been studying Jeremy, who was athletic in build and had one of those faces that was handsome but didn't stand out. Pete realised he wanted to find out more.

'Are you really MI5?'

'Yep, have a look at this.'

Pete scrutinised Jeremy's MI5 warrant card, looked up at his smiling face and considered things. He'd just put a good story to bed and had a second almost completed. He didn't really need another one right now. But he did have a spare hour or so. What the hell! The spook was fascinating .

'I might be able to help. It depends on what you're after,' said Pete carefully.

'I could do with tracing a fast motor vessel. I've got two leads as to who the owner might be; both mix with the great and the not-so-good! Can't tell you what it's about as it's highly sensitive, but you'll be the first to know when the story breaks.'

'That's a bit thin,' said Pete.

'My sources tell me you're a man up for a challenge,' replied Jeremy.

'How's about we go back to my office and see if we can turn something up in the library?'

It was a short walk across to the shiny, glass-fronted building. Pete signed Jeremy in and they made for the library.

Jeremy gave Pete the details of Maryam, her husband and the sheikh, and showed him the photos that Emma had sent to his phone.

'Where do we start looking?'

'First let's look under their names. Let me show you how the manual and electronic cataloguing and indexing work. I suggest you start over here and I start at the other end and we see how we do,' said Pete.

Jeremy looked at the mass of catalogued photos. Bloody hell! If only MI5 had this type of information on people! He was fascinated by the tabloid approach to life. Some of the pictures made the mind boggle and the eyes water. They surely couldn't publish many of them, but he supposed they made for good bargaining tools!

It soon became apparent that Maryam and her husband were landlubbers; they loved high society, opera and the Arts. There was nothing to do with them and boats.

Then Pete struck gold. A colleague had been working on a story about oil magnates and beautiful celebs. There were pictures of the sheikh surrounded by beautiful women and there, amongst the pictures, was the sheikh with a movie star draped across the back of a sleek-looking monster of a powerboat.

'Beautiful, isn't she?' asked Pete. 'I'd love to get my hands on one of those. She looks like a Sunseeker Predator 75 if I'm not mistaken. Like shit off a shovel. I reckon her top speed would be something like forty-seven knots - over fifty miles per hour… Fast boats are a daydream of mine.'

Pete looked carefully through the similar pictures. 'Damn it! None of the photos show the boat's name. Don't worry.' He picked up the phone and chatted to a colleague, and within moments was talking to a specialist yacht broking agency. He spoke to them for a while and then hung up. 'This is the boring bit of the job - the waiting for someone to phone back with the info. And the coffee's cold!' commented Pete.

They didn't have to wait long. The yacht broker advised Pete that a limited number of these boats were built each year. The manufacturer had given him the names of the boats constructed in the past five years. The broker reckoned that it wouldn't take him long to track down whether any of them were owned by a rich Arab sheikh.

Jeremy smiled. It was great to see a professional at work! Pete didn't give away who he was researching. He reckoned Pete could give a lesson or two to some of his younger colleagues. To pass the time, and not wishing to lose an opportunity, Jeremy pulled together a bit of information on Maryam and her husband.

Less than twenty minutes later Pete's broker contact phoned back. He'd identified three such boats which were owned by Arab sheikhs.

'The first one is owned by a Sheikh Tufayl.'

'Voilà!' said Jeremy.

'Her name is *Flying Goddess*,' continued Pete. 'She is usually moored at either Monaco or Cannes and has a full-time captain.'

The information cost Pete €500. On the basis that it would help with a story, he would mark it down to expenses. Pete made a couple more calls and discovered that the boat wasn't in Monaco or Cannes. His contact in Monaco reckoned that the boat left late last year for a refit somewhere or other, but not locally.

'Thanks mate,' said Jeremy. 'I can't tell you much at the moment, but odds-on this morning's work will have been your most profitable yet.'

'Exclusive as and when?'

'Of course, but in the meantime our discussion remains just between the two of us,' replied Jeremy. 'Now if you'll excuse me, I must dash.'

On the journey back, Jeremy phoned Emma.

'That's brilliant!' she said. 'You've got the name, the make and the type of boat and even know that she's being refitted.'

Kate called across to Emma, 'Look at Iceland first. If that's where Basel is, I bet that's where *Flying Goddess* is having a makeover. Have a chat to Jeremy's colleagues and get them to pass the information on to their man travelling to Iceland.'

The morning had gone by fast; it was already 12.15 p.m.

Emma called across to Kate. 'You've got a phone call from a DI Rick Feldon in Manchester.'

'Afternoon. We have pulled in Stone and Wesson,' said a businesslike Mancunian voice. 'The story is that we've linked them with a paedo ring - indecent images, etc. Well, that's what the paperwork says. Could have got it wrong, though,' he said with a chuckle. 'I've made sure that neither of them can see any outsiders. Mr. Stone is complaining vociferously, and his solicitor isn't best pleased - human rights and all that!'

Emma called across, 'Remember to ask him about whether they use outsourcing companies in their police station.'

'Oh shit!' exclaimed Kate under her breath. 'I had quite forgotten.' She asked Rick the question.

'Yes, catering,' came his reply.

'Do me a favour. As far as the two from Dewoodson are concerned, treat all your caterers as hostile! I'll explain later.'

'Will do,' agreed Rick with a hint of surprise in his voice. 'We picked up William Wesson at a property he was valuing. He's like a feral cat and is seriously pissed off.'

'Wesson's computer has been set up in the interview room and we asked him to show us all his files relating to PREH. The little bastard tried to delete the folder they were in. Thankfully we stopped him. Phil Scott is emailing the valuation report to you as we speak. By the way, if you want any more of the clowns at Dewoodson brought in, please let me know. It would be my pleasure. We've spoken to Mr Stone's number two and explained the sensitivity of the situation. He's agreed to close the office until Monday. Also, a couple of suits from MI5 turned up to give us a hand - said they were friends of yours. They're giving the offices a once-over.'

'Excellent work and thanks,' said Kate.

'Good luck at your end. Cheers!' Rick was about to hang up, when he added, 'Do you have a biro at hand? Here are Phil's and my mobile numbers. If you need anything, day or night, please don't hesitate.'

'Thanks Rick and please make certain that no outsiders speak to either of them.'

The email arrived; Kate opened the attachment and printed it off. Rafi scooped it up from the printer. He went through the valuation, marking off the properties which hadn't shown up on the mortgage register. Two of the new addresses were prime high street shop investments, but two were definitely not prime: some elderly light industrial units in Stalls Lane, Heysham, and a commercial property in Castle Street, Peterhead. Both were vacant. Result! Two more possible properties, mused Rafi. He typed Castle Street, Peterhead, into the mapping software. It was next to the docks. He did the same for Stalls Lane, Heysham. 'Oh hell!' he uttered under his breath.

'Found something?' enquired Kate.

'We can add another nuclear power station to our list! The Heysham property is bang next to one.'

Rafi was about to continue when Emma piped up. 'Our contact at the coastguard has traced both of the missing trawlers. *Rosemarie* has just finished a refit at the dry dock in Great Yarmouth and *Highland Belle* is at Troon dry dock. Both are poised to set sail.'

'Well done, Emma,' said Kate. 'Are all the other trawlers at sea?'

'Yep. Except *Northern Rose*; she is still in Peterhead harbour. That gives us three exit points,' said Emma, who marked up the location of the two new properties and the two trawlers on the screen.

Kate stood up and clapped her hands. 'Let us recap on the information we have.' She pointed to the screen. 'We have trawlers poised to leave from three ports. Rafi has located suspicious properties at these five locations, and the terrorists have five missile launchers and sixteen unused missiles.' She scratched her head, as she looked at the screen. 'If we were to assume two targets per missile launcher then how might the properties and targets be paired? Any suggestions?'

'What about putting the properties in Peterhead with, the St Fergus gas terminal and the Cruden Bay oil pumping station - as the targets for missile launcher number one?' asked Emma

'And then there is the Hartlepool property which overlooks the local nuclear power station,' said John, 'but at the moment the second target in this pair is missing.'

Kate nodded.

'Number three could be Heysham nuclear power station – plus perhaps Hunterston nuclear power station up the coast? And launcher number four could then go with the Bacton gas facility and possibly Sizewell nuclear power station,' said Emma.

There was silence.

'Which leaves us with bugger-all for the fifth launcher - could it perhaps be the nuclear train at Willesden Sidings?' enquired John.

'It's all a bit iffy,' said Kate with a note of despondency in her voice.

'But a pattern is emerging,' encouraged John. 'The proximity of the various dots to PREH's properties is too bloody close for comfort for this to be random. If you think back, twenty-four hours ago we had next to nothing!'

*

The conversation was stopped by Aidan cutting in. 'Can you stop what you're doing for a moment? I need to hear your views on a couple of thoughts.' Aidan looked at them from behind his growing piles of paper.

'I still have more to do, but I've reached the point where I'm convinced that a small group of investors have built up sizeable positions in both the long gilt and the interest rate futures and traded options contracts. If the positions I've found at my bank are replicated elsewhere and these investors turn out to be right and the markets *do* crash - the terrorists will make huge profits and there will be lots of bloody noses.'

Aidan turned to Rafi. 'What *if* we were able to stop the markets from crashing - or more specifically prevent interest rates rising and gilts prices falling - *and* limit the impact of the terrorist attacks.' He grinned. 'If we could do this, we could turn the tables on them and wipe out their investments in the derivative markets.'

Aidan paused. 'I would be willing to bet that there are also a significant number of murky players with their snouts in the trough, who we could also take to the cleaners.'

'Wooah!' said Kate. 'That wouldn't be feasible, would it?'

'Aidan, that's brilliant!' exclaimed Rafi. '*All* we need to do is pre-empt most of the attacks and make certain that interest rates and gilts remain stable for - how long - a month?'

'No; far less than that. If interest rates remained stable, in a week to ten days the terrorists' positions in the futures markets would become exposed and they would either have to close them and crystallise large losses, or pay large margin calls. However, if interest rates were to fall, 24 - 48 hours would be enough to crucify them financially. In both cases their investments in the traded options markets would be wiped out.'

'That's all very well and good,' observed Kate, 'but the *if* is a massively big *if*.'

'Yes, I grant you that,' said Rafi, 'but isn't it great to know that the terrorists might not have everything going their way?'

Kate looked at him with that same look she'd given him when she had asked him to work with her. 'You know what I like about you?' her eyes sparkled as she held his gaze. 'It's your unbridled optimism.'

'Hold on a moment!' said Aidan. 'If we go back to when would be the best time to carry out the attacks? In terms of maximum impact - first thing in the morning as the markets are opening, but not late morning or in the afternoon... The London Stock Exchange opens at 8 a.m. and dawn tomorrow is?'

'7.25 a.m., give or take a bit,' answered Emma.

'What are you getting at?' asked Kate.

'We are led to believe the departure time of the trawler in Peterhead is tomorrow early afternoon, aren't we?' said Aidan.

'Yes.'

'If we are right and the trawlers are to be used as part of the terrorists' exit plan, I reckon that all three will leave tomorrow.'

'OK,' said Kate sensing what he was getting at.

'So, thinking about it, I'd be willing to bet that the attacks are planned for tomorrow as that's when the trawlers are leaving, and that they will come between dawn and the markets opening at 8 a.m.!' said Aidan.

'Bloody hell! That gives us less than twenty hours!' said John, quite taken aback.

'We've got too many holes in our hypothesis,' said Kate. 'We've *got* to fill in more of these gaps! To put it bluntly, we have to find the missing targets, the missile launchers and the foot soldiers. In the meantime I'll warn the commissioner of our line of thinking. And remember, not a word of this to anyone, please.'

Greg popped his head around the door at that moment. 'Did I miss something interesting?'

'Yes,' replied Kate, 'Have you been there long?'

'No chance! You are running me ragged. I dropped by to tell Aidan that I've arranged every computer access he should need...

Strange or what?' said Greg. 'There I was working in my office, drawing up a list of all the databases we would need to get into, when the commissioner walked in and asked me – yes *me* – what he could do to help. I explained what I needed. He left as quickly as he'd arrived and not twenty minutes later he came back saying that he'd pulled a few strings. I've had the head of IT from Euronext.liffe, the CME in Chicago and Eurex in Frankfurt on the phone volunteering their services and wanting to know which secure IP addresses we would be using. They've sent me encrypted user names and passwords and authorised me to access all their databases. Their cooperation is one hundred per cent. Simply marvellous if you ask me! Aidan, if I could use your PC for a moment I'll get it set up to access databases you've only dreamed of getting into.'

Aidan smiled, like a young boy being told he was getting the keys to the local sweet shop and got up to let Greg take his seat.

In less than five minutes Greg had Aidan's computer set up.

'Thanks,' said Aidan cheerfully. 'By the way would there be any chance of a better printer? There's going to be a lot of paper.' Looking in the direction of Emma and the elderly printer, he said, 'The old lady over there is getting too slow for me.'

Emma screwed up her face and then smiled at him.

Greg looked at Aidan. 'How big a machine did you have in mind?'

'Anything that prints quickly and has a big memory buffer would be great.'

'I'll see what I can find,' said Greg. Less than fifteen minutes later he was back pushing a printer-photocopier half the size of a desk. 'This little beauty is from accounts downstairs; please look after it.'

John, who had been sitting, contemplating, stirred. 'Why can't we just close down the markets involved and stop the terrorists that way?'

Aidan looked at him. 'In theory yes one could, but the turnover in these markets every hour of the trading day is squillions of pounds. To close the markets for anything other than a short period would be catastrophic for London's reputation. We could close them for a day. The problem is that there are many ways of covering one's tracks and the positions would still be there when the markets reopen. I've identified a number of suspicious contract notes, but it would take ages to look for them all. And this is offshore money, which can be moved electronically via intermediary banks quickly and secretively. It would be nigh on impossible to trace. What makes it really difficult is that we're only focusing on two parts of the market. The terrorists' positions are likely to be spread across a range of products. The two we have highlighted are the most obvious, but Sterling, the FTSE and gold would be good bets as well.'

Kate scratched her head thoughtfully. 'Let us suppose that Sheikh Tufayl is good for £2 billion; his cousin Maryam and Jameel, via their client's moneys, could be good for another £1 billion each and murky third parties put in another £1 billion. If this £5 billion is placed in the futures and traded options markets, and the terrorists get their way, what would their profit roughly be?' She looked at Aidan and Rafi.

Aidan spoke first. 'Conservatively they could make eight times their initial outlay; at the top end maybe fifteen times. Do you agree, Rafi?'

'Yes,' he replied.

'So in round terms the financial markets could be hit with losses of £50 billion,' calculated Kate and after a brief pause continued, 'at which point several banks and insurance companies would get into trouble and the Government would have to step in *again*!'

'Yes, it would be very seriously,' added Aidan.

'Thank you - I just wanted to be clear,' said Kate.

*

Jeremy hurried back into the office and updated the team on MI5's progress. 'Neil Gunton's team is working at full throttle. And on the charity front, things are looking promising. It seems that they use just one travel agency - Fly Skywards Travel. I'm shortly off to pay them a visit.' He looked thoughtful. 'And we've identified who Khalid and Yousif were.'

Kate looked at him blankly.

'Sorry – the people to whom the PhD dissertations were dedicated: Khalid and Yousif were the sheikh's older brothers - cousins of Basel and Maryam. They worked for the family oil company. To cut a long story short, it seems that they were in

Iraq discussing oil deals in mid-January 1991, just as *Operation Granby* got into full swing.'

Rafi looked puzzled. '*Operation Granby?*'

'It was the code name for the British bombing missions. Anyway, it seems an unguided 1000 lb bomb went astray...' He paused, 'A large house was demolished. Khalid and Yousif were inside and were killed,' added Jeremy.

'Why didn't we hear more about it?' asked Rafi.

'According to MI6, as collaborators helping the Iraqi regime with black market oil sales, their family probably feared what the Americans might do, if they made a real fuss,' added Jeremy.

Kate looked serious. 'So our terrorists have a strong motive for revenge!'

*

The buzz of Jeremy's brief visit had gone. Rafi was sitting at his desk. He was tense, his wrist throbbed and his lower back ached. He felt awful. The lack of sleep had suddenly crept up and over-whelmed him.

John finished his phone call, walked over and pulled up a chair next to Rafi. 'Are you alright?'

Rafi gave a small nod.

'I'm sorry to be the bearer of bad news, but I've had a call about Callum's funeral. It's at 2.30 p.m. tomorrow in Clifton, outside Bristol. Kate has suggested that we send some flowers via the undertaker. We obviously can't say that they're from you. How about a card with something like: *Thank you for your friendship and help*. Is that alright with you?'

Rafi sat there feeling miserable and nodded slowly.

'We have his parents' names and address should you wish to write or visit them when this is all over.'

He wasn't one for tears, but in his tiredness they welled up. There was nothing he could do to stop them. John briefly placed his arm across Rafi's shoulder as a gesture of comfort.

Rafi drew a long breath and looked up to the heavens as if to seek divine inspiration. *How can we sort out this horrendous mess?* he wondered.

But then a sudden tranquillity came over him. It was as if Callum was in the room alongside him. Rafi's mind cleared - they needed a game plan to stop the adverse effects of the attacks on the financial system. And for that they would need three things: a huge pot of money, a group of people to whom the Treasury and the Bank of England would listen, and a… Kate called over interrupting his train of thought.

'If you have a spare moment, could you see if you can find another property? We're still a couple of targets adrift.'

As if from nowhere, a possible solution flashed through his mind. His tiredness evaporated. Rafi felt calm, collected and strangely on top of things. He called out. 'Everyone! Do you have a moment? Can we go somewhere quiet to get away from the phones, please? I need to run through an idea.'

'Let me finish this call and I'm there,' said Emma.

John nodded, indicating he would be there as soon as he, too, had finished his call.

Kate put down her phone. 'We can use the meeting room down the corridor.'

John walked into the meeting room just as Kate had started to quiz Rafi. 'Why the meeting?'

Rafi started explaining, hesitantly. 'We're piecing together some of the locations of the terrorist attacks and hopefully we'll soon have a good enough picture to stop much of what they are planning. What's been worrying me is their assault on the financial markets. Their two sets of plans are intertwined. What scares me are the consequences of one or two missiles getting through and hitting a nuclear facility. The loss of life and the long term radioactive pollution would not only be tragic, but would also dent public confidence. The clean-up costs alone could run to billions, plus there would be huge decommissioning costs… Aidan, how big a pot of money do you think that the Government might need to sort out their financial problems if things get really bad? And how much could they take on without spooking the markets?'

'Answering your first question: how long is a piece of string? It could be anywhere between…' Aidan hesitated and the room fell totally silent. 'Let's say in excess of £75 billion as a ballpark figure. It could easily be more. Answering the second part of your question, in the present environment, I reckon £25 billion.'

John looked perplexed. 'But hasn't the Government recently borrowed hundreds of billions of pounds without any difficulty.

So why can't it do it again?'

'There comes a point when investors will simply take fright and walk away,' replied Aidan. 'The Government's annual borrowing requirement is currently running at around £200 billion. And they have been using quantitative easing to sort out their short-term funding needs...'

John still looked perplexed.

'We are talking in terms of the straw that breaks the camel's back,' added Rafi. 'It's all about market sentiment.'

John shrugged his shoulders.

'OK, look at it this way,' said Aidan. 'The terrorists have set up a three pronged attack. They want to hit our economy where it hurts - by creating major energy shortages and electricity blackouts... Crashing the stock market... And forcing the Government to borrow lots more money.'

John cast a serious look at Aidan. 'So, unless we stop them... things will go pear shaped?'

'Yes, and once things start to go wrong for the country's finances, things will rapidly get worse. The Government's credit rating and investor sentiment will plummet. And in no time at all there will be many more sellers than buyers of Government debt.'

'Could the country go bankrupt?'

'Probably not, but if the big investors stopped funding the UK's vast borrowing requirement, then it would get really messy...'

'Could I interrupt?' asked Rafi. 'There may be a way...'

'Pardon?' enquired Kate quietly, as though suspecting Rafi had flipped under the strain. Her eyes still had a sparkle to them and looked at him caringly.

'Well,' said Rafi, 'it's all about finding another source of money. A few minutes ago you mentioned property - as I was thinking about Callum. He'd been visiting a specialist property investor before he was killed. So who's the biggest owner of property and tangible assets in the UK?'

'The Government, the public sector and its various agencies,' replied Aidan. 'I recall from a recent article in the financial press that they have assets worth over £500 billion.'

'Precisely!' said Rafi. 'So why couldn't the Government put

together a contingency fund, such that it did *not* have to go to the debt markets? Instead it could package up these assets into one or more of the new real estate investment trust vehicles - rather like the Swedish Government has done. Our Government could then issue shares in these REITs to those who require payment, compensation, etc., which would be straightforward as they would be listed on the London Stock Exchange.'

'Yes, but I thought that the commercial property market and real estate investment trusts were in the doldrums at the moment.' Aidan paused. 'Sorry, I don't mean to be a wet blanket.'

Rafi looked crestfallen. He thought for a moment. 'OK, how about pepping up the market?'

Aidan looked at Rafi; a smile slowly stretching across his tired face. 'What do you have in mind?'

Rafi's mind was racing. 'You could improve the demand for the REIT shares. What if the pension industry and those retiring could use these investments as an alternative to annuities? The REITs would have better yields than Government bonds and would appeal to many pension fund trustees and those with private pensions.'

'That's brilliant! No, better than that, it's the nuts!' enthused Aidan. 'Real estate investment trusts would take off. Your sleight of hand would easily produce £150 billion for the Government to use, at a manageable cost. *And*, if they raised a bit extra they could use it to buy back gilts and keep prices firm.'

Aidan paused for a moment. 'Your suggestion would need to be packaged properly and explained to the Treasury in terms that they understood. If it went hand in hand with a small drop in long interest rates and the markets remained stable for a couple of days, then the terrorists' derivative positions would become untenable and they'd be wiped out financially.'

'Hold on a moment,' interrupted John. 'Could you explain what a REIT is please?'

'It is just like shares. A real estate investment trust is the property investment vehicle of choice for major investors. All it does is group a number of property investments under one umbrella. Investors can buy shares via the stock market, and they receive dividends instead of rents.'

Kate looked at Aidan and asked, 'Realistically is this a possible solution to the impending financial problems?'

'Yes, *yes* it is!'

'Excellent! Rafi and Aidan, you work on your REITs idea and matters financial, while the rest of us get back to finding the terrorists and the missile launchers,' said Kate.

The meeting had finished. In her relief, Kate stepped over and gave Rafi a hug.

He flinched and jumped back.

'I've done it again... Apologies,' she said, looking worriedly at him. It was as if she had invaded his personal space.

Kate turned to go. Rafi reached out and touched her shoulder; she turned and their eyes met.

'I'm sorry,' he said. 'I ran out of painkillers at lunchtime... My shoulder and back are rather sensitive, not to mention my wrist.'

'I'm glad. No, that didn't come out right - what I meant...'

'Don't worry,' Rafi cut in.

Chapter 4

Kate sat at her desk hoping beyond all hope that crucial missing pieces of the jigsaw puzzle would start falling into place. Her instincts as a detective told her that her investigation was perilously poised. Rafi and Aidan's reading of the position could all be a horrendous miscalculation and if their scenario was wrong, she would not only look a real idiot, but...

Jeremy's phone rang, interrupting Kate's thoughts. John picked up the call and put it on speakerphone. It was a call from Gareth, in Iceland. 'How's tricks? Sorry, Jeremy's out at the moment.'

'It's brass monkeys here! And there's no daylight!' came the reply. 'Got a nice hotel, though I'm not certain if I go a bundle on the cod liver oil or the roast puffin. What the heck! At least the locals are hospitable. I've hooked up with the Víkingasveitin, their Viking Squad, who seem to be a cross between our MI5 and the SAS. We've been inspecting all the shipyards and boatyards around Reykjavík – said it was a health and safety check. We just hit the bullseye at the last boatyard. There was a large yellow-hulled motorboat on a slipway, inside the big boat shed. Didn't look anything like the picture I got of *Flying Goddess*; they have altered her superstructure and given her a new colour to go with her new name: *Golden Sundancer*. I spotted Talal inspecting the boat with a geezer wearing a captain's hat. We didn't want to tip Talal off, so I've backed off.'

'Good news that you've found Talal,' said John.

Kate called across, 'Any chance you could find out exactly what work the boatyard has done to her?'

'While Talal is in there, I can't just walk in and chat to the boatyard manager,' replied Gareth. 'It would be too obvious. As we speak, I am standing outside, waiting to see when they leave, which is why I'm so frigging cold.'

'Rather you than me! But that's great work - do keep in touch,' said John replacing the receiver.

'Now we've found Talal and the sheikh's yacht, what we could do with knowing is when it's due to leave,' said Kate.

'I've an idea,' interjected Emma. 'If I could borrow Aidan for a few minutes and if the people at the Icelandic boatyard speak English, it might work.'

'What do you have in mind?' asked Kate.

'Well... Aidan is the type of guy who could afford a boat like *Golden Sundancer*. If he had a contact suggesting the Reykjavík yard... And he then asks the yard manager about the cost of some work on his boat... Hopefully the manager will be interested in new business and won't consider questions linked to his last four or five fit-outs as suspicious.'

'Good idea,' said Kate, before adding, 'John, see if you can get the contact details of the yacht broker - Jeremy's journalist friend, Pete, has been using.'

'No problems.'

Several minutes later, after a tortuous phone call, John had the broker's name and phone number. 'My God, that was like drawing teeth,' he complained. 'Journalists are too darn protective of their sources for their own good.'

Emma took the piece of paper from Jeremy and dialled the yacht broker's number. 'Hello, I wonder if you could help me. I'm the personal assistant of Aidan Gilchrist, of Maine Leadbetter, international financiers in the City of London. My boss tells me that you're the agents to speak to concerning the purchase of a large powerboat... Good, good, thank you. Could you please give me the details of what you have on your books in the €3 million price bracket? If possible located in Scandinavia, which is where his partner is from... I should mention that he's thinking in terms of spending a tidy sum on getting the boat refitted to her taste – lucky lady!' Emma chuckled. 'Yes, I can give you some contact details... My boss is a bit impatient. Could you perhaps fax me something at your earliest convenience? Within the next ten minutes would be *great*. Thank you.'

As good as his word, within five minutes the yacht broker had faxed through the details of three stunning motor yachts, ranging from twenty to thirty metres in length with prices between €2 million and €3.5 million.

Aidan, briefed by Emma, picked up the phone and spoke to

the Reykjavík boatyard. One could see very quickly why Aidan was a top financial dealer. He oozed charm, but came quickly to the point. It didn't take long before the boatyard manager was chatting openly and describing the boats they'd worked on.

'So, have you refitted anything seriously fast?' enquired Aidan.

'Yes,' came the reply.

'Excellent.' And before Aidan could ask, the shipyard manager helpfully proceeded to give a lengthy description of what they'd done to a Sunseeker Predator 75. 'She's had a complete refit; new colour to the hull. We installed long-range fuel tanks, upgraded the engines and the air-conditioning, done work to the bridge and superstructure to make the vessel more comfortable in inclement seas *and* installed a de-icing kit to help her with the local weather. Basically we've enabled the boat to go virtually anywhere at any time of the year,' said the manager proudly.

'Did you do any work to the interior?'

'Not much needed – we did put in a couple of very large ice boxes.'

Aidan cut to the chase. 'Thank you. My brokers and I are looking at…,' he hesitated and picked one of the details of the boats in front of him at random, then continuing almost seamlessly, 'A seventy-foot motor vessel, currently moored in Sweden. She'll need her engines reconditioning and my partner doesn't like the colours of the state room or the master bedroom. How soon could you start work on her? I'm thinking of putting in a bid this afternoon – subject to survey, of course.'

Aidan paused and listened to the shipyard manager, and then said, 'Oh that would be excellent. You say that the works to *Golden Sundancer* are completed, yes? So you can start as soon as my boat can be delivered?'

Aidan drew breath. 'My partner, Johanna, is rather particular. Would it possible for her to fly over, say, tomorrow or the next day to see the quality of your work on the Sunseeker 75?'

He paused again. 'Oh that is a shame - she'll be disappointed that *Golden Sundancer* is putting to sea later this evening. Thank you very much for your time though, you've been most helpful. I have your name and contact details, so I'll ring again on Monday to discuss the refit works.'

With that Aidan gently replaced the receiver, stood up and

bowed to a round of applause from Emma.

'Good work – no – *excellent* work,' said a smiling Emma. 'I knew you could do it. So we now know that the sheikh's boat is leaving within the next twelve hours.'

Emma did some mental arithmetic. 'That would tie in with a possible rendezvous with the trawler from Peterhead - off the north coast of Scotland tomorrow night.'

'Time is running out,' said Kate. 'We have *got* to find the missing locations and the people who are going to fire the missiles.'

Emma walked casually over to Aidan's desk. 'I didn't realise you had a partner.'

'Ah well, I can be rather deceptive.'

'You can say that again,' said Emma, looking a little crestfallen.

Aidan smiled. 'No you have got it wrong; it is my partner that's the deception.'

Emma brightened visibly.

'Emma, I have a problem,' said Aidan, changing the subject. 'I could do with some more space. I was wondering if you could help. I've printed out the vast majority of the contract notes and I'm swamped with paper!' He flashed one of his charming smiles in her direction. 'Any bright ideas where I could go?'

Emma muttered something under her breath which Kate didn't catch.

'Thanks,' said Aidan. 'But, I need to find a large table or floor: somewhere where I can lay out all this bumph,' he said, pointing to the piles of paper stacked on and around his desk. 'I'm almost there, but the lack of space is slowing me down.'

Kate stood up. 'You two follow me. Pass me some papers to carry.' They left the room weighed down with printouts.

Kate and Emma returned a couple minutes later to collect the remaining paperwork. 'We've put him in the commissioner's conference room and asked Beverley to keep an eye on him and to top him up with coffee. The commissioner is out, so he should get some peace and quiet,' said Kate.

Half an hour later Aidan called Emma. He sounded pleased. 'Could you, Rafi and Kate come up to look at a few things, please?'

They walked into the commissioner's conference room and saw it was now almost entirely covered with paper – not just the large oval table but also the chairs, which had been pushed against the walls, and the carpet as well.

'Thanks for coming.' Aidan greeted them with a grin. 'What do you think? Look at all the Post-its Beverley's given me.'

Emma looked around the room; each pile had a Post-it.

'Is this entire lot colour-coded?' enquired Emma.

'Yep. It hasn't taken nearly as long as I thought it would. I've categorised the contract notes, by colour, into various different types of deal. Things are falling into place,' he said to Emma. 'Rafi's hunch is right: there's definitely something afoot. Let me summarise where I've got to. I've been focusing on the long gilt contracts. The trades, individually, are modest in size, but when put together it's a different matter. Someone has been position building for several weeks. I started with my book at Maine Leadbetter. There are six investors writing – that is selling – put contracts. On the other side of these transactions, Prima Terra have been buying via an offshore account. I then looked at deals done by other brokers and I've been able to piece together a relatively complete picture. The other players buying the put positions are using intermediaries, mainly second or third division international banks.'

John stuck his head around the corner of the door. 'I thought that you might be up to something.'

'Come on in,' said Aidan with a smile. 'I've identified a number of investors whose exposures could lead to huge losses,' he said, pointing to the various piles strewn over the conference room table with pink Post-its. We've two building societies, two insurance companies, one local authority and one metropolitan authority... All have been investing the wrong way around: they should be buyers of these put contracts, not selling them! They have increased their risk exposure exponentially. Darn strange, darn silly and darn dangerous!'

'Their risk management systems should have picked this up, unless the contracts were booked in a hidden holding account,' continued Aidan. 'If they were, no one other than the dealers would be aware of the positions. The expectation would be that they would be traded on for a profit in a matter of days.'

'I'd bet the terrorists have bought off these dealers with large bungs into overseas bank accounts. And with the scale of potential losses you have uncovered, if things go as the terrorists plan -

given the delicate state of the financial sector - contagion would rapidly set in, wouldn't it?' asked Kate.

Aidan nodded.

'Sorry – I've heard you talk about contagion before, could you possibly explain what it means?' asked John.

'If you get measles you're contagious, right? In the financial markets contagion sets in when the troubles of one player are transferred across to another financially healthy player, who, for their part, gets into difficulty and passes the problem on to more players. We saw it happen in the recent credit crunch when a number of banks that had been financially sound, suddenly found themselves to be short of funds. Basically it's a matter of there being too many forced sellers and too few buyers. Prices of assets fall dramatically, which leaves the financial sector lacking capital. In our case, the terrorists have targeted six institutions. And they will very quickly become insolvent. Other banks, insurance companies and financial institutions get sucked into the downward spiral, *unless* the provider of liquidity of last resort, the Bank of England, steps in very quickly and provides sufficient cash to help those in trouble,' said Aidan. 'What makes it particularly dangerous is that the losses will initially be heaped on just six players!'

'The Bank would have to act very quickly and decisively or the downward momentum could become unstoppable,' added Rafi.

'I do not think they will procrastinate, given their recent experience with the banking crisis.' Aidan scratched his head. 'What concerns me is that the UK Government can't keep on borrowing vast sums of money to bail out companies in the financial markets. Very soon they will hit the buffers and find that international investors will not lend to them. Or if they *do*, it will be at massively increased interest rates. And then it will be crunch time.'

'In addition there could be big costs associated with the missile attacks.' Rafi looked thoughtful. 'So part of our plan must be to put across to the Government the downside hazards, in such a way that they can make informed decisions quickly.'

'Good idea,' agreed John. 'What scares me is that the terrorists have resources which rival those of a small to medium sized country. We should not underestimate the damage they are capable of inflicting.'

Kate's mouth was wide open. 'Thank you for describing the scale of the bad news. This is *seriously* frightening. But first things first – we have a lot of loose ends to tidy up and time is short. In order of priority, we must stop the terrorists' attacks or at least significantly limit the damage. And then, Rafi and Aidan, we need you to come up with a solution to stop the markets going into meltdown.'

'And third, pigs might fly,' added John.

'No, thirdly we've got to break this appalling news to our bosses – and soon.' Kate stood up, looking pale and drawn. 'Aidan, thanks for your excellent work.'

Rafi had been thinking quietly about the practicalities of getting the Government and the Bank of England to move quickly. 'One last item, please? Devising a strategy to avert the financial chaos will take time, and time is a commodity we don't have! I'd like to suggest, at our meeting with the chiefs, that we get permission to bring in a small team of financial experts, who could draw up a briefing document for the decision makers at the Treasury and Bank of England.'

'Good idea,' replied Kate.

★

Jeremy returned, positively bouncing. 'Who's been clever boy? I've had a most fruitful time with Dominique, the manager at the travel agent. We looked at the typical characteristics of the tickets they bought. The vast majority were low-cost packages to locations throughout Africa and were mostly last minute bookings on flights which had unsold seats... The typical visit was between one and three months.'

He smiled. 'Then I got Dominique to see if there were any tickets which were out of the ordinary. She wasn't impressed, as there were thousands of them. Specifically, she went searching for business class and full cost tickets, and trips where there were prearranged stopovers. My logic was that if they were recruiting bombers they'd look after them and want them to go to a training camp as well as do their voluntary work.'

Jeremy smiled. 'We have ten. Yes, *ten* individuals who were given favoured treatment by Basel and Jameel's charity. And guess what? One of the names that came out of the computer was that of a Ima Adwafeeq or, if one puts the space in the right place, Imaad Wafeeq, the Bishopsgate bomber! I've passed all the names to my colleagues, who will send through as much information as they can find on each of them. As we speak all the suspects are being traced and will be put under surveillance.'

Jeremy beamed, after a ripple of applause. 'The offer of coffee and doughnuts did the trick. Within half an hour she'd gone back three years and identified all the people who fitted our search criteria. There were literally hundreds of flights that matched. In a tick she had them sorted alphabetically. The number of different names on the list wasn't that great – just below fifty – but only ten had a pre-booked stopover in Somalia. When I pointed out Imaad Wafeeq's name, she went white. She thought I was there to prove she was involved. It took me five minutes to calm her down and to emphasise the importance of keeping what we had found totally confidential.'

'As a matter of curiosity, where exactly were the stopovers in Somalia?' enquired Emma.

'Mogadishu,' replied Jeremy.

'Hold on a minute – where was it that the other PhD student, Miti someone, came from?'

'What a good memory you've got,' said Jeremy. 'You are spot on. Miti Lakhani's family have a business operation in Mogadishu. I wish I had remembered that before you did,' he said with a smile in Emma's direction.

*

Colonel Matlik was punctual. At 5.15 p.m. Kate's phone rang. She was pleased to hear his telltale accent on the line.

'Good evening, I have more news for you,' he said, in his customary laconic manner. 'I received the names and photos you emailed me. You have caused quite a stir. We looked at the mugshots and straight away identified three of them as being highly undesirable. I hope it's OK – I bounced their details on to the FSB, the Russian Secret Service. The phone lines between here and Moscow have been red-hot. It seems that four of them are on their most wanted list! They are using false identities. In reality, they are: Rudnik Miromov and Dakka Dudayev, two former Chechen army officers. The Russians lost track of them ten months ago. The other two are: Aslan Popovskaya and Sergy Kowshaya, whose last known occupation was as part of a specialist Chechen hit squad – they also disappeared. Be advised: all four individuals should be treated with extreme caution. They have no scruples and are trained in everything from unarmed combat and heavy machine guns, to missile launchers and high explosives. In the words of my Russian friends these four are "wermin" – the sooner they can be exterminated, the better! Kornet missiles in their hands are a recipe for disaster.'

'I see,' said Kate hesitantly.

Kate, I must tell you, the next person on your list had the Russians rolling with laughter. He's an Arab, from the Gulf originally. Kaleem Shah trained as an officer cadet at your army's Sandhurst! No doubt your records will confirm this and where he went subsequently. They have him down, until a year ago, as being attached to an international news corps as their minder in the battle zones of the Middle East. We have nothing untoward on the other names you e-mailed me. I have asked a colleague to email you all the details we have on these undesirables. He is sending you copies of both the Russian files and our translation of them. I hope that they help. Sorry to sound like an overprotective father, but if the Russians say they're real shits, tell your SAS to treat them with the utmost caution.'

'Colonel, thank you,' said Kate.

'Unfortunately, I have some further information from the manager of the rifle ranges. It is not news you will want to hear. In addition to the Kornet missile launchers, he delivered four South African 60 mm Vektor mortars and eighty high-explosive shells. They're compact and deadly. Their barrel length is only 650 mm, but they have a range of up to 2 km if the firer opts for a ballistic trajectory.'

'Sorry?' queried Kate.

'The explosive round detonates in the air above the target,' explained the colonel. 'In the hands of a professional, the firing rate, is twenty shells a minute. If aimed straight at its target the range drops to half a kilometre and the shells can go through 500 mm of armour or over one metre of reinforced concrete. Basically, they are nasty little weapons – rather good at attacking soft targets, I would suggest.'

'Such as?'

'In ballistic trajectory mode, their blast radius is thirty metres. They would work a treat against,' the colonel paused, 'Fuel tanks – oil and gas storage plants in particular.'

'That fits in with a couple of the targets we've identified,' said Kate. 'Your information is most timely and thank you for all the trouble you've taken.'

'No problem; we Europeans have a duty to protect one another,' came the reply. 'Look after yourself.'

'I'll try to,' replied Kate, ending the call.

*

Kate raised her voice for all to hear. 'Our worst fears have been confirmed. There are four Chechen mercenaries on the terrorists' payroll.' She picked up the phone again and dialled Neil Gunton, Jeremy's boss. Normally she would have waited for Jeremy to liaise with his boss, but time was critical. She got through on the third ring.

'Neil Gunton speaking,' said a gravelly voice.

'Good afternoon, Kate Adams here.' She cut to the chase. 'The names Jeremy sent you earlier from Immigration – how are you getting on?'

'So far we haven't managed to get much on them. Our analysts suggest that three, possibly four, of them are Chechen. However, we do have chapter and verse on Kaleem Shah. We trained him at Sandhurst. He's been working in Lebanon and the Middle East as a journalist with a number of the international networks.'

'At this end we've had a bit of luck,' Kate replied. 'I'm emailing you the information we've just received from David's friend at the Estonian Security Service. Unfortunately, four *are* Chechens and are as bad as they could possibly get. And we're advised that in addition to the Kornet missiles, they have four South African 60 mm Vector mortars.'

'Oh, hell!' came the reply.

'We're making good progress at this end identifying likely targets,' said Kate. 'And we may be able to eliminate a couple of targets.'

'What do you mean by *eliminating*?'

'Well, if the fifth Kornet missile launcher is on the terrorists' fast getaway vessel… Then there will be eight and not ten UK

130

targets to find,' said Kate.

'What makes you think a missile launcher is destined for their getaway boat?' asked Neil.

'The terrorists have had a large cool box installed, and it is the right size to house the boxes containing the missile launcher and its missiles... We think we know the location of five of the targets, so we reckon we're probably only missing three.'

Kate paused, then went on, 'An alternative view could be that the fifth Kornet launcher is with the Arab, Kaleem Shah, and that he also has two targets. If so we are five targets short... We have a briefing meeting with the commissioner at 6 p.m. You would be welcome to attend.'

'Thank you,' said Neil. 'Jeremy is keeping me well posted. You've pulled more out of the woodwork in the past twenty-four hours than we've been able to over the past two months! I've got a meeting with my boss too,' there was an ominous pause. 'Oh my God! I see what you mean. I've just decrypted your email attachments. These Chechens are mean buggers. I'll speak to the boss immediately and ask that he puts the whole section on standby.'

'Sir,' said Kate in a diplomatic tone, 'the work that you and John's team have been doing points to the terrorists having many people in high places. I understand your list is still growing and includes a special adviser to Number 10, several Members of Parliament and a number of other very well-connected individuals. Should we be worrying about whether any of these people are moles or sleepers?'

'Yes, we should.'

'Well, sir,' said Kate, hesitating briefly, 'Our concern is that if the terrorists were to find out through one of these people that we are on to them, they will move to a plan "B" and change their targets, leaving us totally in the dark. With the Kornet missile launchers they can have a shot at practically any target they like...'

'You're right, Kate, it's a very tricky situation. The potential damage that one of these missile launchers can do in the hands of a professional is unthinkable. Your reading of the position is very similar to ours,' said Neil. 'MI5 agree that it would be better to go after the terrorists at known targets rather than let them slip away and blow the ruddy daylights out of a series of other targets when the whim takes them.'

'Thank you, sir,' said Kate.

'What's your latest thinking regarding when the attacks will come?' asked Neil.

'Tomorrow between dawn and the London Stock Market's opening at 8 o'clock. They'll want as much news exposure as possible to undermine the financial markets, so that they can maximise the huge profits on their derivatives positions. Has Jeremy chatted to you about this?'

'Yes, thank you,' answered Neil. 'I have to dash, we'll talk again soon.'

★

Rafi looked across at Kate. He sensed that she felt pleased with her team's progress, but was shocked by the horrendous possibilities that were opening up in front of her. He looked across at the clock; it was 5.18 p.m. There was less than an hour to go before the evening meeting with the commissioner and the chief superintendent. They were still missing the extra pieces of property information and he was pinning his hopes on Manchester police unearthing something. However, he was worried that they wouldn't have enough time.

Rafi felt out of sorts and irritable. Something he couldn't put his finger on was missing. He stood up and walked around the office. His tired head ached and he was finding it increasingly difficult to concentrate on anything for more than a few minutes at a time. Bloody hell, he needed to get his act together. It was only late afternoon, but it felt like midnight. He walked over and poured himself a cup of black coffee. Back at his desk, he sipped the hot coffee, studied the valuation report again and picked up the last three sets of accounts for PREH, the terrorists' property investment company.

He turned to the most recent balance sheet and looked at the property assets figure. Oh shit! Why the hell hadn't he noticed this earlier? The figure in the accounts was greater than the total set out in the Dewoodson valuation report. Bloody hell! There was £7.4 million unaccounted for! His mind was like a car without synchromesh. He struggled to think of a reason why it might be different. Of course! Development properties could be held in the accounts at cost - and they wouldn't necessarily be

132

included in the valuation report. Rafi stopped and thought. So somewhere there had to be details of the missing developments - probably a letter from the valuer which simply stated that the developments had a value greater than their book cost. £7.4 million wasn't large, but it could conceal one or more key properties. '*Oh yes!*' he exclaimed.

Kate looked across at him.

'That devious little bugger Wesson is still hampering our investigations.'

'What do you mean?' asked Kate.

'We're missing a letter which sets out PREH's development properties. See if Rick can get Wesson to talk and get him to do a search for the word *development* on all their computers.'

John called across the room. 'Want an update from MI5?' It was a rhetorical question. 'It seems that the journalist Kaleem Shah is running a group of suicide bombers. The good news is that they have traced and have under surveillance five of the suspected suicide bombers who received their training in Africa. These are the ones identified by Jeremy at the travel agency he visited.'

'I just hope that they find the rest of the possible suicide bombers – and soon,' added Kate. Her phone rang; it was Beverley, the commissioner's personal assistant. 'Oh dear, yes of course,' replied Kate. She turned to Emma. 'Could you and Aidan tidy up the papers strewn around the commissioner's conference room, please? He's back and would like to use it!'

Rafi sat there thinking. What else might he have missed? He dozed off.

At 5.55 p.m. Kate lightly shook him but he remained out for the count. She paused wondering which bit was safest to shake a little harder. She softly tapped his leg.

Rafi woke suddenly. 'Ooouch!' he exclaimed.

'Don't tell me you've got a bruise there as well!' said Kate. 'Sorry, but I'm running out of options as to what's not damaged.'

'No problem! Was I asleep long?' Rafi sat up to find everyone was looking at him. 'Sleep has been a bit scarce...'

'Time to see the boss,' said Kate.

This was going to be make or break, thought Rafi, as he followed the team up the back stairs to the commissioner's conference room. He was worried, key pieces of the terrorists' plans were still missing. He arrived in the boardroom still wrapped up in his own world, but was brought back to reality by a gentle touch on his shoulder.

'Are you OK?' enquired Kate.

Rafi sensed that a bond had started to form between them. He turned and looked straight into her warm eyes, not two feet away. He hadn't really had the opportunity to look at her face close up - it was her eyes that captivated him.

'A...apologies,' Rafi stuttered, 'I was miles away - again. It's just that the terrorists have been very careful to cover their tracks and plan to attack in several places at once. I keep worrying that I've missed something and it turns out to be costly.'

Close up, Kate's smile and her twinkling eyes had a disarming effect. Rafi wasn't accustomed to such closeness; he moved back a pace to give himself a bit of breathing space and stepped straight into the path of the commissioner, who had entered the room at some speed, aware no doubt that he and David were running two minutes late.

'Sorry sir.' Rafi noticed that he'd scuffed the commissioner's gleaming shoes.

'No harm done,' came the reply, 'Let's get started!'

Rafi turned and looked at Kate whose smile was bordering on a chuckle. She looked at him, and whispered, 'Whoops!'

Kate and Rafi sat opposite each other. The commissioner looked around the boardroom table. 'How are you progressing? As we agreed at our last meeting, this is crunch time. We will have to inform our political masters sooner rather than later. Kate, please update us.'

Kate looked at the faces around the table. They looked haggard. She just hoped she could do herself justice and convey the gravity of the position to the commissioner. The chips were down and she didn't like what she was going to report.

'Sir, let me summarise the position. Many things have happened since our recent phone conversation. We firmly believe that the missile attacks will come in the first couple of hours of daylight tomorrow morning. Through David's Estonian contact, Colonel Matlik, we have confirmation that the terrorists have five Kornet anti-tank missile launchers and three or four missiles per launcher.

As you know, these missiles are lethal pieces of equipment. In addition, we now find that they also have four South African 60 mm Vektor mortars and eighty high-explosive shells.'

Kate paused. 'We've narrowed down the potential targets and I'll come back to them in a minute.' The commissioner nodded.

'Following helpful discussions with the Immigration Office, we have identified two fast track and legitimate ways of getting UK visas, which the terrorists have used to get five people into the UK. Colonel Matlik and his contacts in Moscow have identified four as being former Chechen militia. We have been advised to treat Messrs Miromov, Dudayev, Popovskaya and Kowshaya with extreme caution. We are told that their training and experience is such that they'll give the SAS a run for their money. The fifth person, a journalist called Kaleem Shah, is ex-Sandhurst and has experience of war zones in the Middle East and urban warfare.'

Kate paused again. 'We believe that each Chechen mercenary has a Kornet missile launcher, a Vektor mortar and two targets. Jeremy has been chatting to a senior contact in the SAS, who advises that they are likely to be operating as individuals. As far as the fifth missile launcher is concerned, we think it is for their high speed getaway vessel, *Golden Sundancer*. She is in the North Atlantic, heading, we believe, for a rendezvous point off the north Scottish coast tomorrow evening.'

The commissioner sat bolt upright, unmoving.

'Nine trained suicide bombers have been identified. Kaleem Shah is running them. Jeremy's colleagues at MI5 have traced five of them, but unfortunately Mr Shah and four of the suicide bombers are unaccounted for.'

Kate looked at her notes. 'Moving on to the ringleaders - Jameel Furud, Basel Talal, Maryam Vynckt and Sheikh Akram Tufayl - MI5 has them under constant but discrete surveillance. There is a fifth possible ringleader: Miti Lakhani, who MI5 believes runs their suicide bombers' training base in Africa. Unfortunately he has vanished. Maryam and the sheikh are behaving normally. Jameel is enjoying his golf at a luxury hotel in Marrakech and Basel is on board their getaway vessel *Golden Sundancer*, off Iceland. Three of the terrorists' deep sea trawlers are in port at Peterhead, Great Yarmouth and Troon and are ready to put to sea. This gives them three exit points.'

She looked across at her two bosses. 'Our current informed guesses are that terrorist number one will attack Hartlepool Nuclear Power Station, plus one further target currently unknown.' There was an audible drawing in of breath as the word *nuclear* was uttered. 'They have a vacant industrial property which overlooks the power station,' she explained.

'The second will attack the St Fergus gas terminal and storage tanks and the North Sea oil pumping station at Cruden Bay. Both are close to Peterhead, where the terrorists own two vacant industrial properties. Number three will attack Heysham nuclear power station on the Lancashire coast, where they own a property with a clear line of sight. We think that he will also attack either Sellafield nuclear reprocessing centre or Hunterston "B" nuclear power station.'

The room was silent.

'And terrorist number four will attack the Bacton gas terminal. They own an industrial building in North Walsham, a few miles away. His second target is still unknown. This could be Sizewell nuclear power station, or the Grays liquid petroleum gas storage depot on the banks of the Thames near to the Dartford crossing. But our instincts tell us the missing target will be in London. We had the marshalling yards at Willesden at the top of our list, but MI5 report that there are currently no nuclear containers there, so we are still looking. We have outstanding leads on some development properties that the terrorists own and hope they will fill in some of the gaps.'

Kate paused and took a sip of water. 'Missile launcher number five, we believe, is on board *Golden Sundancer*. Its targets are unknown, but at this point our view is that it is for defensive purposes only.'

Kate shifted in her seat. 'Time is *not* on our side. The facts, as we and MI5 read them, point to the attacks coming early tomorrow morning, shortly after dawn. In the meantime MI5 has its operatives and anti-terrorist officers en route to these lo-cations. They will remain very low profile.'

The frown on the commissioner's face deepened.

'Now for the terrorists' overall game plan, as we see it.' Kate halted briefly, not so much for effect, but rather to collect her thoughts. 'Rafi and Aidan have been looking at the wider picture. This is where things get truly scary. We have reason to believe that the terrorists are trying to engineer the collapse of our already weakened financial system and UK plc. This, we believe, is their primary objective. By so doing, they expect to reap huge profits in the derivatives market.'

Kate paused again and looked across at the commissioner and the chief superintendent. They were looking shocked and sitting bolt upright, like schoolmasters during the saying of grace. Her face was unsmiling. 'We have confirmation that the terrorists control two public quoted companies and ten private companies. These businesses employ over 250,000 people. Through these companies they have in their pockets a number of influential individuals who MI5 advise us are being paid exorbitant fees as consultants or non-executive board members. Included within the 300 or so people are: Members of Parliament, special advisers to the Government and people in strategic senior positions. It is MI5's opinion that a number of these people could be the terrorists' eyes and ears, and could therefore be invisible sleepers.

Kate looked at John, then Aidan 'The terrorists have set up their public sector outsourcing businesses and six other financial institutions to go bust following their attacks. And Aidan says that the terrorists stand to make at least £50 billion if all goes to plan, which will add to the financial chaos.'

Kate glanced down the table at the stony faces of the two chiefs. 'Now for the better news,' she said, with the beginnings of a smile on her tired face. 'Unbelievably, we… Actually, I should say Rafi - have come up with a plan which the Government could use to calm and protect the financial markets. Unfortunately, his and Aidan's cynical view is that our political masters will instinctively move into spin, damage limitation and procrastination mode. This is what the terrorists are expecting. If the politicians procrastinate, all too quickly the downward momentum will become too great for even the Bank of England to stop. However, *if* – and it's a *massive* if – the Government can keep the markets steady, we can beat them at their own game. If interest rates and gilt prices can be held stable, the terrorists' derivative positions will become untenable and they and their co-

137

conspirators will rapidly face huge losses. The scale of such losses would set terrorism back several years and even bankrupt many of their financial backers.'

'Rafi's plan is for the Government to put into place a war chest which will enable them to issue shares in Government Real Estate Investment Trusts, instead of tapping the gilts market. These can be used to meet the potentially large increase in their liabilities. It's ingenious, in that they can draw down what they need, when it's needed. Aidan reckons that this war chest could have £400 billion in it. This would be more than enough to placate the markets under all but the very worst outcomes of the terrorist missile attacks.'

Kate paused. Now for the difficult bit, she thought. 'What we need is complete secrecy. MI5's and our worry is that the terrorists' well-placed sleepers include contacts in both COBRA and the Mayor of London's disaster unit. MI5 are still working on the list of names that John has given them. Our concern, and a big one at that, is that if the terrorists were to be tipped off and consequently changed to a plan "B", we would be completely in the dark as to how to stop them. I appreciate the chances are small, but the hazards are enormous.'

The commissioner almost interrupted, but held his silence.

Kate continued. 'Our advice is that the London Stock Exchange and Euronext.liffe must, at the last moment, not open tomorrow.' She paused, 'Also, we believe that it's too large a risk to take to expect our political masters to fully and quickly comprehend the scale of what they're up against. Spin, procrastination and aggrandisement are so ingrained amongst some ministers that we seriously wonder whether they'll move quickly enough. Accordingly, as of now, Rafi would like to bring together a team of four or five senior City gurus, who will be tasked with drawing up an economic plan for the consideration of our political masters, so that they will be able to make decisions based on facts and not on short-term political expediency. Realistically, by this time tomorrow evening Rafi and Aidan will be ready to drop and won't be in a fit state to pitch a financial recovery plan to the Bank of England or the Treasury. Who knows, the City gurus might even come up with a better plan!' At this point Kate shot Rafi and Aidan a cheeky smile.

'Agreed,' said the commissioner, letting Kate carry on.

'Our next proposal is that the SAS and anti-terrorist squads should be brought in to neutralise the terrorists and to search all the properties we have identified as their bases. The individual terrorists must be stopped from causing destruction, but if feasible they should be allowed to escape to the trawlers. We can then follow them and hopefully pull in all those in charge of the terrorist operation.'

'Lastly, we could do with another Nimrod – AWACS. We have one monitoring *Golden Sundancer*. It would be useful to have a second keeping an eye on the trawler in Great Yarmouth.'

The commissioner looked carefully at the team around him. 'Thank you, Kate. What you're asking David and me to approve, in terms of our careers, is suicide – if you're wrong! I only have one question for you: have you corroborated the facts as if we were taking these bastards to court?' There were nods all around.

'We've sought supporting evidence to confirm each link in the chain,' said Kate. 'The final proof will be if the terrorists are where we say they are. If they're not, we don't have a clue where else to look.'

'So your suggestion is that the SAS and anti-terrorist squads are put in place to prevent the terrorist attacks?'

Kate nodded.

'I have a fundamental problem with this suggestion,' explained the commissioner. 'We're duty-bound to treat this threat with the seriousness it deserves, but with the recognition that if we mess this up, it'll be ranked amongst the biggest police cock-ups on record. The SAS will require full military support at each of the locations, plus field hospital and medical support, in case any of the missiles reaches its target. We don't have the powers to run this scale of operation alone.' Giles turned to David. 'Who do we need to persuade?'

'I reckon we need the say-so of four people: the Home Secretary, the Secretary of State for Defence, the head of MI5 and the chief of staff of the armed services. The Home Secretary is out of the country until tomorrow attending an inter-government conference in Germany. We'll need to get his stand-in. From a practical point of view they'd need to be based here, as this is where all the information is. I agree with MI5: it would be too risky to use COBRA, given the likelihood of there being embedded sleepers.'

The commissioner turned to the chief superintendent and said, 'Are you willing to gamble your career and pension on this?'

'Sir, as I see it, I've no choice. If we don't follow this covert route and MI5 are proved to be right, and the terrorists *do* have moles within COBRA, it would be a total disaster. They would be alerted and could change their targets.'

'Right, it's agreed - you and I will take full responsibility for this if we've got it wrong.'

'Agreed, sir,' said David gravely. 'I have one other issue, but it can be discussed at a later time... I'm uncertain if it would be wise to let any terrorists leave the UK mainland.'

'Perhaps one could view it as letting them move to a location where it would be safe to capture them, and where the chances of collateral damage would be low,' suggested Kate.

The commissioner tipped his head to one side, taking on board her comment. 'Thank you - your observations and the hard work of your team are noted. However, before our political masters arrive for a briefing, I have two strong requests. First, get confirmation that there are only four missile launchers on the mainland. Second, find the whereabouts of the unknown properties.'

'David, will you please phone the Home Secretary's office and see which minister is covering for him and get their phone number? Also, get the number for the Secretary of State for Defence. I met with the head of MI5 a couple of days ago concerning Rafi, and I promised to keep him in the loop. I'll call him and invite him. I'll also speak to the chief of staff of the armed services who, as luck or good planning would have it, is due to have dinner with me tonight at my West End club. I'll arrange for them to be here for a council of war at 8 p.m. I'll then invite the two ministers. Kate and the rest of you, please find me the missing pieces of the jigsaw puzzle.'

As Kate's team was leaving the room, Jeremy turned to John. 'I think we did rather well there, don't you?'

'Yep, I couldn't have put it better if I'd tried,' said John.

They shot an approving glance at Kate, who had heard their

comments.

'Thanks guys, I'm so pleased you kept quiet!'

At that moment the phone next to the commissioner rang. It was Jeremy's boss at MI5. Giles switched the phone to conference mode.

'Evening all. Just a quick call to update you before your meeting ends,' said Neil. Kate and her team moved back into the room and stood by the door. 'We've a lead on Kaleem Shah. There are two suicide bombers with him. One of them used a credit card in Tilehurst, on the outskirts of Reading. Our informed guess is that they're going to attack the Atomic Weapons Establishment at Aldermaston and/or Burghfield, where nuclear warheads are put together. Both sites hold stocks of plutonium. Kaleem Shah, the cell leader, has many years' experience of living on battlefields. It is likely that he will want to lie low somewhere near to the targets.'

'Thank you for the update, Neil. While you're on… Do you happen to know where your boss is?' asked the commissioner.

'He's sitting next to me as we speak.'

'Good evening, Giles,' said the head of MI5.

'Hello Ewan. Can you attend a briefing and strategy meeting here at 8 p.m.?'

'My pleasure. See you then.'

The phone line went dead.

'Right, you've got until 8 o'clock to find me the missing targets,' said the commissioner.

*

Kate looked at her team, seated around her in the fourth floor office. They looked exhausted. She had to keep their adrenaline flowing. 'We have less than two hours to find a way to get confirmation that the fifth missile launcher is on board *Golden Sundancer, and* we have to find the missing properties. Emma please chase up Rick in Manchester. In the meantime, Rafi please decide on who you want on the economics team The commissioner has put his head on the block. Time to tie up some loose ends! We *have* to deliver!'

Emma phoned Rick Feldon in Manchester. After a brief conversation it transpired that the word search of the computers had revealed nothing relating to the missing development properties.

'Wesson is being as uncooperative as ever. He has a huge persecution complex. How long have we got?' asked Rick.

'Well, put it this way, by dawn tomorrow it could be too late.'

Rick went quiet for a moment. 'I'm really getting nowhere with Wesson. He's cantankerous and tired; if I push him any more I reckon he will go into his shell and won't come out again for a long while. And Stone has clammed up and is refusing to talk to anyone.'

'Good luck,' said Kate, and hung up.

*

Rafi's thoughts had turned to the economics team when Kate came and sat on the edge of his desk.

'How do you think the briefing went?'

'Rather well,' Rafi replied. 'You were outstanding.'

'Thanks. This economics team of yours – I'm looking forward to meeting them, especially if they're anything like you and Aidan!' she said with a twinkle in her eye.

Rafi nodded, but his thoughts were already back on the economics team.

Sensing that his mind was elsewhere, Kate returned to her desk.

Rafi started with the easiest choice: the real estate analyst. It would *have* to be Bob Tieson. Bob worked for one of the big US banks and Rafi spoke to him on a regular basis at work. His knowledge of European and North American REITs, and the real estate investment trust sector was second to none. Yes, Bob was his first choice.

He called across to Jeremy who was sorting out a supper order with *Luigi's*. Jeremy sensed that he was needed and gave Luigi carte blanche. 'Supper for, say, ten… No make that fifteen, please. Something we can eat whilst working. And orange juice, water and some strong coffee, please, delivered in, say, three quarters of an hour? Great, thanks Luigi.'

Jeremy put down the phone and looked across at Rafi. 'What can I do for you?'

'I've five people that I need brought in to work with Aidan. Kid gloves approach, but no taking *no* for an answer. OK?'

'Who did you have in mind?'

'The first person is Bob Tieson.' Rafi passed Jeremy the contact details. 'I'll let you have the next four names in a couple minutes.'

'Good,' replied Jeremy, 'That'll give me time to track him down.'

Now for the financials analyst, Rafi thought. He wondered who Callum would have picked. His first idea was the sector's star analyst, Steven Moreland, but both Callum and he viewed him as a bit of a prima donna and he was not really a team player. Rafi moved on to the next name: Matthew Wilson - who worked for a large European bank. Yes, he was highly regarded, very bright and would work well with others under pressure. And he'd been around for long enough to understand how painful extended bear markets could be.

Rafi passed Matthew's details to Jeremy. He now had two excellent people, but neither had any experience of dealing with the Treasury mandarins or the Bank of England. The economist would have to be someone to whom they'd listen. Rafi had a choice of five or six individuals. Then it came to him: why not get someone from the inside? Yes, Alex Lynton – the relatively new senior economist at the Bank of England. Before joining the Bank he'd held down impressive posts in the private sector and in academia. Was Alex a gamble? What if he'd become institutionalised and unwilling to take painful decisions? The more Rafi considered him, the more sure he became of his choice and passed Alex's details to Jeremy.

For the corporate finance specialist – he needed someone who understood real estate investment vehicles. Rafi thought of a name straight away: Donald Hollingsworth. He was a friend from his from his corporate finance days, where he had been Rafi's boss. He still ran a very successful corporate finance team. Several years ago he had become a non-executive director of a leading listed property company. Donald knew his way around the corporate finance market blindfolded and had a good working knowledge of the commercial property market. His experience would be a great help and he was undoubtedly very well connected in financial circles.

Jeremy took the fourth name and what Rafi could remember of Donald's contact details.

'How are you getting on?' enquired Rafi.

'We've tracked down Matthew and my colleagues are working on Bob's whereabouts as we speak.'

The fifth member of the team needed to be able to think out of the box and have a clear and incisive mind. A thought came to him… His sister fitted the criteria perfectly. He scribbled a note for Jeremy. 'Here's the fifth name.'

Jeremy looked at it. 'Saara Khan of Birmingham University. Ah, your little sister; our background research shows her to be an impressive academic and just as unassuming as you are! She's in Birmingham… Do you think that she would prefer a smart squad car or a helicopter?'

'Which do you think would be the faster?'

'Let me make a call.' A few minutes later Jeremy replaced the phone. 'They have arranged a car with a couple of motorbike outriders to keep the road in front clear.'

Jeremy then spoke to his colleagues back at MI5.

'Rafi, we've traced the other four: Donald Hollingsworth and wife are on their way to Dorset, where they have a cottage. We've sent a helicopter down in the direction of the A303 and have the traffic police between here and Yeovil looking out for their car. John has left to collect Bob Tieson; he is working late at his office in the Docklands. I'm collecting Alex Lynton from the theatre – I hope the performance hasn't started! And last but not least, Matthew Wilson is flying into Heathrow. He's been working in Frankfurt. I've arranged for him to be met by a colleague and taken through Immigration and Customs the VIP way.'

'Excellent,' said Rafi with a smile.

Jeremy called across to Kate. 'Do we have any cars left?'

'Of course, but heaven only knows where,' came the reply. 'If you go down to reception I'll get you one.'

'Thanks.'

Rafi sat there, thinking. Would this team of five plus Aidan have sufficient gravitas to stand up to the new Chancellor of the Exchequer? He was a serious politician, but with only a few months' experience of the job it was difficult to predict whether he had become influenced by the highly PR conscious Treasury team. And how would he react when the pressure was really on? Would he understand the seriousness of the huge risks facing the country, or opt for the easier strategy of procrastinating?

'Where have we got to on the London property front?' asked Kate.

'I've been trying to find out the address of the London or South of England property that the fish processing business owns,' replied Emma. 'I've spoken to Land Registry again. Sadly, their system isn't set up for this type of general enquiry. I spoke to Justin again and he's been trawling through their property databases. He says that there are too many permutations, even if you try to narrow down the search criteria, and that it's likely the deal would have been done subject to a confidentiality clause, so wouldn't even be on the databases!'

'Emma,' Kate called across to her, 'the immigration officer, Roger Harewood – the man who keeps the notebooks - is en route back from the West coast of the United States. Could you find the airline and flight number? There can't be many long haul planes from the USA landing at Manchester Airport early tomorrow morning. Then arrange for us to speak to him, in case he can remember something.'

'I'll get straight on to it.'

There was a momentary lull. Rafi leant back in his chair. What else could he be doing on the property front? What seemed like moments later, but was in fact half an hour, he was woken by Kate, standing over him and calling his name.

Rafi looked up into her hazel eyes. A sight to lift the spirits, he thought to himself.

'I thought a short power nap would do you good. Here's a cup of coffee. You'll need it… The first two members of your economics team should be here in five minutes,' said Kate.

Jeremy and John arrived within moments of each other. They had two very angry individuals with them, and took Bob Tieson and Alex Lynton straight up to the fourth floor interview room.

'I think that you had better placate your two friends,' said John as he walked into the office. 'Even though we told them otherwise, they still think they've been arrested. Bob definitely didn't want to come. I had to threaten him with handcuffs. I told him he could speak to his lawyer, if he wanted, when he got here.'

Jeremy came off his mobile phone. 'Saara is making excellent progress down the M1 and Matthew has landed at Heathrow where his reception committee is waiting for him on the tarmac. They should both be here within the hour, hopefully sooner. We caught up with Donald on the A303. His helicopter is en route to the rugby pitch at the Honourable Artillery Company, just around the corner.'

'You better go and greet your two irritable friends. Jeremy no doubt has arranged for fresh coffee and cream cakes as a peace offering... And Aidan is on his way – says he's finished his filing!' said Kate.

Alex and Bob were sitting in silence awaiting their fate.

Rafi walked in with Kate and Aidan following close behind him. He realised that he probably looked like someone who had been dragged through a hedge backwards and sensed that they feared the worst – being implicated as one of his friends. Rafi sat down opposite the two irate individuals, who eyed him suspiciously. Kate sat to his left and Aidan to his right.

Kate started the conversation. 'We will shortly be joined by Donald Hollingsworth, Matthew Wilson and a fifth person who is winging her way down the M1 as we speak. You know Rafi and Aidan Gilchrist? Good. No doubt you want to know why we've hauled you in here.'

Kate smiled. 'You are not in any trouble. Rafi is innocent. He was setup and has been helping us unravel a terrorist plot. It's probably simplest if I get him to explain what is going on and how you can help us.'

Rafi observed the two of them: Alex Lynton, the economist, sat uneasily, whilst Bob Tieson looked as if the father of all black clouds was hovering over his head. Rafi guessed he still had a lot of work to do on the IPO he was launching in a few days' time and didn't appreciate being dragged away from his office, even at this hour of the evening.

'If it makes you feel any better,' said Rafi in a calm and collected tone, 'In ten minutes' time a home office minister, the Defence Secretary, and the heads of MI5 and the armed forces are meeting with the commissioner two floors up. Like you, they have been asked in for a briefing, and like you, have dropped whatever they were doing... We have uncovered a terrorist plot to attack a number of key energy and nuclear facilities in the UK.

They are also planning to trigger havoc in the financial markets, where they have built up massive derivative positions. To cut a long story short, we believe the terrorist attacks will knock market sentiment so severely that the stock market will fall dramatically. And when the terrorists close their derivative positions, this will make the markets *and* the financial system crash.' Rafi paused and then went on. 'Put simply, we have to stop the markets gaining any major downward momentum.'

The silence was interrupted by Bob. 'What do you want us to do? The impossible? Or should we man the printing presses, print money out of thin air and then wave our magic wands?'

'Not quite,' Rafi replied. 'What we need is a plan that can be put in place to calm the markets.'

'Boy, that would be pulling a rabbit and a half out of a hat,' said Alex.

Aidan cut in. 'Rafi has a plan, which we believe you and your colleagues can make a reality. We believe there is the possibility to create listed Government property vehicles – REITs – and use share issues to mop up the liabilities that the Government may face, and to finance gilts buy-backs.'

At that moment a flustered Donald Hollingsworth appeared through the door. Rafi got up and walked over to greet him.

'My God, Rafi, you look terrible!'

'Yes, thank you Donald. Sorry to have ruined your weekend away. Let me introduce you to the other members of the team who beat you here. In the next fifteen minutes you'll be joined by Matthew Wilson – who I believe you know – and by a Dr Saara Khan, who you won't. Aidan will brief you.'

Aidan stood up. 'In straightforward terms, gentlemen, your mission, should you wish to accept it, is to come up with a credible strategy that the Bank of England and Treasury can adopt to avert a financial meltdown. I will bring you up to speed with the minutiae as soon as the others arrive. In a moment Detective Constable Emma Jessop will join us and help us turn this room into our office. And, I understand some coffee is on its way.'

Rafi could sense that they were hooked – their body language had visibly relaxed and there was determination in their eyes.

'If you'll excuse us, Kate and I have a number of things to attend to. Thank you for helping,' said Rafi. 'And so far as the attacks are concerned, there is a team upstairs planning how the SAS can neutralise them.'

*

There was a quiet knock on the office door. Standing outside was Rafi's sister. On catching a glimpse of him, Saara broke into a run. 'I've been so worried.'

'Thanks sis. Me too! Meet Kate, with whom I'm working.'

'You're not under arrest?'

'No,' replied Kate, 'your brother is working with us – he's a godsend.'

Rafi looked at his little sister. She smiled a smile that he would not forget in a long time – its intensity was wonderful. 'I'm sorry to drag you away from home, but we need someone with a clear, logical mind who can act as an independent thinker amongst a team of financial experts.'

'But finance is a blank in my book.'

'Yes, but you know how to structure a hypothesis and set up tests to prove or disprove it. Come and get a cup of coffee and let me introduce you to the team,' said Rafi.

They entered the interview room; it was buzzing and exuded a sense of teamwork and urgency. The conversation paused and Rafi introduced his sister to Aidan's team. 'Saara is here to be your devil's advocate. Forgive her if she asks any naive questions on the finance front; I promise you she'll be worth her weight in gold by the time you've finished. Aidan here will explain what's going on.'

Bob enquired, 'What are the chances of nipping back to the office to collect some papers and download some files?'

'No problem,' said Kate. 'We'll assign you Constable Peter Ashby to act as your chauffeur. Is the gravity of the position understood? *No one* outside this building other than MI5 and the SAS have a clue what's going on. Absolutely *no* talking to anyone! *Got that?*'

'Of course,' replied Bob.

'When Bob gets back could I borrow Constable Ashby?' asked Alex.

'Me too,' said Matthew.

'Emma will make the arrangements for you.'

'Aidan, whilst the others are out could you bring Donald and

148

Saara up to speed, please?' asked Rafi.

'Will do.'

Rafi left to rejoin Kate. He re-entered the office that had become his home.

She looked across at him. 'You look bloody awful,' she said with a soft smile.

'You don't look too good yourself,' Rafi added gently. 'Where do we go from here?'

'Time to ring Rick Feldon in Manchester.'

★

After a long wait Kate was finally put through to a tired sounding Rick Feldon.

'Sorry to keep you waiting, but it is a bit busy here. Wesson is one sandwich short of a picnic and proving to be highly incommunicative. Anyway... When our word search on the computer files came up with nothing, I spoke to the MI5 suits and they have gone through the secretaries' paper files. The good news is they have just found the letter. No wonder the word search revealed zilch – the letter was never saved on the computer. It's being faxed to you as we speak. It gives you two more properties!'

Kate smiled. 'Excellent work Rick; it's just what we needed. Thanks.'

Rafi sat on the edge of his chair; he couldn't wait to get his hands on the fax.

'Oh, by the way, Rick, we think that we're missing one more property,' said Kate. 'One in the South East or London area. It might be worth trying to chat to your man about it.'

'I'll see what I can do,' said Rick, 'And sorry again for not finding the letter sooner.'

'We've got it now – that's what matters.'

Moments later the fax arrived. Rafi read it. It was very straightforward. It confirmed that the value of two properties exceeded their book cost of £7.4 million. Rafi looked at the addresses: development land at Park Avenue, Wasdale Road, Gosforth, and Marfleet Lane, Kingston-upon-Hull.

Rafi went back to his desk and pulled up Google Maps on the screen. He typed in 'Gosforth' and was given the option of either Gosforth NE3 or Gosforth CA20. Rafi clicked on the CA20 link and a large scale map appeared on the screen. With a couple of mouse clicks, Rafi reduced the scale so that he could scan the surrounding area. Oh hell! He recognised the location; it was close to Sellafield nuclear reprocessing plant.

'Kate,' he called across, 'do you have a spare moment?' He showed her the map. 'We have found another location. The terrorists have a property within a mile or so of Sellafield,'

'Oh shit!' exclaimed Kate. 'This isn't what we wanted.'

'But at least we now know where to look,' added John.

Rafi typed in the address of the Hull property and looked at the map.

Kate, standing over his shoulder, said, 'Go east a bit. Thought so – it's just down the road from Easington, where there is a gas terminal and storage facility… And it's vast!.' She looked pleased. 'So, by my calculations, seven targets found… Three still to track down! As long as none of the missing three is a nuclear installation, I reckon we're in with a chance.'

'Or seven down and one to go, if we can get confirmation that the fifth missile launcher is on board *Golden Sundancer*. That would leave only *one* more to find,' said Rafi apprehensively.

'Let's hope you are right,' Kate handed Rafi a pile of papers. 'Could you help me with a bit of photocopying…? There's no one else to ask! I'm putting together corroborating evidence to support what we believe is going on - in case we get a frosty reception upstairs.'

*

Upstairs, Giles and David were preparing for the 8 o'clock meeting.

Air Chief Marshal Sir Nigel Hawser and the head of MI5, Ewan Thorn, were booked to come; however, it was proving more difficult to get the Government ministers to the meeting without telling them why.

Giles had phoned the Defence Secretary. He introduced himself and immediately cut to the chase. 'I've arranged a meeting for 8 o'clock this evening. It is of vital importance; can you attend please?'

'What's it about?' answered a frosty voice. 'I have a social engagement - Covent Garden with the wife. The tickets are like gold dust.'

'I can't talk over the phone, but we would value your input alongside that of the head of the armed forces and the head of MI5.'

'Oh, I see. Yes, I'll be there.'

'Thank you, sir.' Giles gave the minister the details of the venue and put the phone down. He looked relieved; the Defence Secretary, though new to the department, was a level-headed man and a renowned stickler for the minutiae. Once brought on side, he would be an invaluable asset to the team.

His next phone call, Giles mused, was likely to be interesting. The stand-in Home Secretary was a different ball game altogether. He phoned the Home Office, and was put through to the minister's personal assistant.

'The minister is in a strategy meeting and has left instructions not to be disturbed.'

'This is extremely important; I would have spoken to the Home Secretary but he's out of the country,' said Giles.

'Let me have a word with the minister,' replied the secretary.

What seemed like ages later, the minister's voice came on the phone. He sounded peeved.

'What, may I ask, is the purpose of this call?' he asked bluntly.

'When we met at the Bishopsgate bomb location you said you would be available to help 24/7. I have arranged a meeting for 8 o'clock this evening; it is of vital importance. Can you attend please?'

'I'm sorry but I'm busy. I could send my assistant, or we could have the meeting tomorrow morning, say, at 11 a.m.?' replied the minister.

'Sir, under normal circumstances I would have asked the Home Secretary,' said Giles politely, hoping the minister would get the point that the meeting was crucial.

'If I am to consider rearranging my diary, I'd have to know why it's so important that I attend this meeting. I'm booked to give a keynote speech. I'm spearheading the launch of our new data handling unit on immigration statistics. The press will be there. I have a first class speech and it has already been distributed for tomorrow's papers... Unfortunately, I'll have to decline your offer.'

'Sir, this is sufficiently sensitive that I can't tell you about it until we meet, but it is of utmost importance.'

'No. I've made my mind up; you can have my assistant or you can see me at my office tomorrow morning,' added the minister uncompromisingly.

Giles raised his eyebrows, perplexed. 'But it *is* important.'

The minister wasn't pleased. 'Damn it! You won't be getting me to your meeting at this short notice. Do you *know* who you are speaking to? My press conference is far too important an opportunity to miss, particularly as our newly formatted statistics look excellent. Good evening to you.' The phone line went dead.

The commissioner did not rise to the provocation; it was as if he was dealing with a petulant teenager. He dialled the 10 Downing Street hotline, got straight through to the PM's office and asked to speak to the Prime Minister regarding the recent bombing. Within a minute the PM came on the phone.

'How may I help you?'

'Prime Minister, we have a situation developing. It would be helpful if we had your or the Home Secretary's input, alongside that of the Defence Secretary, the head of the armed forces and the head of MI5. I have spoken to the minister covering for the Home Secretary and have been informed that his prior engagement means he's unavailable. I was hoping…'

'When do you want to see me?' came the businesslike reply.

'Eight o'clock this evening at Wood Street, please.'

'I will have to put you on hold - bear with me; I need to speak to my secretary.'

Giles waited, fingers crossed. The recent General Election meant that the Prime Minister was working with a wafer-thin majority and had a lot to contend with.

The PM's voice came back on the line. 'My secretary has rescheduled my diary. Traffic permitting, I shouldn't be more than five minutes late.'

Giles was grinning when he put the phone down. 'There are times when a politician can restore one's faith in the system.'

'You couldn't have asked for a better group of people to pitch our problems to,' said David, who was also smiling.

A couple of minutes later the phone rang: it was a very disgruntled Home Office minister. 'Regarding your recent phone call… For the record, I wish to repeat that I am unwilling to drop this press briefing, unless you explain to me in detail why it is so important I attend.'

David sensed that Giles wanted to get him off the line as quickly as possible, in case the topic of the PM was brought up.

Giles said very politely, 'I've been considering your offer of a meeting tomorrow morning; perhaps I could come over and brief you. Would 11 o'clock at your office be acceptable?'

'Er… yes, that should be fine. Do phone my personal assistant first thing to check the time and venue and that my diary is still free, though,' came the reply.

'Thank you, minister.'

Giles couldn't put the phone down quickly enough. 'Don't repeat me, but that man is a self-obsessed idiot of the first order. Heaven help the country if he ever gets a department to run. Can you see if Kate has made any progress with the missing information? Thanks. I'm going to pay Greg a visit to tell him to implement our emergency plans and get a command centre set up.'

*

Kate and Rafi were collating their supporting information for the 8 o'clock meeting.

Down the corridor Aidan and the economics team had transformed the interview room into their base. Beyond them, the rooms that had been the offices of Chief Superintendent David Pryke and his team had been cleared. Greg and his team were working on turning them into an operations room. A group of desks had been put back-to-back in the centre of the room, with a row of phones and networked PCs with flat screens down the middle. Video-conferencing and LCD screens were being mounted on the walls and secure phone and video links to the SAS command centre, the HQ of the paratroopers and the army's command centre in Wiltshire were being set up. The PM's hotlines were being installed in an adjoining office.

Greg was looking concerned - his assistant was having problems getting two video links working properly. And it seemed that one of the big screens had developed an electrical gremlin, another simply didn't want to work and in addition a touch screen was playing up intermittently.

Aidan and Emma came down the corridor to chat to Greg

about their PC and printer needs. As they walked through the door, they saw that it was a bad moment.

Greg saw Aidan looking at him. 'It's the damn wiring...'

'Can I have a look?' asked Aidan.

Greg waved him across and asked Emma quietly, 'Don't tell me he has a degree in electrical engineering as well?' which Aidan overheard.

'No, I'm afraid not - just as I thought: the same leads in and out. What you have here is an older version of what we have in the office. Emma, see if you can find Rafi; he'll know.'

Moments later Emma reappeared with Rafi in tow.

'Rafi, what do you think? It's similar to the kit we've got in our conference rooms and use to link into our laptops, isn't it? The leads look the same; it's just the screen and the electronics that are older.'

Rafi looked at the leads. 'You're right.'

'Thanks, mate,' said Aidan. He turned and spoke to Greg. 'I just need to make a quick call.'

Aidan spoke to his boss, a main board director of Maine Leadbetter. 'Hi, Russell, it's your erstwhile colleague Aidan here... Yes, I've been working hard... No, I'm not off somewhere with a bit of fluff... Yes, I aim to be back in the office tomorrow... Probably by 10.30 a.m.... Sorry, yes, I'll miss the morning meeting and the early trading... Don't worry, if I get what I'm doing right, it'll be excellent news for the firm.' Aidan paused. 'This brings me to the reason for my call: I've a pitch to some wealthy players first thing tomorrow and I need to knock the socks off them. I've got a favour to ask. Would you ring the security guards on reception and authorise my borrowing the screen from the small conference room and a little bit of associated kit?'

The request was met with silence. Greg and Rafi could tell from Aidan's face that his boss wasn't keen.

'OK, let's say that if it's not back in time, I'll buy a new one. You *do* trust me, don't you? Oh, good. Thanks. Yes, I know I take liberties! See you tomorrow.' Aidan put down the phone. 'I hope he won't mind the small white lie. There's no way what I'm planning to borrow will be back in time. But since the markets will be closed, they won't be much good to him anyway!

Greg, if you could find a van, would you and one of your assistants like to pay my office a visit?'

Greg's expression changed from a scowl to a beaming smile. 'Give me a couple of minutes to draw up a list of what I need and I'll meet you by the back door.'

Rafi looked at Aidan, 'Good move! I hope you've got what he needs.'

'Oh, I don't think that there should be too much of a problem. We have a basement storeroom full of last year's kit which makes this lot look steam age in comparison. This should be fun. I'm willing to bet Greg will think he's visiting Santa's Grotto!'

Kate put her head around the corner of the door.

'So this is where you are! Rafi, I thought you might like to listen in; we have the captain of the Nimrod, tracking *Golden Sundancer*, on the phone.'

As they scurried back to the office, Kate brought Rafi up to speed. 'Twenty minutes ago he radioed in and spoke to John to report that *Golden Sundancer* was on a converging course with a trawler around 250 miles from Iceland, north-west of the Faeroes, in the middle of nowhere.'

Back in the office, the voice of the Nimrod captain could be heard clearly over the speaker phone. 'Your vessel has hove to in close proximity to a fishing vessel, which we've identified as an Estonian trawler, named *Anu Riina*. The captain of the trawler is transferring an inflatable dinghy over to *Golden Sundancer* as we speak. There's a big swell down there and the temperatures are sub-zero... A line has been secured aboard *Golden Sundancer* and her captain is manoeuvring to get the dinghy into the lee of the wind to make it easier to get it on board.

'Can you see what's in the dinghy?' asked Kate.

'Hold on a moment... We've started to get enhanced images from our high magnification camera... Would you believe it! Looks like two wooden coffins... The dinghy and the two boxes are now being pulled on board *Golden Sundancer*... Give me a moment and I'll send through the pictures.'

'While you're at it, could you include any markings on the wooden boxes?' asked Kate.

'Will do.'

'What speed has *Golden Sundancer* been cruising at?'

'Between thirty-seven and forty-one knots - very respectable given the conditions down there. Their de-icing system seems to be working well; unusual, though, for this type of boat.'

'How many do you reckon are on board?'

'Two men; the captain and a crew member are all we've seen... The trawler has disengaged. She is turning south-east and heading for home.'

'Is there any chance of them picking you up on their radar? Seeing or hearing you?' asked Kate.

'Don't worry, we're as good as invisible; we've got our radar-cloaking device on.' The Nimrod captain paused. 'They have completed the unloading of the dinghy and the two boxes have been safely stowed on board.' After a moment's silence he continued, '*Golden Sundancer* is returning to her bearing of 152° and is getting back up to her previous speed. I'll keep you posted if she alters speed or course, or has another rendezvous. Out.'

Kate looked up. 'Emma have you got the pictures?'

'Yep,' came the reply. 'The boxes and their markings are just what we wanted. They confirm the whereabouts of our missing Kornet missile launcher!'

'Excellent, now we've only got *one* missile target to find, not three!' Kate picked up the phone and relayed the good news to the commissioner's assistant, Beverley.

John, who was now back in the room, raised his coffee cup towards Kate, toasting her.

'Here's to your eclectic team. Twenty-four hours ago I wouldn't have given you any odds. Now – who knows? – we might beat the buggers, yet.'

Alex entered the room. 'I thought I'd see how the other half lives. My goodness, it's cosy in here!'

'You should have seen it thirty-six hours ago – none of this mess was here,' replied Rafi.

'No,' said Emma, 'it was all tidied away into the filing cabinets!'

Alex walked across to Rafi's desk and pulled up a chair. 'I am so pleased that you are OK. Might I ask why you chose me, when you could have picked one of the high-profile City economists?'

Rafi looked at Alex. 'It was a no-brainer. How are you getting on with your colleagues?'

'Really well.'

'There's your answer,' he said with a broad smile.

'Thank you and thanks for choosing me. Oh, by the way, your little sister is proving an inspired choice; she's a bright cookie and has us all organised. Chat to you later,' with that Alex turned and left.

Kate looked across at Rafi. 'You don't by any chance have a brother? If so, I'd like to meet him, please!'

'Afraid not.'

She looked at Rafi, her head slightly to one side. 'You are proving to be a most resourceful guy, with some great friends. I'm pleased that I let David bully me into getting you out of Paddington Green!'

Kate and Rafi were finalising the background materials for the presentation to the Chiefs upstairs, when Jeremy bounced into the room.

'Well done tracking down the fifth missile launcher; at last we've *something* to celebrate.'

How he managed to keep up to date amazed Rafi.

'Talking of having fun, we've been over to Aidan's office,' said Jeremy. Greg has had a field day. He's borrowed three large state-of-the-art video-conferencing screens, a large plasma screen and a selection of other useful gismos. The basement store proved to be a real Aladdin's cave. Aidan did a brilliant job of distracting his two security guards and he even got them to lock up the conference rooms before he left, saying that they were to remain locked until 8 a.m. tomorrow. Greg is down the corridor setting up his new toys. How long has the meeting been going on upstairs?'

'Almost an hour,' replied Emma. 'The PM arrived a bit late.'

Kate had finished her collating and walked over to Rafi's desk. 'Well, I seem to be ready. How are you feeling?'

'Given the circumstances, not that bad, thanks. At least my brain is still working; the rest of me feels due for a refit and needs a bit of TLC.'

Kate smiled and whispered, 'When all this is over, I'll see what I can do - as a small thank you.'

'A thank you for what?' Rafi replied.

'You're simply impossible! What planet are you on? If it hadn't been for you, I'd be having a normal night, oblivious to the fact that tomorrow we could be facing Armageddon.'

'Excuse me.' Rafi, still deep in thought, walked off down the corridor to see how the economics team was getting on. He put his head around the door. The six occupants had reorganised the room, with a group of desks in the middle. Alex and Donald were sitting next to each other, opposite Matthew and Bob. Saara was at one end and Aidan at the other. On one side of the room were a couple of PCs and a printer photocopier. A whiteboard, now covered with writing, had been hung on the opposite wall. Plates littered the table. The room definitely had a *work-in-progress* air to it.

'Just thought I'd drop by to see how you were getting on and to let you know that we currently have a good idea where seven of the eight terrorist targets are.'

'And they've traced the two suicide bombers with the journalist Kaleem Shah to the outskirts of Aldermaston, not far from the Nuclear Weapons Research Establishment, as Emma predicted,' added Kate who had arrived just behind Rafi.

Matthew spoke up. 'Emma and Aidan have explained what the terrorists are planning. My view is that you are underestimating the financial downside.'

'But at least we have advance warning,' said Aidan.

Rafi smiled at his sister.

'They're being very tolerant of my lack of finance skills,' she said.

'Have none of it Rafi; this young lady could join my team any day!' said Donald, Rafi's former boss, with a smile.

Rafi turned to leave. The soft voice of Saara follow him down the corridor. 'Rafi, look after yourself.'

*

Back at his desk, Rafi called across to Kate. 'For the life of me, I can't come up with any more ideas where the missing target might be. I'm beginning to feel rather useless…'

Kate looked up. 'Why don't you put your feet up for a few minutes and have a bite to eat. How you manage to still think straight, amazes me.' she added in a caring tone.

Rafi was halfway through a sandwich when Kate's phone rang. 'We're on. Time to face the music!'

As they went down the corridor, Kate put her head around the door of the interview room and asked Aidan to join them.

They walked past a positively beaming Greg, who by the looks of things had the Ops Room fully up and running. He gave a thumbs up sign to Aidan, who acknowledged it with a wave and a grin.

The walk up the back stairs took Rafi back to his school days; it conjured up memories of visiting his house master - the gloomy lighting and the greying wall paint added to his apprehension. The question he was thinking, was 'what would the PM do?'

Chapter 5

The team walked into the commissioner's anteroom, where Beverley was at her desk. 'Giles is ready for you. Do go straight in.' The commissioner's conference room had a very businesslike air to it.

'Good evening,' said Giles Meynell, standing up as Kate entered the room. 'Please be seated. John and Jeremy, would you let Rafi, Kate and Aidan sit at the table and pull up two chairs behind them? Thank you. It's a bit of a squeeze, but I reckon we can manage. Time for some introductions: Prime Minister, Secretary of State for Defence, Air Chief Marshal Sir Nigel Hawser, head of our armed services, and Ewan Thorn, head of MI5 - it is my pleasure to introduce: Detective Chief Inspector John Dowsing of Special Branch, Detective Inspector Kate Adams of our Economic Crime Unit, Jeremy Welby of MI5, Aidan Gilchrist of Maine Leadbetter – a derivatives expert – and Rafi Khan.

After a short pause, Giles continued. This time his gaze was fixed on Kate. 'We have had a fruitful discussion, but before we go any further the Prime Minister and his Defence Secretary would like to ask you some questions.'

'Thank you, Commissioner,' said the PM in a measured voice. 'Three hours ago I had envisaged spending the evening dealing with mundane matters. Suffice it to say, Giles's revelations have come as a serious shock - the intricacy and scope of the terrorists' threat to our energy supplies, our financial system and our country's economic welfare is every bit as grave as anything we have faced since the Second World War,' he looked at Giles reassuringly. 'I'm not going to shoot the messenger. Indeed, I understand that you've been working day and night since Monday. To have come this far with your investigations in such a short time deserves my considerable gratitude.'

The PM paused and looked around the room. 'Unfortunately, all you have accomplished will come to nothing unless our next steps are the right ones. As has most eloquently been pointed out to me, we have to be proactive – not reactive – in the face of these heinous threats.' He looked at his Defence Secretary, then continued. 'There are a number of questions to which we would appreciate candid answers. First of all, why do you believe that COBRA is not the right way forward at this point in time?'

Kate looked across at the PM. 'I wish it were, sir,' she said slightly shakily. She paused and regained her composure. 'MI5's and our worry is that the terrorists have sleepers in place who could tip them off, and prompt them to switch to a contingency plan. At this point in time we've a lead on all except one of the expected terrorist targets. We know that we're up against well-trained and battle-hardened mercenaries. If they were to be tipped off, such is the transportability of their missile launchers that they might simply switch to a plan "B". To answer your question, whilst the chances are small, the downside hazard is too large.'

'Where precisely is the threat of an internal tip-off?' asked the PM.

Kate pulled out some stapled sheets of paper from the small bundle in front of her and passed one to each of the individuals around the table.

'In front of you are the names of individuals we and MI5 can place within the terrorists' web of companies. To put it bluntly, all these individuals are on the terrorists' payroll – whether they know it or not. You will note that there is an executive officer of a metropolitan authority on that list, which falls within the London disaster planning area. On page four is a list of the organisations which the terrorists have infiltrated through their huge outsourcing business and the limited liability partnerships they run. The list includes: the Ministry of Defence, GCHQ, Paddington Green police station, the Home Office...'

'Thank you,' cut in the PM.

'Your list is very impressive, but can it be verified?' asked the Defence Secretary.

'The names come from Companies House and have been given the once-over by MI5.'

'Let us be clear. You are suggesting...' The PM looked at the sheet, 'That a special adviser to me at Number 10, whom I was with not four hours ago, is on their payroll, as are two individuals who provide support to COBRA. Is that correct?'

Kate looked straight at the PM and said simply, 'Yes, sir.'

'The problem is that we have identified two potential moles in COBRA, but we can't be one hundred per cent sure that we haven't missed a third,' said Ewan.

The PM looked at the head of MI5. 'This is *very* disturbing; why didn't I know about this sooner?'

'Unfortunately, Sir, we have only just uncovered them. They're "sleepers", put in place to carry out one or more specific activities. Up to that point, they are in effect invisible. I have seen the documentation relating to one of the limited liability partnerships controlled by the terrorists, on which an MP sits as a non-executive. He gets paid £40,000 per annum for attending just four half-day meetings a year. The going rate for an individual with little business experience would be less than one-tenth of what he's being paid. The fact that this MP sits on a couple of sensitive committees is what concerns us at MI5. Following our investigations into the activities of Maryam Vynckt, we believe that a number of those on the list have received large payments offshore, via Gulf Trade Bank. The problem is that the offshore payments are very hard to trace unless you know exactly where to look,' Ewan paused. 'Therefore, for now, it is difficult to confirm that the list is complete.'

The Defence Secretary looked agitated, but kept quiet.

'So, it's a matter of timing?' asked the PM. 'Whilst the terrorists have their Kornet missiles and remain at large, you believe COBRA should not be activated?'

'Precisely, sir.'

The Prime Minister looked thoughtful. Rafi sensed he didn't agree.

'Thank you,' said the Prime Minister, 'that answers my first question. My second question is: how certain are we that the terrorists have Kornet missiles?'

Kate flicked through her bundle of papers, pulled out copies of the digitally enhanced photos of the two wooden boxes strapped into the inflatable dinghy and passed them around the table.

'The photos were taken under an hour ago. The boats involved are owned by the terrorists... And the markings on the boxes match those stolen from the Russians.'

'Thank you. Now for question number three. Could you please tell me why you are so confident that the four Chechen mercenaries have two targets each?'

'A combination of things, Prime Minister. First, we have confirmation that they took delivery of five Kornet missile launchers and twenty missiles, four of which we know have been fired. This leaves them with sixteen missiles. The photos we have just received indicate that a launcher and probably four missiles are now on board *Golden Sundancer*. This leaves the four Chechen terrorists with a launcher and three missiles each. We have been talking to the army; the launcher, its tripod and the missiles would be too cumbersome for one man to move around quickly. We therefore believe that the Kornet launcher will be used to fire three missiles and then left behind. Each terrorist will then move on to where they have hidden a Vektor mortar and will use it to attack their second target. Our Estonian friends have confirmed that the terrorists have taken delivery of four such mortars with eighty high-explosive shells.'

Kate paused to let what she had just said sink in, and was about to carry on when the Defence Secretary enquired, 'Could they not use the mortars first?'

'Yes, that is entirely possible. But the advice from the SAS is that as the Kornet missiles inflict much more damage, they would be used first,' replied Kate.

The Defence Secretary nodded and she continued. 'If we consider the types of targets close to the terrorists' vacant properties and their weapons - they correspond. The Kornet missiles will be used on the substantially built targets – the nuclear power stations – and the Vektor mortars will attack lighter-weight targets – the oil and gas facilities.'

'OK. Question number four: when and where do you believe that the terrorist attacks will come?'

'Our educated guess is that the attacks will be tomorrow between 7.30 and 8.00 a.m. – from first light to when the Stock Exchange opens. This will maximise the news coverage and the adverse impact on the markets. This theory is supported by the information we have from the local harbour masters, who have informed us that the trawlers are all due to slip their berths tomorrow between late morning and early afternoon.'

Kate passed across more sheets of paper detailing where they believed the attacks would take place.

The PM looked around at his colleagues, who were deep in thought. 'Any questions or shall I carry on?' After a short pause, he moved on to his fifth question. 'Why do you want us to let the terrorists escape and make them believe that they've successfully hit their targets?'

Kate looked behind her at John and Jeremy. Neither showed any desire to tackle this question so she carried on.

'We want to arrest the four main ringleaders: Sheikh Tufayl, Basel Talal, Jameel Furud and Maryam Vynckt and any other people who have been helping them,' expressed Kate. She paused momentarily to collect her thoughts.

'Perhaps I could answer this question Prime Minister?' said Ewan. 'Our intelligence unit tells me that the main ringleaders and the escaping terrorists will meet up. We believe that their destination is Morocco. Jameel is there and confirmation has come through that the sheikh's private jet has filed a flight plan to Marrakech airport. It's scheduled to land at 12.45 p.m. on Monday. We believe the terrorists will leave Britain on the trawlers and rendezvous with their fast motor vessel, *Golden Sundancer*, which will then sail to Morocco.'

'What are the extradition procedures like from Morocco?' asked the Defence Secretary.

'They are a diplomatically friendly country. And we have successfully extradited the £50m Securitas robber from there.' Ewan paused. 'However, the procedure is long-winded and the evidence has to be watertight and well documented. Put bluntly, time wouldn't be on our side. Sheikh Tufayl, a Muslim, is very wealthy and very well-connected. He has the ability to slip the net if he winds up in the hands of the Moroccan authorities.'

'How important do we think these people are?' asked the PM.

'Very,' replied Ewan. 'We're dealing with international players who are in the vanguard of financing terrorist activities. Their bank accounts are in both neutral countries and some less than neutral. Deals struck in the financial and derivatives markets can easily be done via intermediaries – something like the Banco de "we launder your money for a fee". The turnover in the derivative markets is vast. Tracking down such transactions would take time and the profits made would rapidly become untraceable. We believe that we need positive proof of the ringleaders' involvement and can't afford to let them slip away to fight another day. Capturing them *in flagrante delicto* would make it far simpler to freeze their assets and then have them confiscated. If they think that they've been successful, they and their accomplices will be less likely to go to ground.'

Ewan looked at the PM. 'In addition, there would be a feel-good factor from the news coverage following their capture. However, our priority is to scupper their plans and then apprehend them.'

Kate spoke up. 'The four Chechens are dangerous killers. If they were cornered in a public place, it could get very messy and the collateral damage could be large. If we follow them, we can pick them up well away from innocent bystanders. I should make it very clear that we would only wish them to be allowed to escape to the trawlers *if* and only *if* their Kornet and Vektor weapons are out of action.'

The PM thought carefully about what she had just said. 'My last question is: could you please explain your fears relating to the financial markets?'

Rafi glanced at Kate and Aidan. They nodded at him. 'Could I answer that one, please, Prime Minister?'

'Yes, go ahead.'

Rafi thought for a moment about where it would be best to start and eventually decided to start at the beginning, with the description of their three PhD theses. 'John and Jeremy discussed the ringleaders' academic work with a senior lecturer who was a contemporary of theirs - he described their dissertations as being incisive and of exemplary standard. However, to quote him: *If one puts them together, they are the instruction kit for building a financial atomic bomb.'*

The PM shifted uncomfortably in his chair.

'Sheikh Tufayl is conservatively worth $10 billion,' continued Rafi. 'Jameel Furud, through his control of Prima Terra, has around £30 billion of funds under his management; Maryam has, we estimate, a similar sum under her control. While Talal, in contrast, has used the sheikh's money to build up the terrorist infrastructure. They have billions at their disposal, and intend to use it to wreck the Government's finances.' He stopped for a moment, letting the point sink home. 'The terrorist activities should be viewed in the context of the continuing uneasiness in investor sentiment. Their ultimate aim is to trigger another stock market crash, which will enable them to make *massive* profits from their positions in the derivative markets.'

Rafi stopped and looked around the table to check that the guests had taken on board what he'd been saying. 'Aidan has been doing excellent work on the scale of their intervention into these derivative markets.' He leant forward and looked past Kate at Aidan.

'Prime Minister; in a nutshell, if they achieve their ambition they'll saddle the derivatives markets with losses in the region of £50-100 billion,' added Aidan. 'I have identified a sufficient number of contracts to confirm the scale of the numbers involved.'

The Prime Minister looked at Rafi and then at Aidan. 'Well, there is a simple answer: we close down the market and unwind the positions in the derivative contracts.'

Rafi looked at the PM. 'Might I enlarge, please?' he enquired politely.

'Yes,' came the slightly clipped reply.

'Also the terrorists have identified a number of areas where Government guarantees exist. Their aim is to bring billions of pounds of debts and liabilities back on to the Government's balance sheet. For example, by attacking nuclear power stations - there will be colossal clean-up costs, plus the likelihood of large accelerated decommissioning costs. Then there will big costs to stop the outsourced public sector services, that they control, from collapsing. Against the backdrop of a stock market crash, this would put the weakened Government finances into a perilous position,' concluded Rafi.

'This all seems rather far-fetched if you ask me,' commented the Defence Secretary. 'My view is that the greedy bastards want to make a financial killing, nothing more nothing less. Let's stop the trading in the contracts that Aidan has identified and get on with catching them.'

The PM looked at Aidan and Rafi. 'Do you believe that the

Government's finances are in peril?'

'Yes, sir. These terrorists aren't just financially astute and used to dealing with huge sums of money; they are also exceedingly devious and clever. They are determined to inflict as much damage as possible. It is as if they have declared war on our economy.'

Rafi sensed that the Defence Secretary disagreed. 'In the short time available to us, we've looked at the two most obvious derivatives contracts and can confirm that they have built up big positions. I strongly believe that they will have also been trading in Frankfurt and Chicago. It would be nigh on impossible to unwind the myriad of positions they, and possibly their associates, have amassed.'

'This is bloody preposterous!' burst out the Defence Secretary. 'This is all too much. You're exaggerating – trying to play things up for your own self-importance! Have none of this Prime Minister – get on and stop the terrorist attacks. We can let the Treasury and the Bank of England sort out the financial problems next week, as and when they occur.'

Meanwhile, Aidan was doing an excellent impression of a boiler building up a head of steam: his ears had gone red and his eyes had narrowed. He was close to telling the Defence Secretary exactly what he thought of him.

'Do you have a solution?' asked the Prime Minister.

'We believe that we do, sir,' replied Rafi. 'All we ask is that the authorities don't procrastinate. We're drawing up a detailed report for the Chancellor of the Exchequer and the Board of the Bank of England as to how these financial problems can be contained. We would like to put these proposals in front of them as soon as we know how bad, or otherwise, things are going to be. In light of the impending attacks it's our suggestion that the London financial markets do not open tomorrow. This will give us…'

'That is exactly what I suggested!' burst out the Defence Secretary.

'Not quite,' Aidan added quietly. 'Your suggestion was to unwind the terrorists' derivatives positions; ours is to close the markets for a day to give us time to counter their financial attacks. What we have to avoid is procrastination; if the markets pass

167

the point of no return, I'm absolutely certain that financial Armageddon will become an unstoppable reality.'

The Prime Minister looked perturbed.

The Air Chief Marshal spoke. 'Prime Minister, might I make a suggestion? I hear what our friends here have been saying. As I see it, they are experts in their field and we're not. If what they say is correct, it could have damaging consequences that far outweigh the physical damage that the terrorists might inflict. Without a prosperous economy and a fully operational banking sector our democracy would be undermined. Let us focus on stopping the terrorists – their missile and suicide bomber attacks – but at the same time run with Mr Khan and Mr Gilchrist's assertions and get the experts and the top decision makers at the Treasury and the Bank to consider their grave predictions, as soon as practical.'

The PM nodded. 'Thank you, Sir Nigel; that makes good sense.'

The commissioner cast his eyes in Rafi's direction. 'You had something else to say, I believe?'

'Not more pessimism!' exclaimed the Defence Secretary in an irritated tone.

Rafi smiled. 'No sir, actually some good news for once. If we can stop the markets from falling and hold long interest rates where they are until, say, the middle of next week, the terrorists' positions in the derivative markets will become untenable. Their margin calls will become larger and larger, and they will be financially wiped out. This will eliminate several billion pounds from their coffers, damage many of the shadier banks and set back the terrorist cause by months if not years.'

He stopped and glanced at the PM. 'Sir, we have a plan.' He paused, 'Government real estate investment trusts could be created, thus providing the Government with a source of finance that will enable it to meet these impending financial obligations as and when they arise. It will remove the need to tap the gilts markets, *and* will help the Government refinance its increased borrowings resulting from the bail out of the UK banking system.'

'Why didn't you say that sooner?' interjected the tetchy Defence Secretary.

The Prime Minister smiled. 'So there's a silver lining – as long as we take on board your solution and you get it right.'

'Yes, Prime Minister.'

'Right, back to matters at hand,' said the PM. 'The outstanding question that we need to answer is: do the terrorists have a contingency plan "B" in place? And if so, how much damage might a Kornet missile inflict? I'd be very interested to hear your views, Air Chief Marshal.'

'The damage could be extensive. If MI5 are confident that they know where the terrorists are going to attack in all but one of the locations, why give them a second chance by activating COBRA?'

'Ewan?'

'From MI5's standpoint we can't believe our good fortune in finding where the attacks are likely to come from. Why risk tipping the terrorists off?'

'Defence Secretary?'

'We've everything in place to run such an operation from COBRA. And how certain are we that these properties will be used by the terrorists? I believe that the two moles in COBRA should be apprehended so that we can get COBRA up and running, using the advantages that its set up will give us. I'd be willing to take the seemingly minute risk that there isn't a third mole… However, I will fall into line if everyone else believes COBRA isn't the right way forward at this point in time.'

'Commissioner, what are your views on COBRA?'

'The consequences of the terrorists swapping to a plan "B" are, in my opinion, too great a risk to contemplate whilst they and the four Kornet missile launchers are at large. Perhaps, sir, you might like to take a look at the emergency operations room we've set up downstairs before you make up your mind?'

The PM turned to Ewan. 'Please arrest the two COBRA suspects *without* tipping off the terrorists, and see if you can discover how they were going to make contact.'

'Yes, sir. We have them under surveillance.'

The PM looked at Kate and her team.

'We owe you a great debt of gratitude for all your work and insight into the terrorists' activities, and thank you for placing our troubles into context. Mr Khan, thank you for your tenacity. And my thanks to the rest of you.'

Kate took that as the invitation to leave. She and her team filed out of the room.

*

They didn't have to wait long. Jeremy received a call on his mobile. 'Well, I'm damned.' He listened a little longer and then said, 'Thank you.'

Jeremy looked across at John. 'My colleagues have interviewed one of the COBRA suspects. He gave them the phone number he was to ring and the phrase he was to use each time COBRA was activated. They traced the landline number as the ex-directory number of a special press adviser. However, the call was to be redirected through to the voicemail box of a mobile phone. And – would you bloody well believe it? – the mobile is currently located on the outskirts of Aldermaston, 200 metres away from where the suicide bombers are holed up in the horsebox. It's a bit of luck; we had assumed that they were all together.'

*

Kate and Rafi settled down and went through their paperwork to see if they had missed anything that could lead them to the missing target. Hours later they had still found nothing.

Rafi felt exhausted. He turned to Kate. 'I need sleep.'

'How about I tuck you in?' she asked with a mischievous smile.

'Not tonight, thank you,' he replied. 'Could you wake me at 4 a.m. please – or earlier, if I'm needed?'

'Will do,' promised Kate. Rafi walked down the back stairs to the cells, grabbed a blanket and pillow and lay down on his bed. His mind started to clear. He got up, knelt down and for the first time in over a week said his prayers. Then he got into bed, and within moments, he was out for the count.

*

Just before 4 a.m., Rafi was woken by Jeremy. He was groggy and struggled to get his brain back into gear. Strong black coffee was waiting for him upstairs.

'Hey, you still look rough,' said Kate cheerily as Rafi walked in. 'You've chosen a good time to join us. Things are hotting up in the Ops Room. It's like a game of chess. If you come down the corridor with me, I'll bring you up to speed.'

Kate started putting Rafi in the picture. 'Emma, John and Aidan's team are catching up on some sleep down in the cells. The duty sergeant has never known the cells so full of sober people. The Defence Secretary's mood has improved; it seems first impressions were deceiving – in fact he's rather good at his job.' She paused. 'As you'll see, the Air Chief Marshal has brought in a specialist anti-terrorism expert and a couple of senior officers to act as coordinators.'

Rafi tentatively entered the Ops Room. It was buzzing. Kate and he stood out of the way to one side. The video-conference screen to his left was linked up with the SAS command centre. The Air Chief Marshal, Brigadier Harold Sparkman and Colonel Paul Gray were discussing the first operation - the capture of the two suicide bombers and Kaleem Shah at Aldermaston. The colonel gave instructions and two teams, red and blue, were deployed. The plan was to overwhelm the suicide bombers and the journalist at precisely the same moment.

The two suicide bombers were not expected to be much of a problem. They were not professional soldiers, but they did have two large bombs in their horsebox. Speed and the element of surprise were going to be critical.

The SAS commander reported that the two bombers were, to all intents and purposes, tucked up in the living quarters of the horsebox and appeared to be sleeping fitfully.

Kaleem Shah was a different matter. He had had many years' experience of working in war zones. He was undoubtedly a cautious and capable soldier. The fact that he'd opted to sleep a couple of hundred metres away from the two terrorists suggested that he was expecting the unexpected.

The infrared sensors had identified the journalist as lying quietly across the back seat of the Jeep. The vehicle was positioned such that it had a line of sight through to the horsebox and a second 4x4, but was largely screened by twiggy vegetation and small saplings.

It was all quiet in and around the large Jeep and the horsebox. The two SAS teams silently approached the vehicles and waited for their orders.

Rafi watched, totally caught up in the proceedings. Unlike watching TV, this was real. He felt his heart pounding.

Just then Colonel Gray gave the command for the two assaults. There was a momentary delay and then, from a video link, there was the sound of two muffled explosions. The speaker crackled as it picked up the voice of the red team leader who was commanding a team of three against the journalist and his Jeep. 'We've secured the vehicle and have captured the journalist. He didn't put up a struggle. We found two booby traps outside the vehicle. Nothing too sophisticated, but nasty enough to take off a leg.'

The blue team simultaneously descended on the horsebox, found nothing untoward protecting it and seized the two suicide bombers, dragging them from their sleeping bags out into the open.

At that moment a loud bang echoed around the room. The horsebox erupted into a fireball.

'Shit! The bastard had a radio-controlled device up his sleeve,' was heard from the speaker.

'Blue team! Come in blue team!' There was silence.

Two further loud explosions were heard as the terrorists' explosives went up.

The Air Chief Marshal looked at the colonel. 'Not a good start Paul, is it?'

The silence was followed by a muffled voice across the video link.

'Jesus, that was close,' said a shaky voice. 'Two of us are singed, but otherwise fine; two have suffered minor injuries from flying debris, but my corporal has an eighteen-inch piece of aluminium sticking out of his thigh. And the two suicide bombers are in a bad way - one has a piece of shrapnel in his chest. They had no protective clothing on and both are badly burnt.'

'Get the three terrorists out of there and into protective custody. As far as everyone is concerned, the suicide bombers are dead, got that?' ordered Colonel Gray.

'Yes, sir.'

The journalist had attached a small radio-controlled explosive device to the fuel tank of the horsebox, which had ignited around 100 litres of diesel.

Colonel Gray gave the order, 'Initiate phase two.' The dull thud of an explosion in the distance was audible. The video screen showed a section of Aldermaston's outer fence with a gaping hole and a nearby building on fire, billowing black smoke.

'Not bad, eh?' remarked Jeremy, who had materialised from nowhere and was standing next to Rafi. 'Gives the impression to the other terrorists that they were successful, doesn't it?'

'Good work,' added the Air Chief Marshal.

The SAS command centre came online. 'Some plans and a spare timer for a detonator were found in Kaleem Shah's vehicle. The plans mark two buildings that were to be attacked. Both contain low-level radioactive materials; nothing really dangerous, but sufficient to close the plant if released. Odd though, the timer had been tampered with. Whatever the setting, it would have gone off after about five seconds. Also the blue team leader reports that the explosives were packed into rucksacks, just like at Bishopsgate.'

'Thank you,' replied Colonel Gray.

The commissioner was thoughtful. 'Well, that explains why the bomber at Bishopsgate got caught in the blast. He thought that he would have far more time to get away than he actually did. A five-second stroll from the bomb's location to where his body was found fits in with the time delay on the fuse - so he *wasn't* a suicide bomber, just a servant set up by his masters!'

'Interesting,' mused Ewan. 'Ergo, the bombers at Aldermaston were expecting to escape!' He went quiet for a moment, lost in his own thoughts, he spoke out loud. 'I wonder if this attack has anything to do with the Iranians and the UK Trident nuclear weapons programme...? If the terrorists *were* in bed with Iran, it would give them a safe place to go after the attacks... And this sort of attack could appeal to a number of the extremist Iranian politicians. A tit-for-tat attack... I wonder?'

'Ewan, no!' The Air Chief Marshal looked concerned. 'Don't even go there!'

Ewan shrugged his shoulders. 'Old habits... Just trying to put two and two together...'

The Air Chief Marshal spoke over him. 'Now for phase three; the news and the TV crews are all yours, Harold.'

Brigadier Harold Sparkman, who was standing nearby, nodded and phoned a member of the Ministry's press team, who was in bed asleep. 'I've arranged a press conference for you at 7 a.m. near to the Aldermaston explosion. When you're dressed and have had a quick cup of coffee, I'll brief you.'

'Yes, sir.'

Colonel Gray, meanwhile, was giving orders to the SAS red

and blue team leaders. 'Arrange for the vehicles to be removed and the area cleaned. Can you please confirm the terrorists are safely with MI5 operatives?'

'Yes, sir,' came the reply.

'Good. Now how serious are the injuries your team sustained, blue leader?'

'Relatively minor, sir. Corporal Evans looks a bit like a hedge-hog, but he can be patched up! And corporal Winderson suffered concussion when he struck his head in the explosion, but he's got a thick skull – give him a few hours and he'll be right as rain.'

'Thank you, blue leader. All fit members of your unit are to join the red team. A helicopter is on its way.'

Rafi looked at the clock on the wall; everything had happened so quickly. It was only 4.20 a.m., Friday morning.

The brigadier turned to the Air Chief Marshal. 'Press briefing arranged, sir. Our boys on the ground have been told to keep the buildings smoking as you ordered, sir.'

*

Shortly after the Ops Room had become operational, the PM, the Defence Secretary, the Air Chief Marshal, Colonel Paul Gray and Ewan Thorn had gone into a conclave. It was a meeting each of them would remember for years to come. On the table in front of them was a list showing the sum total of all the special forces, marines, paratroopers and army units with urban warfare experience – plus the crack anti-terrorist personnel – that were available. The country's defences were stretched to breaking point. The conflicts overseas and tight budgets had left a gaping hole in the numbers available. Their terrorist adversaries were highly trained and experienced in the deadly art of urban warfare and concealment. A decision had to be made - they agreed that quality rather than quantity had to be the order of the day.

The PM pondered quietly to himself as he listened to the discussion over the allocation of their scarce recourses. He, too, now appreciated just how overstretched they were. Resources were being allocated according to the perceived size of the latent hazard - priority was given to protecting the nuclear installations, leaving the defence of the gas and oil plants bordering on threadbare.

The considered view was that the terrorists would not make their move in the dead of night. And the command centre did not want them to be tipped off by reconnaissance teams being spotted; accordingly, only cursory inspections of the properties and the surrounding areas had been done.

'No sign of any of the four terrorists,' came over the speaker. 'We will wait until all our special forces, marines and paratrooper teams are in position.'

'I hope to God we've got this right,' the Air Chief Marshal murmured anxiously under his breath.

★

'It's now time to see whether the terrorists are where we think they should be,' called out the Air Chief Marshal.

Rafi felt a wave of apprehension flow through him. If he was wrong about the properties and they drew a blank... The butterflies in his stomach turned into a dull ache. He looked at the screens in the Ops Room; they were focused on the nuclear installations. The twilight pictures, from the infrared cameras, gave a distant feel as to what was happening.

The Air Chief Marshal addressed his team. 'Brigadier Sparkman, as discussed, you will coordinate the SAS and the Paras at Hartlepool, Hull and Easington.'

Then he turned to Colonel Turner and enquired, 'Is all in place at the Peterhead properties, St Fergus and Cruden Bay?'

'Yes, sir.'

His next question was addressed to Colonel Gray. 'All ready to go at North Walsham, Bacton, Grays and Sizewell?'

'Yes, sir.'

'Ewan, is all in place at Troon, Peterhead and Great Yarmouth docks?'

'Yes, sir.'

'That leaves me with Sellafield, Prestwick and Heysham.' The Air Chief Marshal spoke via his headset to his SAS contact, glanced across to the video-conferencing screen which linked their Ops Room with the SAS command centre and then at the screen next to it, which showed the paratroopers' command centre.

'Gentlemen, are we ready to go in five minutes?' Affirmative replies came in.

The die is cast, thought Rafi. He touched Kate's shoulder.

She was standing in front of him, gazing at the screens. She turned; her face was white with tiredness. 'This is it,' she said apprehensively. 'We'll soon find out if our hunches were right or if we've got it completely wrong!'

'Hunches... I hope they're a lot more than that!'

'Your confidence is most refreshing,' said Kate. Rafi found his hand next to hers; he gave it an affectionate squeeze. She took half a step backwards and let her body rest against his. She kept hold of his hand as she watched the three screens intently and listened to all that was going on.

The waiting was nail-biting. There were, Rafi estimated, twenty teams of special forces, paratroopers and anti-terrorist personnel out there in the darkness, stalking their prey. Behind them provisions had been made for their support. The scope of the mobilisation made it one of the largest peacetime operations on record.

Rafi held his breath.

Then the five minutes were up.

'Go, go, go!' came over the speakers. The troops swung into action.

On the screens Rafi could see the shadowy terrain over which the soldiers were navigating. Greg's makeshift Ops Room was working well.

At Heysham, a squad of paratroopers were supporting a team of three SAS soldiers. The building had been under observation for the previous five hours. There was no sign of movement and no telltale infrared heat signatures to show where the terrorist was. It was a tall property, to one side of the industrial estate. It was being refurbished and sections were covered in tarpaulins. At the back of the flat roof there was a new scaffolding tower. The SAS soldiers inched forward, carefully checking for booby traps. Eventually the first soldier reached the bottom of the scaffolding tower. He gave a thumbs up sign and pointed to the top of the tower.

His signals were relayed back to the command centre, which briefed the Ops Room. It was then that Rafi heard, 'Infrared shows the target to be lying on the scaffolding boards under the tarpaulins. He's going to be seriously difficult to get at without giving our presence away.'

There was a flurry of movement in a number of the small frames on the screens as the units' progress was fed back to the Ops Room.

The brigadier called out, 'Terrorist located at the Hartlepool property. He's under camouflage netting in the gully of the roof. He has a clear line of sight across to the nuclear power plant. The team on the ground is working out how best to tackle him.'

Rafi felt his hand being gently squeezed, as if to say, 'We weren't wrong!'

'No sign of the terrorists at Cruden Bay, St Fergus or Peterhead,' shouted Colonel Bill Turner.

'No sign of the missiles or of terrorists at North Walsham, Bacton, Sizewell and Grays,' added Colonel Gray, abruptly. 'Wait! A Vektor mortar and twenty shells have just been found on a motorbike parked at the back of the industrial building at North Walsham.'

Colonel Bill Turner spoke. 'An unattended utility van just over a mile from St Fergus has been investigated and a mortar with twenty shells has been recovered. No sign of the terrorist and nothing to report at Cruden Bay.'

The Air Chief Marshal called out, 'They've located a mortar and twenty shells in the panniers of a BMW motorbike parked in an old container on the building site at Gosforth, near Sellafield.'

This was quickly followed by the brigadier. 'A mortar and twenty shells have been uncovered at the Hull property.'

Rafi's pulse was racing. He did a quick calculation: all four Vektor mortars had been recovered, two terrorists and their Kornet missile launchers were still unaccounted for... they were getting there. The smile on his face evaporated, as he realised that it was too soon to be complacent. If just one missile hit a nuclear target then it could be game over.

Rafi listened to the Air Chief Marshal being briefed. The SAS soldiers at Heysham couldn't get at the terrorist on top of the scaffolding without alerting him to their presence. After a short conference, a decision was taken and a message went back. 'Take him out. At all costs stop him firing a Kornet missile.'

The SAS assaulter at Heysham waited unmoving in the

darkness. He had advised command that he couldn't guarantee to immobilise the terrorist with his compact 9 mm sub-machine gun. The SAS snipers behind him also had no clear shot.

He waited for his orders and then moved forward silently. The scaffolding tower had four main legs. He approached the furthest pair, reached into one of the pockets of his assault vest and pulled out a couple of small packages – the special services own blend of plastic explosive – which were spot on for cutting structural supports. Without a sound, he expertly set the charges, then moved back to the other pair of legs and repeated the process. He heard a person moving above him. His pulse rate stayed steady. The terrorist had no line of sight to him and the SAS soldier knew that he'd been as stealthy as a summer breeze; silently, he backtracked around the corner of the building.

He gave the signal that he was clear of the detonation zone and waited for the order from command. When it came, he pressed the miniature magneto in his hand and felt the shock waves of the four explosions ripple through his body. Each of the tower's legs was now missing a section. The tower remained motionless for a moment and then gravity took hold. The scaffolding wall ties had no chance of holding the load. The tower arced outwards from the building and crashed into the ground. The terrorist, who had been under the tarpaulin on the top, spilled out and did a dead cat bounce on the nearby grass. Three darkly clothed SAS men descended on him and stripped him of his weaponry. The Kornet missile launcher and three missiles lay on the ground close to him.

'Beware of any remote controlled devices,' barked the commanding SAS soldier.

*

In the Ops Room the capture of the Kornet launcher, its three missiles and the terrorist was greeted with cheers. The terrorist was still alive, but unconscious and looked to be in a bad state.

Suddenly, flames and dense billowing smoke erupted near to the Heysham nuclear power plant.

'Oh, no!' thought Rafi. Then he remembered it was the army at work, giving the impression that the terrorist attack had been successful.

Kate was still leaning against Rafi. She felt a release of pent-up anxiety. She turned her head and looked into his eyes.

'Your instincts were spot on. You're a star.'

He felt the warmth of her body. 'More like good teamwork,' he replied, holding her gaze with a big grin.

Meanwhile, the brigadier had received confirmation that the terrorist at Hartlepool had a clear view of the nuclear power station. 'Can he be safely taken out?' he asked his opposite number in the command centre.

'Yes, sir. a SAS sniper has outflanked him and has him in his sights.'

'Do it. Just don't risk him firing a missile.'

'Yes, sir!'

A few moments later, confirmation came over the speaker. 'Terrorist taken out.'

This was followed by the noise of a massive explosion at Hartlepool. The brigadier turned to Colonel Gray. 'Crikey! The sappers have been busy – I wonder what they've found to blow up?'

Rafi watched the flames darting high into the air, followed by thick smoke engulfing the area around the nuclear power station. He looked across the screens. The army's pyrotechnic skills were being shown off to great effect at Aldermaston, and now at Hartlepool and Heysham.

★

Daylight would reveal damage to a non-nuclear building at Aldermaston, a smoking zinc factory next to Hartlepool nuclear power station, and fire and smoke coming from the abandoned visitor centre on the perimeter of the nuclear compound at Heysham.

Rafi and Kate were on tenterhooks. Two terrorists with Kornets were still out there. The good news was that at least one of the likely targets – the oil pumping station at Cruden Bay – wasn't nuclear, but what on earth was the other target?

'Nothing to report on the three trawlers,' called out Ewan.

There was a lull in the proceedings. Time ticked by slowly; the two missing terrorists were conspicuous by their absence.

Rafi and Kate hurried back to their office. They looked again through their paperwork, but still couldn't find any clues as to where the missing location might be.

Rafi was worried. Had he let the side down and missed something obvious which could have pointed them to the missing target? The very possibility haunted him.

*

The Air Chief Marshal took the PM, the Defence Secretary and the head of MI5 to one side. 'I would like your permission to mobilise the entire military. We've passed the point of no return. I should have asked for this hours earlier. Unfortunately, at the time I was preoccupied with coordinating the limited resources we had available.' He looked at the PM. 'Sir, we *have* to have a cast-iron insurance policy in place should one of these damn missiles get through to something nuclear. Our ability to deal with a nuclear incident isn't what it should be. We have two terrorists with Kornet missile launchers on the loose. Who knows if they now suspect that we're on to them? We must prepare for the worst eventuality: a nuclear disaster.'

The PM agreed and, on his authority, at 4.45 a.m. all armed services' leave was rescinded. All personnel, including part-time territorial soldiers, all available medical and support Corps, were called to their barracks and put in a state of readiness. Every hospital with an Accident & Emergency Department within 100 miles of a nuclear plant was told to be fully staffed up by 6 a.m. The Home Secretary was contacted and advised to catch the first flight back to London. His ETA in Downing Street was 9.30 a.m.

Every barrack and hospital was told that this was a surprise training exercise, sanctioned by the Prime Minister to test their readiness to respond to a national emergency. The message went out to senior officers that the new Prime Minister wanted to use the exercise as a way of seeing where the problems might be and whether they had the right resources available.

Those in command were left in no doubt that they should prepare for a sizeable disaster or conflict.

The Air Chief Marshal turned to Brigadier Harold Sparkman and Colonel Bill Turner who were standing close by. 'There are contingency plans in place for attacks on nuclear installations. What I want from the two of you is a plan – we'll call it *Operation Counterpane* – which will deal with a serious radioactive leak, contaminating, say, ten to twenty square miles of a densely populated urban area. On your agenda there need to be robust provisions on how to get a nuclear leak covered from the air,

180

arrangements for an exclusion zone with a guarded perimeter, decontamination and triage units, medical facilities, an evacuation and rehousing plan, and a system to monitor the identities of all those displaced. Basically, take what is already there and make it work – big time.'

He was looking perturbed. 'Probably best if you include Len Thunhurst, commissioner of the Metropolitan Police, in your plans. Giles here has brought him up to speed with all our problems and he's aware of the need for secrecy.' He paused, 'The transportation front is what really concerns me. We are short of a couple of squadrons of heavy helicopters. Without them, logistical support in an urban disaster area will be a nightmare. There will be blocked roads and restricted access at a time when speed will be paramount. The number of operational workhorse helicopters in the UK is far below what we'll need.'

Then the beginnings of a smile appeared on the Air Chief Marshal's face. 'I think I'll have a quiet chat with a close friend of mine who runs the Royal Netherlands Air Force. Colonel Turner, you are a logistics expert, please liaise with Ewan and get him to draw up a list of the whereabouts of all private helicopter fleets around the UK. Tell the operators that all helicopters capable of carrying four or more people are subject to a requisition order for the next twenty-four hours. Their helicopters should be fully fuelled, with pilots on immediate standby and ready to join a UK task force by 06.00 hours at the latest. They will be held on call for the rest of the day. Full compensation will be paid if requested. Inconvenienced clients should only be advised that their helicopter is on loan for a rescue operation.'

As of 5.35 a.m. the Royal Netherlands Air Force's base at Gilze-Rijen, fifty kilometres west of Eindhoven, was on full standby and over half of the Dutch military helicopter fleet had been offered to assist the Royal Air Force.

The Air Chief Marshal breathed a sigh of relief on hearing the news - the Royal Netherlands Air Force had one of the most modern fleets in Europe and its helicopters were only an hour away from the east coast of England. Twenty-nine helicopters – Chinooks, Eurocopters and Apache Combat helicopters – were on standby and a direct link had been established with their operations room. This, in one stroke, had more than doubled the number of military helicopters available. He walked over to the PM. 'Sir the deployment of the military is likely to lay bare the level of overstretch.'

The PM nodded. 'Yes, overseas conflicts have tied up too many resources. I believe I've missed a very obvious threat to our well-being - countering large scale terrorist attacks on our own soil... Without guaranteed access to energy, we face an uncertain and potentially bleak future.'

'Air Chief Marshal.' The PM looked carefully at him. 'When this is over, I want you to draw together a team of experts so that you can provide the Cabinet with a briefing paper on how we should shape the armed forces so that they're fit-for-purpose in terms of protecting our country's interests at home.'

'Yes, sir.'

'I have no wish for us to become a police state, but the prospect of a small, but well-funded terrorist cell attacking the heart of our energy supplies is a great concern.'

★

Back in the office, Rafi was still racking his brains about the two missing locations. He was willing to put good money on one of them being the crude oil pumping station at Cruden Bay – its location and its importance to the economy put it right at the top. Then for the other there was Sizewell nuclear power station or Grays liquid natural gas storage depot, but the special forces had still found nothing at either.

Kate and he had been exploring whether the location could be linked to the terrorists' fish processing business and a possible new cold store in the London area. They had checked to see if the terrorists' property company had used any specific firm of lawyers. Unfortunately, they used a different firm for each transaction. They had spoken again to Land Registry, but drawn a blank.

Neil had arranged a special visit to the terrorists' property company's offices an hour earlier, but they were empty. It transpired that they were being moved from London to Manchester. All their computers and files were in transit and MI5 were not surprised to find that they were unable to trace the removals firm.

As a last resort, the commissioner had decided there was

nothing for it but to pull in PREH's directors. There were four of them. Basel Talal was at large in the North Atlantic on board *Golden Sundancer* and the other three, it transpired from one of the director's wives, were on a corporate bonding week with their staff in the Caribbean. The tour company advised that they had chartered a crewed yacht. No one in the marina from which they had sailed knew where they were heading. Their ship-to-shore radio was switched off, as were their mobile phones.

The yacht had left the marina twenty-four hours earlier with the wind a comfortable force three, gusting four. The US Coast Guard advised that with an average speed of eight knots the yacht could be anywhere within a couple of hundred mile radius, equivalent to an area of around 100,000 square miles. Neil had spoken to his opposite number at the US Homeland Security. Four US navy helicopters and all available coastal patrol vessels were dispatched to reconnoitre the possible area. They would try the captain's usual haunts first but, given the scale of the area to be covered, they didn't have high hopes of finding the yacht.

Meanwhile, Kate had rung Rick in Manchester. Wesson was asleep. Rick described the man as unhinged, with a persecution complex. He was still being totally uncooperative.

John had tracked down the flight of Roger Harewood, the immigration officer, and had eventually got through to the captain of the 747 and to Roger.

'Er... Good morning, or is it evening? To what do I owe the pleasure?' said a somewhat surprised and dazed Roger.

John explained about the fish processing business and the need to find their new cold store in London.

Roger sounded very apologetic. 'I seem to recall making a jotting or two. It's hard to keep track of people entering through the immigration fast track process. Unfortunately, I can't recall any details. We're asked to process hundreds of people.'

'Steve said that information in your notebooks might help us,' said John.

'Yes; I've a drawer full of cheap notebooks in which I make miscellaneous notes. As soon as we land I'll go straight to the office and try to find my scribbles on their fish processing business. I hope I didn't throw them away. All I can remember is that the location was somewhere in London. At the moment, I can't recall anything more. We aren't encouraged to muddy the waters. My scribbles aren't welcomed on the files. Just a habit I suppose.'

'A good one,' said John. 'We'll arrange to have you picked up from the plane and taken to your office when you land. Will your wife and family be OK?'

'Yes, no problem there; Felicity is well-organised.'

'If you should remember anything in the meantime, do please let us know. When you get to the office, if for any reason you can not get through on the phone, please fax us with anything you have. The fax comes through to the middle of our office. Steve has put the numbers on your desk. Safe journey.'

John asked to speak to the captain.

'How can I be of assistance?'

'Mr Harewood is going to be helping us with important enquiries when he gets back to Manchester. He seems to have unwittingly uncovered a piece of information that might help us solve a serious crime. We could do with him being as alert as possible when he lands. Could you...?'

The pilot didn't need to hear the rest of the sentence. 'I'll arrange for him and his family to be moved to first class for the remainder of the flight.'

'Thank you. When you land, I will arrange for Mr Harewood to be collected from the boarding gate. Could you ask the control tower to give you landing priority, or should I?'

'No problem, I can do that.'

'This is hush-hush so another excuse would be appreciated. Thanks for your help,' said John.

John thought for a moment, picked up the phone and spoke to Phil Scott, Rick Feldon's assistant. 'Apologies for waking you. I could do with a favour, please. I need to get a Roger Harewood from Manchester Airport to his office in Sheffield, when his plane lands just after 9 o'clock this morning. Time will be of the essence.'

'It's forty miles and at that time of the morning the traffic will be awful. I've got an idea. Can I ring you back?' asked Phil.

'No problem.'

A few minutes later, Phil came on the phone. 'I've pulled some strings and booked the police helicopter. It will be waiting at Manchester airport, and I've arranged for an airport security car to take Roger from the plane across to it.'

'Perfect, thanks very much,' said John.

It was now a matter of waiting. Rafi looked at Kate. It was obvious that neither of them was optimistic.

'What else can we do? How about we get the large scale London maps out again and see if we've missed anything?'

Kate gave Rafi a concerned look. 'I don't know how you do it. You've suffered more stress in the last week than most people deal with in their whole lives and you still keep going with a smile on your face. I'm absolutely shattered.'

He looked at Kate and saw a different, softer side to her.

'It's the company I keep, and an overwhelming desire to stop the terrorists,' he replied.

Kate smiled at him. 'You think the company is tolerable?'

'Yes,' he smiled, 'When you walked into the interview room at Paddington Green, I doubt if you knew how close I was to folding. I shall be in your debt for...' Rafi paused, trying to think how best to express his feelings.

But, before he could finish his sentence, Kate cut in. 'It was David who said I should back you. For my part, I'd have left you to the wolves. But I'm glad that my first instincts proved to be so wrong.'

*

In the Ops Room the planning of *Operation Counterpane* continued at a feverish pace.

Time had slipped by - dawn would soon be breaking.

'They are professionals, hardened in the tactics of guerrilla warfare,' said Colonel Gray to his team. 'If they're half as good as the Russian Security Service say, we can expect them to be invisible right up to the last moment.'

At Cruden Bay in North Scotland, the expectation was for an attack shortly after daybreak. The SAS and paratroopers were waiting, but there was still no sign of the terrorist. However, the indications were that a terrorist had been in the vicinity. An outbuilding behind the vacant industrial unit in Peterhead had been occupied the previous day. Someone had been sloppy. Numerous fresh cigarette ends were found on the floor. In themselves they were nothing out of the ordinary, but in the circumstances they were like manna from heaven. In the FSB files was a miscellaneous

185

comment on Sergy Kowshaya – he was a chain-smoker.

The brigadier's two adjutants were having an increasingly frenetic time coordinating the Ministry of Defence's press team and the release of information to the news desks.

The message they were trying to put across was: 'Yes, there have been three terrorist attacks, but this is a matter for the armed forces and the police, not the politicians. The attacks have been partially successful. Thankfully, no nuclear material has been released. Security has been stepped up at all UK nuclear installations. Another attack couldn't be ruled out. Nothing is being taken for granted and the military has been called in to provide a defensive ring around key installations. This is what the armed forces are trained for and the public should remain calm.'

The Air Chief Marshal spoke to those around him in the Ops Room and those on the video links. 'Daylight will bring with it the real danger as the terrorists will be able to see their targets more clearly and the news cameras will capture any scenes of destruction. Be prepared for anything to happen. We have two highly dangerous terrorists out there. We *have* to find them and stop them.'

*

It was cold at Cruden Bay. A swirling sea mist lapped around the bulbous twin tanks of the oil pumping station, cloaking them in a soft, white blanket. The outline of the buildings was barely visible, making an accurate attack by a terrorist difficult.

Suddenly there was activity. A suspicious movement had been detected one and a half kilometres from the perimeter of the oil pumping station. From nowhere, there was the feint infrared image of an individual kneeling on the ground out in the open, with a missile launcher at his side. The enhanced pictures showed that in the blink of an eye the terrorist had the launcher up on its tripod and was ready to fire at the pumping station. It was clear he knew exactly what he was doing. The nearest SAS soldier was 500 metres to the terrorist's left but, unfortunately, his line of sight was partially obscured by a small undulation in the terrain.

It was too late – there was a *whooshing* sound and seconds later one of the two oil storage tanks erupted into a fireball that lit up the grassland for miles around. The explosion was followed by a series of smaller explosions. It was like a gargantuan Chinese firecracker going off. Dense, grey smoke engulfed the whole facility.

The soldier broke cover and moved rapidly to a point where he could clearly see the terrorist in the distance. On the run, he opened fire. The terrorist seemed unfazed by the bullets whistling around him and fired a second missile into the thick pall of smoke. Another explosion was heard, but this time it lacked the cataclysmic intensity of the first. The dark, clawing smoke belched up into the sky. Anyone downwind was going to have an unpleasant time.

The terrorist's position looked increasingly hopeless; three SAS soldiers with their automatic fire had him pinned down in his foxhole. Suddenly the ground around the terrorist started belching out thick white smoke, creating a smokescreen which rapidly obscured him from the view of the SAS - he was well prepared.

Then, from within the blanket of white smoke, the engine of a powerful motorbike could be heard – it had been stowed under a nearby camouflage net. The terrorist had abandoned the missile launcher and was making a quick getaway.

He appeared at speed from his protective smokescreen, handling the bike with skill. He slipped unharmed through the security force's net and now had an unhindered run to Peterhead and then towards the St Fergus gas terminal. He had foreseen that the security would be tight given the location, but was surprised by the speed of the response.

The team in the Ops Room were briefed on the events: the oil pumping facility had been extensively damaged.

Rafi recalled Emma's earlier comment: 'It's not size that matters, but the throughput of the pumping station. Cruden Bay is where the Forties Pipeline System has its landfall. It can pump over one million barrels of oil a day from the offshore oil fields to the inland processing terminal at Kinneil. Without Cruden Bay the lion's share of the UK's daily crude oil supplies would stop.'

The Air Chief Marshal called out. 'Four of the five Kornet missile launchers and all four Vektor mortars are accounted for. There has been major structural damage at Cruden Bay, but thankfully there are no civilian casualties or injuries. The sappers are doing a great job at Heysham, Aldermaston and Hartlepool. To those not in the know, it's been a seriously awful night. It's as if World War III has broken out in our back yard. We know better.' He paused. 'As a matter of utmost priority we have *got to* find the missing Chechen terrorist or at least his Kornet missile launcher...'

*

The commissioner, who had been watching quietly, leant across and spoke to the Prime Minister and the Air Chief Marshal, 'I think it's time for me to advise the London financial markets not to open.' He picked up the phone and spoke first to his contact at the Stock Exchange, and then to Euronext.liffe. Two minutes later, both exchanges had posted on their dealing screens that they would not be opening due to terrorist threats. Then, as an after-thought, he picked up the phone and spoke to the heads of the derivatives exchanges in Frankfurt and Chicago. To his relief they both agreed to postpone the opening of their exchanges.

*

It was 6.45 a.m. at Sizewell - the grey February dawn was still forty minutes away; the cutting east wind was blowing over the coastal marshland and was forecast to veer around and come from the south-east. Dick Newton and his co-driver, Ted Dyer, had received notice the day before from their controller that their run to the marshalling yard at Willesden Junction in north London had been brought forward by two and a half hours and that the train would be going straight through to Sellafield.

The heightened anxiety of terrorist threats over the past year had resulted in Dick and Ted's timetable being subject to frequent changes. Gone were the days of a regular schedule. But that did not seem to worry them, as they were well looked after. This morning, however, was a first. Never before had they been on the move in darkness and never before had they gone further than Willesden.

In the February early morning air Dick and Ted undertook their final inspection of the two carriages transporting the spent nuclear fuel casks. The radioactivity coming from the sweating casks was within the guidelines. Dick radioed through to control confirming that the freight train was ready to depart at its allotted time.

They had been operating the Sizewell to Willesden Junction run for several years and it had become a regular feature of both

188

their lives. They knew the routine like clockwork and the safety procedures as prescribed by their employers had become second nature.

Back in the warmth of the train's cab, Dick handed his empty coffee mug to Ted and waited for the last few minutes to tick by before their departure time. At 6.50 a.m. precisely, Dick reported in to his controller, released the brake and the train moved effortlessly out of the sidings. The train made light work of its two fifty-tonne reinforced canisters and gathered speed - on the old rails and wooden sleepers - down the branch line from Leiston to Saxmundham.

A few years earlier an early morning start would not have been possible. The 45 mph speed limit imposed on the nuclear freight trains meant that peak rush hours had to be avoided as they caused too much congestion for the commuter trains. Behind the scenes, the speed limit had unofficially been raised to 60 mph. The result was that if Dick and Ted timed their slot correctly when they joined the mainline at Ipswich and went behind the Norwich to London express, they would cause hardly any disruption to the passenger train schedules. In any event, the reliability of the early morning commuter trains was far from good and it was not unusual for their journey to be delayed by one of the many problems encountered by the long-suffering commuters.

There was no real hurry to get to Saxmundham, where they joined the Lowestoft–Ipswich line. They were scheduled to go after the small diesel passenger train which was timetabled to stop at Saxmundham at 7.31 a.m. But, as this morning it was running a few minutes late, Dick brought his train to a gentle stop outside Saxmundham station and they waited for the passenger train to come and go. It was 7.38 a.m. when the nuclear freight train passed through Saxmundham. They were four minutes behind schedule, but in the scale of things this was well within the bounds of normality.

Over the years Dick had become used to Ted's running commentary of the places they passed and his interpretation of what they were. The descriptions rarely changed. It helped the time slip by. There was the alpaca farm and then the small market town of Woodbridge, nestling on the banks of the river Deben, a favourite of Ted's. He would recall how the Viking burial ship at Sutton Hoo on the other side of the river was worth a visit. Then it was on to Ipswich to wait for their slot behind the Norwich to London express train. The intercity train was on time. Dick eased his train through Ipswich station and the tunnel beyond. After that, it was a straight run down to Stratford on the north-eastern outskirts of London. There, they would leave the main line for the North London line which would take them around London, past Willesden Junction and on to the north-west line towards Sellafield.

When their speed limit had been 45 mph, the seventy miles from Ipswich to Stratford had taken two and a half hours, with a couple of stops to let passenger trains past. At 60 mph, the journey would be almost an hour faster and they would need only one stop to let an intercity commuter train through.

*

By 8 o'clock, the early morning news channels had wall-to-wall coverage of the four terrorist attacks. The infernos and the tall columns of acrid black smoke filled the TV screens in the Ops Room.

A drawn and tired looking PM spoke to those around him. 'Thank you for all your unstinting efforts. We can be grateful that we have suffered no casualties and that the nuclear facilities are one hundred per cent intact. However, we still have one terrorist and one Kornet missile launcher unaccounted for. As we don't know where he is or what his target is, I have spoken to the Permanent Secretary for Intelligence Security and Resilience and the director of Civil Contingencies.'

He paused and looked across at his Defence Secretary. 'COBRA will be in session as of 9 a.m. I have told them to have experts on CBRN – chemical biological radiological nuclear – in attendance. And to have all members of ACPO (TAM) – Association of Chief Police Officers (Terrorism and Allied Matters) – available via video-conference links. The Defence Secretary and I will be leaving shortly to brief COBRA.'

The Prime Minister turned to the chief of the armed forces. 'Sir Nigel, I shall leave this Ops Room in your command. Your remit is to take out the fourth terrorist and disable his missile launcher. And please keep all the fleeing terrorists under close observation.'

The PM and the Defence Secretary shook the hands of everyone in the Ops Room and then left for Downing Street.

★

The train journey down towards London was uneventful. Ted kept up his almost constant commentary which was broken only by short conversations with the manager or his assistant at the control centre. They discussed the terrorist attacks. The nuclear trains weren't being stopped; just their schedules had received minor changes. This strategy had been approved by their bosses, who deemed that "Their cargo posed too difficult a target and was thus an insignificant risk,' according to the control room manager.

The controller was in a grumpy mood; he had been trying unsuccessfully to give up smoking and had failed. In his cigarette breaks, Ted chatted with his assistant, a newcomer who had only started working for the nuclear transport company the Monday before. Ted was beginning to wonder if the young lad was stupid. He was charming, but seemed to have little grasp of the importance of his job.

Dick was pleased to find that the intercity train behind them was running late. This meant they could proceed to Shenfield before pulling in to let it pass. They were on the outskirts of London when the young assistant controller came on the radio. 'My boss has nipped out to his car to get another packet of cigarettes and have a smoke.'

Ted sensed unease in the young lad's voice. 'Are you alright?' he enquired.

'Yes, it's just that I wish my boss would get back. I need to go for my morning constitutional – I think it was the vindaloo curry I had last night!'

Ted looked across at Dick and muttered, 'I suppose that means he's desperate for the loo.'

The freight train passed through Romford; it wouldn't be long before they left the main line and started on the next leg of their journey.

The desperate voice of the assistant came on the radio. 'It's no good, I can't wait any longer. My boss should be back soon!'

Dick raised his eyebrows and was going to speak, when Ted cut in. 'I hope he's quick!' He thought back to when he had first driven the nuclear waste trains. The manpower involved in those early days dwarfed the lean efficient teams that had become the norm. Spare capacity was a thing of the past. Forty uneventful years of safe nuclear rail transport had not given rise to complacency, but rather a sense of the mundane had permeated the system and dulled the minds of many involved.

The train was approaching Stratford station. Ted had radioed through to the Control Room. There had been no reply; the manager had not returned from his smoke and the young lad was presumably still otherwise engaged.

As they arrived at Stratford station, the signal for the branch line turned red. Dick brought the train to a halt. As they waited, he noticed that the platforms were almost deserted. After a couple of minutes' wait the light turned green and the train slowly trundled on to the branch line to start its way around suburban London.

Dick smiled. It had been a good run down from Suffolk. He was looking forward to his extended journey up the west coast and wondered if Ted would, for the first time, be lost for words.

*

In Manchester, Detective Inspector Rick Feldon was having a chat over breakfast with William Wesson. His fifteen years of interrogation experience told him that there was still at least one more nugget of information to be drawn from this despicable man. Wesson continued to ignore his questions – he was in denial and his defence was to shower verbal abuse on those around him. Rick was getting nowhere. 'How about we see what's going on in the world?'

A small TV was brought into the interview room. The channels were filled with special news bulletins showing wall-to-wall pictures of the plumes of smoke resulting from the terrorist attacks. Wesson looked without any apparent interest at the pictures. The detective inspector asked him more questions without receiving any response. It was getting hopeless. He was going round and round in circles.

Time was ebbing away. Rick had an idea. It was time for some creative thinking. He left the room and reappeared a few minutes later with a photograph of a middle-aged woman.

Rick put the photo on the table in front of Wesson. 'She's

about the same age as your mother, isn't she?'

There was no reply.

'She worked as a cleaner at Heysham and was killed by flying shrapnel. A slow and painful death, I understand. Now her two teenage children have no close family to look after them,' he lied again. 'What would you and your younger sister have done if your mother had been killed when you were that young?'

Rick pressed on. 'How would you have felt if you and your sister had had no mother?'

Wesson broke down in front of him. Howls and sobs came from the insufferable little man. Rick had no sympathy for him at all. He had one aim and that was to get from him the missing pieces of information. 'Your mother rang. She wants to see you'

Wesson raised his head.

'Why couldn't she have been the person killed by the shrapnel? She always stopped me from doing the things I wanted to and her tongue is as sharp as a carving knife. I don't want to speak to her. In fact, I'd be happy if I never saw her again.'

Rick took a deep breath on hearing the unexpected reply. 'You valued all the properties which were used by the terrorists. We're missing one more address. *You* can help us stop the next attack.'

Wesson didn't move.

'How do you think your sister, who you've protected all these years, will survive as the sister of a murdering, terrorist collaborator? She won't get any sympathy from her mother, will she? Think about it!'

Rick watched the turmoil bubbling up inside the young man. '*Now* would be a good time to tell me the addresses we don't know about.'

Wesson did not raise his eyes. 'All I know is that they have a building which is being refurbished. I do not even know its address, other than it's in Stratford, East London…'

'You must tell me more!'

'I can't! That's as much as I know. You see, I accidentally overheard Talal and a director of his discussing this property…'

'And?'

'When Talal saw me – his eyes were like my father's before he lashed out and hit me. He was livid and shouted at me - *Never repeat what you've heard, if you value your sister's life!* Even if I knew the address, I wouldn't tell you!'

Rick thought for a moment, concluded that Wesson had nothing more to say, pulled out his mobile and phoned Kate's direct line. After several rings the call was diverted to the switchboard. 'DI Adams, please. It's urgent – *Very Urgent.*'

'I'll see if I can locate her; she's not answering her phone.'

The seconds ticked by as if they were the last grains in an hourglass. The telephonist came back on the line. 'She's in a meeting.'

'I need your help, please,' said Rick calmly. 'I have an urgent message for her. *Please* write this down: *Urgent. Ring Me. Now! – Rick Feldon.* As a matter of life and death, please take this message to DI Adams, now!'

'I'm not allowed to leave my desk unless I've got cover.'

'Of course you're not, *technically*, but we're trying to stop the bastards who planned the Bishopsgate bomb from letting another one off. Understood?'

'Yes, sir… I'll go straightaway.'

The phone went dead.

*

In his chauffeur-driven car en route to Downing Street, the Prime Minister thought about the events of the night. Had he been right in not activating COBRA earlier? The Ops Room at Wood Street had served its purpose and had worked well, he mused. Yes, now was the right time to get COBRA up and running.

He mused on the vast powers that the Civil Contingencies Act gave this committee. To all intents and purposes, when sitting, it became all powerful. In the first instance he chaired the committee, but if he was not available, it fell on the Home Secretary or his deputy to take his place.

The PM's thoughts turned to his Home Secretary, whom he had chosen in order to placate the wing of his party he found most difficult to deal with. As he leaned back on the soft leather car seat, he wondered whether the Home Secretary and his department spent too much time courting favourable headlines and news coverage. Increasingly, in the few months since taking power, he realised that he had become progressively more anxious as to his Home Secretary's motivations. The press painted him as good party leadership material and liked his and his ministers' charm offensive. Perhaps his party's wafer-thin majority had prompted his spin offensive and he was jockeying for position in case the PM slipped up.

The PM's attention refocused on the previous week's COBRA meeting, which had been convened to sort out the mess left by the Bishopsgate bombing and to foil any follow-up attacks. The minutes showed it had been a straightforward meeting. It had been chaired by the number two at the Home Office, a loyal supporter of the Home Secretary, with liaison officers from the MoD, the police, MI5, MI6 and the Metropolitan police. This meeting was going to be considerably more difficult. He personally would take the chair.

★

Deep under Number 10, with the Home Secretary away, his number two had taken the chair. He had arrived at COBRA early, sensing it was his opportunity to take control. By 8.45 a.m. he had a quorum. Against the advice of the permanent secretary, he called the meeting to order and had COBRA up and running. He almost caught MI5 with their trousers down. They had the video link, relaying what was going on at COBRA to the Ops Room, working only seconds later.

The minister chairing COBRA appeared very concerned about the impact of the adverse TV coverage and asked for suggestions on how the news stories and the TV pictures could be made to look less grim.

The army at Hartlepool in particular were doing an impressive job. The zinc factory next to the nuclear power station was belching out acrid smoke. Elsewhere, in the words of one TV commentator at Cruden Bay, 'The locals must think that they are on the edge of a war zone, what with all the explosions and the dense smoke.' Aldermaston and Heysham also looked grim.

The Home Office minister relished his time in the spotlight. He cleared his throat. 'First, we must counter these awful pictures with something that will prevent us from looking feeble and, second, we should consider what the terrorists might do next and what we can do to stop them. The second part, I shall leave to the PM who will be joining us shortly.'

The minister looked around the room 'We need to deflect the TV coverage and show the public that we're playing hard ball with the terrorists. I have a colleague working on this. Do I hear any other suggestions?'

'Perhaps COBRA should start vetting everything going on air, as was the case in Iraq?'

'Good idea. We should implement this now,' he turned to his colleague, who had come up with the idea. 'Derek, would you please look after this personally?'

'Yes, sir.'

Derek stood up to leave when the door suddenly opened and the Prime Minister walked in with the Defence Secretary and his personal secretary at his side. The PM, as the screen at Wood Street showed, beckoned Derek to sit down, strode over and stood facing the minister.

The room fell silent.

'Minister, am I right in believing that last night you declined an invitation as the Home Secretary's stand-in to meet with the commissioner of the City of London police force and three very high ranking officers of the State?'

The minister looked most put out and went into bluster mode.

'But I wasn't told who would be there and I was extremely busy. I had a speech to make. I'd already issued a press release and I knew that there would be excellent press coverage. Anyway, I rearranged the meeting for this morning. So no harm was done!'

The Prime Minister's voice took on a steely tone.

'Your judgement call was fundamentally flawed. Events have moved on. You should have been a safe pair of hands on which the commissioner could have relied. Instead you placed personal spin above the needs of your country.'

'That's quite untrue, Prime Minister; the press conference was for the good of the Government.'

The PM beckoned to his personal secretary, who walked over to the minister and placed a typed letter in front of him.

'For your signature,' said the PM.

The minister read the short letter and looked up at the PM, his eyes conveyed hostility. 'Why should I resign at this of all times, when I'm needed here?'

The PM looked at him as if he were a bad-tempered schoolboy. 'That meeting you were too busy to attend last night is still going on. The stakes have been so high that we haven't been able to trust anyone unless they've been within a secure intelligence-monitored environment. Suffice it to say that the two gentlemen missing from this meeting aren't the only moles we've found in senior places.'

'What do you mean…? But *I* am needed here.'

'Sign the letter or I will be forced to fire you.'

The minister was livid and intent on letting everybody know it. He hesitated, signed the letter and was escorted out of the room by the PM's personal secretary.

The Prime Minister looked at the statue-like faces around him. 'I think that we can now get back to business. Let me put you in the picture as to the events of the past thirty-six hours. However, lest you worry that things are being left to drift, let me assure you that a fully staffed Operations Room has been up and running since yesterday evening and is dealing with matters as we speak. The Defence Secretary and I spent the night there, and were there less than an hour ago.'

The PM, with input from the Defence Secretary, gave a detailed description of the events of the past thirty-six hours and the strategy that had been put in place for dealing with the terrorists.

*

A little earlier, back at Wood Street, at 9.39 a.m. Kate's phone had rung. It was the main desk.

'A junior minister from the Home Office is here to see a Mr Khan. I'm advised that you might know something about his whereabouts? He wants to see him, with two senior officers, in an interview room now!'

'Leave this to me,' said John. 'I will tell him this is a very inconvenient time.'

Kate looked at Rafi. They were now alone in the room. 'How are you holding up?' she enquired in a concerned manner.

'OK, but I wish we could find the last terrorist. I'm on tenterhooks with this waiting for Rick Feldon or Roger Harewood to get back to us.'

Kate's phone rang. It was a very disgruntled John. 'The junior minister is *insisting* that he sees Mr Khan. He says that he has a direct order from the Chair of COBRA, his boss. It seems he hauled himself and his press entourage over to Paddington Green police station only to be kept waiting and then to find Mr Khan wasn't there. He was redirected to MI5 headquarters and they sent him here. He's furious - says he'll throw the book at us unless we let him see Rafi immediately. He refuses to understand that things are at a very delicate stage and won't take *no* for an answer. He has told me that he'll use his powers under the Civil Contingencies Act to make us cooperate, or else.'

'I have spoken to Beverley. Giles and David have gone to a meeting with the deputy commissioner of the Metropolitan Police to brief COBRA's police liaison unit and can't be disturbed. I can't find Ewan. So it's down to us. The minister keeps saying that he has to find out how much more Mr Khan can tell him about the Bishopsgate bombing and the recent attacks. Basically, I reckon all the self-obsessed cretin wants is a smokescreen: a story to tell the news teams outside in order to deflect all the bad publicity the Government is getting.'

'Damn it! Why the hell now?' blurted out Kate.

'Because the man doesn't live in the real world!' Tiredness had reduced John's ability to remain calm.

'Sounds like the old saying: "They came to do good; they stayed to do well",' added Rafi.

'Thank you, Rafi,' said Kate in a frustrated tone.

'Anyway,' continued John, 'I suppose we'll have no option but to let him see Rafi.'

'OK, but we keep the interview as short as possible,' Kate replied.

Over the phone she heard John shouting to the duty officer at the reception desk.

'Oh no! Get those flaming journalists away from here! Get the area outside the station cordoned off and keep the bloody press away – at least fifty bloody yards from the front door!'

'Yes, sir,' came the prompt reply.

'Sod it! We need this like a hole in the head,' said John irritably over the phone to Kate. 'You and Rafi – meet me in the third floor interview room. I'll bring the junior minister up.'

'This had better not take long,' remarked Kate to Rafi, who sensed her nervousness.

In the stairwell she stopped him, put her hand on his head and roughed up his hair.

'We can't have you looking kempt.' She pulled his rugby shirt out of the back of his tracksuit trousers and looked at him. 'You'd better take your shoes off.'

'Seriously? My socks stink!'

'Don't worry; it's all part of the illusion.' Kate looked him over. 'Yep, you'll do. You look awful, and yes, your socks reek!' To his surprise, she leant forward and planted an affectionate kiss on his cheek. 'No doubt you'll be worth knowing after a wash and brush up!'

Kate and Rafi were the first to arrive at the interview room. They sat down and waited. Minutes later John and the politician arrived.

'Sorry for the delay,' apologised John. 'The junior minister had to wash his hands.'

The junior minister, flanked by John and Kate, sat opposite Rafi.

'I went to see you at Paddington Green this morning only to find you weren't there. I was redirected to MI5 headquarters – most irregular – and they said I'd have to come here for the full story. I've wasted much valuable time and am in no mood to be messed around. Mr Khan, what I need to know is why you aren't helping the police with their search for the terrorists,' said the frustrated junior minister.

Rafi looked blankly across the table and remained silent.

'Thanks to you we had more terrorist attacks last night. Your resistance and reluctance to help are setting a very bad example to the Muslim community. I am advised that a growing number of extremist youngsters are becoming your followers. This is extremely bad for the country. I am here to give you an ultimatum: either you cooperate or I will throw the book at you and your family, do you hear? What do you have to say?'

Rafi looked at the junior minister: at his pale blue double-cuffed shirt, the light pink tie, the immaculate grey suit and the perfectly combed hair. If things weren't so serious he would have laughed at his pomposity and the bizarre nature of the interview.

'Are you threatening me and my family?'

'Damn right I am! Your type should know what they're up against when they tangle with the Government. You're outside the laws that protect decent and innocent Englishmen. You should be sent home.'

Rafi's temper was rising – valuable time was being wasted. 'I am dark-skinned and a Muslim. Why does that make me and my family undesirable? Answer me that and I'll help you with your questions.'

The minister was silent for a moment. 'It is your damn fundamentalism that's the problem – only permitting one God.' He paused. 'And you debase all other religions and criminalise the pursuit of wealth and personal advancement. Your brand of fundamentalism is not only myopic, but it is detrimental to a modern society. You're all the same: out to undermine our democracy. We will stop you, you know. Your approach to life will be stamped out and the likes of you will be removed from this country.'

Rafi sensed the junior minister was spouting forth a well-rehearsed monologue. 'Is that your view or the view of others?' he said trying to conceal his anger.

'My boss, a senior minister in the Home Office, agrees with me. Fanatical Muslims have no place here. Once our backs are turned, all you want to do is to bring down our democracy.'

Rafi wanted out. Time was ticking away and the idiot on the other side of the table was being absurd.

'Sir,' said Rafi, 'I'm innocent until proved guilty. Find the evidence and then try me.'

The junior minister lost his cool. 'Of course you're bloody guilty – we all know that! The CCTV footage alone will convict you. I've the press outside waiting for me. I need something to tell them which will make a good story to deflect the coverage of all the horrors you've caused. Will you cooperate? Or shall I personally make your life and your family's not worth living?'

Rafi sat there, too furious to answer.

Without warning, John stood up. 'Sir, you're not making any progress. Mr Khan is obviously not going to help you.'

'What the devil are you talking about, Inspector? Don't you know who I am? I'm your boss's boss! I won't take orders from anyone, let alone a junior policeman!'

John kept his cool.

There was a knock at the door. The telephonist burst in.

'DI Adams, I've an urgent message for you.' She passed the

piece of paper across the table to her.

The junior minister grabbed it. 'I'll see that.'

Kate looked at her. 'What did it say?'

'Rick someone asked for you to call him urgently.'

'Oh shit!' said Kate and dashed for the door.

The junior minister was taken aback. He shouted after her. 'You can't leave until I've finished with you. Come back here this instant!'

Kate was long gone.

John stood up and looked piercingly at the junior minister. 'I strongly suggest you stay here,' he said authoritatively. 'The constable outside and I will escort Mr Khan back to his cell - in case he does any *more* damage. You should see the mess he made of the three guards at Paddington Green – nearly killed one of them. He's a third Dan karate black belt. See his right wrist? He felled a nineteen-stone guard and fractured his jaw.'

'Why didn't you tell me this before?' squealed the ruffled junior minister. At this Rafi stood up and started to move towards him.

'No, get back!' shouted John. 'He isn't worth it.'

'Get him out of here!' shouted the squirming junior minister.

'Yes, sir. I'll take Mr Kahn to the cells and return to discuss how we can give your press friends a good story.'

'Do that and don't be long.'

John and Rafi left. John locked the door, turned to the police constable and handed him the key.

'Under no circumstances let him out until the commissioner or I get here. Understood? Whatever the minister says, ignore him!'

'Yes sir. But what about Mr Khan here? Will you be safe with him?'

'Of course.'

'But, what about his karate skills?'

'You shouldn't believe everything you hear!'

'Sorry, sir.'

'Rafi, go and help Kate; I must contact the commissioner before the minister gets on his mobile and does something even more crass.'

Rafi raced back to the office. Kate was on the phone to Rick;

she switched on the speaker.

'I've had another go at interviewing Mr Wesson,' said Rick. 'By accident, Wesson overheard Basel Talal and his property director discussing a building in Stratford, which they said would be untraceable. Basel described it as the jewel in the crown and added that its location was one where they'd make a killing. You're looking for an industrial property in Stratford, East London; it's undergoing refurbishment.'

'Thanks,' said Kate, 'You're a star!'

She hung up and rushed out of the room. Rafi was about to follow her when her phone rang. It was the switchboard.

'There's an urgent message from Roger Harewood; he wanted to check that you got the fax.'

Rafi hung up, rushed over to the fax machine, scooped up the sheet of paper sitting there and ran to the Ops Room, oblivious to all his aches and pains – and his lack of shoes. He briefly looked at the contents of the fax as he ran. It read: *URGENT - I tried to phone. My notes are sketchy. The cold store is a large industrial building located between Billingsgate and the A12 in East London. It is being refurbished. Hope this helps. - Roger Harewood.*

As he passed the meeting room where Emma was, he banged on the door and called for her to follow. Seconds later he barged into the Ops Room, skidded to a halt and shouted to Kate, waving the fax in his hand.

'Roger confirms: it's between Billingsgate and the A12; a large industrial property currently being refurbished.'

Rafi prayed that they weren't too late and that the valuable minutes wasted with the junior minister would not be their undoing.

*

At 9.56 a.m. the PM finished briefing COBRA on the events of the past thirty-six hours.

The video-conference link showing the Wood Street Ops Room was switched on. The PM introduced the Air Chief Marshal, Sir Nigel Hawser, and asked him to update COBRA on the whereabouts of the missing terrorist.

Suddenly, the door behind the Air Chief Marshal burst open and in rushed a scruffy looking policewoman closely followed by a dark-skinned individual with an unshaven face, in a Harlequins

202

rugby shirt, waving a piece of paper and shouting...

Kate and Rafi didn't stand on ceremony and cut across the PM.

'We have found the location of the last terrorist. He's at a large industrial property in Stratford, East London, between the A12 and Billingsgate fish market. It's being refurbished. I hope it won't be too difficult to spot from the air.'

'What's the target at Stratford?' asked the PM.

'Could there be a nuclear waste train in transit near there?' suggested Emma, who had arrived at the door. 'It is the only thing left on our list that could fit.'

'Find out, now!' instructed the Air Chief Marshal to Colonel Turner. 'Find the building and then the target should become obvious.'

At that moment John walked in. He sidled over to Rafi and passed him the tape of the interview with the junior minister. He said quietly, 'I thought that you might like to have the tape as a memento.'

'Thanks...' said Rafi tucking the tape into his pocket. 'They're looking for the last location; it's near Stratford, in East London.'

Meanwhile the Air Chief Marshal was on the scrambler. 'What air cover do we have? A fighter over Sizewell in Suffolk? Excellent! Get it over Stratford as quickly as is physically possible.'

'There's also a Tornado preparing to land at Marham, in Norfolk,' said the squadron leader on a video link with the Ops Room.

'Get it here in double quick time,' ordered the Air Chief Marshal.

'Commissioner, alert the nearest police helicopter and get it to Stratford. The first to arrive will have to locate and take out the terrorist.'

The brigadier called across. 'The Tornado will be at Stratford in seven minutes and the Jaguar from Suffolk will be there in eight and a half minutes. I've alerted the nearest anti-terrorist squad and they'll be in the area in twenty-two minutes.'

'Tell the pilots to look for a scaffolding tower, or a platform on the roof of an industrial building overlooking the railway tracks,' ordered the brigadier.

The colonel meanwhile was getting agitated. He was having a frustrating time finding out where the nearest nuclear waste train was. The clock showed it was just after 9.58 a.m. He'd dialled through on the direct line of the control room coordinating nuclear trains, but he was being given the runaround by the computer-controlled switchboard.

'Oh damn it!' he exclaimed. 'Bloody lift music! What on earth do they think that they are – some poncey retail store?'

A woman finally answered, apologising for the delay. 'If you've come through to me, it means that either the phones in the control room are engaged or the people are busy.'

'Do you work in the same building as the control room for the nuclear trains?' enquired the colonel.

'Yes; they're on the floor above me.'

'Excellent! Go right now and get someone in authority to pick up my call immediately. There's an accident waiting to happen. This is vitally important – do it now!'

With that, the phone reverted back to what the colonel described as 'bloody bog music'. His face had gone from a normal shade of pink through the spectrum to a bright red. A meek voice came on the phone a minute later.

'Please excuse the delay… You caught me with my trousers down. How can I help?' came the response.

'Do you know the whereabouts of any nuclear trains near Stratford?'

'Er… Yes and no,' came an uncertain reply. 'Sorry I'm not that sure; this is only my first week here. The board shows that there's one scheduled to pass through Stratford. My boss has gone outside for a moment.'

'Is there anyone else with you who can help us?'

'Not really, my boss is away from his desk…'

'Find him as quickly as humanly possible.'

'He won't like being disturbed,' came the unfortunate reply.

'Get him now; tell him there's an emergency and you've COBRA on the phone.'

'You what?'

'Just get him, now. Tell him it's a matter of life and death.'

'Will do!'

Rafi looked up at the clock; it was 10 o'clock. He looked around the room. Everyone was holding their breath; there was a deathly hush. Moments later, the voice of an aggravated man came on the phone.

'What do you want?' he barked.

'Do you have a nuclear train anywhere near Stratford?' The colonel barked back.

'Damn it! Who the hell are you?' came the abrupt reply.

'Colonel Bill Turner of the anti-terrorist squad; I have the Prime Minister alongside me.'

'No shit!' was the reply.

'Do as he says, now!' commanded the PM in a stern voice. 'And before you ask, yes, I *am* the Prime Minister.'

'Hold on a moment. Yes, the Sizewell train is running slightly late; it has just left Stratford station and is entering the North London branch line.'

The Colonel shouted down the phone, 'Tell them to do an emergency stop!'

The voice of the controller was heard over the speaker. 'Dick, *STOP! Stop your train immediately;* there's a terrorist threat!'

'Where exactly is the train, now?'

'About 600 metres down the spur line past Stratford.'

'Get it to back up the main line!'

'That's against the rules; I can't do that!'

'Do as he says,' came the uncompromising voice of the PM.

The colonel continued, 'Get all the trains on the main line stopped.'

'One flaming thing at a time.'

'Get them to back up now!' barked the Colonel. 'Get them to do it before it's too late!'

'Keep your hair on! They're starting to back up as we speak.'

There was an expletive heard over the phone, followed by a couple of sentences heavily laced with choice words.

'Did I hear you say that your train has disappeared off the screen… and the radio connection with them has been lost?'

'Y..yes,' stammered the coordinator. 'There was a loud bang and they've effing disappeared off the screen.'

Rafi looked across at the clock; it read 10.02 a.m.

The shaky voice of the controller came back on the line. 'I can confirm that I've lost contact with the driver and the satellite positioning marker is no longer functioning.'

The brigadier interrupted the silence. 'The Tornado is one and a half minutes away.'

Rafi felt spellbound and sick with apprehension. They'd found the missing piece of the jigsaw, but were they seconds too late?

The voice of the Tornado fighter pilot came over the loudspeaker. 'There's been one – now two – explosions! The target is a train, just west of Stratford station.'

The Ops Room meanwhile had been patched into the pilot's on-board camera showing an orange ball of flames erupting high into the air, and the remains of the train strewn across the track - one of the nuclear canisters was missing its front half and the top of the second canister was no longer there. Black smoke spiralled up into the sky, drifting north-west in the light wind.

The Air Chief Marshal spoke to the fighter pilot, who had received the grid reference for the property.

'Can you identify the terrorist's position?'

'Yes, sir,' came the reply.

'Is the building occupied or unoccupied?'

'Hard to tell sir – it looks vacant.'

'If you have him on visual, take him out before he fires another missile.'

*

The terrorist looked across at the burning train wreckage from the top of his scaffolding tower. Radiation would soon be all around him. He launched himself over the side and abseiled from view.

*

You could have heard a pin drop. That was what they were after – London – the business capital of Europe and the venue of the 2012 Olympics.

It was a disaster.

Having foiled the other attacks, Rafi found it hard to take on board the impact of this terrorist success. He had known that the stakes were high and the consequences would be grave if a nuclear catastrophe occurred, but the reality was numbing.

Emma looked at Kate and Rafi. 'Sweet Jesus help us! There's around two tonnes of spent nuclear fuel in the air,' said Emma, with a lump in her throat, 'which is something like 20 kg of plutonium and 40 kg of other radioactive particles on the loose.'

The service chiefs had been trained to work under pressure and they were already making plans to deal with the calamity. The Air Chief Marshal spoke via the video links to the Army HQ at Wilton and then to the colonel standing next to him.

'Activate *Operation Counterpane*. I repeat, activate *Operation Counterpane*. Brigadier, advise the Royal Netherlands Air Force that we need every helicopter they can spare, pronto.'

Colonel Gray spoke to the Prime Minister, who had turned a whiter shade of pale.

'Sir, I suggest that you activate LESLP – London Emergency Services Liaison Panel – immediately. The Metropolitan police are on standby. Although control rests with you and your colleagues at COBRA in the first instance, sir, I suggest that you ask us to coordinate the military element required to contain the disaster, and to oversee the evacuation and the decontamination process for the time being.'

'Carry on,' replied the PM. 'I have two nuclear experts with me who will advise you on the size of the exclusion zone.'

'Thank you, sir.' The video link camera at COBRA was swung round and two middle-aged professors came on to the Wood Street Ops Room screen. They spoke to the Air Chief Marshal and explained what data they would require.

*

En route to the nuclear train, from Colchester Barracks, was a helicopter equipped with radioactivity-sensing devices. Like many others, it had been placed on standby by the brigadier in the early hours of the morning as part of *Operation Counterpane*. The helicopter pilot radioed through that he would be over the train in seventeen minutes.

'For the time being, gentlemen,' said the professors, 'we recommend an exclusion zone of one mile upwind and four miles downwind. We will give you the precise figures shortly after we have the data in from the helicopter.'

The Ops Room was like a hornets' nest. The scale of the task dwarfed anything that had ever been attempted in peacetime.

At last, the helicopter flying at 1,000 feet started to collect and send the data on the radioactivity levels through to COBRA. The professors fed the data, in real time, into the impressive-looking laptops in front of them. As the helicopter flew over the smouldering train, the operator of the radioactivity-sensing equipment let out an expletive and advised the pilot to give the train a wide berth next time. The pilot carried on with a predetermined series of flyovers and sweeps of the vicinity on a grid basis. As the volume of data fed back to the professors increased, it became obvious from their faces that the news was far from good – they had turned an ashen colour.

After what seemed like an age, but in reality was only a matter of minutes, the younger of the two professors started speaking. 'We need to know, Prime Minister, what acceptable mortality rate to put into our models. The scale of the radioactive leak is very large. What level of increased cancer mortality is acceptable? Should we take one additional death per 100,000 people every ten years, or what?'

There was a discussion amongst the COBRA team; a number was agreed on and keyed into the computer model. The other professor spoke up hesitantly. 'I hope you're all sitting down. On the basis of the data, gentlemen, the exclusion zone is: two miles upwind of the train, ten miles downwind and the ellipse at its widest point is six miles wide.'

Rafi looked at the map. A vast swathe of London, from Enfield to West Ham and from Stoke Newington across to Woodford, was now destined for dereliction in perpetuity. It seemed completely unreal – like something out of a disaster movie.

'Air Chief Marshal, we have emailed you the perimeter line of the exclusion zone. It can be superimposed on your maps.'

A hush fell over the two rooms. The second professor spoke solemnly. 'The exclusion zone has an area of fifty-seven square miles and the length of the perimeter is close to thirty miles.'

Rafi looked at Kate. 'I've had enough,' he felt gutted. All his attempts had proved to be inadequate. The terrorists had won through. Tears welled up in his eyes. They'd pulled off the big one. Over fifty square miles of one of the most densely populated parts of Europe would have to be totally abandoned and many people would face horrible deaths.

Haunting thoughts flooded through Rafi's mind. If they had told the junior minister to: *Get lost!*, they could have got the information on the last property to the Ops Room minutes earlier. Valuable time had been squandered. If the nuclear train had been stopped just a few hundred metres sooner the terrorist would not have had a clear line of sight. The knot in his stomach tightened. He turned, walked down the corridor, to break the bad news to Aidan's team.

In a monotone Rafi told them of the missile attack at Stratford, and that one of their team should liaise with the Ops Room to be briefed on the scale of the radiation contamination. The ball was now in their court. He left their room and noticed Kate still standing by the door to the Ops Room.

Rafi walked over to her and took hold of her hand. She turned and looked at him with tears in her eyes. 'Come on, let's go; there isn't much we can do here.' But she didn't move. She stood mesmerised by the screens, like a rabbit caught in the headlights.

'In a few minutes, please,' she replied. 'I would like to see what happens next...'

*

Plugging the gaping holes in what was left of the two spent fuel containers was the immediate task. Access by air was the quickest and safest way to get materials in to cover the ruptured containers. The imperative was to stop further hazardous and highly toxic radioactive waste escaping by entombing the train in concrete.

Operation Counterpane was under way. The army's HQ Land Command based at Wilton, near Salisbury, had been in a state of full readiness and within minutes of the train being hit by the first missile it was already coordinating troop movements, working closely with those in the Ops Room.

Colonel Turner had passed across a long list of all the available UK civilian helicopters. These were now under the command of the Royal Air Force.

All helicopters within 250 miles and powerful enough to lift a concrete hopper were en route to Stratford. The workhorse Chinook helicopters would be the best at transporting the concrete, but as at 10.45 a.m. the nearest was still forty minutes flying time away. The demands of the armed intervention in the Middle East had seriously depleted the modest size of the services' ageing helicopter fleet. On paper, the number of helicopters remaining in the UK looked significant, but in practice the majority were out of action, undergoing repairs or modifications. Thankfully, the helicopter squadron from the Netherlands was now only fifty-five minutes away.

Colonel Turner's team had identified seventeen large building sites with cranes and concrete hoppers. There was a local property development boom going on thanks to the impending 2012 Olympics. Each helicopter was directed to a property development site, where they could pick up a concrete hopper and a crane driver.

It was going to be a dangerous operation, particularly for the first four or five sorties which would be the most at risk when they jettisoned their loads in close proximity to the hot radioactive contents below. In theory, it would be best to use the biggest helicopters first, but in practical terms the colonel opted for a first-come-first-served basis. An added complication was getting the calculations right as to the maximum payload which each helicopter could carry.

The reaction time of the coastguard helicopters was far faster than anything the colonel could have hoped for. The first collected its hopper of concrete within forty-one minutes of the request going out. Having a modest lifting capacity, it was only able to take the hopper a third full, but it was a start.

The pilot and his two crew members were joined by the crane driver and took off with the hopper slung under the helicopter's belly and headed for the plume of dark smoke which was clearly visible in the overcast February daylight. The pilot made his approach from the south-east – upwind. Half a mile from the train, the helicopter gained altitude and the hopper was lowered to the full length of its steel wires. Hovering over a specified spot was second nature to the pilot – even in a force eight gale. This time, it was different. The risks were unseen.

'Bombs away!' shouted the crane driver pulling the mechanical release cord. 'Now comes the slow bit,' he shouted. 'I reckon we'll be here for sixty to seventy seconds.'

'Shout when we can scarper,' yelled the pilot over the noise.

Seventy-five seconds later their task was completed. The empty tubular steel hopper and hawser were ditched; the helicopter banked and headed south.

The co-pilot called back to those behind him. 'What were the readings?'

'OK-ish,' came the reply. 'No more dentist's X-rays for a

while though, I reckon. But we're still below the maximum limit and a bit more shouldn't do us any real harm; just fry a few cells here or there!'

'Are you willing do a second run?' enquired the pilot.

'If no one else is around and we can help stop the radioactivity escaping, do we have a choice?' asked the crane driver.

The co-pilot radioed through to the Ops Room and spoke to the colonel. 'Load safely deposited. Our radioactivity gauge shows that we can do another run. Where's the next helicopter?'

'It's five minutes behind you, followed by two more shortly after that, then there's...' He hesitated, 'A bit of a gap.'

'Sign us up for that slot. Where do we get our next load of concrete from, please?'

The colonel studied the map. His adjutant beside him pointed at a mark on the map, saying, 'I suggest this one,' and relayed the coordinates. The pilot moved on to the new course.

'What did it look like?' asked the colonel.

'Devastation,' replied the pilot. 'There's a river and a canal nearby. You're no doubt aware of where the water goes?'

'Yes,' replied the colonel. 'We're working on how to stop the radioactivity getting into the water courses and then leaching into the water table.'

Multi-tasking was the order of the day. Kate was roped in by the colonel. 'Find me a good location to set up a decontamination unit for the helicopter crews and where we can put the helicopters that have been exposed; ideally a small local airfield away from the public gaze. When you've found it, get the RAF command centre to set up a decontamination unit and field hospital there.'

'Yes, sir,' came the reply.

A private airfield and flying club was found at Stapleford, near the M25/M11 intersection and less than fifteen miles away. She passed the details on to the RAF Control Centre.

'Let me look it up,' said the voice at the other end of the phone. 'Good choice – its main runway will take transport planes. Tell them to expect a couple of Hercules planes within the next forty-five minutes. Get them to clear the area to the west of their runway number 28/10. We will put the contaminated helicopters there.'

Kate phoned the flight centre, half expecting the phone to be answered by an unhelpful individual. It was answered by the manager of their Club House. Kate explained that the RAF needed to borrow their facilities.

'No problem. We've been listening to the flurry of radio traffic for the past half an hour. Is it as bad as they say?'

'I'm afraid so,' replied Kate.

'What can we do to help?'

'You can expect two Hercules transport planes carrying medical supplies within the hour. They won't be staying long, as they've other deliveries to make,' said Kate, who went on to give details of their requirements.

'We'll clear out the student accommodation block. It'll make a good medical block and decontamination facility. I've only one favour to ask: if you could ask the transport planes to land on the tarmac part of the main runway and not on the grass section, it would be much appreciated,' said the manager.

Back at the train, the first five sorties flown by the lighter coastguard helicopters had started to cover the ruptured canisters with concrete.

'Bloody pyramids!' commented the adjutant. 'The train line is on an embankment and the concrete pours down off the carriage on to the sloping ground. The base layer of the concrete gets wider and wider but the pile doesn't get much higher.'

The crane driver in the back of the first coastguard helicopter overheard this conversation and shouted to the pilot, 'Suggest they add salt to the concrete; it'll speed up the setting time.'

The first heavy-duty Chinook helicopter did the sixth run and took almost two full hoppers. This was closely followed by eleven more Chinook sorties.

By midday, the ruptured canister and train were no longer visible, buried beneath a small hill of concrete. Phase One had been completed successfully.

*

Meanwhile, the irate junior minister had been let out of the interview room and was now en route to 10 Downing Street, where he had been summoned to attend a meeting with the head of PR at the Cabinet Office.

*

Phase Two, which had commenced simultaneously with Phase

One, involved the establishment of the exclusion zone.

Four Apache helicopters were tasked with marking the thirty-mile long boundary of the exclusion zone and the location of the fourteen decontamination centres. They used a combination of electronic and smoke beacons.

From listening to the conversations, Rafi had gleaned that the main problem was the large amount of radioactive material that the south-easterly wind had picked up and was depositing over a wide area.

The Kornet missiles had thermobaric warheads. These, it seemed, were different to conventional explosive weapons and used the oxygen in the air instead of carrying an oxidizer in their explosives. As one of the army officers explained, 'They produce more bang for their bucks. Unfortunately there was water surrounding the spent fuel rods. The thermobaric explosion will have extracted the oxygen from the water and liberated hydrogen gas, which will have made the bang even bigger. The ferocity of the blast vaporised much of the radioactive material and blasted it high into the sky. The radioactive plutonium is heavier than lead, so thankfully it won't travel far. It is the lighter and more highly radioactive isotopes in the spent fuel that will cause the problems. They will stay airborne far longer and are responsible for the unexpectedly large size of the exclusion zone.'

16 Air Assault Brigade, the army's premier rapid reaction fighting brigade from nearby Essex and Suffolk, parachuted in 750 troops using Hercules transport planes. They were joined by soldiers from the 1st Royal Tank Regiment's Nuclear Biological and Chemical Unit, stationed alongside RAF Honnington in Suffolk, who landed at London City Airport within fifty minutes of the first missile exploding. They were transferred by helicopter to the locations of the fourteen decontamination centres and were tasked with helping clear the ground.

Other soldiers had already started securing the perimeter of the exclusion zone: they were stopping people from entering and directing those leaving the exclusion zone towards the nearest decontamination centre. The public were left in no doubt that the soldiers carried live ammunition and were prepared to use it, if necessary.

Meanwhile, 3,000 soldiers were being airlifted in from all

round the UK to reinforce the cordon around the perimeter as quickly as possible. Commercial planes had been commandeered to assist with the troop movements.

Companies of soldiers were tasked with supervising the evacuees and corralling them into the holding areas, located adjacent to each of the fourteen embryonic decontamination centres and the adjoining medical centres which were triaging the casualties and dispensing radiation tablets. It was calculated that over 1,000 decontamination shower units would be required to process the majority of the 900,000 people in around ten hours.

Rafi couldn't work out where all the planes and people came from. The screens showed the skies full of parachutes. Rapidly, it all became a blur. He stood watching but taking little in.

One question that had been exercising COBRA was how to make certain that the inner exclusion zone was completely cleared of people. A ninety percent rule was adopted. Speed was of the essence. Those who could be moved quickly were dealt with first. Reluctant individuals would be strongly encouraged to leave later in the afternoon.

The squadron of twenty-six helicopters that had flown in from the Netherlands, combined with the armada of private helicopters, were a godsend. Every available decontamination unit and the associated medical support teams within their range were commandeered and delivered to one of the fourteen decontamination centres. The ingenuity of the Royal Engineers and the soldiers from the Royal School of Military Engineering at Chatham and at Minley in erecting the decontamination centres tipped the balance. By the early afternoon 1,250 decontamination shower units were up and running.

Specialist army units moved in to coordinate the mammoth task of clearing the exclusion zone. They were joined by the Territorial Army's Medical Services and Veterinary Corps.

Thanks to the forward planning, *Operation Counterpane* had sufficient numbers of paratroopers in planes around the UK ready to take off. Within eighty minutes of the missile explosion the thirty-mile perimeter had a significant military presence guarding the electronically tagged line. The line in the densely built-up areas was zigzag in shape. The smoke beacons marking the locations of the fourteen decontamination centres were clearly visible.

600 Regular and Territorial personnel from the Royal Military Police, Provost Staff and Guard Service arrived to work alongside the local police forces and emergency services. Their first job, with the paratroopers, had been to systematically block all the roads and side streets out of the exclusion zone so that no vehicles at all could leave the area. Lorries and cars were commandeered and used as barricades. Tempers flared as people were forced to walk to safety.

A one-way road system was established to funnel the traffic away from the exclusion zone. In the opposite direction the local police assisted by the Territorial Army established express ways to enable troops, the emergency services and their equipment to get to the perimeter of the exclusion zone. To stop the civilian movement of traffic and keep the roads moving for emergency vehicles, a curfew was imposed on the whole of the Home Counties.

The helicopters that had completed their sorties with the decontamination equipment and medics were tasked with flying in Territorial and Regular Army soldiers in protective clothing to work with the paratroopers to create corridors within the exclusion zone. These corridors channelled people towards their nearest decontamination centre. Those who couldn't walk were transported by army vehicles.

One of the hardest parts of the operation was to stop panic setting in. All radio, cable and TV stations carried the same content. There was a message from the Prime Minister, followed by an explanation as to what was going on and what people should do.

Appeals for help with the rehousing of those dispossessed went out to councils and people living away from the exclusion zone.

*

The brigadier and his team were in charge of identifying and unblocking bottlenecks. The decontamination centres were their main headache. They implemented a fast track system. At the holding areas alongside the decontamination centres, units were set up, screening people for alpha, beta and gamma radiation. Where 'within nominal' readings were detected, people were given potassium iodate tablets, sent away from the exclusion zone and told that they didn't need to be decontaminated.

Initially, those people from the fringes of the exclusion zone were found to have negligible levels of radiation and were sent on their way, but soon the contamination levels rose as the radioactivity travelled with the wind and a point was reached where everyone had to undergo decontamination. Logistical problems were experienced as families found that they were being split up in the process. Contaminated children not of school age were allowed to have a parent with them. All other schoolchildren separated from their parents were fast tracked and moved to nearby schools to be reunited with their families as quickly as possible.

It was a bitterly cold day. Thankfully, many of those who had been out in the open had the benefit of wearing heavy winter clothing and much of the radioactive material was removed by simply stripping them of their clothes.

Once naked, the radiation readings were taken again. For those with external contamination and whose skin was intact, it was a relatively uncomplicated procedure: a thorough wash under a shower of warm water and a good scrubbing with a soft brush or surgical sponge. These soon ran out and were replaced with strips of towel. The small proportion with more severe contamination was moved on to a second decontamination section for more thorough treatment.

The brigadier and his team had devised a processing system which enabled those running the holding areas and the decontamination centres to keep track of people's identities. Bar coded hospital wrist and ankle tags were used and these gave details of whether the person's identity had been confirmed before they had been parted from all their belongings. This data was cross-referenced with a central database, along with their digital photograph and their basic biometric details.

London City Airport was turned into a transport logistics centre. It was cleared of all its civilian traffic and became a military airport. The runway, at 1,319 metres, was long enough for it to take the CN-235 tactical military transport and Hercules planes. Its close proximity to the exclusion zone was a stroke of luck.

Nearby, on the southern edge of the exclusion zone, the army had set up its field HQ. The coordination of people's movements, prioritising the casualties and the problems of the long queues at the emergency decontamination units were an administrative nightmare. Logjams became common place as the system struggled to deal with the huge numbers. Nevertheless, substantial progress was being made.

An SOS had gone out to all neighbouring countries which could get decontamination equipment into London City Airport within three hours. The Belgians, Dutch, French, Germans and Irish all contributed to this urgent request from COBRA. By midday their transport planes started landing with their cargoes of decontamination equipment, medics and medical supplies. By early afternoon, planes were stacked high above the southern approaches to the airport, waiting for a landing slot.

*

Phase Three was proving more difficult. How were the watercourses to be dealt with? Radioactive particles had been thrown violently into the air by the explosion. Those that entered the nearby canal, the River Lea, or the water table would be transported slowly towards Docklands in the City of London. Unless they were stopped quickly, the scale of the exclusion zone would have to be widened, threatening Docklands and the eastern fringes of the City of London. Colonel Gray's team was given responsibility for coordinating this.

*

Rafi and Kate stood at the side of the Ops Room looking on in awe. The Air Chief Marshal's military machine was an impressive sight. The scale of the operation beggared belief. By early afternoon the last task given to the Wood Street Ops Room in respect of Stratford had been completed and an exhausted Air Chief Marshal handed over to COBRA and the command centre in Wilton, near Salisbury.

Under the watchful eye of the brigadier, the focus of the Ops Room moved back to coordinating the capture of the terrorists.

Rafi became aware that Ewan was standing next to him.

Ewan had a pretty good idea of what was going through Rafi's mind and put his arm around Rafi's shoulder. 'You know, had it not been for your early warning, we would be faced with a catastrophic disaster far bigger than anything we are witnessing.

Your forewarning gave the Air Chief Marshal the opportunity to take the unprecedented step of putting the whole UK military machine into a state of readiness a full five and a half hours before the train was hit. Your determination to beat the terrorists has enabled us to have a response time we could never have dared dream of. I know it won't make you feel much better, but thank you.'

*

While all eyes were on the unfolding disaster at Stratford, MI5 had been tasked with the surveillance of the two Chechen terrorists who were on the run. Without their Kornet and Vektor missile launchers they no longer posed a serious threat to national security. The PM, in approving the plan to let the terrorists run, had made it crystal clear that if they posed *any* danger to the public they should be stopped by whatever means necessary. The object of the exercise now was to round up the terrorists, their associates and the ringleaders.

Sergy Kowshaya, fired up by the success of his missile attack at Cruden Bay and his escape from the hail of bullets, had in a well-executed move swapped his motorbike for an elderly car. Unbeknown to him, however, he was being observed. He opted for a circuitous route up the coast to retrieve the Vektor mortar he'd left in the utility van the afternoon before. The van was parked on the grass verge in front of a terrace of cottages, just over a mile to the north-west of the St Fergus gas terminal.

Sergy made good time to the van and, 300 metres short of it, he steered over to the bushes at the side of the road, stopped dead and inspected the scene in front of him. All was quiet. He felt under his leather jacket for his Stechkin automatic pistol. He paused and then continued on his way towards the van. Adrenalin pumped through his veins. He knew he would be vulnerable as he approached the van. If the security services were on the ball, there was the possibility that they could have pieced together the location of his second target. If so, they would be watching the surrounding area like a hawk for all unexplained movements.

He stopped his car in front of the van, pulled out a set of keys from his jacket pocket, walked over and opened the van's sliding side door. On the floor were two heavy-duty workman's tool bags. He lifted them up, turned and made for the small gap in the hedgerow a few metres away. He dropped to his knees, opened the first bag and lifted out the Vektor mortar. In moments it was pointing through the gap towards the St Fergus gas facility and storage tanks over the slight hill in the distance. He had already calculated the sets of angles of trajectory and compass settings required in ballistic mode. The missiles would explode above the main gas storage tanks.

In the second tool bag, lying next to the mortar, were twenty missiles. He pulled opened the top of the bag, picked up a missile and, in one fluid movement, dropped it down the barrel of the mortar.

'Svoloch!' he swore in Russian. The damn thing had misfired; either the firing pin was damaged – but he'd checked it the day before – or it was a dud missile? If so, there was an outside chance that the missile could go off at any moment. The odds were that it was a dud, but did he want to risk it exploding as he got it out of the barrel?

Sergy then did what he would never have done on the battlefield: he left the mortar where it was, put his hand into a side pocket of his jacket, fished out a small explosive with a timing device, armed it and placed it in the bag with the nineteen remaining missiles. He stood up, returned to his car and left the scene, heading towards a small industrial unit on the outskirts of Peterhead.

He was in contemplative mood; he was €3 million richer after his success at Cruden Bay, but destroying the St Fergus facility would have earned him a further €1 million. He abhorred the sense of failure, but whether he had €3 million or €4 million in the bank made little difference – he was now richer than in his wildest dreams.

Moments after Sergy's car had disappeared out of sight, the three special services men who had been watching his every move broke cover. They had known that the terrorist would suffer a misfire, as they had removed the firing pin, and had watched Sergy place an explosive in the bag with the missiles. The nearest soldier was seventy-five metres away. He spoke with his commander. It was agreed that the terrorist had left an explosive with a time delay to cover his tracks. It was now time to decide whether to investigate or wait for the big bang. The SAS soldier ran crouching close to the ground. If it had been him, he would have set the device to explode in ten minutes in order to give him time to get well away from the scene.

He opened the bag. His eyes locked on to the small explosive device. It was a small but lethal piece of plastic explosive with a sophisticated timing device. The digital readout showed 0:37. Delicately, he picked it up and walked fifteen paces out into the field, placed it on the ground, turned and ran for cover.

Sergy wound down his window; it was a bitterly cold day and the heater of his old car barely made an impression on the wintry air flooding inside. He heard the dull bang of the explosion; it was far quieter than he'd anticipated. His mind put two and two together. Koit, the Russian bastard, had sold them duds. He wound up the window and thought unspeakable thoughts. Suddenly, not having the full €4 million rankled.

Twenty-five minutes later and still thinking foul thoughts, Sergy arrived at the industrial property that had been his base for the past twenty-four hours.

Away from prying eyes, he swapped his car for an old moped and changed into scruffy sailor's clothes. Unbeknown to him, the front of the property was being watched. It was on Rafi's list.

Sergy opened the back door to the industrial unit and left via an overgrown dirt track on a short cut through an adjoining property. He came close to losing those watching him, but as he turned into Catto Drive his moped chugged straight past the nondescript MI5 communications vehicle coordinating his surveillance. Instead of heading straight for the harbour he went to a truckers' café a mile away. Here he consumed a hearty English breakfast washed down with several cups of coffee, read a tabloid newspaper and watched, with pleasure, the awful news on the small television secured to the wall. The team, watching his every move, kept their distance.

Just before noon Sergy paid, got on his moped and headed slowly towards the docks. He counted three police cars with lights flashing pass by. They paid not one jot of interest in him. At the docks, he parked a short distance away from the trawler *Northern Rose*, went into a warehouse and came out moments later carrying a crate of supplies. He headed towards the trawler and climbed on board as she was slipping her mooring lines.

Sergy stood on the deck for a few moments, as if he was looking for a colleague, and then went below deck. *Northern Rose* motored out to sea and set a course northwards; one that would take her safely past Rattray Head. An hour later she changed course to north-north-west, heading towards Duncansby Head, the Orkney Islands and the Pentland Firth.

The MI5 team were pleased to see Sergy safely on board. Now he was away from the public, the prospect of collateral damage had receded.

Meanwhile, the Nimrod aircraft tracking *Golden Sundancer* picked up *Northern Rose* as she headed northwards. The navigator spoke to the Ops Room and COBRA, and gave a predicted rendezvous between the trawler and *Golden Sundancer* north-west of the Pentland Firth, around 18:00 hours.

*

Dakka Dudayev, the terrorist who had caused the carnage at Stratford, left the industrial building in a sports hatchback and had, so far, evaded detection. The team tasked with tracking him had become worried; he was thought to be making for North Walsham, but, an hour and a half after the Stratford attack, his precise location was still not known.

There were sighs of relief when he was seen turning off the M11 on to the A11. Dakka motored up the A140 to Aylsham and on to North Walsham.

When Dakka entered the industrial estate he saw smoke and flames coming from the industrial unit, two down from where he'd stored his Vektor mortar and the twenty high-explosive shells. Parked right in front of his factory were a fire engine and a police car. The whole area had been cordoned off. He did not hesitate. He casually turned his car around and headed for Great Yarmouth.

Those watching him were pleased to see him leave.

On the outskirts of the town, he slipped off the main road into a housing estate and headed for a lock-up garage. After swapping his casual attire for nondescript fisherman's clothing, consisting of a duffle coat and patched trousers, and his sports car for a moped, he slowly made his way to the ship repair yard.

At the docks, Dakka Dudayev left his moped a couple of hundred metres away from where *Rosemarie* was berthed. He walked calmly down the road, through the ship repair yard, past the dry dock, on to the dock side and stepped aboard *Rosemarie* as her mooring lines were being cast off.

At just after 4 p.m. *Rosemarie* motored out to sea, turned south on to a bearing of 179° and ratcheted her speed up to an impressive fourteen knots. She, it was thought, was heading for the Straights of Dover, with a likely rendezvous point with *Golden Sundancer* somewhere beyond the Isles of Scilly.

A second Nimrod was on station to monitor *Rosemarie*'s progress in case she put into port to offload her human cargo.

★

In Scotland, the industrial property at Prestwick had been under surveillance by a special forces and MI5 unit since the early hours of the morning. Alistair Hartnell, Basel Talal's number two, had been identified as a passenger on an internal flight from London Stansted to Prestwick the night before. Hartnell was lying low in the industrial property. He had been joined by an unidentified man late in the evening. His colleague, it transpired, was Kim Chindriani, the man responsible for recruiting potential suicide bombers.

Neither was viewed as being particularly dangerous, but rather were seen as two rats abandoning the sinking ship. Just before midday they were observed leaving the property in a small car and were followed to the dry dock and ship repair facility just up the coast at Troon harbour. They left their car in the ferry car park and casually sauntered across to the ship repairer's quay where they boarded *Highland Belle* a whisker after 1 o'clock. A few minutes later, the trawler set sail and settled on to a course of 233° at a speed of thirteen knots. She was heading for the North Channel. No doubt she would leave the Mull of Kintyre to starboard and head north-west out into the Atlantic to her rendezvous with *Golden Sundancer* in the early hours of the following morning.

On board the trawlers there was sadness that some of their colleagues had not made it. The terrorists had been operating independently and had only been briefed on their targets, but had found out from the news channels that two of their colleagues had been killed at the scene of the attacks. However, the coverage was music to their ears. The combined effect of their attacks

222

sounded devastating. The fires were still burning at Cruden Bay; dark plumes of smoke were coming from Aldermaston, Hartlepool and Heysham, and at Stratford they'd hit the jackpot.

*

The sheikh and Maryam were also being closely watched. MI6 had sent a team to find Miti Lakhani, but had no news of his whereabouts.

In Luxembourg, Maryam was acting as if it was a normal working day. She was due to remain there until Tuesday, when she was booked to fly back to the Gulf. The reports were that she was looking very pleased with herself.

The sheikh, likewise, was doing nothing out of the ordinary and had spent much of the day at his palatial home, sunning himself by the pool.

*

In silence, Kate and Rafi had left the Ops Room to get a coffee. After a short break they ventured back.

The commissioner saw them enter and walked over to speak to them. He looked at Rafi with tired and slightly bloodshot eyes. 'I see that the weight of the world is on your shoulders. You should be congratulated and should not feel guilty! Only two out of nine attacks were carried out. Cruden Bay pumping station will be repaired and will be out of action for a matter of months not years…'

'But we let Stratford slip though the net,' said Kate.

'It was not your fault – understand that! The information came in in sufficient time. It was the system that screwed up and not you – please remember that.'

He looked carefully at Kate. 'Time you both got some well-earned rest. Rafi, your flat in its present state wouldn't be very welcoming. My sincere apologies for turning your life upside down. We totally misjudged you. Perhaps we could put you up at a hotel?'

'Thank you,' Rafi replied gratefully.

'Have a rest. But then, I'd appreciate it if you could come back and listen to what your economics team has to say. They have a meeting scheduled with the PM and the Chancellor of the Exchequer this evening, followed by the Bank of England early tomorrow afternoon. If you could be back in action by, say, 6.30

p.m. it would be appreciated.'

'Yes, sir.'

Giles turned to go back to his allotted space on the central desk, when he caught sight of Saara, who was in deep conversation with the brigadier. 'Your little sister is quite remarkable! For an unassuming person she packs one hell of a punch. Her understanding of things nuclear and her ability to decipher the experts' suggestions is impressive. If your parents were around they would be very proud of you both... Kate, please look after Rafi. The outside world still views him as public enemy number one. He deserves some proper TLC. Remember, we need him fighting in our corner until all the terrorists have been rounded up and the financial gremlins have been slain.'

Rafi was ready to drop. His head ached, his eyes hurt and was finding it increasingly difficult to take in what was going on around him.

Kate gently tugged at his sleeve. 'You have been working non-stop for nearly four days. Time to get some shut-eye. First, though, we need to visit accounts to sort out some accommodation for you.'

As they walked down the back stairs towards the accounts office, the prospect of staying in a budget hotel filled Rafi with horror.

'Are my credit cards working?' he inquired.

'Should be by tomorrow,' Kate replied. 'I'll ask Jeremy to arrange for them to be returned to you as soon as is practical.'

They arrived at the accounts department. 'Hi,' said Kate. 'Let me introduce you to Rafi Khan.' Kate explained their requirements and the importance of confidentiality.

Rafi interrupted her. 'What I need, please, is a comfortable hotel where I can pay the bill in a couple of days' time. Unfortunately, my credit cards are still with MI5.' He thought for a moment. 'Could you please book me into a suite at the Savoy?'

'That'll cost a flaming fortune,' commented Kate.

He looked at her. 'I'm exhausted. I could do with a hotel where I know it'll be really comfortable and quiet, and where the service will be first class. The prospect of a soft, comfy bed and a luxurious duvet at the moment is worth its weight in gold. Don't worry, as soon as you've got my credit card working again, I'll pay for it.'

'The Savoy shouldn't be a problem,' said the accounts woman. 'Although I can't say that we've ever used them before. Let me give them a ring.' She found the number, dialled and began talking to their corporate reservations department. In a matter of minutes she had everything lined up.

To Rafi's surprise she booked a two-room suite in Kate's name.

'It's the commissioner's suggestion,' said the accounts woman. 'He said that Rafi needed someone to vouch for him as, in the eyes of the public, he is still a terrorist.'

It slowly dawned on Rafi that he had been oblivious to all the press coverage of the past week and the vilification to which he would have been subjected.

'Fine,' replied Kate with a gleam in her eye. 'Good idea. Come on, let's go.'

On their way to the car, Kate picked up an old pork-pie hat and a scarf, and handed them to Rafi.

As they were getting into the car, Neil Gunton arrived. 'Goddamn it! We so nearly stopped them from doing any serious damage. I'm willing to bet that Stratford will be a defining point in the history of this country... People will soon be talking in terms of BS and AS – Before Stratford and After Stratford. Even in my book, the sheer scale of Stratford is mind-blowing.'

Neil paused. 'Sadly, though, I doubt if people will ever appreciate how much carnage your actions prevented. I was talking to one of our boffins; he described what a thermobaric warhead could have done to a waste storage pool at a nuclear power station. In his words, *It would have made Stratford seem like an inconvenience*.' Neil gave Rafi a pat on the back, shrugged his shoulders and went on his way.

Chapter 6

Thanks to the curfew, the traffic was unprecedentedly light. On their arrival at the Savoy Hotel, Kate went in and sorted out the formalities, whilst Peter, who had been driving, and Rafi waited in the car. She returned clutching a key card.

Rafi put on the pork-pie hat and wrapped the scarf around his neck and lower face. He felt a bit of an idiot. They said their thanks and goodbyes to Peter and then made their way to the lift.

'Are you very, *very* wealthy?' Kate asked, while they were waiting. 'One night here costs about the same as my monthly mortgage payment!'

Rafi was too tired to explain that he simply wanted comfort and was willing to pay any price for it. The last week had been worse than anything he had ever known and he yearned to put it behind him.

They arrived at the door to the suite. Kate opened it. 'Wow! This looks fantastic. Do you normally live like this?'

'No, I have a two-bedroom flat in north London. This is the first time for me as well.'

Kate looked at him with a smile. 'What makes you think that I haven't stayed in a place like this before?' she hesitated. 'I have a confession to make. I hope you don't mind but I've changed our suite from a two-bedroom to a one-bedroom, so that they could give our booking to a displaced family.'

Kate looked at him anxiously, waiting for his reply. She felt as if she'd been caught doing something wrong at school.

Rafi was too tired to care – he just wanted to get some sleep. He smiled at her as she opened the door. 'Fine by me,' he replied in a deadbeat manner.

The apartment was opulent; a modest entrance hall gave way to a spacious sitting room, with windows overlooking the Thames below and the Millennium Wheel down the river to the right. To one side of the sitting room was a door leading into a spacious bedroom containing the father of all king-size beds and a large en suite bathroom.

They were travelling light; they didn't even have a toothbrush between them.

Kate went to explore the bedroom and bathroom and came back proudly clutching a sumptuous white towelling robe in one hand and a toothbrush in the other.

'What more could a girl want?' she asked rhetorically, eyes shining.

Where she'd got her second wind from, Rafi didn't know. He was desperate to just crash out. 'I'm ready to drop; let's toss for who's going to use the bathroom first,' he suggested.

'No need to do that,' replied Kate, 'Women and children first. I have already got the water running. In the meantime, will you order something to eat?'

Rafi looked at her. 'I'm too tired for food; can we see what's in the bar?'

Unlike other hotel rooms he had been in, this hotel apartment had its own bar area. He opened the refrigerator. 'What would you like? Gin and tonic, fresh orange juice, wine, smart mineral water – you name it we've got it.'

'Orange juice and a large gin and tonic, please.'

'There's some great-looking chocolate and the nuts look good. How about cashew nuts, crisps or chocolates with your drink?' asked Rafi.

'Anything. It all sounds great.'

Rafi dug around in the refrigerator, carefully choose a few items and handed them to Kate, before taking a few for himself to a nearby armchair.

Kate was smiling. 'Thank you for all you've done. I hope that when this is over we'll be able to get to know one another better.'

'What was that about?' pondered Rafi. He was too tired to consider whether it was an offer of friendship or something more.

Kate took her two drinks, placed them by the side of the bath. 'I won't be long. If I fall asleep in the bath, feel free to wake me. In the meantime, I suggest you make yourself comfortable and have a stiff drink or two.'

Rafi looked at her. 'You can do the drinking for both of us.'

'How silly of me, I forgot you don't drink.' And with that, she turned and walked off towards the bathroom. As she went, she unclipped her hair and gave her head a shake. A mass of deep auburn hair sprang out.

It was the first time Rafi had seen her with her hair down. He gazed at her. She looked after herself well – her slight frame, though not curvaceous, was nicely proportioned and well toned. Her shoulder-length wavy hair looked soft and would undoubtedly be a stunning feature when washed and brushed. He was too tired to think any further.

The sound of the running water stopped. Soothing splashes washed through the air. Rafi poured himself another large glass of fresh orange juice and looked out of the window. London seemed calm and still.

He mulled over the twist of fate - this part of London had been spared the ravages of the explosion at Stratford. His mind wandered – had the wind been blowing in the opposite direction, it would have covered the City, and for that matter the West End of London, under a deadly blanket of radioactivity. Would the closure of the City of London have stopped the terrorist leaders from cashing in on their profits? Of course not; they would also have positions in Frankfurt and Chicago. His tired brain left it there.

Rafi stood gazing out over the Thames, drinking his orange juice and enjoying the tranquillity. He heard the bathroom door open and turned to see Kate emerge, snuggled into a soft white bathrobe, clutching an empty glass in her hand.

Her face lit up as she smiled. 'This is my idea of heaven.'

Rafi looked at her approvingly and replied, 'Mine too. Would you like a top-up?'

'I think I can do that, thanks. You can have that bath you deserve – and undoubtedly need,' she said, holding her fingers over her nose like a clothes peg.

As he walked past her to the bathroom he smelt a sweet orange aroma. The bathroom had the same smell, which now reminded him of her. He smiled as he discarded his scruffy clothing. He was looking forward to getting back into his normal clothes.

The hot, gushing water of the shower was wonderful. He eventually got out and, after wrapping himself in a luxurious towel, walked back into the bedroom. The room was peaceful; Kate had turned off all the lights except for the small lamp on his side of the large bed. She was sound asleep, her damp hair framing her face against the background of the white duvet and pillow. Lying on the floor was her bathrobe. She stirred slightly; she looked beautiful – stunningly beautiful. She snuggled further under the duvet and continued her well-earned sleep.

Rafi slipped off the bath towel, slid under the crisp duvet and turned the light out. As he drifted off to sleep, he reflected that something good had come out of the worst week of his life.

*

Rafi awoke to find the curtains half open and noticed that it was dark outside. Kate was sitting at a small table by the window in her bathrobe; her mass of hair was neatly brushed and resting strikingly on her shoulders. He looked carefully at her face and the splashes of freckles on her cheeks and across her nose – she had an innocent schoolgirl-like quality. He liked what he saw.

'Late lunch is served,' she said. 'Hope you don't mind but I've taken the liberty of ordering a selection of things: a couple of starters – smoked salmon or pâté – followed by medium-rare steak or Dover sole, a couple of delicious-looking gooey chocolate puddings... and loads of fruit.'

Rafi opted for the pâté and the fish, letting Kate finish off both chocolate puddings.

Whilst they were eating, Kate thought about the person sitting opposite her. What was it about Rafi that made her want to be in his company? His inner strength? Perhaps they were soulmates? She hoped so. She worried that she had shown her feelings to him too soon.

'I hope that was alright changing suites,' said Kate, coyly.

Rafi looked across at her lovely face. He'd been working alongside her for almost four days and hadn't fully taken in how beautiful she was. 'I'm glad you did,' he replied. 'If I wasn't more enthusiastic earlier, I apologize. I didn't know whether I was coming or going with tiredness.'

She smiled and poured a cup of steaming coffee. They sat there, sipping their coffee and enjoying each other's company.

When they had finished their late lunch Kate got up and, looking at Rafi, said, 'I have some bad news. Well, not that bad... Our time here is running short. We have got forty-five minutes before we have to leave. But before we go, I think we should get that off,' she said, pointing at him.

Rafi raised his eyebrows.

She gave a beaming smile. 'No, not what you are thinking. I meant that dirty Elastoplast bandage. Whilst you were asleep, I asked the manager for a medical kit.' She opened the first aid box and pulled out a pair of scissors and a roll of bandage. She leant forward, took his hand and carefully cut the plaster from top to bottom. She finished and moved closer.

'I fear this is going to hurt. If it's anything like strip wax, it'll hurt like hell – sorry.'

She pulled the plaster with a sharp, prolonged tug. There was a quiet ripping noise as it pulled the hairs out of his arm. This was accompanied by the sharp hissing sound of Rafi sucking air in through his teeth.

As Kate moved back, her bathrobe fell open across her chest, revealing a lovely and distracting sight. 'That wasn't too bad, was it?' she said.

'It was an eye-opener,' he replied.

'I'm here to please,' she quipped and then realised why Rafi had gone quiet and was staring at her. She leant across and kissed him delicately on the cheek.

'All in good time; unfortunately, we have things to do.'

'Queen and Country and all that,' he mocked.

'You've got it in one,' she grinned, pulling her bathrobe closed. 'Let's get you bandaged up.'

Tenderly she strapped his wrist. 'Your bruises still look very impressive. Are they painful?'

He smiled at her. 'In comparison to your strip wax treatment, not really!'

'Time to get dressed,' said Kate. 'The manager has sent up a selection of clothes for both of us. They've hung them in the wardrobe. Have a look and see what you think. I've got a bit of tidying up to do in the bathroom.'

They dressed in casual but smart new clothes. Rafi chose a white shirt, charcoal grey flannel trousers, dark blue blazer, black moccasin shoes and in case he had reason to venture outside, a smart blue wool overcoat. Kate opted for a light camel-coloured trouser suit, a creamy-white open neck shirt and a dark brown wool and cashmere overcoat. She looked stunning.

'I hope your credit card is going to be working soon; there's no way that mine will withstand the damage that I've run up since we got here!' said Kate.

'Don't worry; we can sort it out mañana.'

'It must be nice to be rich.'

'Yes, it must be. Unfortunately, this isn't how I normally live,' replied Rafi.

'Well, I'll want to be with you when it is like this.' Kate chuckled and winked playfully at him.

Rafi looked down at the clean dressing on his wrist. 'And whenever I need cheering up all I have got to do is look at this bandage and think of you!'

He pointed to the old hat and stripy scarf draped over the back of the sofa. 'Will I need these?'

'How about these instead?' asked Kate, pointing to a new dark blue scarf and trilby hat. 'You know, we really must get going. Jeremy and John are waiting for us downstairs.'

Sure enough, a large unmarked police car was waiting outside.

*

They sped through an eerily quiet London.

'The curfew is still in place,' John told them. 'Thankfully, almost everyone is keeping their heads down. The people from COBRA and the PM have been on the radio and television to try to stop people panicking and advising them to stay indoors.'

John turned left at Trafalgar Square, into Whitehall. 'I hope you're going to be on your best behaviour,' he said as he turned right and stopped the car in front of the tall metal gates guarding Downing Street. John showed his police warrant card to the armed guards standing at the gate and they were let through.

'We've been asked to act as your minders,' said Jeremy. 'Heaven only knows how long it'll be before you get to see the Prime Minister. It must be chaos in there.'

*

John stopped the car in front of Number 10. Kate and Rafi were ushered in.

To Rafi's utter surprise, they were met in the front entrance hall by the Prime Minister, with outstretched hands. He then led them through to the inner sanctum of Number 10. As they started walking he looked at Rafi. 'I like the disguise,' he said with a grin.

231

'You'd make a good gangster.'

The PM stopped. 'I am afraid that there is a lot going on at the moment. Kate, I need Rafi for ten minutes or so. Would you and your colleagues see how things are progressing downstairs in the COBRA meeting?'

Kate nodded.

'Mr Palmer here will show you the way.'

A dark-suited young man beckoned Kate to follow him.

'Rafi, I've arranged for you and your economics team to meet here at 7.30 to discuss your concerns. We'll be joined by the Chancellor of the Exchequer and a couple of people from his team.'

The PM strode on, with Rafi following close behind. They arrived at his study door. The PM beckoned him into the room. They'd been in there for only a few seconds when the phone rang.

The Prime Minister took the call. 'My apologies, Rafi. I have the Mayor of London on the line. I am likely to be some while, perhaps you could find DI Adams and catch up on what's been happening with the terrorists? If you go next door, I'll arrange for someone to show you the way.'

Rafi walked into the empty, adjoining office. He looked around, plumped for the comfiest chair, sat down and waited.

A few minutes later, a smart, but soberly dressed woman appeared.

'Excuse me for keeping you,' she said with a hesitant smile. 'I've been asked to show you the way to COBRA. Please come this way.'

'Thank you,' said Rafi, getting up a little unsteadily.

They passed through a further set of security checks and descended some sets of stairs.

Rafi looked at the woman he was following. Her clean-cut, formal white shirt and black skirt were unremarkable, however her neat blonde hair was eye-catchingly beautiful.

When they arrived at the subterranean briefing room, the woman turned. 'I will come and get you when the PM is free.' Her businesslike face was transformed by a fleeting smile.

Rafi saw Kate chatting to a swarthy-looking man and went over to join them.

'I was updating Kate on our progress,' he told Rafi. 'We are

232

making headway, but it's a massive large task. No doubt you want to know about the escaping terrorists? But first let me introduce myself. I'm Craig – MI5.'

The young officer looked the opposite of Jeremy: short, thickset, dark haired – and almost uncouth.

'*Golden Sundancer* is currently going like a bat out of hell round the Western Isles of Scotland, averaging almost forty knots. Her rendezvous with *Northern Rose*, north-west of Pentland Firth, went without a hitch. We now expect her to rendezvous with *Highland Belle* west of Stanton Banks, just before dawn tomorrow. *Rosemarie* is heading for the Straights of Dover. We estimate she'll rendezvous with *Golden Sundancer* south of the Isles of Scilly, in the early hours of Sunday morning. The question is, are we right in believing that *Golden Sundancer* will head for Morocco?'

He fell silent for a moment, as if collecting his thoughts. 'The Navy has checked what vessels it has between the Scilly Isles and Morocco. At Gibraltar, they have *HMS Scimitar* and *Sabre*: two sixteen-metre fast patrol boats, capable of thirty knots plus. There is nothing else in the vicinity which can get close to matching *Golden Sundancer's* speed. I understand that the boffins at the Admiralty are currently hatching a plan.'

Craig paused. 'Jameel is still in Marrakech where we've an agent keeping an eye on him. The sheikh's private jet is scheduled to land there at 12.45 p.m. on Monday. He's hired a helicopter for the afternoon and his plane is scheduled to take off again at 22.30 that evening.'

Kate nodded.

He continued. 'We've looked at all the ports within range of the helicopter from Marrakech, in the time available. The Moroccan Atlantic coastline is long, but thankfully there are only three ports that we believe fit the situation: Safi, Mohammedia and Casablanca. For a number of reasons, Safi is the one our anoraks confidently predict they will use.'

'So, how are you going to capture them?' asked Kate.

'The Prime Minister wants them captured alive,' answered Craig. 'The bosses believe that there's a better chance of success if we seize them when they are all in one place. The plan is to have a vessel, with SBS personnel aboard, waiting for *Golden Sundancer* in Safi. They then overpower the terrorists and whisk them away to a waiting submarine.'

'So quite simple, really,' said Kate, with a grin.

'Why aren't they using the SAS?' Rafi queried.

'The special boat service, or SBS,' replied Craig, 'Is the Royal Navy's special forces unit – it is every bit as formidable as the SAS, but is, in essence, the aquatic version. In many quarters they're rated more highly! Things will have to be done quickly, which could complicate matters. The terrorists and their masters will probably be in our grasp for only a few hours. At *Golden Sundancer's* present rate of progress, she'll arrive in Safi early Monday afternoon, which gives us only twenty-four hours to prepare an appropriate welcoming party.'

'How's the plan going?' Rafi asked.

'Hold on a moment,' said Craig, 'Let me make a call.' Several minutes later he put down the phone. 'It seems we've arranged for two resourceful female Naval Lieutenants – Anna Gregson and Janet Steiner – to be flown to Gibraltar. They're on their way as we speak, together with some special kit for our SBS friends.'

Craig continued explaining the plan. 'Obviously, we don't want to scare the terrorists' leaders away. A fast motorboat moored in Gibraltar has been identified. We ruled out *HMS Sabre*, as there's no way we can disguise her military parentage – one sight of her and the terrorists would run a mile. Furthermore, the Moroccan Authorities wouldn't take kindly to the Royal Navy operating within their territorial waters. So we're renting, or purchasing if we cock up, a Sunseeker Manhattan 56 called *Puddle Jumper*. She has a top speed of some thirty-two knots and is fast enough to get down there before them. *Puddle Jumper* is being given the once-over and provisioned as we speak.'

Craig paused, as if searching for an elusive word. 'The awkward bit is that we have a hiccup or two on the resources front. SBS's M Squadron, which deals with maritime counterterrorism, should be on standby. They're, er… rather busy at the moment. They're in action in the Middle East. The Air Chief Marshal has secured the services of two of their team who are cutting short their current operation and will be joining those on board *Puddle Jumper*. We had hoped for more, but so be it. The special forces command centre is sending SAS soldiers to Marrakech Airport and to the ports of Safi, Mohammedia and Casablanca. The last

234

two, just in case our intelligence has ballsed up.'

A grin spread across Craig's face, his white teeth framed by his tanned face. 'A bright spark at the Admiralty has dreamt up a cunning plan. Our two naval officers and the two SBS operatives on board *Puddle Jumper* are to be joined by two retired civilians.'

Kate tilted her head to one side in surprise.

'Yes, I know you must think that they're off their rockers. The Navy has trawled through their records for recently retired naval officers who had seen active service and who could go along as parent figures to keep up the illusion that those on board are civilians. The retirement age for many very able officers is early fifties.' Craig grinned. 'They couldn't believe their luck. They found a retired couple who are both still fleet of foot. Adrian Bell is a highly experienced commander and a master navigator, with considerable experience of active service. As a youngster, Adrian commanded one of the three *HMS Scimitar* class, fast training craft during the Cod War in the North Atlantic. They were at that time the fastest wet hulled military craft in the world. And it gets better: the commander's wife, Helen, also has twenty years' experience in the Navy. So we have two capable "parents" to look after our boisterous rabble. The two naval officers will become their *daughters* and the two SBS operatives will be the *boyfriends.*

'Not surprisingly,' continued Craig, 'The husband and wife were a bit taken aback to be volunteered. They were at home in their garage, varnishing their dinghy. They're currently packing their sailing gear. Two, twin-seat Harrier jump jets are waiting for them at the nearby Thorney Island army facility and will fly them to Gibraltar.

'The two *parents*, as I call them, together with the two naval officers, will arrive in Gibraltar in the next couple of hours. *Puddle Jumper* should put to sea an hour after they land. The SBS officers will rendezvous with her in the next twelve hours. I understand a wet jump is planned.'

Craig paused. 'As I was saying, the terrorists' boat, at her current rate of progress, should make Safi by Monday early afternoon. Our team on *Puddle Jumper* plan to arrive under the cover of darkness, late on Sunday night.'

A frown fell across Craig's face. 'Getting them away is also proving difficult. It is rather embarrassing as a world power, but we seem to have all our submarines in, er… The wrong places or in dry dock for repairs, and the four new Astute class submarines are still not in service. The cutback in numbers, without the new replacements, has left the Navy decidedly short. The earliest any submarine can be off the coast of Safi is 15.40 on Monday. However, those at the Admiralty are a tad uncomfortable – well, that's an understatement – as the only one that could get there in time is one of their Trident Class nuclear submarines with all her nuclear missiles on board. It seems that the prospect of having our terrorists on board her is beyond the Admiralty's comfort zone. Out of the frying pan and into the fire! However, they have been won over by the PM. She's broken off from her current manoeuvres and is sailing at full speed to be on station Monday afternoon.'

Rafi was about to ask a couple of questions, when his guide appeared at the door and beckoned him over.

'The Prime Minister will see you now,' said the secretary.

Rafi was ushered up the rather claustrophobic stairs to the PM's meeting room. He wondered how Aidan and his team of five were getting on, and whether the PM and his new Chancellor of the Exchequer would tackle the impending financial problems head-on. His thoughts moved on to the huge risks now faced by the markets.

Rafi stopped outside the meeting room – he felt apprehensive. What if they'd reached mental overload and wanted none of his bad news? The future would be bleak.

As he entered, he was greeted by the sight of fourteen tired and slightly dishevelled-looking people. Aidan and his team were sitting along one side of the table. There was an unoccupied chair next to Aidan, to which Rafi was shown.

The PM stood up to greet Rafi. He looked pale and in need of some well-earned rest. On one side he was flanked by his private secretary, the head of press communications and the Defence Secretary, and on the other side, by his Chancellor and three people from his Treasury team. The PM did the introductions.

Rafi, meanwhile, looked around the shiny, dark wooden table. There was a grim feel to the room. His eyes caught those of Saara's. They exchanged brief smiles – she seemed at ease in the exalted company. Aidan and his team's faces looked strained, as if they were expecting a hard time.

The PM called the meeting to order. He was forthright. 'Gentlemen, we are here at the request of Mr Khan. Yesterday he asked me to consider the risk our weakened financial markets are now facing and, if we agree with his predictions, he has asked that we listen to a strategy to stop our markets going into meltdown when they reopen on Tuesday. Mr Khan advises me that the main item on the terrorists' agenda is not the physical disruption of our energy supplies, but rather financial chaos.'

The PM turned to his Chancellor. 'I appreciate that it is only a few months since you took up your post. The final decision as to how we proceed rests with you. I shall back your judgement and the proposals you put before the Cabinet tomorrow, in advance of our statements to the Commons on Monday afternoon.'

The PM paused. 'Before we start, I must reiterate that we are here as a group seeking to work as a team.' He paused. 'If Mr Khan is correct, the challenge that faces us is gargantuan. He has made it clear to me that the terrorists expect us to hesitate and to drag our feet before we react. If we do, Mr Khan has in no uncertain terms advised me that we may not regain control of the financial markets. We have to consider whether Mr Khan's hypothesis has substance. We must not shirk our duty, even if it means that we get bad press for taking a robust approach when others are unable to see the dangers facing us.'

The mood of the room was sombre. 'Before we start,' said the PM, 'I should like to thank Mr Khan for his foresightedness and Mr Gilchrist and his team from the City and academia for their Herculean efforts. You have been able to focus on the financial problems at hand without being overwhelmed by the practical and human issues that we face as politicians. Gentlemen, the stakes are high.' He turned to his Chancellor. 'Is there anything you would like to add before we listen to Aidan and his team's concerns and recommendations?'

'Not at the moment, thank you.'

'What then, please, are your proposals?'

Aidan spent a few moments detailing the expertise of those sitting next to him and turned to Rafi's former boss, Donald, to make the presentation.

Donald stood up and walked over to a whiteboard which had been set up at the end of the room. He was confident, without being arrogant.

'Our objective, gentlemen, in these uncertain times, is to provide the financial markets with a sense of certainty and confidence. We are facing two problems. Firstly, the terrorists have created a black hole in the Government's finances and, secondly, Aidan has proved beyond all doubt that if the markets fall sharply when they reopen, the terrorists will make massive profits from their investments in derivatives. When I say massive, I mean tens of billions of pounds... And this will depress the markets even further.'

Donald paused and turned to the Chancellor. 'Put this on top of the vast sums that the Government has to raise for the foreseeable future to balance its books, add in widespread blackouts, a stock market crash and large scale disruption to the UK economy... Quite simply, international investors will go elsewhere in their droves. Already there has been a significant shift in sentiment, as reflected by the currency markets where sterling is taking a hammering... To put it bluntly, I have major doubts as to whether the extra money required post Stratford can be borrowed in the markets. This would mean going cap in hand to the International Monetary Fund, and even they might not have sufficient funds to solve our problems...'

*

Night was closing in on *Golden Sundancer*. She was making good headway against the swell. The captain, Basel Talal and Sergy Kowshaya, the Cruden Bay terrorist, were on the bridge. They were in an upbeat mood.

Sergy looked out of the window at the spray coming over the bow. 'We make port by midday Monday, yes?'

The captain glanced across at his charts. 'Probably around 14:00 hours – later if the weather gets bad.'

Sergy shifted his eyes across at Basel. 'The Sheikh will be there to thank us – personally?'

'Yes, of course and Jameel Furud will be there also.' Basel sensed that Sergy was uneasy. 'You did well at Cruden Bay.'

'But it was Dakka who hit the jack pot.'

'Cruden Bay was simply brilliant... And you are now rich

238

beyond your dreams,' said Basel soothingly. 'What are you going to do with your money?'

'I am my own keeper. My family were all killed by the Russians… I hope to buy a big olive grove and find a nice woman.'

Basel smiled. 'For someone with so much money - you don't look very happy?'

'Yes it is true, I feel sad… I'd be a €1 million richer if the bastard hadn't sold us dud mortars… The damn shells wouldn't go off - St Fergus should have been destroyed, just like Cruden Bay,' replied Sergy. He'd had enough of the talking and went back to gazing out of the window at the waves and the spray.

*

Back at Number 10, the meeting with the Prime Minister was winding down. Donald had finished his presentation. Aidan got up and went over to a couple of large boxes in the corner of the room from which he pulled out smartly bound reports. 'Gentlemen,' he said as he handed them across the table, 'You'll find in these the numbers behind our proposals.'

'I am grateful to you for your incisive work,' said the PM. 'Any questions?'

'Just one,' replied the Chancellor. 'Timing is going to be tight. You and I will be making our announcements to the House on Monday afternoon. Am I right in assuming that we don't want the terrorists to know that we're onto their conspiracy, whilst they're still at large?'

'Yes,' replied the PM.

'So, the financial rescue plan shouldn't be revealed until the terrorists have been captured, which is expected to be… When?'

'Around 3.30 p.m. on Monday afternoon,' answered the PM.

'So that means we must speak for at least ninety minutes before being able to make any concrete announcements?' queried the Chancellor.

'Possibly longer, if the capture doesn't go to plan,' replied the PM.

The Chancellor looked thoughtfully at him. 'If you were to set the scene and explain how the Government is tackling the enormous problems associated with Stratford, and what the future holds, then I could run through the financial issues. Would that be OK?'

'Yes, that's what I had in mind,' agreed the PM.

'Then if things are delayed, I shall just have to make sure that I have some other worthy proposals I can talk about, which will use up time,' said the Chancellor with a small frown. 'I have been given a lot to consider. Mr Gilchrist, I am extremely grateful to you and your team for letting me have advance warning of what to anticipate. I hope I can live up to your expectations.' He glanced back at the PM. 'Perhaps I could retire with my team to work on Monday's speech. I will report my proposals to Cabinet tomorrow evening?'

'Yes, please,' replied the PM. 'Is there anything else?'

'I have an observation,' said Rafi. 'If the wind had been blowing in the opposite direction, the City of London would have become the no-go area. I believe the terrorists would have thought of this, so my thinking is that they could have sizeable positions in both the Frankfurt and Chicago derivatives markets. I think we should strongly suggest that they do not open on Monday.'

'Good point,' said the Chancellor. 'Leave that with me.'

The meeting had finished. The PM spoke to Aidan's team. 'Would any of you like to watch Monday's proceedings from the Gallery?'

'If it's alright with you, sir,' Aidan replied, 'we would prefer to watch with a couple of trading screens in front of us in order to see what the other markets make of the speeches.'

Saara spoke up. 'I would like to take up your offer, please. I am ashamed to say that I've never been into the Houses of Parliament. This would make a good first time, I think.'

'Of course.'

'If you'll excuse me,' said the Chancellor. He picked up his papers and, deep in thought, headed for the door, followed by his team.

Aidan hovered by the door. 'How on earth did you manage to get all that documentation together so quickly?' Rafi asked.

'It was a close run thing. We brought in a couple of Donald's team to help with the word processing behind the scenes, plus we did a great deal copying and pasting from existing documents. A couple of large printer/photocopiers were shipped in from my offices and in the end we borrowed the PM's secretarial team for the collation and binding of the documents. I reckon we did quite a good job!' answered Aidan proudly.

'Truly outstanding considering the circumstances,' replied Rafi.

'Would you like to join us for a quick bite to eat?'

Rafi was about to say yes when the PM beckoned him to stay behind with his permanent secretary.

'Unfortunately, it seems I still have a few things to do. Let's get together for lunch soon, though.'

The room emptied leaving just the PM and Rafi. The tense atmosphere that had characterised the previous meeting remained. The PM picked up the phone and Kate was shown in. 'Sorry, I don't have that much time; I have another meeting due to start in five minutes. I wanted to speak to you both. I had considered leaving it until this was all over, but it didn't seem appropriate, given all you've both gone through and done.'

The PM drew breath. 'It's not possible for me to fully express my gratitude. Your foresight has given us the opportunity to come out of this disaster with some vestige of hope for the future.' He had a serious look on his tired face. 'Mr Khan and Inspector Adams, were I to be in a position to grant you a request, what might it be?'

Rafi looked at the Prime Minister and then across to Kate. He sensed that his first wish had been granted. He had found someone with whom he would enjoy spending time; hopefully a great deal of time. Rafi returned his gaze to the Prime Minister. 'I'm not certain whether I need anything, thank you, sir.'

'But come now, there must be something?'

Rafi thought for no more than a few seconds. It dawned on him that here was an opportunity of a lifetime – he could do something that would have made his hard-working parents proud. Rafi took a deep breath. 'Well, here goes. Would it be possible for there to be a Royal Garden Party at Buckingham Palace, where those invited are drawn from Muslim communities throughout the United Kingdom? Not the movers and shakers, but rather the quiet, hard-working, first-class citizens who help to make this country tick. For too long they've been unappreciated and disenfranchised.'

The Prime Minister thought for a moment. 'Yes, I like your

idea of acknowledging those who quietly get things done.'

'Also, it would be much appreciated if my flat could be given a bit of a tidy up!'

The PM smiled and nodded. 'Consider it done.'

'Detective Inspector, is there anything we might do for you?'

Kate thought for a moment. 'Could I have a couple of weeks' leave starting as of Monday evening? I'd like to recharge my batteries and get to know someone I've recently met,' she said with a grin.

Rafi felt a warm glow building inside him. He looked across at Kate approvingly. The Prime Minister nodded. 'I suggest that you speak to your boss and say that I asked you to spend a couple of weeks overseeing Mr Khan's recuperation, following the un-fortunate events at Paddington Green.'

'Sir, there is one other thing,' said Rafi. 'It's more a comment rather than a wish. I'm not a vindictive man; however, in my experience as a fund manager, the vast majority of people in positions of influence get there because they're good at their job or, in a few cases, because no one else is willing to pick up a poisoned chalice.'

Rafi put his hand into his pocket and pulled out a tape. 'I have here a recording of the interview between a junior minister and me. He was sent with a press entourage by the stand-in Home Secretary to interview me minutes before the Stratford missiles were launched – no doubt to use his actions as spin to deflect what was going on elsewhere. This is the original tape. There are no copies.'

Rafi hesitated. 'Sir, the contents are, I believe, political dynamite. On second thoughts, Prime Minister, you would be better off *not* listening to it. Hypothetically speaking, if it transpired that the Stratford missile attack could have been averted, had it not been for an obsession with spin which fatally delayed key information getting through, it would damage politicians and politics irreparably. And currently, there's more than enough to sort out; starting a blame game would only be counterproductive.'

Rafi hesitated again. 'As I see it, a growing number of politicians spout forth initiatives and policies, but have little or no idea of change management and the workings of the real world. They've become obsessed with spin and looking good in the eyes of the media and have forgotten about implementation.'

The PM looked tense.

'What I ask,' continued Rafi, 'Is that whoever listens to this tape should consider whether or not spin interfered with the course of events. For example, without the obsession with spin, would the train have been stopped sooner and thus been outside the terrorist's line of sight? If they agree that the Stratford attack could have been prevented, I ask you to set up a task force to report on how the Civil Service can change the way *they* and *politicians* deal with the media, such that the current practice of spinning, giving misleading information and part-truths, becomes a thing of the past. As I see it, at the moment too many senior politicians have little more than political research and think tank experience, and have become obsessed with perception rather than practicalities and substance.'

The Prime Minister looked at Rafi. 'Are you telling me that this tape is evidence that spin by a member of my Government prevented you from stopping a terrorist attack? And that this is the only copy?'

Rafi nodded and said, 'I couldn't possibly comment Prime Minister, but I can assure you, you do not want to hear the contents of the tape.'

The PM thought for a few moments. 'I shall do as you request and if the head of the Civil Service confirms that the contents are as inflammatory as you say, I shall indeed ask him to undertake a full root and branch review of how politicians, their spokespeople and the Civil Service deal with the media.' He stopped, deep in thought, for what seemed like a long time, but was probably no more than a few seconds.

'I will go further; if spin has corrupted the system, I will introduce an independent verification process.' The PM paused. 'It will be overseen by a select committee, whose members will be chosen by a secret ballot of MPs. This committee will be tasked with bringing into the open blatant spin, barefaced lies, half-truths and white lies. Offenders will henceforth have to face this committee and if they are not cleared of wrongdoing, they will have to make a public apology and correct their errors on the record. Furthermore, their apologies will be added alongside the relevant sections of Hansard requiring amendment or clarification. The committee will have teeth to investigate and bring people to account; these powers will include the ability to suspend members of both Houses and, in extremis, debar the individual from public service.' The PM went silent again for a moment, then went on, 'On reflection, I am prepared to go further and widen the powers of the committee to include all public officials who blatantly deceive in order to further their or their party's own ends.'

'Thank you Prime Minister.'

The door to the office opened. 'Your next meeting is ready to start, Prime Minister.'

'Thank you, SJ.'

The PM looked at Kate and Rafi, and held out his hand. 'It's time for me to be elsewhere. Thank you both again for your help.'

They shook his hand and left.

*

Back in the hotel suite, Kate put her arms around Rafi's neck, her warm brown eyes gazing into his.

'What now?' asked Rafi.

'Silly question! How about we get some food – I'm starving – and turn in for an early night?' she said with a wicked glint in her eyes.

'Great idea. What would you like to eat? The room service menu is impressive.'

'I'm glad you're paying,' she said with a smile. 'I could eat out for ages on some of these prices.'

'We deserve some pampering, or at least I thought your orders were: lots of TLC.'

'That,' said Kate, 'could be on the menu for dessert.'

They settled for a light supper. After the meal they snuggled up on the large sofa, enjoying the tranquillity.

'Would you mind if we paid an impromptu visit to my brother and my parents on Sunday?' asked Kate. 'I think they need a bit of reassuring after the past few days.'

'Sounds like a great idea. Are you sure we are not wanted elsewhere, though?'

'I've cleared it with David - thanks.'

'Where exactly do they live?'

'Just outside Colchester.'

'Sounds like an excellent idea.'

The conversation moved on to what they could do during Kate's two-week break, which was scheduled to start as soon as the terrorist leaders were in captivity.

'I don't feel like going far away,' Kate said.

'Before this all happened, I'd booked a suite at a hotel in Cornwall for ten days. What do you think?' enquired Rafi.

'Is it a very smart hotel?'

'It's family run – by all accounts it's comfortable and has good food,' said Rafi.

'But what about the beds?' queried Kate.

'They should be fine,' he replied.

'They?' asked Kate sleepily. 'Would it be too forward if we continue to share a bed?' Kate planted a kiss on his cheek and snuggled up.

Rafi smiled. The prospect of having Kate as a girlfriend appealed. 'I'd like that very much... I'll ring the hotel in the morning.' He didn't get a reply; Kate was sound asleep in his arms.

*

The next morning, Rafi awoke to the buzzing sound of the bedside phone. He reached over and picked it up. His watch showed the time to be 11.45 a.m. He recognised the voice at the other end but could not initially place who it was. The quietly spoken woman introduced herself as SJ from Number 10.

'Could you come in to see the Prime Minister again, please? I've arranged for a car to collect you. It'll be waiting outside your hotel in thirty minutes.'

'No problem,' Rafi replied, replacing the phone and sitting up.

Rays of daylight crept around the edges of the curtains, casting a soft warm light around the room. Kate's side of the bed was empty. Rafi lingered for a moment realising that he missed her company. Then he reluctantly slipped out of bed, aware of his bruises, and headed for the sitting room. On the side table was a note: *Thought you needed a lie-in. Sorry not to be here - have things to do at work. See you later. Love, Kate.*

*

Forty five minutes later Rafi was walking in to 10 Downing

Street. He was met at the door by a smiling SJ. She looked at him and felt she couldn't fully work him out. His mugshot had been plastered over the papers as *public enemy number one*, but he was one of the good guys. He'd had a rough time by the looks of things, but his eyes told another story. They were alive and bright.

'The PM sends his apologies, his meetings are running late. While he is busy, he thought you would like to be brought up to speed on the terrorists' whereabouts. But first, how about a cup of coffee?' asked SJ.

Rafi nodded, and followed her to a coffee machine.

'This is how the other half lives,' remarked SJ apologetically.

'Home from home, where I worked was open plan and my desk was practically on top of all the others.' Rafi paused as he realised he had used the past tense. He sensed that that part of his life was over.

'How about a nice biscuit or two,' she said bending over just in front of him to open a cupboard door.

To Rafi's surprise, he found himself wondering how such a meticulously dressed secretary could suddenly look provocative.

'If you would like to follow me... I thought we could borrow one of the meeting rooms.'

As Rafi followed SJ, a stray thought flitted through his mind – what would she look like with her hair down and in casual clothes? Undoubtedly she'd be very beautiful. His musings were halted as they reached their destination, a small meeting room, where SJ beckoned him to sit opposite her. She gave him a radiant smile.

Rafi was suddenly aware that he was staring 'Sorry I was miles away...' He felt uneasy and wondered what SJ would say next.

'The PM tells me you are a remarkable man, and that you helped avert a number of other major disasters.' SJ paused and smiled. Her soft blue eyes locked on to his. 'The PM asked me to look after you...'

Rafi searched for a good reply but his mind was focused on SJ's beautiful face. 'That's good,' he replied, weakly returning her smile. He wondered if SJ realised how uncomfortable he felt. He took a sip of his coffee and looked down at his bruised and swollen wrist, partly to avoid making eye contact.

'Is it as painful as it looks?' asked SJ sympathetically.

'Not really, I've sort of got used to it now, thanks to the painkillers,' replied Rafi. He sensed his brain was beginning to work again, and decided to take the initiative. 'Do you like working at Number 10?'

'Yes, I do.'

'The hours must be very long at times…' Rafi took a mouthful of his coffee.

'Yes, and the working weekends and late nights can wreak havoc with the social diary.'

Rafi looked down at her left hand - there was no ring. 'Your boyfriend must be very understanding…'

Seeing that Rafi had relaxed, she smiled. 'That's a nice thought. If only one could find the right man. I seem to attract all the wrong ones.' Someone just like you would suit me perfectly, she thought to herself.

He smiled and looked into her lovely blue eyes… 'Don't worry, your luck will turn when you least expect it.'

'Thank you,' replied SJ.

'I am serious,' added Rafi. 'A week ago I was on my own and then through the most bizarre circumstances I met Detective Inspector Kate Adams… You have everything going for you… the right man will come in to your life.'

SJ looked carefully at Rafi. In the space of a few minutes he had turned the tables on her. He was now making her feel uncomfortable… That Kate Adams was a very fortunate woman… It would be nice to swap places with her. 'How precisely did you meet Kate?' asked SJ.

'I was in the cells at Paddington Green police station and she came to interview me…'

'So you reckon I should get myself locked up… I'm not certain if I'd have a job to go come back to though!'

Rafi laughed. 'The mind boggles… The prospect of you ending up in prison is difficult to picture. I'd opt for something far less extreme. Like Kate you are on the side of the good, so you won't have to go looking for trouble.'

'But it might be fun,' said SJ with a disarming grin. 'Perhaps when this is all over, you and Kate could give me some pointers?' Before Rafi had a chance to reply, she looked at her watch. 'You should be elsewhere… It's time for you to pay COBRA a visit.'

Rafi finished his coffee. 'I'm ready when you are.' He hesitated, and not knowing where the thought came from, blurted out, 'It seems to me that you and Kate are very alike… under the surface that is.' He fell silent, suddenly feeling embarrassed to go any further with his line of thinking.

SJ felt a strange feeling come across her. So he really did like her… with a bit of planning on her part she would arrange for their paths to cross again. She stood up. 'Come on, you really should be elsewhere.'

A few minutes later they arrived at the door to the COBRA meeting room. As Rafi walked in he sensed a new feel to the room. The urgency and horror of the day before had given way to a businesslike atmosphere. Inside the door was a face he'd got to know very well over the past few days. Jeremy greeted him warmly and they fell into conversation.

SJ smiled and glanced at her watch. 'I'll come and get you in seventy minutes,' she turned and left.

*

Jeremy looked at Rafi. 'Where would you like me to start in bringing you up to date?'

'*Golden Sundancer* and the trawlers, please.'

'It's all go at sea and in the air there are two Nimrods tracking them. The Great Yarmouth trawler left port at 16.00 hours on Friday and, as you know, turned south. She entered the Straights of Dover around 22.30 yesterday and is currently heading towards the Lizard Point off Cornwall. On board is Dakka Dudayev, the Stratford bomber; a real hard case.

'I'd say so!'

'The trawler from Peterhead offloaded Rudnik Miromov, the Cruden Bay terrorist, onto *Golden Sundancer* north-west of the Pentland Firth at 5 p.m. yesterday evening. *Golden Sundancer* then headed at speed around the Western Isles. The Troon trawler rendezvoused with her at 03.00 south-west of Stanton Banks where she picked up Talal's number two, Alistair Hartnell, and the recruiter of the suicide bombers, Kim Chindriani. Since then *Golden Sundancer* has been flying down the west coast of Ireland at a very impressive 40-46 knots. She's currently just west of Bantry Bay. Our calculations point to the Great Yarmouth trawler, *Rosemarie*, and *Golden Sundancer* rendezvousing at 19.00 hours this evening south-west of the Isles of Scilly. From there, we believe that they'll head for Morocco and the port of Safi.'

'What's Maryam up to?'

'She's carrying on as usual in Luxembourg, playing at being a real socialite. Wining and dining seem to be her middle names. The commissioner is arranging a visit to Luxembourg to tie in with the capture of the other terrorists on Monday afternoon,' Jeremy drew breath and pointed to the screens around the room. 'On the home front, the army's pyrotechnics continue to be impressive: there's still a good mix of dark smoke, explosions and flames from Cruden Bay, Aldermaston, Hartlepool and Heysham. Even though numerous announcements have been made that no radioactivity has been released and the terrorists missed their nuclear targets, the TV crews love it. I feel sorry for the local residents, but at least it's in a good cause.'

'How's it progressing at Stratford?' asked Rafi.

'Basically, it is a huge mess and it is still taking up masses of resources. Thankfully, *Operation Counterpane* has got most people away from the exclusion zone relatively quickly. The genius part was getting others to look after them. It's worked magically. The reaction of the provincial cities, and in particular the rural communities, has been beyond anyone's expectations. Trains have been running constantly from the London terminals since Friday morning, transporting the refugees to their destinations. Fleets of coaches have poured into London from across the country, with offers of accommodation and homes for those who got on board. The major retailers have been brilliant. In some instances people have been getting on their coaches with a blanket, a duvet or just a towel or coat around them. En route to their destination, stop-offs to department stores have been arranged to fully clothe and re-equip the travellers. The Dunkirk spirit has been unbelievable. Only a small minority of those dispossessed have caused trouble; the vast, vast majority have been grateful for the help and to be evacuated,' said Jeremy.

'What are the radiation levels like?' Rafi enquired, concerned.

'The experts got their initial calculations for the exclusion zone spot on. The Royal Engineers, with the help of specialist building contractors, have completed the demarcation and the clearing of the perimeter of the exclusion zone and I understand that plans are afoot for work to start tomorrow on the foundations for the perimeter wall. There have been attempts at looting and to get items that are now, of course, radioactive out of the exclusion zone, but the army patrols have been up to the task and have clamped down firmly on such activities. There are 3,000 battle-hardened troops with experience of Iraq and Afghanistan policing the perimeter – next to nothing has got out.'

Jeremy paused. 'The scientists have put in place plans to counter the problems of the leaching of the radioactive materials into the water table. Fingers crossed they'll get it right, or else the City of London and Docklands will be in trouble.'

Jeremy chatted at length, detailing how the exclusion zone was being cleared of people and how the location of London City Airport was a godsend. 'It must be a nightmare for the air traffic controllers, what with all the transport plane movements. Thankfully, only one pilot got the approach wrong and nearly ended up in the water!'

Jeremy hesitated. 'Your interrogator, Andy, phoned me earlier today.'

Rafi involuntarily tensed up.

'Nothing untoward,' reassured Jeremy, sensing Rafi's unease. 'In his investigations he came across an individual with long standing links to your family.' Jeremy passed him a piece of paper with a name and phone number on it. 'I think you might know him?'

Rafi looked in surprise at the name: *Major Charlie Staveley*. Then he smiled. 'Yes, I remember him well. He was my maths teacher at Haileybury.'

'Andy interviewed him about the money he paid first to your grandfather and then to your father. All he would say was, "It was a long time ago... Haileybury had strong connections with the Stepney Boys Club which assisted families in the East End of London – this was my way of helping." Andy reckons that the major was hiding something. You might like to drop by and have a chat with him one of these days.'

'Thanks,' said Rafi, still completely puzzled, 'I'll do that.'

Their conversation returned to Stratford and the terrorists.

Out of the corner of his eye Rafi saw SJ enter the room and

realised that his time with Jeremy was up.

Rafi felt a delicate tap on his shoulder, turned and saw her smiling face just behind him.

'Time to come with me.'

Rafi nodded, said his goodbyes to Jeremy and followed her up to the ground floor of Number 10 and the PM's anteroom.

'You must be beginning to get to know this room rather well,' SJ commented.

'Yes, I can recommend the service – it's excellent,' Rafi grinned. He seemed to have said the right thing. SJ nonchalantly preened her hair, turned with a little wiggle of her hips and left the room. A few minutes later she was back holding a tray with a cup of tea and some chocolate biscuits.

'Thank you.'

She smiled. 'I only try to please. The PM will be ready to see you soon.'

After only a few moments Rafi was shown by SJ into the adjoining room.

The PM got straight to the point. 'Rafi, the head of the Civil Service has listened to your tape,' he began and then paused. 'He says that if I heard its contents I could not, with a clear conscience, deny knowledge of what went on, should it ever get out into the public domain. He confirms that it is political dynamite. It is clear that the Home Office and a number of its ministers took spin to an unprecedented level. Thank you for bringing this matter to our attention.'

Rafi nodded.

'I have commissioned a report on "Media briefings and dissemination of information and data by ministers and public servants". I have asked for proposals from the head of the Civil Service for a select committee to monitor this area. Henceforth, we have to make those who use lies, half-truths and false statistics as tools of their trade openly accountable,' said the PM.

'Thank you,' replied Rafi.

'I was saddened to learn we came within a whisker of averting the Stratford disaster, only to have people, who should have known better, get in the way. By the way, the junior minister in question has resigned his seat. I understand he's going to try his hand at something well away from the public gaze.'

With that the meeting was over and Rafi was ushered into the entrance hall of Number 10 where he found Kate waiting for him.

'Have you had a useful morning? I missed you. Your friend SJ,' she said with a wink, 'phoned. She asked if I could come and collect you. So here I am. There's a car outside and if it's OK with you, our next port of call is Wood Street.'

Rafi nodded; he was becoming accustomed to being at people's beck and call.

'We're going to give John, Jeremy and the team a hand with the logistics for rounding up all those suspected of being on the terrorists' payroll. Actually, that's a bit of a white lie; they want me – and I rather like your company – hence the *we*!' she said with a big grin. 'I reckon I'll get withdrawal symptoms when this is all over,' she paused. 'Will you come with me?' asked Kate, slightly flummoxed by Rafi's deadpan expression, and then added quickly, 'don't worry; if you don't want to tag along I can easily drop you off at the hotel on the way.'

'I'll come… I'd love to. Sorry for being slow, it's just that my thoughts were on what the PM has just told me.'

Rafi leant forward and gave Kate a kiss on the cheek. 'Come on, we can't keep the car waiting. Remember you promised me some TLC and I'm going to enjoy cashing it in… With interest!'

*

They had been in the Ops Room at Wood Street for less than five minutes when Jeremy appeared. 'I thought I might update you. The list of highly paid non-executives on the terrorists' payroll is quite something. Several of the names are dynamite. For example, we have identified *six* Members of Parliament who are implicated.'

Jeremy yawned. 'Sorry… where was I? Yep, we've checked through the bank accounts of the two COBRA members caught with their snouts in the terrorists' trough. It seems that they received their money from our old friend the Gulf Trade Bank. They've been very naïve and stupid. Thankfully, they weren't sophisticated enough to use an offshore account. The bribes went straight into Building Society accounts. Those who *have* been using offshore accounts will be harder to pin down and no doubt they will be the ones really worth catching – *c'est la guerre!*' He smiled and added, 'John and his team have done great work; the fun bit is going to be hauling the culprits in.'

Jeremy paused. 'The bosses at MI5 are gobsmacked by how much John and his team have turned up in such a short time. They have people working around the clock going through bank statements and corroborating the evidence. There's a real buzz down there. One of these days I must show you around!'

'Who do you think ran the UK end of the slush fund?' Kate asked.

'Maryam, we reckon, looked after the money side of things via bank accounts funded by the sheikh,' answered Jeremy. 'At the moment we aren't sure who did the recruiting or the management of those on their payroll.'

'When will the arrests take place?' asked Rafi.

'As soon as the terrorist leaders are in our custody,' replied Jeremy. 'Oh – by the way – you remember that a BlueKnite employee turned a blind eye and let the bomber in at Bishopsgate? Well, it also seems that the controller looking after the nuclear trains only joined a year ago and was also on their payroll. Last week he received £15,000 from the Gulf Trade Bank; big coincidence or what? No wonder he took so long to get back to the control room and employed such a half-wit to work with him.'

'Thanks for the update; now, if you'll excuse me, I've got a few loose ends to tidy up.' Kate smiled at Rafi and added, 'Do make yourself at home!'

Rafi's attention turned to the large screens on the walls. One showed a press conference, describing the full impact of the nuclear sabotage. It included a report on what had happened in the previous twenty-four hours and on the progress being made. All roads into the exclusion zone were now dead ends. The one-way – out only – system was being enforced rigidly at the army-controlled checkpoints.

Rafi felt a shiver go down his spine as he saw pictures, from the previous day, of masses of people corralled in one of the open air holding areas. The footage followed the process of decontamination; people being stripped of all their belongings and clothes, and taken to a purpose-built shower marquee, next to a prefabricated building. Large signs in many languages had on them: *Radiation risk – NOTHING to be taken beyond here.*

The TV cameras showed heart-rending footage of people arriving at the checkpoint and being forced to give up all their possessions. The pictures included those of a confused little girl being made to give up her favourite teddy – she was crying and couldn't comprehend what was going on. The scene brought a tear to Rafi's eye.

The report contained footage of mobile phones being handed out to each individual or family. The mobile phone companies had literally cleared their warehouses and the stocks in their shops. Free pay-as-you-go phones with credit vouchers for calls were issued to those coming out of the decontamination centres. Those with missing family members were given a phone number they could call to give information about the people they had lost. A number of local sports halls became rendezvous points for the missing people.

The TV commentator commended the Dunkirk spirit. The attitude wasn't, 'How much is this going to cost?', but rather, 'What can we do to help those who have lost everything?' The newscaster then announced that there would be a public holiday on the Monday, as a mark of respect for the loss of life and the suffering.

Rafi watched a piece on how the National Health Service was holding up. All the hospitals within 200 miles of the disaster area were flooded with people. A number of five star hotels had been requisitioned and turned into specialist radiation treatment units. Those with radiation poisoning were being sent on to one of these new specialist hospitals, with instructions from on high that everything should be done to make them feel comfortable. Elsewhere patients were seen on trolleys and makeshift beds. Against the odds, the system was holding up.

The armed forces were stretched beyond anything anyone could ever have envisaged. By late Friday afternoon, 10,300 troops and specialist professionals had arrived to enforce the perimeter of the exclusion zone, to run the decontamination centres and to clear the exclusion zone of people. All military bases remained on full alert.

The RSPCA worked with the armed forces and Territorial Army's veterinary teams to deal humanely with those animals found in the exclusion zone. It was a gruesome and demanding task. The RSPCA gained permission to run their own decontamination units for mildly contaminated pets, where the owners could be identified.

Rafi was enthralled when the bulletin turned to the problems associated with the leaching of the radioactive materials into the water table. In particular, the River Lea and its canal were near to the wrecked train. An ingenious solution had come from a company based just south of Newcastle, which made a polymer for – amongst other things – nappies. It rapidly turned liquids into jelly like substance which would remain stable for over a month. They had dispatched eight lorry loads with a police escort and arrived in London late on Friday afternoon. Their cargo was applied to the water flowing in and around the exclusion zone. The main problem related to the River Lea. A decision had been taken to divert the Lea into the King George reservoir just to the north of the exclusion zone and from there the water was being pumped straight into the mains as, unfortunately, the large Coppermills water treatment plant, a mile to the south, through which the water normally passed, was now out of action.

According to the reporter, decisions were being taken on how the River Lea could be redirected on a permanent basis. He listed the few solutions which were being considered - including diverting it into the River Roding - and concluded that drinking water shortages would be a feature for months to come. However, the good news was that the critical problems were being resolved and there were high hopes that radioactive materials would not leach out of the exclusion zone.

Rafi spotted Colonel Turner and his team looking at a screen showing a large chart. Curious, he went over to investigate. The screen showed the precise location of *Golden Sundancer*. She was still heading south.

It was late evening. Tiredness was rapidly overcoming Rafi – he felt ready to drop. The pressures and excesses of the last week had caught up with him again. He'd lost track of where Kate was, so he left a message for her and cadged a lift back to the hotel. Once there he grabbed a cold drink, had a quick shower and climbed into bed. Sleep came quickly.

*

Rafi awoke on Sunday morning to find it was almost 9.30 a.m. Kate was already up and dressed.

'Hi there, sleepyhead; your timing is perfect. I've ordered breakfast and the hire car is waiting for us downstairs.'

They enjoyed their breakfast, and by 10.15 a.m. were on their way.

Rafi took his trilby and cashmere scarf and a couple of the Sunday newspapers with him.

The Home Counties curfew that had been imposed on Friday morning had been lifted at midnight on Saturday. The roads were unduly busy as the exclusion zone had severed the roads towards East Anglia.

Their destination was the Suffolk/Essex border, where Kate's family lived. They talked about her family and about her early years. It became obvious that she'd had a very happy childhood living in Kenya, where her parents had been farmers.

'Then the carefree days ended,' Kate recalled with sadness in her voice. 'When I was twelve my grandfather died. We returned to England so that my father could sort out his affairs. The death duties were far larger than my father had expected and a decision had to be taken... Sell up in England to meet the huge tax bill and return to Kenya, or sell up in Kenya and live in the family home in Suffolk. My father chose the latter and following that decision everything changed. My schooling went from a relaxed private school to a large state school. My friends in Kenya loved outdoor activities: riding and hunting for creepy crawlies. Everything was tame in England. The weather was awful for five months of the year and people spent so much time indoors.'

'Was it that bad?'

'I had nothing in common with my new peer group at school,' she said. 'I was teased for my strange accent. My parents had promised that I would go to a good private school but it was not to be. My brother, Marcus, and I were sent to the local comprehensive school. It was only meant to be for the first year while my father sorted out the family's finances. However, it soon became apparent that money was very tight due to the size of the Estate Duty tax bill and the large running costs of the house.'

Kate paused. 'Marcus is fifteen months younger than me. He contracted diphtheria as a child and was on death's door for over a week. He pulled through, but the illness had made him partially deaf. In Kenya he grew up as if poor hearing was a minor hindrance. He was well catered for at his school and had the full attention of his own nanny to work with him at home. Sadly, in England things were totally different. Marcus didn't fit into the education system, which lacked the flexibility to cater for his special needs.'

'I remember,' continued Kate, 'my parents discussing our education. Basically, they felt that I needed to stay at the same school as Marcus, as he relied on me to protect him from bullies. So I stayed there for my A levels,' she sighed. 'I spent my gap year helping my father, working for the family business. It was then that my relationship with my parents crumbled. They had expected me to go off to university to read business studies or agricultural economics and to then return to the family business. I didn't do that do that.'

'Why not?'

'I had other ideas. I wanted to go into the police. I had a massive row with my parents, left home and enrolled at a police training college. At last, I had found something I really enjoyed doing. I shouldn't brag, but I sailed through with flying colours. Whilst I was a young constable I studied part-time at the Open University Business School and five years later graduated with a BSc in Business Studies and Accounting. It was hard work, but in my heart I guessed that one day I'd want to go back to Suffolk and work alongside my brother, helping the family business, so I chose a degree I could use when I returned home.'

Kate paused. 'Sadly, things went from bad to worse with my parents. While I was at the police college I became friendly with Maurice. My parents did not approve of him as my boyfriend. I refused to back down and after a stormy weekend at home they disowned me.

'That must have been hard.'

'It was, and then my love life went to pieces. I was working long hours. Maurice wanted us to socialise and party more and in the end we went our separate ways. Kate smiled. 'I focused on my work and studies and moved from the Met to the City of London police force.'

'My relationship with my parents by that stage was nothing

more than an exchange of Christmas and birthday cards.'

They had reached the Suffolk border. 'Are we getting close?' Rafi asked.

'Yes, not long now,' replied Kate, who noticed that Rafi was deep in thought. 'Are you OK?'

'I'm fine thanks, I was just thinking about family and friends. I was wondering if on our way back into London we could drop in and see an old teacher friend of mine, Major Charlie Staveley. Would you mind doing that? He lives just outside Hertford, in Great Amwell.'

'Good plan – why don't you give him a ring now?' suggested Kate.

His phone call successfully completed, Rafi saw National Trust signs to Leverthorne Hall and Leverthorne Vineyard, which they seemed to be following. Alongside the roadside was a tall brick wall. A large splayed back entrance, with impressive black wrought iron gates came into view. To Rafi's surprise they drove through the gates up a tree-lined driveway. Leverthorne Hall was nowhere to be seen.

'Would you like to see where I grew up?' enquired Kate with an impish grin, as they turned a corner. In the distance was a large Georgian mansion which could be described as impressive by anyone's standards.

'Not bad eh?' said Kate. 'Marcus and his family live in the west wing. My parents have the coach house and stable block. My brother has let most of the main house to the National Trust on a peppercorn rent. Says it makes life much simpler and lets him get on with the running of the estate and its businesses as a proper commercial venture.'

Rafi looked at Kate. 'So, all along, things like the suite at the Savoy were second nature to you!'

'If only! As far back as I can remember, living here was a continuous round of penny-pinching. Just try to imagine: two acres of roof, rising damp, old wiring and cranky central heating… To name but a few of the house's redeeming features – they all cost a fortune.'

Kate glanced at Rafi; there was sadness in her eyes. 'This is going to be difficult. I have not seen, let alone spoken, to my parents for many years. In the beginning I tried, but they would not answer my calls. I have kept in touch with Marcus. It was especially difficult when he found a girlfriend and wanted to get married, but my parents refused to let him have the reception here if I attended. In the end, he and Susannah decided not to get married. That, as far as my parents were concerned, was the final straw. The last time I went home was with Maurice. This time it's with you in tow. Please don't be surprised if this is a very short and fiery family reunion.'

'Apart from Saara, I don't have the luxury of having a family,' commented Rafi. 'It's got to be worth a shot at patching things up between you and your parents. It's just a shame that all the good work you've been doing has to be kept quiet until the terrorists are caught.'

'A blaze of publicity might have been useful,' mused Kate, 'but this way we'll see if there's any real affection left for me.'

The car stopped.

'Whatever happens, you've still added one extra person to your life: me.'

Kate turned her head and looked at Rafi. He could see the beginnings of tears welling up in her gorgeous eyes. She leant over and kissed him.

'Right, let the charm offensive begin.' Rafi groaned as he eased himself out of the car seat. His bruised lower back had not liked the prolonged car journey.

Kate smiled. 'Be your normal self. They get us warts and all.' She gave his hand a squeeze and headed for the open front door. Rafi followed, with his trilby tilted over his eyes and the scarf round his neck and lower face.

He marvelled as he stepped inside. The entrance hall could have contained his flat. They approached the National Trust booth where a kindly woman greeted Kate with a big smile.

'Hello, Mrs Hindmarsh - isn't it? I didn't recognise you straight away.'

'Don't worry dear – it's been over ten years. How lovely to see you again.'

'How's...' Kate hesitated, 'Danny?'

'On excellent form, thank you. I have three grandchildren. He works in Sudbury now, in an office opposite the church. He would be pleased to see you, so do drop by if you can.'

'Thank you, Mrs Hindmarsh, I'll do that next time I'm up here. Today is a bit of a fleeting visit.'

Mrs Hindmarsh nodded in a knowing manner and they proceeded on their way.

They walked into a cavernous central hall. It was devoid of furniture. Its stone floor had small squares of black stone inlay to give it a criss-cross pattern. The main feature in the central hall was the grand sweeping staircase. There was a pair of large double doors to the left which led through to an impressively furnished drawing room. In front of Rafi the open double doors framed a view through what looked like a music room and on to the largest set of French windows he could ever recall seeing, with a vista down to a lake and a gazebo. To the right of the hall was a grand dining room.

'How many could you seat?' he asked.

'Oh, I think we had about sixty in there for my twenty-first,' she replied nonchalantly. 'Come on, enough of the sightseeing; let's find Marcus.'

Kate took hold of his hand and led Rafi off to the right of the dining room, past a winding, back staircase, past a billiards room, down a long passage and past the kitchens. They climbed up a second set of back stairs and there in front of them was a normal-looking front door.

'Welcome to my brother's flat,' said Kate with a broad smile. She rang the doorbell.

They were greeted by a beaming Marcus. 'Great to see you, Kate. And if I remember correctly from your phone call, this must be Rafi?'

'Yes,' said Kate.

'Susannah will be with us shortly; she's sorting out the final touches to lunch. Let's find Mother and Father. I have told them that you've a boyfriend with you, but not that it's Rafi! I didn't want to mess things up, so I thought it might be simpler for you to explain how your boyfriend has gone from being a terrorist to a good guy.'

They walked down a small corridor, the walls covered in pictures of Africa. Marcus looked at Kate. 'Happy memories!'

'Yes,' came the reply, 'The best.'

They came to a cosy sitting room with an open log fire

brightening the cold February day. On the other side of the room was a large sofa and, parked in the middle of it, were two elderly people, who stood up slowly. They weren't doddery but time had started to take its toll. They looked apprehensive. Kate walked forward and gave her mother a kiss on the cheek, followed by a hug. She turned to her father, stretched out to shake his hand, had second thoughts and gave him a peck on the cheek and a hug. Rafi sensed that her parents were surprised by Kate's attempt at reconciliation. They sat down. Not a word had been spoken. Marcus did the introductions.

'Mr Rafi Khan, it is my pleasure to introduce you to our parents: Major Sir Percy Gant-Adams and Lady Yvonne Gant-Adams.'

'You will no doubt have seen his picture in the papers recently,' added Kate quickly. 'He's been working undercover for us. The full story will come out next week. We've only known one another for a week but I can assure you he's a real catch and my first boyfriend in ages.' And with that she planted a caring kiss on Rafi's cheek.

Wow, that was brave, Rafi thought. Talk about light the blue touchpaper and stand well back! Kate's parents looked on awkwardly. But the tension eased as Susannah walked in carrying a tray with a bottle of champagne and some orange juice. She exclaimed in delight when she saw Kate. The tray was put down next to Marcus, who uncorked the bottle with a pleasing pop, charged the glasses and passed them around.

The major lifted his glass, looked at the bubbles and took a sniff of the bouquet. Then he stopped, looked at his daughter and said, 'Please forgive me for not standing up again, but I would like to propose a toast.' He raised his glass in the direction of Marcus and Susannah.

'First I should like to toast our hosts without whom this reunion would not have happened – thank you both.' The glasses were raised and an appreciative sip was taken by all. The major turned his gaze to Kate.

'The second toast is to Kate, my long-lost daughter. Your mother and I look forward to you telling us what you've been up to. Marcus tells me that you've been heading up a team involved with the Bishopsgate bombing?'

261

'Yes, Daddy – and a bit more besides.' The conversation stopped in its tracks. It was as if Kate's career was of little interest to her father.

Rafi felt annoyed, but tried not to show it. He looked carefully at the major. In his youth he must have been a dashing and well-built man, and his wife must once, he guessed, have been a slightly willowier version of Kate. She had the same auburn hair and warm brown eyes.

Susannah looked at her watch. 'Lunch will be in ten minutes. Please excuse me while I put the vegetables on.'

There was a silence. Rafi waited for someone to break the ice. Kate's mother beat him to it. 'Tell me Kate,' she said in a frail voice, 'I have been reading the papers. I am confused. How precisely did you manage in the space of a week to turn a terrorist suspect into a boyfriend?'

'It's a long story. Rafi was set up. I was sent to see if he had information that could help us prevent more terrorist attacks. That was last Monday. Since then Rafi and I have been working flat out unravelling the terrorist conspiracy.'

'I see, dear,' came her mother's uncertain reply.

Marcus got up and recharged the glasses.

'Don't you drink?' asked the major.

'No, sir,' replied Rafi. The major looked at him and hesitated before saying, 'Do please call me Percy; it will make things less formal.'

Rafi sensed that uttering those few words had broken the ice. 'Thank you, sir.'

The major continued. 'Where do you come from?'

'It's not a very interesting story,' Rafi replied, hoping to avoid the subject, but he was encouraged to continue.

Rafi took a mouthful of the orange juice and then began. 'My father owned a bakery in the East End of London. I was educated at Haileybury and then studied for my Bachelors and Masters degrees in London.'

The major nodded, hoping for more.

'Up to a week ago, I was a senior fund manager in the City of London. The rest, as they say, is history.'

Kate skilfully switched the conversation to Leverthorne Hall and its vineyards. It transpired that Marcus had studied through the Open University Business School and had specialised on the marketing and product development side of Business Studies.

In the words of his mother, Marcus had turned the estate around. 'There is now a small rural business park with a growing number of successful cottage industries and he has found an excellent farm manager to run the 3,500-acre farm.'

'How big is 3,500 acres?' Rafi enquired.

Kate looked at Rafi as if acres to square miles was a ratio he should have known, and replied, 'Five and a half square miles.'

'Oh, really!' exclaimed Rafi. There was laughter. He sensed that the tide had turned.

'Lunch is ready,' echoed through from the dining room, where Rafi soon found himself sitting next to Lady Yvonne, and opposite the major and Kate.

Given the circumstances, lunch was a relatively jolly affair. There were a few hesitant pauses in the conversation, but the sheer joy of Kate and her brother being back together again, under the roof of the family home, was plain for all to see. They sat next to each other and chatted away at ten to the dozen.

After lunch, the small talk continued over coffee and Rafi found himself the centre of the conversation. It seemed her parents found it simpler to talk to him rather than to Kate, lest they unintentionally reopened hidden wounds.

Rafi's background, his education, hobbies, work and involvement in uncovering the terrorist plots were all discussed.

Kate looked across at her parents. 'Did I tell you that I have also met Rafi's sister, Saara? When I saw the two of them together, it reminded me how much fun we had when we were living in Kenya... all the grief of the last decade seemed irrelevant; I just wish we could be that happy again,' she paused and fell silent.

Her parents, who were sitting comfortably on the sofa, seemed overcome by emotions. The major looked at Kate and then his wife. 'Kate, I agree; we did have a good time in Kenya. I am sorry that moving here caused such friction and hardship. Yes, we should strive to find that happiness again.'

'But with a few more coats and jumpers,' added Marcus with a laugh.

Coffee had long been finished. There was a brief lull in

the conversation. Kate looked at her watch, time had flown by, it was coming up to 3.30 p.m. She explained that they had a second visit to make on their way back to London, as a teacher-friend of Rafi's had invited them for afternoon tea.

They said their goodbyes and promised to be back soon.

Back in the car, Kate looked radiant. 'Thank you for being so patient and courteous through all the interrogations.'

Rafi looked into her warm eyes. 'My pleasure. It was fun, and I am hugely relieved it all worked out.'

'Yes; after a shaky start – I can't believe how well it went,' said Kate.

They had an uneventful journey and in what seemed like no time at all they were pulling into Gypsy Lane. They stopped in front of a red brick house. Great Amwell was only a couple of miles from Haileybury College.

The major's front garden was well-kept. They walked up to the front door, rang the bell and stood there, holding hands.

A stooping silver-haired man answered the door. Rafi instantly recognised him – he had aged well, but was looking a little unsteady on his pins.

They were greeted by a jovial, 'Come on in, come on in, it must be cold standing out there.'

'Thank you,' said Rafi and went on to introduce Kate.

They entered the modest-sized home and headed for the sitting room, where they were greeted by a roaring open fire.

Charlie beckoned Rafi to sit on the sofa next to the fire.

'Your timing is excellent – the kettle has just boiled. Let me look at you first though, young Rafi, it's been too long since I last laid eyes on you.' He stood there gazing at him. 'Thank you for your phone call. It's a shame that you got caught up in this terrorist mess. I wondered whether you might make contact after I'd had that visit from MI5.' He paused, as if uncertain what to say next. 'Why don't you have a look at some photos whilst Kate and I put the kettle on?'

Charlie picked up an old leather-bound photo album from the sideboard and handed it to Rafi, then disappeared with Kate into the kitchen.

Rafi opened it. It contained pictures of the major's life. There were a couple of photos of him in his early school days at Haileybury: one of him playing cricket, which rekindled memories of Rafi standing in almost the same spot, bowling right arm off breaks. The chapel and the large central courtyard looked just the same.

He moved on a few pages to see a very handsome, young man dressed in army uniform with a dark brown moustache and closely cropped wavy brown hair. The sparse text under the photos showed that he'd been posted to Palestine and had initially served under Allenby, before being posted to India.

He turned the page and there was a picture of a beautiful Indian woman in a nurse's uniform standing in front of a large hospital. This was followed by a series of casual snaps of him and her taken during their outings. Rafi looked carefully at the photos; 1945–46 seemed to have been a very special and happy time for them. Then there was a sun-bleached photo showing the nurse and her family, all dressed up in their finest; looking very splendid in palatial surroundings. In the centre was the person he assumed to be the head of the family; he looked intimidating. A couple of photos of a kindly looking servant carrying a tray laden with glasses, cups and saucers followed.

'What?' Rafi exclaimed. He recognised the servant. He was his grandpa, Mansur Khan. His gaze fell upon the nurse in the picture. It couldn't be! He couldn't believe it – it was Lateefa, his grandmother, in her early twenties. He was confused. Why was Charlie holding hands with his grandmother in many of the pictures? The last photo showed them standing formally next to each other. There was a look of sadness in their faces.

Rafi turned the page. It contained a short press cutting on the death of Mansur. This was followed by another cutting which showed the mangled car in which his parents had died a few months later. The next page was blank; there were no more pictures, except for the penultimate page, on which there was a photo of Charlie standing next to a young lad, with his arm around his shoulder, a beaming smile across his face. Rafi remembered the occasion. It was taken in the summer near the end of his third year at Haileybury. He had taken four or five wickets in an inter-house cricket match. Charlie, who had been watching, insisted that a photo be taken for posterity. Rafi hadn't seen the photo until now. He sat deep in thought, and was interrupted by the clattering of a trolley on which the afternoon tea had been placed. Charlie and Kate sat down and passed around the tea.

Charlie looked carefully at Rafi's face. 'I was distraught,' he said. 'I really wanted to marry your grandmother. Sadly for both of us, it wasn't to be. In those days, family honour ranked above individual feelings and sensibilities.'

'Pardon?' asked Rafi.

'There's no easy way to say this,' said Charlie. 'I met Lateefa, your grandmother, in India just before its partitioning with Pakistan. We fell in love and then calamity struck: she told me that our relationship had to end, but she would not tell me why. I didn't find out until later that she was carrying my child and had been disowned by her family. Had it not been for your grandfather, Mansur, a servant in her household, it would have been a disaster. He sought me out and explained why Lateefa had broken off our relationship.'

Rafi could see the beginning of tears in Charlie's eyes.

'I had been transferred to the Green Howards and was being posted to Sudan. I had so wanted to go back and see Lateefa, but there just wasn't time. And to have become a deserter from the army would only have made things worse. When I told Mansur that I *had to* go, I had expected him to be angry with me. Instead he smiled and asked if he could help. It transpired that he had been in love with Lateefa since his childhood.'

Charlie looked sadly at Rafi. 'The partitioning caused large-scale and violent cross-border migration of Muslims, Hindus and Sikhs. It was this upheaval and Lateefa being without family support that prompted Mansur to find me. I was impressed – he had it all planned. He asked me to arrange passes for Lateefa and him to get to England. Mansur then found Lateefa and they emigrated there. I helped them with what little money I could.'

'So my father was your son?' Rafi exclaimed, finally understanding what Charlie was trying to tell him.

'Yes.'

'Why on earth didn't you tell me before now?'

'I promised your parents that I would not interfere,' said Charlie.

'Hold on a minute!' said Rafi. 'Did you have anything to do

with my going to Haileybury and Saara going to a private day school?'

Charlie nodded. 'After decommissioning I went back to my studies, became a teacher and then accepted a job at Haileybury. Several years later, I had been visiting a school in Stepney with which Haileybury had long-standing links and, as good fortune would have it, on the way home I stopped off at a local bakery in the East End of London. I unexpectedly met Mansur again. He looked much older, but I recognised him instantly.'

Charlie poignantly related how he had returned the following weekend and had met Mansur and Lateefa. 'I had a tear-filled reunion with your grandparents. We talked about Jansher, their only son and decided that the past should remain in the past – it wouldn't have been fair on them for me to come back into their lives. I asked if I could help them with their finances. They were too proud to accept any help. In the end, they allowed me to help with the education of any grandchildren that they might have.'

Rafi smiled. 'That explains why I went from a deprived state school to a smart private boarding school!' He was overcome by emotion.

Charlie sat quietly waiting for Rafi's response.

'Wow,' replied Rafi. 'So as of today the number of my close family relatives has doubled.... Let me give you a hug.' Rafi embraced him warmly and then sat back down. 'I always knew Mansur as grandpa. Could I call you grandfather?'

Beaming, Charlie nodded, not trusting his voice.

'Saara will be delighted; I can't wait to tell her face to face.'

'Unexpectedly, Mansur wrote to me once or twice a year keeping me up to date as to what your father, Jansher, was doing. It was just like him to be so thoughtful,' said Charlie.

The conversation drifted back to when Charlie had first met Lateefa, Rafi's grandmother. 'She came from an immensely powerful and wealthy family. They commanded respect for tens if not hundreds of miles around,' said Charlie. He went on to describe the close-knit community in India before independence, the partitioning and painful birth of Pakistan. Charlie talked about the British Army families – the nannies and the family helpers – and about his relationship with Lateefa - 'it should have progressed to marriage,' Charlie's voice faltered. 'It broke my heart to lose her.'

'Did you meet my mother, Ameena?' asked Rafi.

Charlie hesitated. 'No... I'm sad to say, I did not...'

'Why the hesitation?' enquired Rafi. 'Is there something I don't know...? *Please* tell me, if there is...'

'OK, then..., your grandpa was approached by your family in Pakistan who sought an arranged marriage between your father and Ameena, a distant cousin. It transpired that the eldest son of the head of the family had fallen for Ameena, but his parents wanted him to marry the daughter of a wealthy merchant. Mansur reluctantly agreed to Ameena coming to stay for a couple of months, as a guest, but on the condition that your father was not to know about any suggestion of an arranged marriage.'

Charlie paused. 'Your parents enjoyed one another's company and fortunately it didn't take long for them to fall in love. They got married seven months later in a small ceremony.'

'Thank you,' Rafi thought for a moment. 'Could you tell me about my family in Pakistan?'

'Your cousins are very powerful people. Their fiefdom stretches over an area of thousands of square miles. Perhaps you should pay them a visit one day,' suggested Charlie.

*

It was approaching 8 o'clock.

'I'm afraid we should be going soon,' said Rafi. 'We've got an early start tomorrow.'

'Would you like to stay for a quick bite of supper?' asked Charlie hopefully.

Rafi was about to decline the offer when Kate interjected, 'That sounds like a lovely idea.'

The conversation switched to Kate, her family reunion and her teaming up with Rafi to track down the terrorists.

Rafi talked about Saara and he promised to visit with her. After lengthy and fond goodbyes, they finally left at 10 o'clock.

*

The journey back into London was slow but straightforward and they arrived at the packed hotel just after midnight.

Rafi opened the door to their room and found a white envelope lying on the carpet. It contained two messages: one from Kate's boss and one from Saara.

Kate picked up the phone and spoke to David. It was a short call. 'We'll be picked up from the front of the hotel at 07.30. He wants me at work early.'

She passed the phone to Rafi who dialled his sister's number. There was a delay before the phone was answered. He guessed he'd woken her up.

They spoke briefly and she updated him on the meetings she and Aidan's economics team had had with the Chancellor of the Exchequer and representatives of the Bank of England.

'They're playing their cards very close to their chests. Heaven only knows what the Chancellor is going to do and say tomorrow. At least it's a bank holiday and the markets will have to wait until Tuesday morning to digest things,' said Saara. 'I'm going back to Birmingham tomorrow evening. I've missed a couple of deadlines and don't want to let my colleagues down... And I'm missing Steve.'

'How are you getting home?'

'Coach of course,' came the reply. 'I got the ticket booked for me earlier today by a helpful man at Number 11. I can't wait to get back to normality. Let's talk soon when things are calmer. Please give my love and a hug to Kate. Tell her Steve and I look forward to seeing you both in Birmingham. Bye.' He put the phone down. He felt guilty, as he had not told Saara about their grandfather. He wanted to tell her face to face, but was it fair to keep the news from her?

Kate meanwhile had slipped into the bathroom. She washed quickly. Back in the bedroom she undressed and slipped under the luxurious duvet. Her thoughts turned to Rafi. She hoped he would not be long...

Rafi finished his drink, turned the sitting room light out and went to see where Kate had got to. The bedroom lights were on, but she was fast asleep. Moments later he slipped into bed and turned off the light. He lay there thinking back over the day. Unexpectedly, it had been a very good day.

Chapter 7

After a good night's sleep and a quick breakfast, Kate and Rafi were at their desks in Wood Street by 7.45 a.m. on Monday.

Soon, though, Rafi found himself alone; Kate had disappeared to work with John and the rest of the team downstairs.

The office felt strange without the pent-up tension of the previous week. Rafi tidied his desk and then browsed the Internet to see how the main overseas markets were trading. He looked at Bloomberg's news page first. There, at the top of the 'Breaking News', was a headline that made him smile: 'International markets closed - in respect for all those who lost their lives in London'. Rafi clicked on the link to read the story. It explained how the chairmen of the major international banks operating in London had got together and asked their home stock and derivatives exchanges not to open for the day as a mark of respect, and the idea had snowballed. Rafi smiled; the Chancellor had arranged things in a very appropriate manner.

After forty minutes he'd run out of things to do so decided to see how things were progressing in the Ops Room. There Rafi was greeted as one of the team – basically no one took much notice of him! He looked at the screens and listened to the discussions going on.

Puddle Jumper had arrived at Safi in the early hours of the morning with its crew of six. They had cleared customs. *Golden Sundancer* and the sheikh's plane were some five hours away.

The atmosphere ratcheted up a notch as Giles and David walked in, accompanied by Len Thunhurst, the Commissioner of the Metropolitan Police, John, Kate and the rest of their teams.

Rafi noticed that video links had been established with regional police command centres. Those around him spoke of *Operation Dry Clean* and explained that it would be the largest series of coordinated arrests ever undertaken.

Giles started the video link briefing. 'The need for secrecy is absolute. Details of the arrests and the names will not be released until Len Thunhurst is satisfied that it's safe to do so. The terrorists' network of contacts should not be underestimated – let us not forget that two members of COBRA have been arrested. *Operation Dry Clean* will commence as soon as we receive confirmation that the ringleaders have been apprehended. There will be hell to pay if they are tipped off and give us the slip at the last moment. The capture of the terrorists is scheduled for 3.30 p.m. this afternoon, give or take a bit. Until then we must keep our actions under wraps. Len Thunhurst will be in charge of the UK arrests and I shall be overseeing the arrest of Maryam Vynckt in Luxembourg.'

Len took up the proceedings. He congratulated Giles and his team on their work and turned to Emma. 'The floor is all yours.'

Emma looked worn out. She was a little hesitant at first, but soon got into her stride. She pointed to the electronic presentation on a second screen, which was linked to the conference rooms of those listening. Emma explained, using the diagrams on the screen, the relationship between Basel Talal's venture capital business; Jameel's Prima Terra; Maryam's Gulf Trade Bank and the sheikh, who was the chief financier. She also mentioned the raft of public and private companies controlled and manipulated by the terrorist leaders. Jeremy nodded approvingly.

Emma paused to take questions and then put a new slide up on the screen. This contained a very lengthy list of names and addresses linked, where available, to mugshots of the people involved. She turned to Jeremy. 'Thanks to the work of MI5, we have so far been able to trace 289 of the 323 people we are interested in. MI5 will be seeking your assistance to find the missing individuals.

'For those on our list,' she continued, 'We've adopted a colour coding of red, blue and black. The names in red are individuals who have been complicit in the recent terrorist activities and for whom we have more than sufficient evidence for a prosecution. The blues have direct connections with the recent activities, but more evidence has to be gathered before we've got a watertight case. The names in black are circumstantially linked: while we believe that they've been very much involved in the terrorists' plans, we need more information before we can confirm their involvement. The red names are our first priority. However, all the names are important as they'll complete the picture of what the terrorists have been planning and will corroborate the case against those we're going to prosecute.'

Emma pointed to the screen. 'As soon as we have a person in custody, we'll give their name on our list a yellow background. That way we can quickly see how things are progressing.'

'Thank you, Emma,' said Len turning to the video camera. 'Many of the people you will be arresting are sleepers. Do not feel any sympathy for them – they are *all* implicated. Once in custody, we need to build a complete picture and identify any loose ends that we may have missed. Emma and her team, with the help of MI5, John and his team, have prepared a dossier on those you'll be arresting. It will provide you with background details of what these individuals have been doing and how they've crossed the line. I do stress that each and every one of them should be treated with caution.'

Len paused to let his last statement sink in. 'The resources of this terrorist operation have been likened by MI5 to those of a small to medium-sized country. They have on their payroll some of the most dangerous mercenaries we have ever had the misfortune to deal with. And be warned: some of the people on this list are very well connected. And please be aware that these sleepers or invisibles, who would usually go unnoticed, are extremely valuable to us. The fact that we don't catch them with a smoking gun should not lessen the gravity of their involvement.'

The commissioner turned to Jack Fisher, one of John's team, who blushed as he stood up. His voice started as a quiet squeak. John passed him a glass of water and gave him an encouraging smile. 'Jack has spent the last couple of days, with the help of MI5, unravelling the terrorists' network of outsourcing companies working for the public sector. What he and the rest of the team have unearthed makes for unpalatable reading.'

The commissioner nodded towards Jack, who had recovered his composure. 'You'll see there is an extensive list of companies, limited partnerships and businesses, which are controlled by the terrorists. Key individuals in these companies have been listed above. Their paper and electronic records will be needed so that we can identify the internal chains of command and see exactly what they have been doing.'

Len concluded matters with a stark warning. 'We have good reason to believe that several of these people have a direct line of communication with the terrorist leaders. Until we have all the key leaders in custody we must, under *no* circumstances – I repeat, under *no circumstances* – let the cat out of the bag that *Operation Dry Clean* exists. Is that clearly understood?'

Fifteen minutes later, after a series of searching questions, the video links were turned off and connection was re-established with those tracking *Golden Sundancer* and the sheikh's plane, and those planning the capture of Maryam in Luxembourg.

*

Colonels Turner and Gray and a reduced team came back into the room, which was rapidly reverting to a mini war room. On the central screen there was now a large electronic map showing Morocco and the north-west coast of Africa.

The clock on the wall gave the time as 11.06 a.m. The Prime Minister was scheduled to stand up in front of the House of Commons in less than three hours. Even though it was a bank holiday, these were exceptional times and the House was in emergency session.

Rafi turned his attention to the activities in Morocco. The chart showed a red dot which was making its way across the screen following a thin yellow line towards Marrakech. It was about 700 miles away. There was a second red dot 100 miles offshore tracking a thin yellow line along the coast towards the port of Safi. Then he spotted another red dot by Marrakech and a number of blue dots.

Kate tugged at his arm; she was also looking at the central screen. 'I reckon those red dots are the sheikh's plane, *Golden Sundancer* and Jameel. The blue ones must be the good guys - so the blue one in Safi must be our friends on board *Puddle Jumper*.'

Rafi pointed to the fine yellow line which stopped about fifteen miles off the coast. 'That, I presume, is where the submarine is to rendezvous with *Puddle Jumper*.'

One of the colonel's adjutants walked over to chat to Kate. 'It's all starting to come together nicely. The next few hours should be interesting! We have patched into the SBS command centre which is overseeing the operation at Safi. There's a

Nimrod offshore at 40,000 feet monitoring the location of *Golden Sundancer*. She has her cloaking device on so she'll be invisible to the terrorists. She'll pick up the video pictures and radio communications from the SBS men on board *Puddle Jumper* and the SAS teams on the ground. She'll then relay them to the command centre where they'll bounce them on to us.'

The adjutant thought for a moment. '*Golden Sundancer*, at her current speed, should reach Safi between 13.30 and 13.45 hours, our time this afternoon. She has slowed down a bit; it seems she's sailing into a steep swell. The sheikh's plane is scheduled to land at Menara airport, Marrakech, at 13.00 hours. If the switch to the helicopter goes quickly, they could be at Safi by 14.00 hours... We would prefer there to be more of a time gap before the helicopter arrives.'

'Are they going to be well prepared?' asked Rafi.

'The terrorists still seem blissfully unaware that we are on to them,' continued the adjutant. 'The two SAS operatives we have undercover at Marrakech Airport have reported that the helicopter is unguarded, with just the pilot waiting. The sheikh meanwhile has two minders with him on board his jet. Both are big gorillas of men, but definitely not in the same league as the two Chechen mercenaries on *Golden Sundancer*.'

The adjutant pointed to the map. 'In Safi, we have two highly experienced SAS soldiers - Major Mark Piggot and Sergeant Colin Blake. They have identified four heavies watching the harbour and if they're anything like the Chechen mercenaries, they'll have a real skirmish on their hands. Thankfully, the industrial part of the port is relatively deserted. In contrast, the nearby fishing boat quays are a hive of activity. From the location of the four heavies, we believe that the helicopter plans to land on the quay in the industrial part of the harbour, close to where *Golden Sundancer* is likely to berth.'

The adjutant paused and looked across at the screen. 'As good fortune would have it, our friends on board *Puddle Jumper* seem to be in just the right place. Now that we're certain Safi is the rendezvous point, the three SAS men at Mohammedia and the three at Casablanca are, as we speak, driving down the N1 to Safi. Roads permitting, they'll be there in good time.'

'What's Jameel up to?' asked Kate.

'He finished a round of golf half an hour ago and is currently in the hotel bar. He's packed his bags and ordered a taxi to the airport ten minutes ago. He's the proud possessor of a couple of tracking devices: one in his shoe, which he left unattended whilst playing golf, and another in his hand luggage!'

*

On board *Puddle Jumper* the atmosphere was calm and relaxed. The retired commander and his wife were sitting on the aft deck, enjoying mugs of tea. They were joined by a scantily clad Lieutenant Anna Gregson, with a colourful caftan wrapped around her waist. She was followed by a similarly dressed Lieutenant Janet Steiner.

'Been enjoying the sun?' enquired their *mother*.

'It's fantastic up on the foredeck,' replied Anna.

'Any idea where your *boyfriend* Clive is?' the commander asked.

'Yes; he and Jim have gone on a bimble – said they had to see a man about a dog,' replied Janet.

The commander nodded. 'We've got about two and a half hours before we will have company, according to our friends.'

'In which case,' said Janet, 'Time for a bit more sun on the foredeck.'

'Remember the sunscreen,' said their *mother* tossing a bottle in Anna's direction.

'Thanks *mum!*'

As the two women left for the bow of the boat, Jim and Clive climbed back on board and walked over to chat to the commander.

'That was quick; I thought you were chatting to your SAS friends, Mark and Colin?'

'We were. And we've sorted out what equipment we have between us. They're rather well tooled-up. As long as a small army doesn't arrive, they should give us more than enough cover.'

'What do they make of the four heavies guarding the helicopter landing area?' asked the commander.

'Piece of piss!' replied Clive. 'The way they handle themselves and their guns, they're no more than local hoodlums. All they seem to do is smoke cigarettes and talk; not one of them has even done a recce, which is good news.'

'It's the two Chechens on board *Golden Sundancer* that we have to be careful of,' remarked Jim. 'Oh, by the way, we reckon that *Golden Sundancer* will moor up 100 metres across from where we are.'

*

In the Ops Room, Rafi turned his attention to the flat screen TV. He watched the commentary preceding the PM's speech in the House of Commons, where a political correspondent was standing inside the Houses of Parliament with a senior opposition MP on either side of her.

'Gentlemen,' began the interviewer, 'Will there be a call for a vote of no confidence and will the Prime Minister survive this afternoon?'

'My party will want to find out why things have gone so badly wrong and will wish to see those who have let this country down take responsibility for their negligence,' replied the first MP.

The interviewer turned to the second politician. 'It's going to be very difficult for the PM and his Chancellor to put a lid on the financial fallout from Stratford, isn't it?'

'Undoubtedly. It's going to cost the country tens if not hundreds of billions of pounds. This could sink our economy, our currency and scare the living daylights out of the markets. The last thing that we need is political uncertainty. I hope that the PM will find a way of getting the opposition parties involved with the process of getting the country out of this mess.'

The interviewer looked at the first MP. 'If there's a call for a vote of no confidence, what will the implications be?'

'The Government has a tiny majority and will seek to tough things out. It's more likely that pigs will fly, than for a recently elected Government to give up its reins on power.'

'Thank you, gentlemen, and with that we return to the studio,' concluded the political correspondent.

*

The special forces command centre and the Air Chief Marshal were in discussion with Clive and Jim. As things currently stood, the helicopter would land in Safi only minutes after *Golden Sundancer* berthed. Jim asked whether it might to possible to get them more time to overpower those on board before the helicopter arrived.

276

Accordingly, at Marrakech airport, a quick-thinking and inventive SAS operative borrowed the jacket of an airport worker and walked up to the helicopter. He had a water bottle filled with oil hidden in his pocket. The bottle had a tube – commandeered from a drinks machine – tightly inserted into its top which went down his trouser leg.

The disguised SAS man sauntered over to the pilot to enquire whether the helicopter would be requiring the help of a baggage handler. He was summarily sent away. As he left, he walked towards the back of the aircraft and stopped to tie his shoelace under the tail's rotary engine. Job done. He got up and walked off. On the concrete apron behind him was a fresh puddle of oil.

The SAS man walked back to the airport buildings and found an airport security official. He explained that the helicopter he'd visited seemed to be leaking hydraulic fluid from its engine.

'It's probably nothing, but should someone look at it? We don't want it to fall out of the sky.'

The security man had shrugged his shoulders and begrudgingly gone off to tell his boss. Nothing happened for some while. It seemed that the message hadn't got through.

However, some minutes later, a relieved SAS man reported that a man dressed in overalls was on his way towards the helicopter. The conversation between the man and the helicopter pilot looked animated. The pilot eventually got out, looked at the fluid on the concrete and with a shrug of his shoulders agreed to let the man look at the engine. This entailed the engineer walking back to collect his tools and a stepladder.

There was a noticeable smile on the face of the officer in the special services command centre; the engineer was in no hurry and was slowing things up, just as required.

The sheikh's plane landed at Marrakech Airport on time. It parked away from the passenger planes, next to a group of small private aircraft not far from the helicopter. Those on board were quickly cleared through customs and immigration. The sheikh met Jameel on the tarmac and they were seen smiling in the bright sunshine, next to their two heavily built security guards. However, on hearing the news of the delay, the sheikh hunched his shoulders and scowled.

★

At Safi, *Golden Sundancer* had turned on to the final approach to the harbour. As things stood, she would now arrive comfortably ahead of the helicopter.

Jim and Clive, with assistance from Mark and Colin, their SAS back-up, had three groups of people to take care of: six on board *Golden Sundancer*, the four heavies on the harbour side and the five people on the helicopter – fifteen hostile people. It was the two Chechen mercenaries on board *Golden Sundancer* and the two bodyguards with the sheikh to whom they would have to pay special attention.

The command centre made it clear that the mission was to capture all the terrorists alive. Casualties, if at all possible, should be avoided, but in the last resort be limited to the bodyguards and the heavies on the dockside. The politicians wanted the terrorists unharmed.

*

The Prime Minister was due to stand up in the Commons in less than fifteen minutes. Tension was rising in the packed chamber.

*

Back at Safi, preparations were complete. The plan was straightforward. When *Golden Sundancer* arrived, the two female naval officers would act as attractive distractions; meanwhile, Jim and Clive, the two SBS officers would slip on board via the swimming platform at the stern, neutralise those on board, then wait for the sheikh and his entourage to board the vessel and overpower them too. Mark and Colin would take care of the four heavies on the dockside.

The commander was standing next to the radar screen on *Puddle Jumper*. 'I can see them on our radar; they're approaching the outer harbour. ETA: four minutes,' he said into his radio.

Colin confirmed that he had got *Golden Sundancer* in his binoculars. 'The captain plus one are on the flybridge and two people are sitting on the foredeck, leaving two people below deck.'

*

Big Ben struck twice. Rafi, who had been following events in Safi on the screens, switched his attention across to the TV.

The Speaker of the House called: 'Order, Order! Pray silence for the Prime Minister.'

The Prime Minister rose and moved to the dispatch box in front of him. He waited a few seconds. A hush fell over the packed House of Commons. Uncharacteristically, the PM took off his wristwatch and placed it face up on the dispatch box. The estimate he had been given was for the submarine to pick up of the captured terrorists at around 3.30 p.m. Maryam, meanwhile, would be smuggled out of Luxembourg. Only then could he reveal what had been going on. So much could go wrong. There were bound to be delays. It would therefore be something like two hours before he and his Chancellor could announce the full story.

There was a sense of anticipation in the air. The future of the Government lay in his hands. The next couple of hours would be crucial.

'I come before the House with a heavy heart. The Stratford disaster will haunt us for years to come.' The PM's demeanour mirrored his words.

'My Government and I wish to pay our humble respects to all those who have suffered from this disaster and to all those who will suffer from radiation poisoning in the future. I am mindful of all those who have lost everything. The efforts of the police, the armed services, doctors, nurses and emergency services deserve our thanks and praise. I pay tribute to all those who have played a role in the rehousing of those who lost their homes. In recognition of the deeds and acts of friendship, in future, the second Monday in February will be a public holiday. It will be a day to remember all those who suffered and a day to reflect. I hope that Stratford Day will become a day of good deeds and community works.'

One could have heard a pin drop.

'The financial implications of the disaster will be explained by the Chancellor of the Exchequer shortly. He will set out what the Government will be doing to help those who have been caught up in this heinous and barbaric attack.'

The PM paused. 'The trials and tribulations that now face our country are greater than at any time since the end of the last World War. It is imperative that unity and common purpose prevail.'

★

Rafi listened to the PM give an update on the tragedy, which included details on the dead, the dying, the dispossessed, the army's progress in guarding and clearing the exclusion zone, its size and the problems they had overcome to stop radioactive materials polluting the water table and travelling down the River Lea.

The PM moved on to his policy initiatives. 'The General Election, which was held less than a year ago, produced a finely balanced result. The number of votes cast for the two main parties was almost identical and the vote for the Liberal Democrats gave them a creditable third place. Ninety five per cent of the votes cast at the election were for the three main parties. The manifestos on which the election was fought were as similar as the political pundits could remember; indeed some called for a hung Parliament to bring in the dynamism and skills of the opposition parties.'

He paused. 'The recent exploits of a few of my former ministers have highlighted the misguided and muddled thought processes of political apparatchiks. Their goal was to ingratiate themselves with the news gatherers and the media rather than to focus on doing their jobs well. For this I am deeply sorry. We were elected to run the country on behalf of the people and not to look good and score points as if we were on a TV game show. Last week, presidential style, single-party politics was the order of the day. As of Friday morning this all changed. It is our duty to pull together, work in harmony and deal with the aftermath of this tragedy. Therefore, this afternoon, my Chancellor and I shall be setting out my Government's proposals which are designed to take us forward, with one voice.'

The PM glanced across at the opposition benches as he spoke. 'Until such time as the country has recovered and its economy is prosperous again, I will be forming a Coalition Government and a new collective Cabinet drawn from across the political spectrum of this House. The Cabinet's composition will be along the lines of Parliamentary committees. This morning I had an audience with the Queen and I also met with the leaders of Her Majesty's two main opposition parties. We have agreed to identify a range of topics which will henceforth be outside the Punch and Judy nature of politics and will become a matter for consensus between the leading political parties. This will enable the Government to deliver long-term strategies and not quick fixes. The country will require this if it is to fully recover its dynamism.'

The PM had the complete attention of those listening to him.

'A State of Emergency will continue until such time as the after-effects of Stratford have diminished. Lest those of you sitting on the back benches or in the Upper Chamber feel left out, Parliament will have a major role to play in scrutinising the legislation that will be put forward by the Coalition Government - a National Government. Transparency and genuine debate will be key elements of this process.'

The PM hesitated and looked across to the Speaker of the House. 'This Government recognises that responsibility has to be taken for the disaster. The air has to be cleared to forestall any accusations that there might be in this House. I have accepted the resignations of the Home Secretary, a minister and two junior ministers in the Home Office. I will talk about their replacements shortly.'

This statement was met by gasps.

The PM continued resolutely. 'I have also accepted resignations from all those public servants in charge of nuclear safety matters and the board members of the company responsible for running nuclear freight trains. My Cabinet has arranged for a number of senior executives from leading energy and industrial companies to be seconded to take their places in the short to medium term. I am pleased to report to the House that a distinguished former leader of an opposition party has agreed to work with the new Home Secretary, as the Home Office minister with responsibility for Homeland Security. He has put on hold all his private business activities and speaking engagements. Some might say that the Home Office is a poisoned chalice; others might view it as an opportunity. I am pleased that the former party leader takes the latter view.'

The PM paused and took a sip of water, looked at his watch, and continued. 'I shall be announcing the details of my Cabinet reshuffle over the next twenty-four hours; this will include the name of the new Home Secretary and the other key ministers of State. I have not asked them yet, as many of them sit on the benches opposite me and today their role is to hold this

Government to account. In picking the new members of the Cabinet, I have borne in mind that there is no substitute for real world experience. The pendulum has swung too far. Too many members of the Government have little or no experience outside the political arena. This is unhealthy and undesirable.'

The camera swung around the House. The brooding menace which had been in the air over the opposition benches had lessened. The inclusive proposals had taken those in the Chamber by surprise – so far so good.

*

Golden Sundancer had her fenders out on her port side. With a delicate touch, she was brought alongside the harbour wall about eighty metres across from *Puddle Jumper*. The captain and Basel were on the flybridge. The muscular frame of Dakka Dudayev, the Stratford terrorist, could be seen standing at the stern. The slight figure of Kim Chindriani, one of the recruiters of the bombers, was at the bow. They threw lines to the two heavies waiting at the edge of the harbour wall. The ropes were passed round heavy metal bollards and back on board. Bow and stern springs were attached and a gangway was put in place.

'That leaves Sergy Kowshaya, the Chechen terrorist, and Alistair Hartnell, Basel's number two, below deck,' said Mark over the radio from the shadows of the harbour side. 'What are the odds that they are suffering from seasickness?'

As if on cue, two very dishevelled and ashen-looking men stumbled on deck and walked shakily down the gangway to dry land, both dropping to their knees and kissing the ground.

'Excellent, excellent,' said a voice from the command centre. 'Kowshaya definitely looks below par.'

Meanwhile, the retired commander, his wife and two *daughters* had come out onto the foredeck of *Puddle Jumper* to watch the arrival of their neighbour. Janet waved to the man standing on the harbour side by the bow of *Golden Sundancer*. Unnoticed, Clive and Jim slipped over the stern in their grey, lightweight wetsuits, and sleek air tanks strapped to their backs.

The command centre had briefed the two SBS men. 'We've identified a blind spot, three to four metres from the stern of *Golden Sundancer* at her waterline, on her starboard side. Suggest you wait there.'

They slid out of sight below the water, hugged the harbour wall and quietly surfaced at the specified blind spot. They shed their air tanks and flippers, and waited for the signal that the coast was clear and it was safe to climb on board via the swimming platform. Sergy Kowshaya and Alistair Hartnell meanwhile had returned below deck.

*

The Prime Minister was now thirty minutes into his speech. He was talking about nuclear power and the importance of the UK being self-sufficient in energy terms. 'The security of our energy supplies is crucial. In a modern society, energy is a cornerstone on which the foundations of a civilised way of life are built. We have suffered the devastating impact of a nuclear disaster. Maintaining the status quo is no longer an option. In the last Parliament a decision was taken which seemed to be the simplest and most convenient zero carbon option.' He paused and looked around the House. 'The go-ahead was given for £50 billion to be spent on a new generation of nuclear power stations for the 2020s. This, in hindsight, was rushed and did not address the scale of the risks involved… With nuclear power there is an infinitesimal probability of things going wrong, but when they do, the hazards are *so* extreme that they dwarf the benefits. The debate should have focused on how self-sufficiency could have been achieved *without* nuclear power... As things currently stand, in these times of terrorist threats, nuclear power has become too vulnerable, and too risky. However, it may still have a role to play, *but only when* the transportation, storage and security risks have been addressed, in a thoroughly uncompromising manner. Then and only then can it be brought back onto the agenda.'

The PM looked up at the camera. 'With this in mind, a Ministry for Energy and Scarce Resources will be created. It will be tasked with moving forward energy savings, the development of sustainable and efficient renewable energy technology and the efficient use of this country's energy resources. It will work with the Treasury and provide the stimuli required to make us use our existing natural resources wisely. The Treasury's role will be central to our move to energy self-sufficiency and nuclear-free electricity generation. Accordingly, I have commissioned a report from a panel of experts on how Britain can deal with the impending fifty percent energy shortfall. Their detailed findings will be discussed by my new Cabinet, and we shall place our proposals before Parliament at the earliest opportunity.'

The PM paused, looked down at his watch and continued. 'In particular, this panel is considering clean coal technology, carbon capture and sequestration techniques. The Victorians recognised the importance of sanitation and built a network of sewers to counter the threats of disease. We now recognise the threat of climate change. With this in mind, the panel is looking at the benefits of building a network of pipelines to collect carbon dioxide from the largest carbon polluters so that it can be stored cost-effectively underground.' He rearranged his papers, looked at his watch again and continued. 'British coal is an energy source steeped in political emotions. It transformed our country's economy during the Industrial Revolution. It is a valuable resource which we have prematurely discarded. The country has a couple of hundred years of retrievable reserves and, unlike oil and gas where exporters act like a cartel, with coal there is a free market with over 100 countries exporting it. Clean coal will play an integral part in our future and our ability to become energy self-sufficient and environmentally responsible...'

*

A movement on the main screen caught Rafi's eye and his attention shifted. The Air Chief Marshal was speaking to the SBS command centre.

News had just come in from the six SAS soldiers travelling to Safi. Two trucks had collided on the bridge at Azemmour, blocking the road to all traffic. Unexpectedly they were facing a slow 45 km detour via the next bridge upriver at Maachou and were likely to miss the party. Colonel Gray was not pleased.

*

The PM had moved on to a new topic. 'On the Homeland Security front, we must of course ensure that coordinated attacks, as suffered on Friday, never happen again. Over the past few years the security associated with airport travel has been tightened up. However, the security associated with our land borders has been shown to be unfit for purpose. Our immigration rules and methods of identifying who is legitimately in this country and who is here illegally are too lax and seriously wanting. I am not a believer in identity cards nor in Orwellian Big Brother-style interference in people's lives, however, the system must be improved.'

The PM glanced across to the opposition benches. 'I will ask the new Home Office minister in charge of Homeland Security to draw up proposals which will provide transparency as to who is in our country. Biometrics will be used for the unique identification of individuals. The software, I am advised, is available to facilitate this. I repeat: this is *not* the thin end of the wedge for the full-scale issuance of identity cards. One secure biometric database will be created and it will be used to confirm a person's identity. Name, date of birth, contact address, photograph, fingerprints, iris scan and other such biometric data, as appropriate, will be stored on the database. Biometric information will be gathered at police stations and specialist Homeland Security offices free of charge. Visitors to the UK will be required to provide biometric data at their point of entry.'

The PM took a sip water. 'This database will be available online for a restricted number of users, so that they can confirm a person's identity. However, these users *will only* be able to confirm that the individual *is* who they say they are, by checking their biometric details online. We have become accustomed to having our PIN number checked when we withdraw cash from a cashpoint machine - this will be a broadly similar process. No part, I repeat, *no part* of the database will be available for downloading. In future, an individual's biometric information will be checked as part of the process of obtaining a passport or driving licence and verification will be real time, online at an official office. Furthermore, as from 1 September, all new car insurance policies will require named drivers - each of whose identity will need to be verified against the biometric database.'

'Over a relatively short period of time, users of public services such as, for example, the National Health Service, social and local authority services, tax offices and the Electoral Register will be required to be on the biometric database. However, I stress that each database will remain separate. It is *fundamental* that they do. The State does not wish to invade people's privacy, but it does need to know the names of the people in our country, have a point of contact for them and know the basis on which they are here. It is currently not possible for the Home Office to give an accurate estimate of the number of people in the UK. *Too* many people are off the radar screen. The numbers run into hundreds of thousands. This is totally unacceptable. Those who are here illegally or without the appropriate documentation will be identified. There will be duplicates and anomalies, and these will be investigated by the authorities.'

The PM paused to let what he had just said sink in.

*

At the airport, the sheikh was beginning to get annoyed by the delay. He pulled out a wad of banknotes and gave them to one of his bodyguards, with instructions to hurry the mechanic up. Minutes later, as if by magic, the mechanic reappeared carrying an aluminium stepladder on his shoulder and a large toolbox. He set up his ladder and climbed up to the rotary engine, then removed a side panel and looked in. He stood there for a minute, seemingly tinkering around. He closed the panel, gave the pilot the thumbs up and walked slowly back to the buildings.

The helicopter was ready to get on its way to Safi. The thirty-minute delay was all that had been needed.

*

Once again Rafi's attention shifted to the action at Safi.

Dakka Dudayev had left *Golden Sundancer* and was enjoying a cigarette on the quayside. Janet and Anna waved at him and his brief acknowledgement was taken by them as an invitation to go over to him. They hopped off *Puddle Jumper* and, in a carefree manner, walked around the harbour towards Dakka, with their caftans flowing in the wind. The material was bunched up and tied around their hips, thus obscuring the small pistols that were tucked into their bikini bottoms. Under their hair, out of sight, were miniature headphones, and tiny microphones were hidden in their bikini tops.

Janet approached Dakka as if he was the first red-blooded male she'd seen for a very long while. Anna stood nearby, looking on shyly. The two women giggled like teenage girls. They looked beautiful, flirty and helpless.

On *Golden Sundancer*, the captain and Basel were still on the flybridge. Dakka was on the quayside and this left the three remaining individuals below deck. It would soon be time for Clive and Jim to make their move.

Over the radio came the voice of Mark, one of the SAS men. 'The captain is calling up the harbour master about refuelling. There's no reply. He is sending Sergy to investigate.'

Sergy hesitantly walked up the gangway, and then off along the harbour side. As he passed *Puddle Jumper*, he received a friendly 'Good afternoon' from the commander's wife who was sitting in the sun on the aft deck.

Sergy was about to discover the problem. The harbour master was lying unconscious at his desk – he had received a knock out blow from Colin, the second SAS soldier, who had also bugged the room and placed a small gismo looking like a Coke can in the rubbish bin. It was a radio-controlled device containing some of the strongest knockout gas known.

*

Rafi's attention switched back to the TV. The PM was in his stride. His sound bites were excellent.

'Stratford has shown how a few kilograms of radioactive waste can blight a vast area for millennia. The UK owns tonnes of highly toxic radioactive waste. Post Stratford the threat of being able to disperse radioactivity over an aggressor's city will be as strong a deterrent as annihilating it with a Trident missile. We can therefore put to one side the next generation of Trident missiles and switch to lower cost, but highly effective *dispersal missiles* which will make use of our stockpile of radioactive waste. These dispersal missiles will include radioactive isotopes that will glow in the dark, so that there can be no misunderstanding as to where the radioactive fall-out is located. The switch from Trident to dispersal missiles will save tens of billions, and we will channel these massive savings into higher education and academic research. This will counter the underinvestment which higher education has suffered over the past three decades - during this time we have seen the relative rankings of our universities on the global stage slip. Despite this, fourteen of our universities are in the top 100 in the world; twenty-five are in the top 200 and forty-three are in the top 500. These are figures we can be proud of. UK higher education is an area of international excellence. We shall build on this excellence and it will benefit our economy.'

The PM then paused and again looked at his watch. It was coming up to 14.30 – he and the Chancellor still had a lot more talking to do.

*

Kate nudged Rafi and pointed towards the screens and the action taking place at Safi harbour.

Mark, who had been carefully watching *Golden Sundancer*, gave the all-clear. Clive and Jim slipped quietly on to the bathing platform. They peeled off their waterproof suits to reveal dry clothes underneath. Silently, they moved forward, their automatic pistols drawn. Basel Talal and the captain were on the flybridge, chatting, whereas Sergy and Dakka were ashore. That left Kim Chindriani and Alistair Hartnell below deck.

Mark's monitoring device pinpointed the location of the two people in the cabins. Clive and Jim crept silently through the boat's main stateroom and proceeded down the stairs to the cabins. They were directed towards the two men on their bunks.

Forty-five nail-biting seconds later Jim's voice came over the speaker: 'Both men are inoperative. They're gagged and tied up. Please advise when we should expect our next customer.'

Two terrorists down, six more terrorists and six bodyguards to go, Rafi thought to himself.

*

Along the quay, Sergy arrived at the harbour master's office. He quietly approached the shabby front door, which was closed. His hand was tucked under his loosely fitting shirt. Concealed forty metres away, Colin noted that he was undoubtedly armed. Sergy looked around before he pushed the door open and entered the tired-looking building. He closed it behind him. A torrent of what Rafi could only imagine were Chechen swear words were picked up by the listening device.

Sergy was obviously far from pleased. He pulled out a small walkie-talkie. The bug picked up his conversation with the captain. 'The harbour master is pissed out of his mind; sprawled out cold across his desk with an empty bottle of Scotch in his hand. I'll sober him up and come back to the boat. Out!'

Colin listened in and pressed the red button on the small grey box in his hand. The knockout gas in what looked like a Coke can was released into the room. Six seconds later there was a resounding thump as the Chechen's body hit the floor. Colin moved unobtrusively from his hiding place and skirted around the back of the harbour master's office, out of the line of sight of those on *Golden Sundancer*. He put on a clear plastic gas mask, pulled out from his back pocket a scrunched-up flannel hat and placed it on his head. He stood there, waiting for the all-clear signal from his colleague who was observing the captain on the flybridge. As Basel Talal turned to descend the stairs to the main deck level, Colin casually walked around to the front of the harbour master's office, and slipped quietly inside.

A minute later Sergy was trussed up like a Christmas turkey, as was the harbour master, just in case either woke up, which, given the circumstances, was highly improbable. Both men would be out for at least two hours; far longer if either of them suffered from a weak heart or asthma. Colin radioed in that the two had been tied up and, on hearing that the coast was still clear, sneaked out of the office, making sure that the door was left slightly ajar to let the fresh air in to disperse the knockout gas. He then walked around the back of the buildings to join Mark who was watching the heavies as they waited for the helicopter.

*

As Sergy was being tied up in the harbour master's office, Clive and Jim received a warning through their ear pieces from Mark that Basel Talal was on his way to his cabin. He was ambushed. Not being trained in unarmed combat, he didn't stand a chance and didn't see what was coming. Unconscious and securely trussed up, he was left by Jim in his cabin, propped up in a chair.

Outside, on the quay, Janet and Anna were doing their best to chat up Dakka.

He was interested in them, but his training told him that there would be time later. He spotted the captain descending from the flybridge and turned to leave.

In their earpieces the two women received an order: 'Slow him down; we don't want him on board for a couple of minutes. Will advise when it's safe for him to board.'

Janet called after Dakka. 'Before you go, would you by any chance have a bottle of vodka we could borrow? Our parents are so boring; they don't like people drinking on board. Please, please; we would make it worth your while!'

Dakka stopped and gave the two attractive women an appraising look. 'Wait there and I'll see what I can find.'

Janet moved alongside him and followed him towards the gangplank.

'We need another thirty seconds - do not let him board,' came an urgent voice over the communications link. Anna broke into a run, caught up with Janet, tripped and went flying on to the concrete quayside. She let out a howl and a series of expletives. Janet bent over her friend who was spreadeagled on the ground. 'Sis, are you alright?'

'Oow, I've really hurt my knee.'

Dakka stayed where he was.

Janet helped Anna to sit up. Blood was streaming down her leg from a nasty gash in her knee.

Dakka looked down at Anna and then in a matter-of-fact manner said, 'I'll fetch the first aid kit.' He paused briefly and then added, 'And a bottle of vodka. Wait here.'

*

Moments earlier Mark had given a warning to Jim and Clive that the captain was on his way below deck.

The captain sensed something was wrong as he was about to enter his cabin. As he turned to investigate, he was felled by a strong blow to the side of his neck.

'Damn it! Clive,' exclaimed Jim, 'You nearly took his head off.'

'Yep, But how was I to know he was going to turn around.'

The captain was securely bound up and dumped on his bed.

Clive and Jim waited silently and out of sight at the bottom of the stairs.

Dakka meanwhile, went to a cupboard in the stateroom and pulled out a bottle of vodka, then turned and collected the first aid box from the stern deck. He walked down the gangplank to the two women huddled on the quayside. He handed them the bottle and the box. 'Put the box on the gangway when you've finished. I'm busy now. I'll see you later for my reward.'

Meanwhile, Clive and Jim had climbed the stairs and were waiting in the stateroom. Their earpieces kept them informed as to where their target was. Dakka walked down the gangplank and through the open door into the stateroom. His sixth sense told him he wasn't alone. He spun around to see Jim coming at him. Instinctively, he shifted his weight from one foot to the other and let fly a lethal drop kick which caught Jim just below the shoulder, knocking him backwards. Jim started to pick himself up, but was too slow: Dakka was on him, his powerful hands locked around Jim's neck, pinning him to the floor.

There was an almighty crash. Dakka slumped unconscious across Jim's body. The remnants of a heavy glass decanter were scattered across the carpet.

Jim struggled to regain his breath, as Clive hauled the muscled man off him. Moments later, Clive had Dakka's arms tightly secured behind his back with reinforced plastic handcuffs.

'Thanks,' said Jim, as Clive carried on immobilising the terrorist.

Jim got up slowly. 'For a heavy man, he sure moved quickly! I reckon the bastard has either broken my collarbone or dislocated my shoulder.'

'No good asking you for a hand in getting him down below, then?' Clive dragged Dakka across the stateroom and, with a series of loud bumps, down the stairs.

He reappeared a few moments later. 'I've put him with the captain. Right, let's have a look at you.' Clive stood in front of Jim. 'Lift your arm as high as you can. Is that all you can manage? Does it hurt here?' He prodded Jim's collarbone area.

'Not much.'

'Think of something nice; your girlfriend with no clothes on - got the picture?'

Jim nodded.

Clive took hold of his arm and with a quick upward motion relocated his shoulder back into place.

'Jesus!' screeched Jim. 'That was painful.'

'Come on, let's see what you can do with your injured arm. Can you hold a gun?'

Jim nodded.

'You will be useless in a fight unless the opposition has a blouse on,' commented Clive.

*

'Six out of six accounted for on the boat. This leaves the four minders on the quayside and five in the helicopter.' Rafi smiled as he listened to the radio transmission.

The sheikh's helicopter was about fifteen minutes away.

Meanwhile the Nimrod picked up the mobile phone conversation between the sheikh's bodyguard and one of the heavies on the quayside. 'Is everything OK? I've tried to ring the captain but there's no answer.'

The heavy standing on the quayside looked across at *Golden Sundancer*. 'All quiet here. The captain has gone below; probably getting ready to meet you.'

'Good. We'll be with you shortly.'

Rafi made a mental calculation. The operation was running about twenty minutes behind schedule. He hoped the PM and his Chancellor had sufficient material to keep on talking, then noticed that the PM was being handed a folded piece of paper.

Colonel Gray, standing nearby in the Ops Room, had arranged for its delivery only a few minutes earlier. The note read: *Terrorists on boat at Safi have been captured. The helicopter with the sheikh and Jameel onboard is en route and expected to land in the next fifteen minutes. We estimate it will take sixty to seventy-five minutes to wrap things up.*

At the dispatch box the Prime Minister was handed a sheet of paper. He slowly read the message - his face gave nothing away. He then turned and passed it across to his Chancellor, who read it, smiled and tapped the pile of files on his lap. The PM took a deep breath and continued. He was a professional, carrying on if his prolonged speech was the most natural thing in the world.

'The role of our armed forces has to be reconsidered. Our military forces must be properly equipped to defend us against terrorist attacks. We have to change our strategy and start fighting − not with brute force but with minds and souls. Post Iraq we have surrendered the moral high ground. Our international image is tarnished. We must rebuild trust in ourselves and our country.'

The PM was in flowing form. 'It is time to restore our sense of fair play and equity. Warfare has changed. It has moved from the macro level and large theatres of war, to the micro level and local operations. We need to refocus our military prowess and twin our military might with our anti-terrorist expertise. Stratford has been the wake-up call to end all wake-up calls. We have to be able to counter terrorist attacks on our own soil and have the wherewithal to deal with major calamities should they ever arise again. We must have personnel and equipment fit for purpose. I have asked the head of the armed forces and the Defence Minister to prepare a briefing note to this end for Cabinet. Part of their brief will be to consider the valuable role that the Territorial Army and former military personnel can play. In particular, they will look at the specialist skills they can offer, and will advise on how they might be appropriately rewarded for their part-time commitment to our military activities.'

*

On the dockside, Anna's knee had been patched up by Janet. The two women slowly walked back to *Puddle Jumper* clutching the first aid box and the bottle of vodka. They had been informed via their earpieces that Dakka had been overpowered.

Anna smiled; the gash to her knee had been worthwhile.

On board *Puddle Jumper*, she was given a hot cup of tea with sugar by the commander's wife.

The commander was deep in thought, looking over the charts in front of him.

'What are you looking at?' asked Janet.

'I reckon it's always a good idea to know exactly where every-thing is, just in case things turn interesting and one has to leave in a hurry,' came the reply.

The sound of an approaching helicopter caught their attention and that of the four heavies.

Across on *Golden Sundancer*, a mobile phone started ringing in the cabin where Basel had been stowed. Clive opened the door and pulled the phone out of Basel's trouser pocket.

It was Jameel. 'Baz, Jamie here; we'll be landing in a couple of minutes. The sheikh is most pleased and wants to congratulate you personally. He says he's looking forward to the London markets reopening tomorrow. And he says by then, he'll have jumped up the world's rich list by umpteen places. His positions in Frankfurt and Chicago should also show fantastic profits; he's going to close all his positions tomorrow and send the markets spiralling down. We're all going to be fantastically rich it'll be difficult to count the noughts! Baz, are you there?' Jameel heard the sound of a lavatory flushing and a muffled voice.

Clive hung up and smiled.

The helicopter hovered over the area, next to where the heavies were standing, preparing to land.

Clive and Jim rummaged around in the captain's and Basel's cupboards. Jim found a Panama hat and gaudy striped shirt. He slowly took off his top and replaced it with the loud shirt, put the hat on his head and walked up to the stateroom to join Clive, who was wearing the captain's hat and a tight-fitting white jacket.

They pulled up two chairs and positioned them so that they were partially facing away from the open door, yet would be visible from where the helicopter was landing. They could be seen from the quayside enjoying a drink. It was as though the captain and Basel were casually waiting for their guests to arrive.

Mark and Colin, who had been patiently waiting in the shadows, spoke quietly to each other.

'I can see my targets, but can't get near them,' said Colin.

'Not much cover to help me either,' remarked Mark.

A crisp voice from the command centre cut in. 'If necessary take them out and move on - and provide backup for Jim and Clive. Remember, it is the sheikh and Jameel we want unharmed. If the others get in the way, so be it. Got that?'

Under the noise of the helicopter landing, the quiet pops of the silenced guns were inaudible. The two heavies who had moved back to the nearby buildings slumped to the ground with bullet holes to the chest and forehead.

Rafi winced, but told himself that the stakes were too high for niceties. It all felt a bit unreal.

*

Mark and Colin shifted their location to get a better line of sight. The rotors were still whirring when the two remaining heavies, with their heads held low, ran forward and opened the side doors. The two bodyguards were the first to step out; they were closely followed by Jameel and the sheikh. The group started walking towards *Golden Sundancer*. Jameel and the sheikh were at ease, smiling and talking to each other. They didn't notice anything untoward, until it was too late.

Jim, with the brim of his panama hat pulled down at a jaunty angle and his bright shirt catching the light, waved energetically to Jameel, raised a glass in the air and returned to his conversation with the captain.

Anna and Janet stepped off *Puddle Jumper* and made their way towards *Golden Sundancer* with the first aid box. They arrived just before the group from the helicopter. Their flimsy flowing kaftans caught the eye of Jameel, who strolled over to say hello.

Meanwhile, the sheikh and his two bodyguards headed towards the gangway. Then, one of the bodyguards heard the spluttering of silenced gun fire and turned to see the two heavies, who had greeted them, lying on the ground by the helicopter. He let out a loud warning shout and pulled out his gun.

Over the radio came the command from Mark, the closest SAS soldier: 'They've gone hostile. Take them out.'

There was more spluttering of silenced guns. The sheikh's two bodyguards fell on the spot where they had been standing.

The helicopter pilot, sensing danger, fired up his engine, but wasn't fast enough. Colin broke cover, sprinted across and with his gun pointing through the window, beckoned the pilot to turn the engine off. The sound from the rotor blades faded.

The sheikh lunged forward to grab his bodyguard's gun, which was lying nearby on the ground.

'I wouldn't do that if I was you,' warned Clive, who was standing on the gangway, his gun trained on the sheikh. 'Move once and you lose your manhood; move twice and you lose your mobility!' The sheikh froze. Clive walked towards him, slowly.

'What do you want?' he growled.

'Maryam sends her best wishes. She's set you up; her freedom for yours. She has all your account details and, with you behind bars, she gets everything,' he said, enjoying the wind-up.

'The devious little harlot,' spat out the sheikh.

Clive swung him round and secured his hands tightly behind his back with plastic handcuffs. He spoke to the command centre. 'The sheikh has been apprehended.'

Anna, meanwhile, had been standing less than three metres from Jameel when the shooting started. Jameel stood there, transfixed, watching as those around him fell. He returned his gaze to the beautiful woman standing near him. There, in the palm of her

295

hand was a small shiny revolver.

'Don't move,' she ordered. 'At this range I can choose whether I hit you in the heart or perhaps the head. Either way, if you move you're dead.'

Jameel stood still. 'Who are you?' he asked.

'Silence!' Anna ordered, or you leave here in a box.'

'What's going on?'

'Silence!' ordered Anna again. 'You'll get explanations in good time.'

Jim walked over. 'Need a hand?' he enquired.

He didn't wait for an answer. He swivelled Jameel around and with a firm grip secured his hands behind his back with a pair of handcuffs, and then proceeded to frisk him. 'He isn't armed; he's all yours.'

'Thanks,' said Anna, 'Why do you boys get all the fun?'

Jameel looked from Anna to Jim. 'Who are you?'

'Friends of Maryam,' came Jim's reply.

*

At that moment, an urgent message came through to the command centre from the Nimrod. 'Moroccan air traffic control has picked up a distress call from the helicopter pilot.'

They played it back. 'Sheikh Tufayl, a worthy friend of Mohammed, has been kidnapped by hijackers at Safi docks. The hijackers have a large motor vessel. There have been shootings and killings; we are all in grave danger.'

The pilot had started to repeat his message, facing away from Colin, when he heard the thump of the butt of his gun against the window. He turned, looked down the barrel of Colin's gun and fell silent.

'Moroccan air traffic control has informed the police and the Royal Moroccan Air Force,' came the message from the Nimrod.

'Time to get out,' ordered the command centre. 'We suggest you take *Golden Sundancer*. Get out of there quick. You probably have less than five minutes before the local police arrive and less than half an hour before fighter planes come to have a look.'

Clive shouted to Mark. 'We have to get Sergy. I left him trussed up in a cupboard in the harbour master's office.'

The two men left for the office at a sprint.

The command centre was speaking to the commander on

Puddle Jumper. 'There isn't time to transfer the prisoners to your vessel. Take command of *Golden Sundancer*; check she has enough fuel and prepare her for immediate departure. Suggest you take your local charts with you and leave now.'

The commander grabbed his charts and a few personal belongings and called across to his wife to gather up all she needed quickly. They ran as fast as they could in the direction of the terrorists' boat.

★

The PM was winding down his speech. 'I have set the scene for the next phase of British politics. It will be consensus politics. The three largest political parties speak for ninety five percent of those who voted in the recent general election and their representatives in the Cabinet will have much work to do.' He paused as the members of the minority parties stirred with disaffection. 'However, I recognise that it would not be a good idea to leave out members of the minority parties, especially those representing the regions.'

The PM looked across to the minority parties and their representatives. 'I am aware that there are some very able people who sit in this House, who are not members of one of the three main parties. Rest assured, you will have a role to play. I have been heartened by the generous offers of help that have come from Scotland, Wales and Northern Ireland. As part of the Union, all parts of the UK will have responsibility in shaping our countries' future. London has been the powerhouse that has driven the UK economy for decades. Post-Stratford, it is an inevitable truth that London's economy will struggle, with nearly one-sixth of its population displaced and almost one-twentieth of its land now unfit for human habitation. Our capital must now be joined by cities across the UK in the quest to regain our competitive and prosperous economy. Regional cities must pick up the baton and push our economy forward.'

He glanced to his left towards the Speaker. 'These are exceptional times. I propose to break with tradition, if the Speaker permits, and ask the Chancellor of the Exchequer to follow me with his proposals on how to get this great Country back on its feet. After the Honourable Member has set out his proposals, I shall face any questions the Members of this House might wish to put.'

The Speaker nodded and the PM picked up his watch.

If all went to plan the Chancellor would need to speak for just less than fifty minutes, plus the time it took to capture Maryam. Then the news of the terrorists' capture could be made public and the round-up could begin.

The PM stood aside to let the Chancellor move to the dispatch box. The Chancellor took off his watch and placed it to one side in front of him. He had with him his notes and a small pile of different coloured wallet files, which he stacked neatly next to his watch.

The polite silence continued for the Chancellor. Rafi sensed that the fireworks were being reserved for the questions after his speech.

The Chancellor's face was strained and unsmiling. His voice was unruffled, but sombre. 'Our economy and the Government's finances have suffered a second massive blow. Just as we thought we were coming to terms with the first shock to the system - the debilitating effects of the global credit crunch - we have been hit by a nuclear catastrophe. We face financially perilous times which will necessitate significant changes in order to steer our economy back to safe waters.'

Those in the Chamber sat in silence as they waited for the gravity of the position to be fully revealed. 'I will, this afternoon, set out how the Government plans to remedy the position and I shall be introducing a range of initiatives to facilitate the rebuilding of our economy…'

*

The commander had reached *Golden Sundancer* - a big sister to *Puddle Jumper*. He bounded up on to her fly deck. 'Phew!' The ignition key was still in place.

He turned the key and pressed the ignition buttons. The turbo diesels roared into life. He ran through the checks.

He was talking to himself under his breath. 'The auxiliary fuel tanks are both empty, but the main tank is probably good for 100, maybe 150 miles. That should be more than enough. This is going to be fun!' He never dreamt that he would find such heavy duty power again. 'It's going to be like the Sabre class vessels; what a way to feel young again!'

He called across to Lieutenant Anna Gregson. 'Cast off and stow the fore and aft springs - then man the bow line.'

In the direction of Lieutenant Janet Steiner he shouted, 'Prepare to stow the gangway. And Jim, man the stern line.'

The commander saw the door to the harbour master's office swing open. Clive and his SAS colleague, Mark, were carrying the deadweight of the bear-like terrorist; they had an arm under each of his shoulders, leaving his feet to drag along the ground. They were doing something more than a trot, but they were still over 200 metres away. The commander did some mental arithmetic.

Meanwhile Colin had handcuffed the helicopter pilot to his joystick and as a parting gesture fired a couple of bullets into the helicopter's radio and fuel tank. For the time being at least the helicopter would be going nowhere. He then tidied up the bodies of the six bodyguards and left them sitting on the concrete with their guns on their laps.

The commander called across to Jim. 'Move the stern painter to the starboard side and make certain it can run freely around the bollard on the quayside. Stand by the cleat until you receive further orders.'

'Aye, aye, sir. Runs freely,' came the reply.

'Lieutenant Gregson, check that the bow painter runs freely and prepare to cast off.'

'Runs freely, sir.'

The commander turned to his wife who was standing behind him. 'Darling, would you please find a boat hook and when I say "Cast off bow", push hard at the quayside wall and swing the bow out into the harbour?'

He turned and looked astern. 'Jim, when I call "Cast off bow", let out three metres of mooring line - no more - and hold her until I say "Cast off stern". Mind there are no knots to snag the rope – and watch your fingers!'

'Aye, aye, sir.'

In the distance there was the wailing of police sirens. They were getting closer. The two special services men were making good progress carrying the unconscious terrorist. They only had a few metres to go. The commander waited patiently for them to reach the gangway. Sergy was unceremoniously dragged on board by the SAS officer and Clive.

The commander shouted, 'Stow gangway, cast off bow, let out stern line and, darling, push!' He then eased the control for the port engine forward and the starboard engine slightly into reverse. The boat, which was still secured to the quayside with a stern line to her starboard side, turned on a sixpence. At that moment he caught sight of the first police car. Moments later, the bow was facing the opposite side of the harbour and was swinging round to face out to sea.

The commander called out, 'Cast off stern!'

Jim, thinking of his fingers and the taught rope, took out his razor-sharp knife and cut the lines secured to the rear stanchion. At that moment the commander pushed forward the throttles to both engines. The vessel was like a wild stallion that had been tied down and suddenly allowed to run free. With the engines roaring, the stern dug deep into the water. The commander by now had the throttles towards their maximum revs.

The commander shouted, 'Lieutenants: stow the fenders and prepare for sea.'

The harbour water was like a millpond. *Golden Sundancer*, with the power of her two turbo engines propelling her forward, gracefully lifted her bow up out of the water and on to the plane.

The commander looked over his shoulder and saw that the first police car was 150 metres away. *Golden Sundancer* was almost up to her cruising speed. He smiled. He was enjoying the feeling of the immense power beneath his feet.

'I'll give a prize,' shouted out the commander, 'To the first man or woman who can cause a distraction on the quayside. A car's petrol tank perhaps? We want them to keep their heads down until we get out of range.'

Clive passed Anna his rifle. 'See if you can hit something.'

With the skill of a trained professional, she picked up the rifle and fired at the nearest police car. At that moment there was a huge explosion which ripped apart the nearest harbour building, followed by a second explosion further down the quayside. The quayside was torn apart and a plume of dark smoke erupted from the tall storage tank behind the buildings. The police car screeched to a halt and the policemen dived for cover.

Clive shot a glance at Colin standing nearby and laughed.

'Damn good shooting!' he exclaimed and gave Anna a firm pat on the back. Her bemused smile stretched from ear to ear.

Hidden from view, in the palm of the of Colin's hand, was a small radio-controlled transmitter which had set off the explosions. He grinned at Clive. 'So nice, for once, to be properly prepared for a retreat.'

The commander called down. 'See if you can hole *Puddle Jumper*'s hull. She's the next fastest vessel in the area and we don't want her coming after us.'

Anna and the two SAS soldiers trained their rifles on *Puddle Jumper*. Flecks of spray appeared along her waterline as the shots reached their target.

The commander on the flybridge had the engine throttles forward to their maximum. He looked at the rev counters. The port engine had crept into the red. He eased it back to below the red and, at the same time, balanced the revs on the starboard engine. *Golden Sundancer* was making forty-nine knots. She was pure poetry in motion. He cast an eye over to the chart which he had been studying carefully earlier in the day. The channel posed few problems. Phase one was complete. It was time for phase two: getting out of Moroccan territorial waters, into the freedom of international waters and on to the rendezvous with the submarine twenty miles off the coast.

Jim, who had climbed up on to the flybridge, called out, 'Permission to come on to the bridge, commander,' as he mounted the last step.

The commander turned around. 'Yes. Jim, could you sort out the radio? I need to find out from command centre what the incoming Moroccan Air Force is up to. In a few minutes we'll be in open water. I need to know which direction they are approaching from.'

Jim sat down next to the radio and changed the settings.

'Here you are, commander.'

'It's all yours Jim; I've the charts to work on.' The commander called down to his wife. 'Darling, could you come up to the fly-bridge?' She bounced up the stairs like a young rating and he gave her some instructions: 'Right, your task is to steer a course of due west and to keep an eye on the two rev counters, the temperature and oil pressure dials. Anything untoward, please shout! We're making straight for international waters.'

The swell in the Atlantic Ocean had eased, and the waves, though several metres tall, were long and well spaced out. *Golden Sundancer* was skimming across the water; being light on fuel helped. These were the conditions in which she thrived. She looked and felt spectacular - like a thoroughbred. The commander's wife delicately adjusted the throttle, applying a little more power, lifting the revs to a fine whisker below the red. The roar decreased a few decibels as she eased back the throttle to a point where the pitch of the engines sounded pleasing and not laboured. They were doing a very respectable forty-eight knots.

The commander recalled that Morocco had signed up to the international convention. Their territorial waters ended twelve nautical miles from land. It was an easy calculation: fifteen minutes to freedom - then he could start to breathe a small sigh of relief.

'Jim, what's the position regarding the fighter planes, please? And also enquire about the weather - those clouds over the bow look like rain in the offing.'

The radio crackled; it was the control centre. 'Are you receiving me, commander?'

'Jim here,' came the reply.

'Tell the commander that you'll shortly have company. A Mirage F1 fighter has been scrambled from Sidi Slimane Air Base some 235 nautical miles to your north-east.'

'North-east,' repeated the commander. 'Yes, I have it on the chart.'

'We'll advise when she's airborne: ETA from take-off is eleven minutes. Radio traffic suggests that the pilot is in no hurry - the control tower is telling him to pull his finger out, but the plane hasn't started taxiing to the runway as yet. And an old Northrop F-5E Tiger II has been scrambled from Meknes Airbase, 225 miles north-east of where you are - ETA from take-off is thirteen minutes. We'll advise when airborne. Radio traffic from the control tower suggests that the plane is undertaking its final checks as we speak and could be airborne shortly. To add to your problems, there's a Floréal class frigate at Casablanca. She's received orders to put to sea and has on board a Eurocopter

Panther. She's 140 miles away. She'll pose no problem unless she launches her paraffin pigeon which is armed for anti-surface and submarine warfare. You've potentially three bandits to avoid. We're working on a plan.'

The commander reached over and took the microphone from Jim's hand.

'We're heading due west from Safi harbour. We will reach international waters in…' He paused, looked at his watch, and then continued, 'In thirteen minutes forty-five seconds. Please advise the submarine to make her rendezvous point fifteen miles due west of Safi harbour. Please advise her ETA.'

*

Back in the Operations Room the events unfolding off the Moroccan coast had ratcheted up the tension. It was unheard of for a Trident class nuclear submarine to surface in open water when there were potentially hostile aircraft around – and so close to another country's territorial waters.

*

The commander surveyed the scene. He was having fun: *Golden Sundancer* was a joy to handle. His mind went into overdrive. He could clearly visualise in his mind's eye where he was and where the three hostiles were going to be approaching from.

The radio crackled to life. 'I've spoken to your pickup vessel; she'll be at the rendezvous point in forty-six minutes. You asked about the weather – expect some heavy rain showers.'

The commander looked at his watch. Yes, that should give him enough time so long as neither of the fighters got their act together and took off within the next three or four minutes. It was going to be a very close call. He called across to Jim, 'Get me Clive and the two SAS chaps here; we need a council of war. Tell Lieutenant Steiner to see how many life rafts she can find and ask her to take them to the aft deck. And get Lieutenant Gregson to see if she can find an inflatable dinghy, an outboard, and some life jackets, and to put them on the aft deck as well.'

The commander spoke into the radio. 'Do you have any news for us?'

'Yes, as good planning would have it, they kept back one of the Harrier jump jets that flew you and your wife to Gibraltar. She's fully armed and took off two minutes ago. Her ETA is

303

forty-one minutes.'

'Thank you,' replied the commander. The seconds were ticking by.

The longer it was before the fighters took off, the better their chances. He could pick out dark rain-laden squalls in the distance. A small smile crept across his face.

*

The Chancellor was in sombre mood. He was explaining to the House the consequences of the terrorist attack at Stratford and was setting out his proposals to persuade the public and industry to make the best use of energy and to encourage the diversification of the UK's energy resources.

'I shall be announcing a range of tax incentives to encourage the production and use of efficient and renewable energy sources, and to progress carbon sink technology to enable coal-fired power stations to move to zero emissions...'

*

At this point, Rafi's attention was pulled back to the big screen and the running commentary from the command centre.

Jim had returned to the flybridge with Clive and the two SAS men.

'Right,' said the commander, 'we've got ourselves a spot of bother. Two Moroccan fighters have been scrambled to intercept us and a frigate with a Eurocopter on board is putting to sea. In the short term it's the two fighters that concern me.'

The commander pointed at a spot on the map. 'The Trident submarine will reach our rendezvous point here in forty-two minutes. The Moroccan Mirage could be there in nineteen minutes and an elderly Northrop Tiger should follow a couple of minutes later. That will leave us unprotected, with nowhere to hide, for around twenty minutes. How many life rafts do we have?'

'Two,' came the reply from Jim.

'Excellent, get Lieutenant Steiner to inflate them and tell her to keep them tied down! Also, find out from Lieutenant Gregson what's happening with the search for a dinghy and an outboard.'

'She's found a twelve-foot inflatable with a ten horsepower outboard,' called back Clive.

'Perfect! Get it inflated and ready for sea – and make sure that

304

the outboard has petrol in it,' said the commander. He turned his attention to his charts. 'We'll reach international waters in five minutes. A couple of minutes later we should reach…' he pointed to the group of black clouds over the bow, 'That weather front, then we will launch the life rafts and I'll change *Golden Sundancer's* course and head her north, on autopilot, towards the two fighter jets.'

Clive raised his eyebrows.

The commander turned to the four special forces men around him. 'Here is the plan. You've got seven minutes from now to get the terrorists into the life rafts. Jim, you and Lieutenant Gregson will remain on board with me and my wife. The rest of you will go with the terrorists in the rafts. Once the rafts are in the water, we'll need to put as much distance as possible between the rafts and the fighters.' He paused. 'Let's hope that their attention is drawn to *Golden Sundancer* and they don't even think of looking for us elsewhere!'

The commander looked at Jim. 'Have you got anything more in your bag of tricks?'

All the special service men nodded in unison.

'Before I jump ship, could you wire up an explosive device, for which I can set the timing?' asked the commander.

'No problem,' replied Clive.

'Plus another bomb which can be detonated from the dinghy? And can you arrange for there to be a radio so that I can talk to the fighter pilots?'

'No problem.'

'Will one of you please disable the tracking devices in both life rafts and put a radio in each?' ordered the commander.

'Consider it done,' said Jim.

'As soon as the dinghy is fully inflated we will launch her, abandon ship and leave *Golden Sundancer* on autopilot heading at top speed up the coast. I'll come back in the inflatable and meet up with the two life rafts. If we can buy ourselves ten minutes before the first fighter spots *Golden Sundancer*, she'll put over eight miles between us and the fighters. Anything more is a bonus and will make it harder for them to find us.'

'Four minutes to international waters.' The commander's wife called out,

The commander turned to Clive, 'Time to get a move on.'

The four special servicemen ran down the steps to the lower deck to fetch the captives, who were bundled on to the floor of the rear deck.

'The two Chechens, Chindriani, Hartnell, you and I,' said Clive pointing to Colin, the nearest SAS man, 'Will go in one raft. The sheikh, Basel, Jameel, their captain, Lieutenant Steiner and Mark, the SAS major will go in the other.'

A minute and a half after they'd entered international waters, they reached the edge of the squall. The sea around them had darkened and the wind had strengthened – the telltale signs of looming heavy rain. Moments later the downpour hit them. The commander brought the vessel to a stop.

The terrorists were manhandled quickly into one life raft, then the other and, with their guards safely on board, the rafts were cast off.

The commander pushed the throttles forward and majestically *Golden Sundancer* lifted her bow out of the water.

Meanwhile, Lieutenant Gregson had the inflatable fully functional and Jim had rigged up two incendiary bombs.

'We will leave the precise timing until we know the status of the fighter planes,' said the commander.

'Of course, sir,' replied Jim.

The radio crackled back into life. 'The Northrop Tiger has completed its taxiing and is taking off as we speak. ETA thirteen minutes and counting.'

'Right!' shouted the commander. 'Life jackets on. I'll slow the boat down, let you get off, set the autopilot and come and join you.'

Jim looked at the commander. 'Old man, you realise that falling into the "oggin" at fifty knots will feel like hitting wet concrete?'

'Jim, get on your way and set the bomb to go off in twenty minutes. Your concern is noted,' replied the commander.

'Aye, aye, sir.'

'Throw me a life jacket, and shout when you're ready to leave ship.'

Seconds later came the call, 'Ready to disembark.'

The commander eased the throttles back. From the flybridge

he watched the three quickly and safely climb into the small inflatable dinghy and fire up the outboard engine. He picked up his small hand-held compass and tucked it into his trouser pocket, set a new course on the autopilot, pushed the throttles forward to their top setting, turned and bolted down the stairs, heading for the swimming platform.

The commander stood for a moment on the edge of the platform, watching the water churning at his feet. With a sharp intake of breath, he held his nose, knelt down and rolled slowly side first into the water. The compass in his pocket dug into his thigh as he hit the rushing water. He felt like a human skimming stone. Then there was darkness. The next thing he knew, he felt a strong pair of hands holding him as he gasped for breath. The inflatable dinghy was bobbing at his side in the pouring rain. Lieutenant Gregson and Jim, using his one good arm, grabbed him and dragged him on board. His wife put the small outboard into gear, turned the little dinghy and headed for the two life rafts.

Shaking from cold and shock, the commander fished inside his pocket and pulled out the small brass-encased compass. He opened it – it was still in one piece. He handed it to his wife and gave her the course to steer before flopping back down onto the wet floor of the dinghy.

*

The Ops Room and the command centre were on tenterhooks. The presence of the two Moroccan jets was going to make things very difficult and a major diplomatic row was the last thing the Government needed right now.

Colonel Gray sent a message to the House. The Chancellor was advised that he would have to speak for at least another forty minutes before the PM could reveal his hand.

*

The Chancellor leant forward and tapped the pile of folders in front of him, sending an acknowledgement to the Ops Room. He pulled out a red folder. 'I now wish to tackle one of our "sacred cows". It is a matter which has held back our economy and resulted in a disproportionate and inefficient allocation of capital away from production. At the present rate of decline, manufacturing's share of output will soon be less than ten percent.'

The silence was broken by MPs shuffling in their seats in anticipation of what was to follow.

'We live in a country where our home is our castle. Where we live is an integral part of our well-being. Those of us with above average salaries have the ability to occupy homes near to where we work, homes that are very comfortable to live in, but which are also very expensive. Too many of those who provide our public services and make our economy and our lives operate efficiently and harmoniously have been priced out of the market. They have been forced either to move long distances away from where they work or to live in substandard accommodation. Furthermore, the lack of appropriate accommodation near to where they work has prompted many individuals to leave their public sector jobs. Nurses, teachers, firemen, street sweepers, policemen and many, many more who work to make our lives better view owning a home as an impossibility; something they would love to afford in the right location, with the right amount of space, but that is financially out of their reach.'

The Chancellor looked up at the camera. 'Our love affair with housing has created exorbitant house prices and a dearth of affordable housing. These two factors are two of the – if not *the* – key factors driving social exclusion and social deprivation.' He paused for effect. 'Why should we have to live in homes which have prices far exceeding their building cost? Economists maintain that it's all to do with the immovable laws of supply and demand, but I have a different perspective; one borne out of the necessity to rectify the current inequity. The current housing market solutions for those on low salaries – namely, affordable housing, equity sharing and the like – make house ownership for the less well off a very risky business. Were these shared equity schemes a stock market product, I am sure that they'd be out-lawed by the Financial Services Authority as being far, far too risky for a family's largest investment.'

★

Rafi watched intently as the Chancellor paused and took a sip of water. The Chancellor still had a lot of talking to do, before the terrorists were captured, and only then could he get onto matters relating to Stratford and the economy. Rafi wondered how he would fill the time. Would his initiatives be new and innovative, or re-cast proposals which had already been announced? Rafi hoped that they would be the former. Now had to be the time for the Chancellor to be bold and housing was a good place to start…

★

'I now turn to another fundamental problem with affordable housing and housing for our armed forces and their families. This housing *is* low cost. It provides *small* residential units, *not* family homes, and encourages poor quality buildings. Furthermore the specifications of these low cost houses are environmentally unsound. We are stacking up problems for future generations: ghettoisation and the creation of the "haves" and the "have-nots". Our housing, when energy is a scarce resource, must be built to environmentally sound standards. The further we make our key and low paid workers commute, the less environmentally sensible it is - and the less able they are to enjoy their work and their home lives. In London, too many key workers lose over two hours a day commuting, not because they want to, but because they have to. For too many, between ten and fifteen hours a week are wasted. This is very poor use of people's time; it spoils people's quality of life and does not foster a contented society.'

The Chancellor moved up another gear. 'This Government will introduce a new ownership structure: *indexhold*. Indexhold is an uncomplicated structure: it simply uses the tried and tested legislation for leasehold property which will form the basis of the legal relationship between the freeholder and the indexholder.' He paused for a moment. 'Key workers and members of the armed forces will be able to purchase homes through indexhold ownership. These will be long leasehold interests at a nominal rent. The purchase price for the indexhold interest will be the gross building cost. It is the high cost of *land* that has pushed up property prices and driven away key workers from city centres. Indexholds will enable people to own their home, but at a sensible price, will provide new housing that is environmentally up to standard and will rebalance the fairness of the position.'

★

Rafi was amazed; what a remarkable concept, so logical, and so straightforward! It would, over time, dramatically improve the lifestyle of key workers and be tremendous for the economy - there was a need for hundreds of thousands of new homes and this would provide house builders with an environmentally friendly product to champion. He listened intently as the Chancellor continued.

*

'When the owner of an indexhold interest decides to move and sells their home, they will receive their initial purchase price *plus* a sum representing the inflationary increase. The freehold will be owned by a public body or a charity and they will have the first right of purchase on a sale. They can be expected to exercise this option to buy back the indexhold interest as the price will be significantly below that which the property could be sold for on the open market. At this point, the indexhold interest will then become available for sale to another key worker or soldier on another long lease.'

'In practical terms, the money raised by selling indexhold interests will be used to build the right types of homes, with high environmental standards, on land owned by the state. This proposal will assist those wishing to live close to their work in our large towns and cities, but will also be extended to rural communities to enable locals who are being priced out of their villages to remain there or get back into them.'

The Chancellor let slip a small smile. 'There will be another benefit. As there is a guaranteed blue-chip purchaser of the indexhold interest, namely the freeholder, mortgage lenders will factor this into their interest rate charges. Gone will be the days when the less wealthy are penalised for having poor credit histories, low salaries or small deposits.'

*

Rafi realised that he had been listening in awe, completely distracted from the events at Safi. Something good *would* come out of the Stratford catastrophe. The Chancellor had, in a single stroke, introduced an initiative that would, over time, improve the lives of hundreds of thousands, if not millions, of people - *and* free up capital which could be deployed in more productive areas of the economy.' This was a very timely and socially astute initiative.

Rafi glanced across to the clock. It had been several minutes since the commander had jumped ship. From the dots on the screen he could see that *Golden Sundancer* was making an excellent turn of speed away from the dinghy and the two life rafts.

Suddenly over the radio came the voice of a Moroccan fighter pilot in heavily accented English. '*Golden Sundancer!... Golden Sundancer!...* I have you on my radar – bring your boat to a stop. I say again, bring your boat to a stop!'

In the Ops Room the Air Chief Marshal spoke to the command centre. 'We have to keep the two Moroccan fighters interested in *Golden Sundancer* and looking in the wrong place for about twenty minutes. Get the Harrier pilot to engage the two fighters in conversation and to tell them that there are British nationals amongst the hostages on board - and that they should shadow the motor vessel. I repeat, we've got to keep them looking in the wrong place! The dinghy and life rafts won't show up on their radar, so they will be safe until the rain clears and the planes fly directly overhead.'

The seconds passed by. The Moroccan pilot would by now have *Golden Sundancer* on visual. What would he do? He had been warned that there were hostages on board. At 48–50 knots *she* could outrun anything that the Moroccan Navy possessed. A further command was heard.

'Stop or I *will* open fire!'

'Northrop Tiger, come in *Northrop Tiger*,' said the Harrier pilot. 'Be advised that there are British Nationals on board… *Do not engage!*'

In the rainswept dinghy, the commander leant across to Jim. 'If you hear any cannon fire, please push your little red button. The pilot will think it's all his doing.'

There was silence and then a further command to 'Heave to' was heard. *Golden Sundancer* carried on regardless. In the distance there was the distinctive sound of a short burst of gunfire. No doubt the fighter pilot had aimed across the bow.

Jim pressed the little red button. Seconds later the deep boom and shockwave of the explosion reached the dinghy. He squinted through the rain, but could see nothing.

The radio fell silent.

*

Back at the command centre there had been initial consternation when the pilot had opened fire and seconds later *Golden Sundancer* had literally disappeared from the Nimrod's screens.

'Oh my God!' the intelligence officer standing beside the team leader was heard to say. He'd just arrived back on duty and had missed out on the recent shenanigans.

Over the speaker came the voice of the Northrop Tiger's pilot. He was calling up helicopter support.

The stern voice of the Harrier pilot meanwhile was demanding to know what the hell the Northrop Tiger pilot thought he was up to.

Meanwhile the Eurocopter on board the frigate *Mohammed V* had taken off to investigate. The sky was going to get busy and the nuclear submarine still had to make its pickup.

'Right,' said the chief in the command centre to the Nimrod, 'Where exactly is our Harrier relative to the helicopter?'

'She'll be there in fifteen minutes and the Eurocopter will be there two minutes later.'

'Excellent.'

Meanwhile the Harrier's pilot was demanding that the two Moroccan fighters keep looking for survivors until the helicopter arrived.

*

In the rainswept dinghy, the commander was still dazed. The swell that had hardly inconvenienced *Golden Sundancer* was making life uncomfortable for those in the little open-topped inflatable, which was barely making four knots. Slowly, the commander calculated that they would get back to the life rafts in twelve minutes and the submarine would surface just minutes later.

*

The Nimrod continued to pick up the radio traffic between the Moroccan fighter pilots and their control centre. There was consternation. The Northrop Tiger pilot was describing the size of the explosion.

Jim had placed his explosive charges next to the cool box, which housed the four thermobaric Kornet missiles, which in turn weren't far from the main fuel tanks full of diesel vapour. The overall effect was impressive. One moment *Golden Sundancer* had been there, the next she'd literally disintegrated into a fireball. Her debris had vaporised. When the flames and smoke cleared there was no sign of her.

A minute later the second Moroccan jet fighter arrived to find nothing but clear ocean. The presence of the RAF Harrier fighter thirteen minutes away, bearing down on their two planes, was causing concern at the Moroccan control centre.

*

Rafi listened to the colonel who was talking to the RAF command centre. 'We have the makings of a major diplomatic incident if they piece together what's really going on under their noses. Tell the Harrier to keep talking and to get them to stay where they are...'

*

The contents of the Chancellor's third coloured folder grabbed Rafi's attention. It was as though he'd been through the Treasury's 'good ideas box' and was bringing them out, one at a time.

The Chancellor started to outline a new corporate structure. 'The *not-for-profit corporation* will primarily be used for public sector bodies.' His voice was clear and authoritative.

'The structure of a not-for-profit corporation will be similar to that of a public limited company,' he added in a businesslike manner. 'Just like a PLC, it will have a Memorandum and Articles of Association. The difference will be that this corporation will have *custodianholders* instead of shareholders. The custodianholders will have limited liability, as is the case in companies limited by guarantee. The custodianholders will have the same role as shareholders, in that they will be responsible for holding the management to account. Custodianholders will be drawn from the managers of the business, its employees, its funders, local organisations, locally elected politicians *and* those who receive the services. The last group, the service users, will have the *largest* number of votes, but no group will have a clear voting majority.'

The Chancellor seemed to be enjoying himself ...

*

Rafi's attention was pulled back to the action going on off the Moroccan coast. The distant Nimrod reconnaissance plane reported that the dinghy had rejoined the two life rafts. All three

313

specks on the rain swept ocean were ready, waiting for their rendezvous. The squall was clearing and they would soon be clearly visible to a plane flying overhead. Eight miles away the radio traffic between the Harrier and the two Moroccan jet fighters had been concluded. The Moroccan pilots viewed it as job done and had turned back to their bases minutes before the Harrier arrived.

The seconds ticked by.

The Harrier arrived, over the spot where *Golden Sundancer* had exploded, and waited for the Moroccan helicopter to get there so that a final search could be carried out.

The helicopter, in theory, posed a grave threat to the submarine, but with the Harrier in position that threat could be neutralised.

The command centre spoke to the special service personnel on board the life rafts. 'Activate the homing device. You have less than seven minutes to get on board the submarine.'

Jim felt under his shirt and switched on his personal homing device for ten seconds – not 200 metres away, the submarine picked up the signal.

The order went out: 'Make surface and prepare to take on board visitors.'

The sight of the Vanguard class submarine breaking surface at speed surprised those in the dinghy. They knew she was big, but relative to the life rafts she was huge!

'The helicopter has you on its radar and has changed course to investigate - the Harrier is shadowing,' came the message from the Nimrod. 'Captain, you have less than six minutes before the helicopter has you on visual.'

*

Rafi sensed the tension in the room. It was going to be a close-run thing.

*

In a flurry of activity, a squad of naval ratings descended on the two life rafts and the dinghy. The ratings and three of the special service men hauled the eight uncooperative captives out of the life rafts and manhandled them across the deck to the door at the bottom of the conning tower. They were followed by those from the inflatable dinghy. Meanwhile, Jim had slashed the buoyancy

314

tanks of the dinghy and the life rafts and lashed them together, so that they would sink under the weight of the outboard engine.

The Nimrod was tracking the hostile helicopter and speaking to the submarine's commanding officer. 'You have ninety seconds before you're in firing range. The Harrier has taken up a position above and behind the helicopter and continues to shadow her.'

As Jim hurried through the conning tower door, the command, 'Secure hatches!' rang out.

With seconds to spare, the submarine commenced her dive into obscurity and vanished from the radar screens.

Meanwhile, the Harrier and the helicopter pilots were in conversation.

'The possible vessel has disappeared,' advised the Harrier pilot. 'I suggest we call it a day.'

'We give it, say, ten minutes and we return to base? Yes?'

'Affirmative,' came the Harrier pilot's reply.

*

Over the speaker Rafi heard, 'All eight terrorists and all eight service personnel safely picked up. Diving and going into silent mode. Will speak later; ETA Devonport in forty-eight hours.'

'Bravo Zulu, out.' A cheer went up. A sense of relief filled the air. The submarine was heading back to Plymouth with its cargo safely on board.

*

The Chancellor was still going strong. He had been going through the contents of the orange folder in front of him and was explaining how the Government proposed to improve the transparency of corporate ownership, and how it was going to remove the tax deductibility of losses and associated costs incurred by those speculating on naked options. Rafi didn't catch precisely what he was explaining, but from the attentive nature of the faces around him he was still having the impact of a magician pulling rabbits out of a hat. His audience was enthralled.

*

Meanwhile in Luxembourg, as soon as *Golden Sundancer* had reached international waters, Giles gave the signal to the local police team. The gendarmerie was waiting outside Maryam's offices. Her arrest had been authorised by the Chief of the Luxembourg police. The evidence he had been shown was overwhelming and, off the record, he had agreed that a trial in London with the other three terrorists would be the simplest solution. Neither spoke of extradition. A British SWAT team, including a couple of SAS operatives, was standing by.

When the knock at the door came, Maryam was found entertaining a group of EU politicians in her boardroom. Their lunch had stretched right through the afternoon. For her part, she was celebrating.

Maryam, with the support of her influential guests, put up an impressive verbal fight, protesting her innocence. Things nearly turned ugly when she summoned her two bodyguards, however, the local gendarmes were prepared for resistance and the bodyguards were quickly outnumbered and overpowered.

In the commotion Maryam was bundled out of the room by two SAS men, down the service lift into a waiting car and transported to the nearby airport. At the same time, a substitute with a coat draped over her head was taken away to the local gendarmerie to keep up the pretence. Nineteen minutes after the main group of terrorists were safely on board the submarine, Maryam was in custody aboard a private jet taking off for the UK.

*

At that moment, Colonel Turner gave the order for a message to be passed to the Chancellor of the Exchequer, who was still speaking at the dispatch box.

There was shuffling behind the Chancellor as he was handed a small folded slip of paper. He finished what he was saying, paused and then opened out the sheet so he could read the message. He read it twice. All eyes in the Chamber were on him. The silence was deafening.

'Mr Speaker, I have been informed of a development; one which this House should be made aware. If the Speaker will permit, I believe that the Prime Minister should communicate this important news.' The Speaker nodded.

Rafi grinned as he thought about the Chancellor's stalling for time and the excellent initiatives he had produced.

The PM was passed the message, he read it, stood up and moved to the dispatch box. He hesitated, a ripple of uncertainty spread around the Chamber. 'Thank you, Mr Speaker, I have some breaking news. I can inform the House that we have just received information regarding the terrorists who committed the recent atrocities.' He straightened his shoulders and stood upright. The PM looked calm and confident. No doubt under the surface he was jumping for joy, but he was a master of his trade. 'I can inform this House that special forces units have in the past few minutes successfully apprehended nine terrorists. They have captured the four leaders of the terrorist cell, the two mercenaries who wrought the carnage on Stratford and Cruden Bay, a recruiter of the Bishopsgate bomber and two accomplices.'

The PM paused to let the House take in the implications of what he had just said. 'Furthermore, I am able to report that the two mercenaries involved in the attacks on Hartlepool and Heysham are safely out of action, as are the three who attacked Aldermaston. I am advised by the intelligence services that we now have in custody the leading players who conspired against us and wrought such terrible damage and grief on our country.'

There was a brief silence as the news sank in. Then, en masse, the MPs sitting behind the PM rose to their feet and started clapping and waving their order papers. Applause and cheers from the other side of the House soon followed.

Rafi watched as the Speaker let the House enjoy the moment before calling, 'Order, order; pray let the Prime Minster continue.'

'Whilst the terrorists were at large, I can reveal that we have been waging a war of deception against them. The terrorist attacks on Aldermaston, Heysham and Hartlepool were in fact foiled and what you witnessed on television were the army's pyrotechnic skills being put to use. Attacks on the St Fergus, Bacton and Easington gas facilities were also foiled, as was an attack on the nuclear reprocessing plant at Sellafield. Sadly, these seven successes were overshadowed by the tragic events at Cruden Bay and Stratford. The catastrophic damage suffered at Stratford greatly saddens me. Memories of this attack will haunt me, forever.'

He paused to let the words of his last sentence sink in. 'As we face up to the enormous losses incurred at Stratford, it is impossible to contemplate what the position might have been had the terrorists succeeded with all their planned attacks. Suffice it to say that we would have lost over fifty percent of our electricity and gas supplies and would be facing horrendous radioactive contamination in five locations.'

The PM looked up at the camera. 'We owe a debt of gratitude to the commander-in-chief of our armed forces and his colleagues, who in the early hours of Friday morning responded to our intelligence sources and set in motion a vast damage limitation strategy. *Operation Counterpane* was set up to counter the anticipated attacks. It was the commander-in-chief's foresightedness that enabled help to be at Stratford within minutes of the disaster occurring. We owe a huge debt of gratitude to the Royal Netherlands Air Force whose unreserved assistance was outstanding. And the Government's thanks go to all those who ably and promptly came to our aid, in our time of need.'

Applause rippled around the Chamber.

'The terrorists' plotting was uncovered last week by the City of London police, during their investigations into the Bishopsgate bombing. The police and MI5 were helped to a significant degree by a tenacious individual whom they had wrongly arrested in conjunction with the Bishopsgate bombing. There are very many people to whom I would like to pay tribute. Their resolve helped stop the majority of the terrorist attacks, and their unstinting work following the Stratford disaster has been far beyond the call of duty. They know who they are. They did their jobs not to gain from being in the spotlight and to spin their story, but because it was in their very nature to fight against those who sought to bring this country to its knees. Their identities will be revealed in due course, but for the time being, let them relax in the knowledge that what they have done has been exceptional.'

The Chamber reverberated to loud cheers from all sides.

'The past few days have been doubly difficult. We have been on the trail of the terrorists, but have feared that they might be tipped off that we were on to them, only to disappear from our radar screens and then go on to commit a series of horrendous attacks about which we had no intelligence. The terrorists used their huge wealth to build a network of clandestine informants and to extend their influence far wider than we could hitherto have anticipated. They took advantage of the opaque intricacies of our corporate system and our lax border controls to manipulate and steer events to their own end. The extent of their plotting will be revealed over the next few days.

'It is with humility, regret and deep sadness that I have to report to the House that my Government has been tarnished by this episode. The terrorists used a significant number of people to assist them. I am advised by the police and MI5 that the terrorists had in place a significant number of influential sleepers or moles, who in return for excessive remuneration became their eyes and ears. The identity of these sleepers has caused the intelligence services and me grave concern.'

Gasps echoed around the Chamber.

'For example, MI5 identified two members of COBRA who were on the terrorists' payroll, which is why an Operations Room was set up at the City of London police headquarters in Wood Street. The scale and magnitude of the recent attacks has made me realise how vulnerable we are to those with immense wealth, who take it upon themselves to either attack our society or use their money to influence those around them. Our freedoms, love of material things, and the chasm between the vastly wealthy and the rest of us have made too many people easy and obliging targets. It is with great sadness that I have to report that a large number of people in senior positions took huge sums of money for nominal amounts of work and did not seek to question what was going on – they were in reality working for the terrorists. They should have guessed it was too good to be true. Furthermore, in their greed, many were all too happy to receive this money in secret accounts offshore. Little did they appreciate that they were being groomed, and that they formed part of the terrorists' information network.'

Rafi watched as the PM was forced to pause as the House reverberated with retorts of: 'Shame, shame!' The noise grew to a crescendo, as the displeasure was voiced in no uncertain terms.

'Silence, silence!' boomed the Speaker of the House.

The PM continued. 'MI5, working with the City of London police force, have identified over 300 well-connected individuals who were on the terrorists' payroll, directly or indirectly.'

More gasps were clearly audible.

The PM paused and looked around the House. 'It is with sadness and displeasure that I have to report to the House that six members sitting in this Chamber succumbed to the terrorists' financial advances and thus became part of their network.'

A shocked silence gave way to calls for justice to be done. It took the Speaker a full four minutes to suppress the noise before the Prime Minister was able to be heard again.

'I should remind everyone that under British Law a person is innocent until proved guilty. Sergeant-at-Arms, are you and your colleagues ready?' enquired the Prime Minister.

'Yes, sir!' came the clear reply.

'Are you in possession of the list of the Members' names, for whom arrest warrants have been issued by the City of London police in connection with aiding and abetting the terrorists' attacks at Stratford and other locations around the UK last Friday?'

'Yes, sir!'

'With the Speaker's permission, I would ask you, please, to proceed.'

The PM sat down while the sergeant-at-arms – the head of Parliament's police force – walked over and passed the arrest warrants to the Speaker, who looked at the papers and then solemnly asked her to proceed.

The Members' names were slowly read out one by one. They were not in alphabetical order, which only added to the dramatic tension. The six included a newly appointed junior minister and a backbench MP from the Government's party, an MP from each of the two main opposition parties and two MPs from the smaller parties. Protests of innocence rang out around the Chamber. Shock and incredulity spread around the House, as Members who had hitherto been seen as whiter than white had their names called out. Only one MP put up a real struggle, whereas the others left with whatever dignity they could muster.

The Prime Minister watched as the door closed behind the last to be escorted out. The hubbub and mutterings gradually subsided. 'If the Speaker will permit, it would be helpful if the Chancellor of the Exchequer could now complete his outline of the Government's financial proposals, before he and I put ourselves before the House to answer questions.'

'Agreed. Pray continue.'

Rafi was on tenterhooks. How much of their advice would

the Chancellor take on board? He looked at the faces of the opposition MPs on the TV screen. There was a look of bewilderment.

'Thank you, Prime Minister,' said the Chancellor. 'I have outlined a number of initiatives to enhance economic activity. I will now turn to our proposals of how the Government is to deal with the huge costs associated with the Stratford disaster.' He paused and then went on, 'As Members are no doubt aware, the credit crunch and the various state bail outs have necessitated significant Government guarantees and a substantial increase in borrowings. We shall *not* be undertaking any further borrowings. *Indeed,* as things stand it would not be *possible* to do so without, risking the UK's credit rating, and triggering steep rises in interest rates and gilt yields. This would be very counterproductive.'

There was utter disbelief on the faces of those opposite him.

'So how then can we meet these new and very large financial liabilities?' The Chancellor paused whilst those in the Chamber were left to imagine the starkness of the position. 'I am pleased to report that we have a plan. Under this plan the costs associated with the disaster will be met via the issue of shares in new Government Real Estate Investment Trusts – REITs. The value of the public sector's property and tangible assets is around £900 billion, or thereabouts. A proportion of these assets will be transferred into these Government REIT vehicles, which will be listed on the London Stock Exchange. We will compensate each and every person who lost their health, their home, their possessions or their business as a result of the terrorist attacks by transferring to them shares in the Government REITs. A cash alternative will be provided by a consortium of banks who will offer a cost-effective trading facility.'

'The sums involved will be large - in addition to the compensation costs there are a number of other significant costs, such as the decontamination and decommissioning costs of our nuclear power stations and the payment of guarantees… At present, the best estimate I have for Stratford and the associated costs is £195 billion. A full breakdown will be published by the Treasury in the next twenty-four hours.'

There were gasps around the Chamber – the figure was far larger than anyone had expected. The House fell silent once more and the Chancellor continued. 'I also propose to use part of the proceeds of the REIT share sales to repurchase long dated gilts,' continued the Chancellor.

Strike one for the terrorists, Rafi thought. This would underpin gilts prices and be the first nail in their financial coffin.

'The Treasury's best estimate is that the cost of the dividends on the Government REIT shares sold to third parties will be no more than £1.5 billion for the next fiscal year, rising to £3 billion in the following year, and will therefore be well within its scope to manage, without recourse to rises in national taxation.' He paused momentarily and looked at the shadow chancellor opposite him.

Strike two: the Government funding requirements would remain on track. The second nail in the terrorists' financial coffin has been hammered home, thought Rafi.

'I shall also be introducing proposals which will allow pensioners and those planning for their retirement to invest in London listed REITs as an alternative to annuities. This will provide the REITs market with liquidity. Furthermore, I am advised by leading actuaries that the yield advantage of REITs over gilts and their inflation hedging characteristics will reduce the deficits of many pension funds.' The Chancellor let those around him take in what he had said about Government REITs. He now had to move on to a particularly difficult area.

'Our economy,' the Chancellor continued, 'our financial service industries, the City of London and our currency were badly bruised by the recent banking crisis and will be further injured by the nuclear disaster. To rebuild them we need a period of currency and interest rate stability. It is well known that the five criteria for our entry to the Euro have been long debated; this debate has been against the background of a strong currency and a positive economic outlook for the UK. Some eminent economists have argued that Stratford has materially changed the risk–reward relationship. They have advised me that the risks to our well-being, and to our economy, of being in the Euro are now significantly less than if we were to go it alone and keep Sterling.'

'Wait for it…' thought Rafi.

'I have considered their arguments and have concluded that Sterling is part of our heritage, our identity, and our economic independence, and it should only be given up *in extremis*. So, in how desperate a position do we find ourselves? We have found a workable solution to meet all the costs associated with Stratford and this will inject billions of pounds into our economy. And we *will* make a start at reducing the scale of unfunded public sector pensions, which will improve the Government's finances. The introduction of not-for-profit corporations will make our public sector services more efficient and will reduce the need for future tax increases.'

The Chancellor stopped and looked around the Chamber. People were on the edge of their seats. Back in the Ops Room Rafi suddenly wasn't sure what to expect.

'On the other hand, I have had to consider how much damage speculators might cause if they try to decimate our currency. Therefore, whether or not we join the Euro rests on whether or not we can hold our currency stable.'

The tension was palpable.

'So, are we, or are we not going into the Euro?' wondered Rafi.

'Early yesterday, senior representatives of the Bank of England flew out to meet with the largest international Central Banks to ask for their help in supporting our currency and to determine the level at which support would be forthcoming. Without this support we would find ourselves in exceptionally difficult times and joining the Euro would become a necessity. The results of these deliberations should be available to me now.'

There was movement behind the Chancellor. He turned round and was passed a large white envelope by the PM. He opened the envelope, pulled out two sheets of paper and read them. His face gave nothing away, but before he spoke, he pulled out a handkerchief and mopped his brow.

'As of ten minutes ago, the Federal Reserve of America, the European Central Bank, the Chinese, Japanese, Indian, Saudi, UAE, and four other Central Banks have all agreed to support and be aggressive purchasers of Sterling, until such time as the UK economy has recovered from the recent catastrophe.'

Sighs of relief were heard around the Chamber.

'The support level has been set at a figure four percent below Sterling's trade weighted exchange rate as at close of business on

Thursday evening.'

The Treasury had taken Aidan's brief *and* added their own magic – Sterling was to remain independent! They had done a superb job. Rafi looked at the ceiling, let out a small whistle and smiled. Strike three! Sterling was to be protected. The third and final nail had been hammered home. The terrorists' positions in the derivatives markets had become untenable and they would be sitting on truly massive losses when the market reopened in the morning!

A weary, but relieved-looking Chancellor surveyed the packed House of Commons. 'Details supporting the initiatives I have set out this afternoon to the House will be published as soon as is practical – the printing presses are running as I speak. The events of the past few days have required much soul-searching and reprioritising.' He paused and looked across at the shadow chancellor. 'I commend these proposals to the House.' He sat down to growing applause from the House, which was taking its time to assimilate all he had put before them.

The Prime Minister rose to take his place at the dispatch box. 'If the Speaker will permit me, I should like to tidy up a few loose ends. The reshuffle I spoke of earlier will be far-reaching. I have scheduled meetings with the leaders of the main opposition parties for later this evening. I will be speaking with many of you over the next twenty-four hours. I have received assurances from the party leaders sitting opposite me that they will place the interests of the country first.'

The PM paused for dramatic effect. 'Where spin rules, reason is wanting, honesty is wanting, public service is wanting and the role of this House is overshadowed. Spin and self-aggrandisement are unacceptable. We owe it to the people of this country to consign spin and subterfuge to the past.' The PM paused and looked across at the opposition benches.

'It can be expected that members of competing parties will find themselves working together running the Ministries of State. Undoubtedly, there will be differences of opinion over some issues, but this should not stop efficient Cabinet Government. This House, its committees and the Upper Chamber will have the important role of scrutinising, improving and approving the proposals put before them. The Government has many difficult decisions to make in order to steer our country forward in an appropriate direction. What I am proposing is a move away from presidential-style politics to one where the Government is, as it was decades ago, fully accountable to Parliament. Our collective aim must be to get things back on to an even keel, to rejuvenate our economy and to rebuild our damaged international reputation. I commend these proposals to the House.'

With that the PM sat down to applause from all corners of the Chamber. He looked exhausted.

The Speaker called for the Leader of Her Majesty's Opposition. Silence returned to the Chamber as he stood up and raised aloft a pile of papers.

'I thought I'd been well-briefed by my team when I came to the House this afternoon.' Slowly and theatrically he lowered the pile of papers, turned and placed them where he had been sitting. 'I won't need them.' He looked across at the Government benches. 'If my sources are correct, the Prime Minister has personally been working non-stop for the past three days as part of the effort to prevent the terrorists' attacks, for which I thank the Honourable Member. I shall be meeting with him later today and again tomorrow. Following these meetings, I shall report back to this House any concerns I might have. In the meantime there is much to digest and, in the circumstances, it would be churlish of me to find fault for the very sake of finding fault. The two Honourable Members opposite me have, with great openness, sought to provide leadership and the wherewithal to enable our country to extricate itself from the horrendous tragedy of Stratford.' He cast his eyes upwards towards the television camera.

'I should like to pay my respects to all those who have lost and those who will lose their lives as a result of this nuclear catastrophe, and to thank all those in the emergency services, the armed forces and the intelligence services who have helped in our hour of need. I'd like to express my sympathy to all those who lost their homes or businesses in the "Isle of Stratford", and to thank all those people and companies who helped selflessly.'

With that, the leader of the official opposition party sat down. The eyes in the House, as if following a tennis ball at Wimbledon, moved along the front row and focused on the leader of the third political party. It was his turn. He had a reputation for holding strong environmental views and a nuclear disaster was something he had warned against over many years. Would he use the events of last Friday to put the knife in? So far, the Home Secretary, a couple of lower ranking ministers and a number of quango employees involved in the nuclear industry had resigned. Would he try to make this a resigning matter for the Prime Minister as well? He stood up and looked around the silent Chamber.

'It is on the record that my party places huge importance on environmental issues and has a profound distrust of matters nuclear.'

The House sensed that things were going to get interesting.

'The Stratford nuclear disaster will haunt us for generations to come and its occurrence is political dynamite. Its consequences will be felt by every individual in this country. A lesser Government might have tried to spin its way out of the quagmire. Instead, this Government has come here today with a rational, inclusive and cohesive plan, which I believe will provide the foundations for this country to prosper again and will bring environmental and sustainability issues to the centre of our culture.'

'I look forward to meeting with the Prime Minister later today and again tomorrow morning. I shall come back to the House and report more fully on these discussions and will raise such questions that I believe require answering.' He paused and in a sombre tone added, 'I, too, wish to pay my respects to all those who have suffered and to convey my great thanks to all those who have helped in this time of crisis.' He looked around the House and sat down.

*

One of the colonel's team was beckoning Rafi to pick up the phone nearest to him.

It was Aidan. 'What do you think?' he enquired.

'That's unfair,' an ecstatic Rafi replied, 'you're the one with the screens in front of you.'

'The currency markets are seeing big support for Sterling. Several early punters bet on it going through the floor and have had their fingers burnt. The support since the Chancellor's statement has been unprecedented. And, Rafi, the terrorists and their banks will be sitting on some mind-bogglingly large losses when the derivatives markets open tomorrow! Did the PM and the Chancellor perform some kind of miracle, or what?'

'Better than I could have prayed for,' Rafi replied.

'Basically, things are looking marvellous! Must dash - see you around Rafi. Bye.'

Rafi called across to anyone within earshot, 'Aidan says that the markets loved the PM's and the Chancellor's speeches. And that the terrorists and their bankers are being taken to the cleaners.'

Colonels Gray and Turner and their teams looked ready to drop. But they looked happy as they packed up their kit – the military operation was complete. The Wood Street Ops Room had served its purpose well.

*

Len Thunhurst and his team were jubilant. It was their turn now as the focus swung onto the arrest of those implicated with the terrorist activities.

A spreadsheet visible on a large screen showed the tally of the arrests. The table showing the names in red, blue and black – slowly at first, then more rapidly – turned yellow as the arrests continued.

Rafi looked up at the TV screen. A well-known political commentator was attempting to sum up the activities of the afternoon. The words *unprecedented*, *remarkable* and *incomparable* were used frequently in his report. He finished by saying that it had been a great day for British democracy.

Rafi looked back across the room. The large screen showed *Operation Dry Clean* to be progressing well. The number of arrests was continuing to rise swiftly.

Chapter 8

Rafi had had enough.

Kate walked over and gave him a hug. 'Let's get some rest. I'm no longer needed here.'

'Fine by me,' replied Rafi.

'I'm afraid it's time for normality to resume. No more chauffeur-driven cars. How about I get us a taxi?'

Rafi nodded. Fifteen minutes later they picked up an evening paper and got into the black taxi waiting for them. The February evening was bleak and cold.

'Where to?'

'Clapham, please,' answered Kate.

'The traffic is awful – it could take a while.'

'No problem,' Kate looked at Rafi. 'Is it OK if we pick up our stuff from the Savoy tomorrow? I hope you don't mind, but I rang the hotel and told them that they can let someone else have our room.'

Rafi smiled at her. 'What else have you been up to?'

'Oh, there's one other bit of news,' she grinned. 'As of now, I'm sort of on holiday. I've been ordered to spend two weeks helping you convalesce!'

Rafi smiled, 'that's the best news I've heard in ages.'

'And it gets better. I thought you might like to get this back,' she said, passing him his wallet and personal effects from Paddington Green.

'Thank you. I can now pay for *Luigi's* and the hotel suite. And I can do some clothes shopping.'

Kate gave him a big hug. 'That sounds like fun – I hope I am included! By the way, how did you get on with the hotel in Cornwall?' she enquired.

'They have found a small suite for us. I told them we would be arriving tomorrow, early afternoon and staying between ten days and a fortnight,' replied Rafi.

Kate curled up against him on the back seat.

'So much for me going out with a butch police officer,' he whispered into her ear.

'Don't be silly,' came the soft reply. 'They employ me for my brains and not my body!'

As the taxi approached Clapham, on Kate's say-so, it turned into a tree-lined street off the Common and pulled up in front of a red brick terraced house.

'Home sweet home,' beamed Kate as she joined Rafi after paying the driver.

'Come on, let's get inside, it's freezing cold out here.' Kate unlocked the front door and they entered a small communal area, with two front doors. 'Mine is the upstairs flat.' There was a clunk as she unlocked her front door.

'Good lock,' Rafi commented.

'Yes; you never know who might come calling.'

Inside, on the mat, was a pile of mail – most of which looked like junk. Kate scooped it up and headed upstairs. Her flat comprised a sitting room, a small kitchen, a cosy bath room and a good-sized double bedroom at the back of the house. The place felt like a deep freeze.

'Is your central heating not working, by any chance?'

'Sorry. I turn the thermostat down when I go out. Don't worry, it'll soon get warm.'

Kate scurried around – closing the curtains and lighting the gas fire in the sitting room before heading off towards the kitchen.

Rafi joined her and they stood there waiting for the kettle to boil. 'Long-life milk, I'm afraid. Sugar?'

'No, thanks.'

'Come on, follow me – let's get warm.' Instead of going towards the sitting room, Kate turned right and headed for her bedroom.

It was a friendly looking room; simply furnished. In the middle of the wall, facing the window, was a large double bed. Kate placed Rafi's mug of coffee on one bedside table and hers on the other. He looked across at her, wondering what exactly she was going to do next. She slipped off her shoes, stripped off her coat and hopped fully clothed into bed.

'It's cold in here – I could do with your body heat to warm me up,' came the suggestive but gentle request.

Rafi sat on the side of the bed and took his coat and shoes off. 'Come on, I'm freezing!'

He climbed under the duvet. Kate was right – the bed was freezing. Rafi moved over to her side and snuggled up. She wrapped her arms around him; her gorgeous eyes were inches away from his. He lay there staring into the sparkling deep brown colours, savouring the warmth of her body next to his. She moved forward and kissed him softly on the lips. He was in heaven.

'If it's alright with you, I thought we could have something from the freezer for supper and spend the evening in bed. How's the coffee, by the way?' asked Kate.

Rafi hadn't touched it yet. He moved back to his cold side of the bed, took a couple of mouthfuls and returned to her warmth. He lay there thinking - what a long time it had been since he'd had a girlfriend… And he had known Kate scarcely a week! What were things coming to? Rafi felt happier than he could remember.

'Tell me about the hotel we're staying at,' asked Kate.

'It's just outside Newquay. It's got four stars and overlooks the Atlantic Ocean.'

'Did you say the bedrooms were nice?' enquired Kate.

'Yep.'

'And?'

'They have big, comfy beds!'

'Just what the doctor ordered,' replied Kate, who snuggled closer to him.

The proximity of her body, which was now nestling partly on top of him, made it difficult to concentrate. He wondered what she was going to do next. She leant forward, gave him a lingering kiss on the lips and wriggled her body. The effect was electric. She kissed his cheek and, to his disappointment, rolled off him and slipped out of bed.

'Why don't I rustle up some supper?'

He watched her slim figure disappear out of the room and lay there enjoying the warmth of the bed and the anticipation of things to come. This was the first time for a long while that he had felt relaxed, comfortable and truly happy.

Kate reappeared a few minutes later, clutching another cup of hot coffee. 'I guessed you wanted to stay warm.' She left again leaving him to his drink and thoughts. Rafi sipped at it, savouring its warmth. After several minutes he got up, and went to see what Kate was doing. The temperature in the flat had returned to a comfortable level now. He looked around him as he walked down the corridor to the kitchen and sitting room. The place was small, but homely. It was very different to his flat in Hampstead. On reflection, he came to the surprising conclusion that he preferred it. This place had the essence of Kate and that made it special.

He walked into the kitchen.

'The pizza will be ready in about twenty minutes; sorry, the oven takes ages to get hot. In the meantime, I'm going to have a bath. I'd invite you to share it with me, but we would get stuck – it's rather small. The sitting room is nice and warm now though. Perhaps the news might be worth listening to?'

Rafi turned and went into the sitting room. He picked up the remote controls and switched on the television. He eventually found the 24-hour news channels and flicked through them. On the first one he saw a photo of himself and heard the reporter saying: 'Mr Rafi Khan has been instrumental in enabling the police to catch the terrorists…'

Rafi flicked to another channel. CNN was running a bulletin on the money markets and the American commentator was interviewing a foreign exchange trader who was describing the day's trading.

'Been quite a day! That British Finance Chancellor caught us on the hop. We thought Sterling was going to be a one-way bet down through the floor, but when we found out that our Fed, the ECB and the Central Banks of China and Japan – to name but a few – were piling in to support Sterling, we knew that the speculators were beaten. And as if that wasn't enough, the British Finance Minister then found a couple of hundred billion pounds without tapping the bond markets. *And* then he set out how the £1,100 billion unfunded public sector pension deficit will be tackled … The currency markets have given up the fight. The steam has literally gone out of trying to short Sterling. It's been quite a day; one I'll remember for a long time!'

The TV interviewer switched across to a stockbroker. 'Tell us, Irvine, about these new UK Government REITs.' Rafi listened to Irvine tell his American audience how it was the US who had created the Real Estate Investment Trust structure some decades ago. His view was that the UK Government had done something that some saw as brave, while many others looked at it thinking, 'Gee, why on earth haven't *we* done that?'

Before being cut off by the interviewer, the broker gave a throwaway remark that made Rafi first smile, then chuckle, 'What has captivated us is this new UK not-for-profit corporation: like a public company but controlled by custodianholders - the people - and not shareholders. The change in accounting methods *alone* will bring huge efficiency gains. It's a great idea and will knock the stuffing out of our game theory junkies; hats off to the UK Chancellor!'

'What are the prospects for tomorrow?' asked the interviewer.

'It should be business as usual,' came the reply.

The cameras panned back to the interviewer in the CNN studio.

'Well, there it is! An extraordinary day on the money markets; the UK currency and its economy seem set to fight another day. Who would have thought it? It's a big surprise. Tomorrow the world's eyes will be on the reopening of the UK financial markets. The omens look good, but who knows? Will the London Stock Market hold its nerve or will it be a bloodbath?'

The timer in the kitchen started bleeping. Rafi switched off the TV. Kate was still in the bathroom.

'The bleeper's gone, what should I do?' Rafi called out.

'Could you see if the pizza is cooked? If it is, could you put it in the top oven to keep it warm?'

'Will do,' Rafi replied as he went back into the kitchen. Its size suddenly struck him; it was a fifth of the size of his. Small it might be, but nevertheless it worked well – like Kate, he thought to himself.

The pizza was cooked. He opened the tin of baked beans which he found on the side and poured them into a saucepan. How long had it been since he'd had baked beans? Ages. Probably university, he thought. With his larger than average salary his diet had gone somewhat upmarket. He gave the beans a stir.

Rafi's mind wandered and he found himself wondering what a young detective inspector might earn. Probably little more than a university research fellow, he guessed. It then dawned on him that, following the events of the last few days, he was effectively unemployed.

At that same moment his thoughts took another turn. He smelt a sweet fragrance. This was followed by a sexy hug from behind.

'A penny for your thoughts?'

'Oh, it's just dawned on me that I'm out of work.'

'That's good news! Now you can do something worthwhile, and not just because it pays handsomely. You know, when I saw your bank statements I could hardly believe what a fund manager was paid. On average, you were earning more in a month than I earned in a year. Though, I suppose that those of us protecting Queen and Country do it for the job satisfaction, and to eat baked beans rather than caviar! How's supper coming along?'

'Pizza is cooked and the beans are hot.'

'Why are we standing around?' Kate had two trays quickly laid. 'Water or orange juice? No good offering you wine or a G&T, is it?'

'Orange juice would be great.'

'Do you mind if I have a glass of wine?'

'Not at all.'

In the sitting room, Kate put her tray on the floor in front of the gas fire and pulled across a small coffee table from alongside the sofa; she then lifted her tray on to the table and sat down cross-legged. Rafi looked down at her; she was wrapped in an old, fluffy pink dressing gown, with a nondescript towel wrapped tightly around her head – but she looked gorgeous.

Rafi sat on the sofa and felt the warmth of the fire. He tucked into the food – it tasted good. He watched Kate open a bottle of wine, fill her glass and sip at its contents.

She caught him watching her. 'Have you ever drunk alcohol?'

'Not really. My parents, well my mother in particular, were strict Muslims and I grew up in a teetotal household. I suppose it was at university that I decided not to drink. I saw too many people getting smashed for no good reason, which really put me off.'

The conversation switched to their journey to Cornwall. Kate was amused to find that he didn't have a car. 'How about I drive and you pay for the petrol…? Deal?' asked Kate.

'But remember I'm unemployed!' chuckled Rafi.

'Yes, but thankfully you have a bank balance which should tide you over for a year or three.' She yawned. 'Sorry, I have been surviving on catnaps for the past few days. If I stay up much longer, I won't be able to see straight, driving down to Cornwall tomorrow.'

There was a lull in the conversation which was soon broken by Rafi. 'Would you mind if I went and showered?' he asked.

'Good idea. I'll clear up. Would you like a cup of coffee?'

'More orange juice would be nice, please.'

'I've put a spare towel on the chair in the bathroom. It looks old but it should be OK, I hope.'

He saw what she meant. The towel had definitely seen better days. He picked it up and was surprised to find that its shabbiness belied its softness. Definitely fit for purpose, he thought.

Rafi shed his clothes and looked at himself in the mirror. His wrist still looked puffy and badly bruised. It was still an angry purply-blue colour. He'd got rid of the bandage as it had become the object of too much attention. From what he could see, his back boasted some seriously impressive bruises, but thankfully they all looked far worse than they now felt.

The shower cubicle was compact. At the third attempt he worked out how to get in and turn the water on without wetting the floor or getting dowsed in very hot or very cold water. He stood there, enjoying the warm water splashing over him. He looked around for some shampoo, washed his hair and picked up the bar of soap. It smelt of exotic eastern fragrances – very feminine. He gave himself a good scrub from head to foot, rinsed off the soap suds, turned off the shower and stepped out into a steam-filled room. He dried and walked out into a dark corridor with the towel around his waist.

He could see a small strip of light coming from under Kate's bedroom door and headed for it. Slowly, he opened the door. Kate was sitting in front of her dressing table looking into the mirror. She turned and looked at him. Her tired, freckled face was devoid of make-up - she still looked lovely.

He walked over to his side of the bed, shed his towel and climbed in.

'I'll be with you in a moment,' she said and with that the light on the dressing table went off. The room was now only lit by the small light on her bedside table. She walked over to the door, unwrapped the towel from around her head, took off her dressing gown and hung them both on the back of the door.

Rafi lay in bed spellbound. The curves on her slim body were accentuated by the soft lighting. She turned her head and caught him ogling at her naked behind.

She slowly stepped backwards, then sideways. He felt his pulse race. She had a great body.

'Do you like?'

He was captivated. 'Yes, very much!' he eventually added.

'Flattery will get you everywhere.'

Rafi watched as she climbed into bed. She turned off the light, disappeared under the duvet and came up for air with her head on his chest. The curtains were drawn but small shafts of dappled light came in around the edges from the lights outside. She slowly moved up and kissed him. 'I'm a very lucky girl…' Her voice trailed off as she sat up, letting the duvet slide off her shoulders. She ran her finger tips across his exposed chest. His body twitched, as inch by sensual inch she drew imaginary patterns on his torso. He gazed at her lovely face framed by a mass of silky hair.

Kate lent forward and kisses followed the lines her fingers had taken, lingering along the way at his small dark nipples. Little electric shocks raced through his body. Her fingers, meanwhile, had moved on with their gentle caresses.

Rafi was in seventh heaven. He felt her kisses gradually move back up his chest to his neck and the hollow beneath his right ear.

'When I first laid eyes on you a week ago, in my wildest dreams I'd never have guessed that you and I would get this close.'

*

Rafi awoke to the sound of light-hearted singing coming from the kitchen. Kate's dressing gown was no longer on the back of the door. He sat up and looked around her bedroom.

The door opened quietly. Kate slowly put her head around it. 'Oh, good, you're awake. I wondered when you were going to come around. I've got a cup of black coffee for you. Thought you could do with a caffeine boost. Did you sleep well?'

Rafi smiled and nodded as she came to sit next to him.

'I've finished packing. I didn't know what I'd need so I'm travelling light; a good excuse for some shopping. And I've rung the Savoy and they said all our belongings are packed up and ready for collection. And some good news: MI5 have spoken to the hotel and asked for the bill to be sent to them. They left you a message: *Thank you and sorry we roughed you up*.'

Rafi grinned and sipped at his hot coffee. Kate leant over and gave him a kiss.

'How long do you need to get ready?'

'Would fifteen minutes be OK?'

'Great. I thought that we could eat brunch on the way.'

*

Kate's car was a small, old-looking, Volvo. She drove through the London traffic quickly and confidently. They arrived at the Savoy in what seemed like record time and stopped near the front door.

Rafi walked behind Kate into the crowded hotel foyer.

At the main desk they were greeted by the manager, who seemed pleased to see them.

'I'm sorry you're leaving us. I hope you had a pleasant stay.'

'Every bit as good as I hoped,' Rafi replied.

'Your luggage is being collected as we speak and will be waiting for you at the front door. I hope you will visit us again soon; it was a pleasure to have you both here… I'm sorry, I nearly forgot – I have some messages for you.'

There were messages from Kate's parents and from Emma and Saara sending their best wishes. None of these needed an immediate reply. The last one, though, was from Jeremy. Kate read it and passed it to Rafi.

As he read the message, Rafi felt the colour drain out of his face. Their nightmare had not ended. The terrorist from Heysham had escaped from hospital – heaven only knew what he was capable of doing, even with a broken arm and collar bone.

'So now what?' he said in a shocked tone.

'Doesn't look good, does it? We'll speak to Jeremy in the car and take it from there.'

They said their goodbyes to the manager and put the luggage, which seemed far more than Rafi could remember, into the Volvo's boot and across the back seat.

They turned into the traffic on the Strand and headed west towards the Hogath Roundabout and the M4.

As they drove along the raised section of the M4, Kate turned on her hands-free phone and called Jeremy. His phone went to voicemail, so she left a message. 'Hi, Kate here. I'm on my mobile. Chat soon.'

The traffic on the motorway was surprisingly light and they made good progress out of London, past Heathrow and on towards Reading.

'How about brunch?' asked Kate.

'Great idea,' replied Rafi.

'There's a service station coming up shortly – is that alright with you?'

Rafi nodded. Baked beans and service station food, both in the space of twenty-four hours – how things were changing for him!

As Kate was pulling over towards the service station exit, her phone rang.

'Hi, Kate,' said Jeremy in a businesslike tone, 'Sorry to break in on your well-earned holiday, but something has come up. Aslan Popovskaya, the terrorist we captured at Heysham, has escaped from hospital. We haven't got a clue where he's heading, but given all that has been going on recently he's likely to be like a bear with a sore head. Where are you off to?'

Kate gave Jeremy the hotel details.

'I'll get a fax sent with his mugshot, just in case.'

Kate passed the service station, indicating to Rafi that they would stop at the next one.

There was a stony silence in the car.

'Why would he come after *us*?' Kate asked Jeremy.

'Well, I suspect it is Rafi he's after. Who has had their face plastered over the papers recently? And who, according to the news coverage, helped the police and messed up the terrorists' plans, robbing them of their multibillion payout?'

'OK, I get your line of thinking. But no one knows where we're going – or do they?'

'No, you're right, but better safe than sorry.'

'Do you have any leads on where Popovskaya might be?'

'We have one long shot which we're following up. Colonel Matlik and his Russian contacts have sent us details of all the other mercenaries that they have on their most wanted list. We have distributed the photos and names to all airports and ports, just in case one of them comes over to help Popovskaya. The new face recognition and gait assessment software at Heathrow airport has picked up a potential match. A brute of a man travelling on a Polish passport arrived there from Budapest an hour and a half ago. He has an uncanny resemblance to a former Chechen army officer, Radu Dranoff, and is on the list we have just received. We gave his and several other passengers' luggage a spot check, and at the same time picked up his mobile phone number. I have a team tracking his mobile phone calls and his movements. At the moment he is on a coach heading for Oxford. I have got another call… Must go. Do please keep in contact.'

'Will do and thanks for the call.' Kate flicked off her phone. They sat in silence until they arrived at the service station just after Swindon.

'Well, what a way to start our holiday!' said Rafi who looked across at Kate's strained face.

'You know what our problem is?'

'No,' he replied.

'You and I have become too hot a story. One sniff of us being in Cornwall and the flaming paparazzi will be all over us like locusts. Hey presto, within less than twenty-four hours the terrorists will know where we are.'

Rafi nodded. 'Well, at least Jeremy has a lead and the new Chechen arrival is probably only here to get Popovskaya safely out of the UK.'

'I hope you are right. Do you know what I love about you, Rafi? It's your optimism.' Kate leant across and gave him a peck on the cheek. 'Come on, my tummy is rumbling. I need to keep my energy levels up for all the exercise we're going to take in Cornwall.'

They chose their food in the cafeteria, Rafi pulled out his wallet and paid at the till. Then he noticed that in amongst his other banknotes was a damaged £20 note which hadn't been there when he had last looked. Attached to it was a Post-it with a scribbled message: 'You might like to frame this as a souvenir!' It was signed by Jeremy. Rafi smiled to himself.

Breakfast was far better than he'd imagined. Kate tucked into a full English breakfast. He looked across at her slender frame and wondered where she managed to put all that food. She scowled as she caught him staring.

'I wish I had your metabolism,' he chuckled.

'Is that why you were staring? What a disappointment – I thought you were ogling!'

The journey was uneventful but then, thirty miles from Newquay, Jeremy phoned again.

'Hi guys!' He sounded upbeat. 'I've got some news for you. Our Chechen with the Polish passport received a phone call half an hour ago. It was from a mobile phone which we've traced to outside Lancaster, which is near where we had Popovskaya in a secure hospital unit. Putting two and two together we think that our two Chechen mercenaries are on their way to meet up. Thought you might like to know. I've sent a fax with their details to the hotel. I'll keep you posted. Goodbye.'

It had been a one-sided phone call as Kate hadn't been able to get a word in. Jeremy had sounded upbeat, but both Kate and Rafi felt it had been an act. She put her hand on Rafi's knee. 'Even if we jump to the conclusion that they are after you, at least we'll have one, maybe two days before they'll know where we are. Jeremy and his team will look after us; don't worry.'

Rafi sat staring out of the window.

Kate looked subdued. 'This is no way to start a relationship. Let's chill out for the next couple of days and I promise you, Jeremy will keep an eye on our backs. If you want to start worrying, save it until after the paparazzi have found us. Then we'll both be in the frame.'

Rafi looked into Kate's eyes and at her lovely face. 'I'd hoped to leave the nightmares behind. But at least I've got you with me. I agree. No worrying until our whereabouts are common knowledge.'

For the last half-hour of the journey they played a game, trying to guess what the hotel would be like. They knew it stood on its own headland and overlooked a long, sandy bay.

'You're a pessimist,' concluded Rafi.

'Yes, but with low expectations things must get better.'

'Is that why you decided on me as your new boyfriend?'

'Of course, how much worse could it have got? A man locked up as a suspect in a terrorism case, uncooperative and with a useless wrist to boot. Plus, smelly – no, *really* smelly – unkempt, and that's just for starters.' They laughed and the mood in the car became lighter.

In contrast, outside the weather had turned foul. They followed the signs to Fistral Beach, drove past a windswept golf club and there in front of them was the Headland Hotel, an imposing Victorian-style red brick building, overlooking the Atlantic Ocean and the surfers' paradise, Fistral Bay. Its long driveway went through its own small golf course.

The strength of the wind was driving the rain horizontally. Kate drew her car up near the front door and they sat for a while looking at the heavy rain. She looked at Rafi with a grin. 'Where did we put the overcoats?'

He smiled. 'In the boot, of course!'

'Will we get more soaked making a dash for the front door, or getting our coats out of the boot?'

'I have a better idea.' He picked up Kate's phone and dialled a number. When he got through he asked whoever was on the other end of the line, 'Would you by any chance have a spare umbrella or two? We're stuck ten metres away from your front door and we…'

A friendly voice interrupted him. 'It is rather nasty outside. I'll get the porter to come and help you in.'

Wielding a large umbrella in high winds and driving rain was a skill that Rafi hadn't considered until then. They were ferried one at a time into the hotel. Kate went first and Rafi followed, wet at the edges but not soaked.

He walked into the reception area. Kate was standing in front of a roaring open fire. She was beaming.

'This is just brilliant. I think I'm going to like it here.'

To his surprise she bounced over and flung her arms around his neck, giving him a kiss that was more appropriate to the privacy of one's own room. Kate finished her show of affection and drew back, noticing that Rafi had started to blush.

'Oops, I seem to get a bit carried away at times,' she said to no one in particular. The hotel was busy for off-season February. Rafi wondered if, like the Savoy, it had also taken more than its fair share of those left homeless.

At the reception desk they were greeted by an attentive receptionist who arranged for their luggage to be taken up to their room. Next to their key was Jeremy's fax. It contained mug shots of Radu Dranoff and Aslan Popovskaya. Rafi studied Kate's serious face as she read it. She then passed the fax to him. The three pages of information made disconcerting reading. Popovskaya was made of stern stuff. In his fall from the scaffolding tower he had fractured his left collar bone and broken his left wrist and arm in several places. And now he and Dranoff were on the loose, most likely after them.

'Shame that Popovskaya is right handed...' Kate was politely interrupted by the receptionist.

'We've filled up since last week. Please forgive us if the service is a little slower than normal. We've managed to find you a comfortable bedroom, though.'

Rafi took the key and, holding Kate's hand walked across to the small lift. They got out on the second floor. The corridor leading to the room was spacious and newly carpeted. Kate squeezed Rafi's hand in anticipation as they stood in front of the door. He opened it and they walked in. In front of them was a modest-sized sitting room with stunning views over the long sandy beach and the ocean. A large arrangement of flowers on the side table added to the welcoming atmosphere.

'Where is the bed?' asked Kate, sounding like a young girl itching to explore. 'How about I try this door?' she said with a bounce in her step and disappeared into the next room. 'Rafi, look what I've found!'

He followed her and there in front of him was the wonderful sight of Kate lying on her back, spread eagled across a large king-sized bed, and bouncing up and down.

'This is great! I couldn't have chosen better if I'd tried. Nice, comfy bed – let me change that, a nice, big, comfy bed – great views and peace and quiet. Fantastic!' Kate rolled off the bed, stood up in front of Rafi, and looked into his eyes. 'Promise me one thing,' she said. 'Let's forget the terrorists and enjoy the now. Tomorrow can look after itself. It usually does.'

He pulled her close to him and kissed her.

Kate pulled back and straight away sensed Rafi's disappointment.

She paused and spoke just before Rafi was going to. 'I could do with using the bathroom for a moment. Could you do me a favour and find out when they finish serving afternoon tea?'

A short phone call later, Rafi returned to the bedroom and called to Kate through the closed bathroom door. 'Tea ends in just over an hour.'

'Excellent... I'll be with you shortly.'

Rafi walked back into the sitting room, picked up and put on his jacket, and turned the lights off. He walked over to the balcony doors; it had stopped raining. He opened them and stepped outside into the bracing wind.

Motionless, he stood looking out over the dark ocean, letting the fresh, salt laden air wash over him. He shivered and was about to turn to go back inside when he felt a pair of warm arms wrap around him. He was grateful for the body warmth. Kate nestled closer to him, then backed off. Following her unspoken instructions he turned. Her long sleeved blouse was unbuttoned. A gust of wind flapped open the soft material revealing a naked body... She moved forward and whispered a request into his ear.

*

Some while later Kate and Rafi lay curled in each other's arms. He placed a kiss gently on her cheek. 'I'm going to have to keep my eyes on you! Taking me unawares like that. Whatever will you think of next?'

Kate grinned.

'No don't tell me! You look so innocent, but underneath you're a right little minx...'

She poked him gently in the ribs. 'Yes... but it takes two to tango!'

Rafi looked at his watch. 'By my reckoning we have half an hour before they stop serving tea.'

*

Afternoon tea was as Kate had hoped: scones, clotted cream and strawberry jam in front of an open fire. They chatted, sitting comfortably on a huge sofa while time sped by.

But their cosy little world was shattered when Kate answered a call from Jeremy.

She filled Rafi in. 'MI5 has intercepted a phone call;

Popovskaya and Dranoff have met up, not ten miles from the hospital that Popovskaya escaped from. Unfortunately, they have lost them and have no further information. Neil reckons that they'll lie low for a couple of days to let Popovskaya recover and then come after us. An SAS team is on its way to watch the hotel and to protect us. They should be here later this evening and we have been advised to sleep in another bedroom - incognito.'

★

They dressed for dinner, and then moved into the new bedroom the proprietor had found for them.

Dinner was enjoyable; they ate hungrily and chatted, but the vivacity had gone. The nightmare wasn't over yet.

Whilst they were having coffee, Jeremy phoned. 'An SAS team of three are keeping watch over the entrances to the hotel. They like the fact that the hotel is so exposed because it makes it difficult for Dranoff to creep up unnoticed. I hope to be with you in about twenty minutes.'

Sure enough, a short while later Jeremy appeared accompanied by a casually dressed individual.

'Please let me introduce you to your SAS bodyguard: Corporal Brett Johnstone. He'll be your shadow whilst Dranoff and Popovskaya remain at large. Have you eaten already?' enquired Jeremy.

'Yes,' replied Kate, 'but I can always find room for another pudding! Do come and have dinner – you'll like the food.'

'Excellent,' grinned Jeremy.

'How about I find us a nice, quiet table and see if I need to borrow a tie?' suggested Brett.

He reappeared a few minutes later. Jeremy and Kate were deep in conversation. 'Dranoff and Popovskaya have disappeared off the face of the earth. We tried to lock on to their phone signals, but their phones are turned off. These two definitely know what they're doing.'

Jeremy and Brett tucked into a hearty dinner.

'Neil is sure that you're their target - payback time for those who got in the way,' said Jeremy. 'We have considered other possible targets, but we keep coming back to the fact that Popovskaya will be feeling pissed off, and *you*, Rafi, seem the perfect person on which to vent his anger. What worries us is

343

who arranged for Dranoff to come to the UK to help Popovskaya. We thought we had all the main players under lock and key, and incommunicado. We know Miti is on the run in Africa, but we don't believe his influence goes this far. There has to be someone else out there – part of the terrorists' web – who is pulling the Chechen end of the strings. We're looking again at the teams run by Kaleem Shah and Kim Chindriani to see if we missed someone, but haven't found anything yet.'

Jeremy paused. 'Neil doesn't think they know that we are on to them. My colleagues are keeping an eye out for stolen guns or vehicles reported between here and their last known locations.'

'When do you think that they will come for us?' asked Kate.

'Unfortunately,' said Jeremy calmly, 'As soon as the paparazzi are on to you, your location will become public knowledge. Realistically, you could expect company any time from to-morrow early afternoon. Neil would like you to stay put, so if they do come for you, the SAS can protect you. The alternative is for you to go into hiding and wait for them to come after you… which I wouldn't recommend.'

The conversation moved on to the terrorists captured at Safi.

'They're due to arrive in Plymouth tomorrow. I shall be there to greet them; one of the perks of my job!' said Jeremy.

'How badly were the terrorists damaged by their investments in the markets?' asked Brett. 'Jeremy has been describing what they were aiming to do, and how they got caught with their pants down!'

'I spoke briefly to Aidan earlier today,' Rafi said. 'He says that the markets have been remarkably resilient. But in the areas where the terrorists were playing the derivatives market, prices have moved sharply against them. They're sitting on some truly massive losses. With Maryam, Jameel and the sheikh unable to make contact with their dealers, their positions will be sold. Aidan reckons their collateral will be too little to cover their margin calls. As a result the dodgy banks that acted as intermediaries will also be put through a financial shredding machine.'

Jeremy smiled. 'Good – serves them right.'

'Aidan is optimistic that several other shady people will be caught red-handed. He's been liaising with Neil, who's following up a significant list of very interesting leads. Maryam, it seems, is in bed with a number of European investors, many of whom are super wealthy, very well connected and of dubious character. Time will tell if they are just plain greedy or are in fact crooks,' added Rafi.

After dinner, Brett and Jeremy walked with Kate and Rafi to their room. Brett had been given a room on the other side of the corridor, near the top of the stairs, and proceeded to set up a selection of listening and monitoring devices in their room and along the corridor.

Rafi and Kate said their goodnights and retired to their new twin bedroom. Rafi sat tentatively on the edge of his single bed.

'I'd been *really* looking forward to this evening,' said Kate. 'Now we're stuck with single beds and bugs!' she grinned. 'Would you like a good night's sleep or company?'

'Both please.'

'I wonder how we might manage that?' Kate said with a grin. She headed for the bathroom. 'There's no bath but we do have a big shower,' she called to Rafi.

As if he had read her thoughts, moments later he was standing at the bathroom door in his next to nothings.

'You don't hang around,' said Kate.

To Rafi's delight the shower had a range of settings. He was under a warm torrent when Kate joined him and changed the setting to a fine drizzle.

'Now where would you like me to start?' Kate picked up the bar of soap and smelt its inviting scent. 'How about your back?'

Rafi turned round and faced the shower wall.

'I hope this doesn't hurt,' said Kate as she looked at the bruises on his back.

He felt her fingers softly glide on the silky lather, gently massaging his muscles. They slowly worked their way from his shoulders down to the bottom of his back, skirting around his bruises. She was in a playful mood.

Kate recalled her first sight of him in the interrogation room. He had looked ordinary and cheerless. Then seeing him after his shower in the changing room at Wood Street police station, partially undressed, it had been a revelation. She smiled, he was gorgeous. His body was willowy but manly... The soap slipped out of her fingers. As she bent over to pick it up he tickled her.

Kate let out a loud shreik.

Moments later, there was a loud bang as the bathroom door flew open. There on the other side of the steamed up glass was the outline of a man holding a gun. Rafi's heart missed a beat as the faces of Radu Dranoff and Aslan Popovskaya flashed into his mind. He stood petrified, his pulse racing. Time stood still.

'Sorry mate, I thought you had unwanted company!' came an embarrassed voice. The door closed and Brett, the SAS man was gone.

Rafi stood motionless under the hot drizzling water. 'Are you alright?' asked Kate.

'I guess so,' replied Rafi shakily. He still had the outline of the gun framed in his mind. 'That gave me quite a shock.'

Kate changed the shower's controls and, under a torrent of water, quickly hosed off the sea of bubbles.

'Brought reality back with a bang... Ehh?' and gave Rafi a hug. 'Let's get you dry and tucked up in bed'.

*

The low morning sun streamed in to the bedroom through the small gaps around the curtains. A ray of light danced on Rafi's face. The daylight had woken Kate half an hour earlier. She had come round to find Rafi asleep in her arms, with his serene face close to hers, and had carefully examined every inch of it many times over. Kate smiled as she thought about the man lying next to her.

The fluttering of Rafi's dark eyelashes brought her out of her daydreams.

'Good morning darling. I hope you slept well,' she said softly.

'Like a log.'

Kate lent forward and gave him a kiss. 'How about breakfast in bed?'

'Nice idea. What about a full English breakfast with orange juice and coffee, in say half an hour? And we don't even need to use the phone to order.'

'Pardon...? Oh, I forgot that our SAS friends are listening in.'

*

Half an hour later there was a knock at the door, and Brett entered carrying a tray laden with their breakfast. 'I hope you don't mind me using the spare key?' He put the tray down and smiled at Rafi and Kate snuggled up in a single bed. 'And I hope I didn't barge in on you.' He grinned, turned and left.

Their breakfast was interrupted by a phone call from Jeremy. 'There's no sign of Dranoff or Popovskaya. Have you seen the morning papers?'

'Not yet,' replied Kate.

'Well, there's a picture in one of the tabloids of the two of you having dinner. If that's not a red rag to a bull, I don't know what is. The terrorists now know exactly where you are. Brett has asked for you to stay in your room. Sorry if it cramps your style, but…'

'That's alright,' butted in Kate. 'Rafi and I'll be fine.'

The rest of the morning passed slowly. Rafi read the papers and was in particular fascinated by an article in *The Independent* which gave details of the exclusion zone around Stratford and provided a summary of the building works that were in progress, and of those planned. It showed maps and explained how the transport and key utilities were being rerouted around the newly named 'Isle of Stratford'.

Kate meanwhile lazed around, read a magazine and wrote postcards to her parents and her brother.

They opted for an early lunch in their room.

'Now what?' enquired Kate. 'I'm fed up with writing cards and reading.'

She picked up the hotel brochure. 'Hey Rafi, do you like swimming? There's a heated indoor pool. I wonder if Brett would let us go for a swim later?'

'If you can find me a pair of trunks, I'll be there,' replied Rafi.

Kate got up, rummaged around in her suitcase and pulled out two swimming costumes. 'I packed these just in case - I love water.' She held up a black Speedo one-piece and then a couple of scraps of blue material. 'A friend got me the bikini in Brazil a couple of years ago, but I haven't had the courage to wear it!'

'I can see why,' said Rafi with a big smile.

'Would you like to see it on?' enquired Kate.

'Yes please.'

Kate disappeared into the bathroom. Several minutes later she reappeared. 'So what do you think?'

Rafi looked at her. The Speedo swimsuit fitted her like a glove

- flattening out her contours, giving her figure the look of a teenager.

'This is what I usually wear. It's not very flattering is it? Now what do you think of this…?' She peeled off the one-piece, revealing the skimpy bikini.

Rafi's eyes were drawn to the small blue triangles which accentuated her subtle sexy curves. 'You look amazing…'

Kate moved towards Rafi, her fingers playing with the thin blue strings that held the flimsy bikini together. 'Now if I pull this and this…' she said, stepping forward in her nothingness, 'You get just me!'

*

At 4.30 p.m. Brett knocked on the door and entered carrying a tray of Cornish cream tea. 'Hope I didn't wake you, but I thought you might like some sustenance.' He put the tray down on the side table. 'I have some news. Jeremy phoned. He hopes you are not getting bored stiff, and says that Jameel and co. are safely in custody on English soil and are *seriously* disgruntled. All they want to know about is what the long gilts index and interest rates are doing. We haven't broken the bad news to them, as yet. Oh, by the way, Maryam is under lock and key at a safe house. Neil Gunton is looking forward to playing her off against the others.'

'Thanks Brett,' said Kate, 'And thank you for watching over us.'

'My pleasure. Let me know if you need anything else. If not, I'll be back at supper time,' he smiled as he left.

Kate picked up the bedside phone and rang reception. 'What time does the post go…? OK, thanks.' She leant forwards and kissed Rafi warmly on the lips. 'I have to nip downstairs to buy stamps - the post goes in five minutes. Sending cards to the family is something we always used to do… I thought my parents would like a card showing the hotel and its beach.' Kate dressed quickly and went downstairs.

Wrapped in a bathrobe Rafi sat by the window. It was dark outside. The floodlights accentuated the driving rain. He sat there thinking of very little. Next to him on the table, was a Sig Sauer P226 revolver, which had been given to him by Brett. 'Its small size,' Brett had explained, 'Means you can carry it on you without showing a telltale bulge. All you need to know is that it has seven

.38 calibre rounds, which will stop a man if you hit him anywhere in the torso. Remember, it has a safety catch on the thumb side for right-handers. This little beauty has only a modest kick; aim a little low unless you've had time to cradle the gun properly.' Brett had shown him how to hold the gun. 'Be instinctive and please bear in mind that if you are aiming at a person thirty feet away, your accuracy as an amateur will be in the order of six feet. So please be extra careful of bystanders!'

Rafi recalled his fervently hoping that he would never have to use the gun. Kate had put hers in her handbag. He'd left his on the table; he didn't know what else to do with it.

He watched as a pair of bright headlights arced down the windswept drive. They belonged to a silver Range Rover. It parked opposite the hotel and out stepped a well-built man wearing a flat hat, plus fours and a checked sports jacket; he also had a Barbour jacket slung over his left shoulder.

If it had been me in this rain, Rafi thought, I'd have had the Barbour on and not draped over my shoulder. Rafi watched as the man glanced around, turned and strode towards the front door.

Rafi sensed something wasn't right. The man's face was obscured by his hat and coat. He was walking straight towards the door; in front of him was a large puddle. He didn't walk around it but straight through it, and that's when Rafi noticed his shoes. They were heavy, black, scuffed leather boots – the sort one would associate with a navvy or a soldier. He was thickset and his gait wasn't that of a well-heeled City gent.

'Oh my God!' Rafi gasped and jumped to his feet. He felt certain he had just been looking at Dranoff. He picked up his gun and bolted out of the room, running down the corridor barefooted, with his white bathrobe untied and streaming out behind him. As he passed Brett's door, he banged on it and shouted, 'Dranoff's downstairs and so is Kate!'

At the top of the stairs an elderly couple shrieked as he ran past them. Rafi grabbed the banister rail with his good left hand and swung round and down the wide stairs.

In a couple of bounds he'd reached the half landing. As he headed down the last flight of stairs, the man came into view - he was walking through the reception area. Rafi focused on what little he could see of his face. Yes, it was Dranoff!

Neither of the SAS men from outside was following him. Rafi saw Kate sitting across from the bottom of the stairs, sticking a stamp on to her postcard. Dranoff was just on the other side of the glass divide between her and the reception area.

Her eyes looked up and met Dranoff's as he pushed through the glass swing door between them. Out from under the Barbour jacket came a sawn-off shotgun.

'No! It can't end like this,' thought Rafi. He let out a blood-curdling scream, flicked the safety catch off and pointed his pistol towards the terrorist. He couldn't shoot at him - there were too many people close by and with the gun in his bruised hand he could hit practically anyone within ten feet of what he aimed at. But he *had* to shoot to distract Dranoff and to draw his fire. Still screaming, Rafi fired at the plate glass window next to Dranoff.

There was a loud bang and a crash of splintering glass.

Dranoff swung his gun round and fired both barrels. The wooden banister rail at Rafi's side erupted into a swarm of flying splinters, as he fell headlong down the stairs.

For Rafi everything went pitch black.

Chapter 9

Slowly, Rafi opened his eyes. He could see nothing. He couldn't move; his head was in a vice. Where was he? To his left there was, he thought, a faint red glow and a dull bleeping noise. He tried moving again but nothing happened. His head ached, as did his stomach, right arm and thigh. He picked up the smell of disinfectant. It suddenly dawned on him; he was in hospital.

Rafi felt something warm in his left hand. He squeezed it wondering what it might be. It moved and squeezed him back. A grey shadow moved into his line of sight. His eyes began to focus. There, sitting by him, was Kate.

'He's coming round!' she called out in a croaky voice. Rafi's head was immobilised. He couldn't see who else was there. The door opened and light flooded in. He could see Kate's face out of the corner of his eye. She looked tired; her eyes were red and puffy.

'It's so good to have you back,' she whispered, holding his hand firmly, as if he might leave.

He saw a nurse bending over him. 'How do you feel?' she asked.

'Sore,' he replied.

'How's your head?'

'Sore.'

'Your leg?'

'Sore.'

'Your side?'

'Sore.'

'Your right arm?'

'Very painful, thank you.'

'It's to be expected, I'm afraid… What's the last thing you can remember?'

He hesitated, as his mind lurched back to the hotel reception area and the stairs.

'When Kate saw Dranoff… Just before I was shot,' he replied.

'Excellent; that's good news – no amnesia.'

Rafi felt his strength ebb away as he was asked a series of further questions. He fell silent.

'Nurse, how is he?' asked Kate.

'Considering everything, surprisingly well. I will fetch the doctor to look him over.'

The nurse reappeared with a doctor in tow. The doctor carefully checked Rafi and his wounds, then turned to Kate.

'The bang to his head gave him severe concussion. Thankfully there doesn't seem to be any long-term damage. The antibiotics are fighting the infection to his wounds. I've never known someone add cat excrement to twelve bore cartridges… Very nasty, indeed.'

He paused. 'There may be some more splinters to be removed; it was difficult to pick them all up on the X-rays. The wounds to the right side of his stomach and chest are mending well. His wrist is badly sprained and his elbow has been relocated and should mend well too.'

He looked at Kate and Rafi. 'I've never seen such bruising. The initial X-rays appear to show that there are no broken bones, but I'd like to run a few more tests before we remove his neck brace.'

'Thank you,' said Kate. 'Can I chat to him?'

'Yes, but don't tire him. No more than a couple of minutes, then let him sleep.'

Rafi looked up and saw tears in Kate's eyes.

'I thought I'd lost you!' She slowly bent over and kissed him.

'How long have I been here?' he enquired.

'Nearly four days. I feel awful that we let you down.'

Rafi tried to smile, but his head and face remained immobile. 'That's OK. Silly question, but where am I?'

'Plymouth Hospital. You were making an awful mess of the hotel's carpets. There was a retired doctor on holiday in the hotel. He managed to stem the bleeding and insisted that you were taken to the nearest hospital with a major accident and emergency unit as quickly as humanly possible. He gave you less than an hour if you didn't get into a good A&E Department. Luckily, an SAS helicopter was nearby. The retired doctor insisted on staying with you for the journey.'

'Just as well,' said the surgeon standing by his bed. 'You lost a large quantity of blood and needed a lot of patching up. Thankfully, underneath the mess you weren't as badly shot up as we had thought. You should thank Mr Welby for tipping us off about the shotgun cartridges smelling foul and the potential infection problems. You succumbed and ran a high fever for the first couple of days, but we were able to limit the complications. We've managed to help your natural defences fight the bacteria with some strong antibiotics.'

Rafi looked at Kate. 'Have I missed anything while I've been out of action?'

'Not really. I've kept some newspapers for you to read, just in case.'

'Thank you...' Rafi mumbled and drifted back to sleep.

He remembered little of the next thirty-six hours. There were fleeting moments of consciousness followed by more sleep. Whenever he awoke, Kate was there beside him, holding his hand. Painfully and slowly, he returned to the land of the living.

*

One morning his neck brace was gone and he was no longer pinned into position flat on his back. The nurse showed Kate how the electric bed worked and how to adjust the mattress so that Rafi could sit up.

The curtains were opened and daylight streamed in. As he was slowly brought up into a sitting position, Rafi looked down to see his right arm bandaged up and his side, from his ribs to his knee, covered in dressings. He felt light-headed and his bottom felt burning hot. Kate smiled at him. Her face was tired but gone were the puffy red eyes.

'Thank you for saving my life,' she said as she held his hand. 'I shall always remember...' She couldn't continue as the horror of the gunfight flooded back.

'Was anyone else hurt?'

'There were a few minor cuts from flying glass, but otherwise you were the only casualty other than Dranoff, who was taken out by Brett, the SAS soldier, following you down the stairs. Popovskaya has been captured and is safely locked away. It was all a bit of a cock-up,' Kate explained. 'The two SAS men watching the front entrance of the hotel missed Dranoff. How did you know it was him?'

'Hunting and shooting types driving smart Range Rovers in smart shooting kit don't drape their Barbour coat over their shoulder in the pouring rain and don't wear scuffed, heavy, black boots. When I couldn't see his face, which he'd covered with his hat and a Barbour slung over his shoulder, I guessed it might be Dranoff. I picked up the gun and ran to warn you.'

Rafi stopped speaking for a moment. 'When he saw you and pulled out the sawn-off shotgun and swung it towards you, I thought I was going to lose you.' There were tears in his eyes. He couldn't see Kate's as she'd turned away.

Another person had entered the room – it was Colonel Turner. 'Good to see you in one piece. Sorry about the cock-up. Thanks to your quick thinking, a real disaster was averted. I hear you got peppered by the sawn-off shotgun. and that your dive for cover behind the wrought iron banisters saved you. They tell me that the wooden handrail was blown to smithereens. The SAS man behind you was very impressed by your reactions: shooting to attract the attention of the terrorist and diving at the same time. He wondered if you had military training.'

Rafi grinned. 'Simple good fortune - I missed my footing as I looked for the darn safety catch and for something to shoot at. I couldn't aim straight for the terrorist – there were too many people I could have hit. I actually tripped just as I fired at the big glass window.'

'Good work all the same. I'm pleased to see you on the mend. I'll drop by when you're up and about for a debriefing.' The surgeon appeared at the door. The colonel excused himself and left.

Rafi spent the next half an hour being brought up to speed on his various injuries. 'There's quite a number,' said the surgeon, running through them as if they were on a shopping list. 'A posterior dislocation of the elbow which has been successfully relocated; fourteen stitches in the head and two drill holes as a result of the emergency surgery to relieve the pressure; six pellets in the thigh and buttocks and several more in the flank, which went into your intestines and lung – we've patched them up, but I had to remove a small part of your lung.' The surgeon paused and smiled. 'With a good convalescence, you'll soon be right as rain.'

'Thank you,' replied Rafi weakly.

*

Time passed slowly, but Rafi started to feel stronger and more able to face the world.

During a further inspection of his wounds, Rafi asked, 'Doctor, how much longer will I be in hospital?'

'If you can find somewhere quiet to convalesce and someone to care for you, you should be able to leave tomorrow.'

'Tomorrow would be great,' replied Rafi

A kindly physiotherapist arrived and went through a gentle exercise regime aimed in particular at his elbow. This was followed by a dietician who talked about what he should eat whilst his intestines and body mended. Late in the afternoon the surgeon and doctor reappeared. They were pleased with Rafi's progress. They chatted with Kate and, to Rafi's surprise, announced that if he wished he could be discharged and could return to the comfort of the hotel. Kate was given a series of contact names and numbers, plus a schedule of when he should attend the local surgery.

'Any ideas on what we should do for clothes and headgear?' Kate asked the nurse. After a short discussion, Kate opted for the short journey to the town centre to buy Rafi what he needed. An hour later she reappeared carrying a couple of large bags.

'Sorry to have taken so long.'

Rafi dressed in comfortable, warm clothes. With Kate's help he stood up and for the first time in days he looked at himself in the mirror. He was horrified by what he saw. His eye sockets looked skeletal. Two thirds of his hair was missing. A jagged scar with stitches ran from just above his hairline to the top of his head and his bruised scalp was a dark reddish purple.

His legs felt wobbly and he sat down on the bed more quickly than he'd intended – to the great discomfort of his unhealed wounds.

Kate spoke to the nurse about the practicalities of getting back to Newquay. They opted for the simplest solution and took a taxi. The journey seemed to go on forever. Rafi didn't know how or where to position himself. His body ached and his head

355

throbbed. They drew up in front of the hotel at 8 o'clock.

The cold wind cut through his clothes. Kate helped him inside and across to the lift. The area at the bottom of the stairs looked very different. There were temporary carpets. Boarding covered the plate glass window which separated the reception area from the seating area at the bottom of the stairs and also the stained glass window on the half landing. Builders' dust sheets were draped all over the banisters.

Kate had phoned ahead to check with the hotel that they were still welcome. The proprietor and his wife were there to greet them. It transpired that they felt their staff had let Rafi and Kate down, revealing their whereabouts to the tabloid press. The £500 bung that the chambermaid had received had been donated to a local charity. She'd kept her job on the basis that her apology was accepted. She was there waiting at reception with a bunch of flowers. She stepped across and passed them to Rafi. She took one look at him and crumpled, promptly bursting into tears.

'I am sorry; I just did not think. The journalist was so convincing. Will you forgive me, please?' she stuttered through her tears.

Kate put an arm around her. 'You weren't to know. At any rate he probably would have found us sooner or later. At least it's all in the past and we're still in one piece… Your flowers look lovely. Thank you. Perhaps you could help us find a vase?'

Rafi was exhausted by the time he arrived at their room. He slowly shuffled into the bedroom and sat gingerly on the bed. His backside hurt like hell. He curled up on his left-hand side. Kate cradled his head in her lap.

For the next two days he remained holed up in the suite. His wounds were healing well and he started to get his energy back. Kate, it seemed, was enjoying her role as nurse.

On the second day the phone hardly stopped ringing. Saara, the major, Kate's parents, her brother and Emma all wanted to hear how he was and to pass on their love and best wishes. Jeremy phoned to apologise that he couldn't drop by as he'd been given another assignment, which necessitated a bit of travelling, but he looked forward to seeing them soon.

In the middle of the afternoon, while Rafi was sound asleep, a call came in from the Prime Minister. Rafi was very groggy. The

PM enquired after his health, conveyed his best wishes and hung up. A nice touch for someone so busy, Rafi thought.

While he recuperated, Rafi went through the newspapers. Post-Stratford, things were slowly returning to normality. In particular, there was one small article by Pete Lockyer which caught his attention: it showed a picture of Maryam in a smart suit sitting in a stately drawing room. Apparently she had not gone to prison, but was helping the police with their enquiries. Strange, he thought, and made a mental note to ask Jeremy what was going on.

In their little world, the hotel proprietor had been doing his best to protect them from any further unwanted press intrusion, but the situation was becoming untenable. Camped outside was a small village of TV crews and reporters. Kate and Rafi needed to do something or they would get no peace and quiet for the rest of their holiday.

An idea came to Kate and she phoned Jeremy to get Pete Lockyer's number. She then phoned Pete to ask if he would do an interview. He jumped at the invitation and said he would be there first thing the next morning.

As dusk was falling, the hotel proprietor arranged for Kate and Rafi to be smuggled out in the back of a van. The afternoon trip to the doctors was otherwise straightforward. The nurse looked at the notes from the hospital and set about changing Rafi's dressings and bandages. Fifteen minutes later he only had one dressing left on his side. All the others had been removed as she was pleased with how he had healed. Kate arranged a follow-up session for the last of his stitches to be taken out and they returned surreptitiously to the hotel.

Psychologically Rafi was feeling much better. His headaches had gone and seeing the wounds on his body almost mended had been a real tonic. That evening they went downstairs for dinner. As he passed through the reception, Rafi observed that the repair work was almost complete.

In the dining room, they were met by the restaurant manager. 'Excuse me for saying, but everyone is curious to see how you are mending. They have seen the mess and, like me, find it incredible that you're still alive.' He beckoned them forward. 'Your table is at the far end by a window overlooking the sea. It should be quiet, except you will have to walk past everyone.'

'Not a problem,' said Rafi as he shuffled in. He became aware that the room had fallen silent and dozens of pairs of eyes were staring at them. As they approached the table, Rafi noticed that the two seats had their backs to the room and were facing the window and out to sea. 'Could you move our places so that we can look into the room? That way we won't look as if we're avoiding everyone.'

Moments later Rafi sat down gingerly. The restaurant manager reappeared with the menu.

Kate asked, 'Is the person I noticed as I came in the retired doctor who helped Rafi?'

'Yes, he's sitting over there with his wife.'

'Thank you.'

The menu was mouth-watering. Kate was in her element. Her healthy appetite had returned, helped by the long runs and swims she had enjoyed while Rafi was resting. She made her choice. Rafi was still hesitating and when the waiter returned, Kate passed him a sheet of paper.

'Sorry, but you're still on a strict diet; it won't be long before your fully mended and you can have grown-up food again!'

'At least I won't have to cut it up!' he said, moving his right arm in its sling.

'I'm so pleased you are on the mend. A serious look replaced Kate's radiant smile. The helicopter flight down to Plymouth felt like the longest journey of my life. The retired doctor who tended your wounds was a godsend. I honestly thought you might not make it.'

She hesitated. 'Would you mind if I asked him and his wife to join us for coffee? He was so brilliant…'

'That's a great idea.'

Kate got up and walked down to the doctor's table. He and his wife were pleased to accept the invitation, and at the end of the meal, they joined Kate and Rafi in the sitting room for coffee. Like everyone else they were keen to find out what had really been going on. Rafi thanked him several times over.

'Just pleased to help,' replied the doctor, 'And the helicopter ride was a first.'

'I only found Rafi a few weeks ago – I couldn't bear to have lost him so soon,' said Kate.

The conversation covered a wide range of topics. The doctor chatted about his time working in Manchester and the increase in gun and knife crime that he had witnessed. He explained how he had had his arm twisted a number of years ago and had attended a special training session on how to deal with gun crime injuries... 'I'm pleased it came in useful,' he said with a grin

After half an hour of talking, tiredness overcame Rafi. He said his goodnights and retired upstairs, leaving Kate chatting to the doctor and his wife.

Back in the bedroom Rafi undressed with difficulty and surveyed his body. In many places, it was hard to see where one bruise ended and another started. His wounds were still sore, but the burning heat had gone out of them.

He curled up in bed. Next thing he knew it was morning and Kate was sitting at the bottom of the bed, in her running kit, eating breakfast.

He smelt the hot food. It made him hungry.

'Good morning. I hope you don't mind me starting,' she said. 'Not at all. What's on the menu?'

'Scrambled eggs, croissants, fresh orange juice and coffee. By the way, we've got Pete Lockyer due here in about an hour.'

Pete was early and caught Rafi in his dressing gown. Kate ordered breakfast for him and his cameraman, whilst Rafi slowly got washed and dressed. She explained the ground rules. 'Please treat Rafi as a close family member. We do not want anything published that he will regret. We will chat openly to you, on the understanding that you clear what you write with Jeremy's boss, Neil Gunton, at MI5.'

Judging by the size of his frown, Pete was none too happy with that suggestion and Kate picked up on his reluctance.

'It's quite simple. Much of what Rafi and I will tell you has been kept under wraps. There may be things we tell you that could jeopardise the investigations into this awful affair. Don't worry; there should be enough to keep you in stories for weeks!'

Pete gave his word. 'And having seen today's newspapers I appreciate your reticence,' he commented. 'The photos weren't very nice.'

Rafi caught the end of the conversation and glanced across to

Kate.

'One of the guests took a series of photos of you at dinner last night and you looked quite awful in them. The proprietor was very upset. He'd asked all the guests to respect your privacy whilst you were convalescing. The culprit was the same reporter who passed the bung to the chambermaid. He got a guest to take the photos using a special hidden camera.'

'Quite how marketable is our story?' Rafi sighed.

'Red-hot,' replied Pete. He paused. 'Would you want paying?'

'What sort of sum would we be talking about?' asked Rafi, and Kate shot him a glowering glance.

'The full inside story, handled properly over a number of weeks or even months, would net you a six, maybe even a seven, figure sum for an exclusive. Basically, you could name your price. Is this going to be a very expensive trip for me?' enquired Pete.

Rafi looked across at Kate. She slowly shook her head.

'I think it would be churlish not to take the money,' said Rafi.

'But…' interjected Kate. She looked horrified.

'Seriously. Consider if the money was not for us, but for the hospices helping those with radiation poisoning. They must be overflowing. How about Pete's paper running an appeal to raise money for the hospices helping those suffering? The appeal could go alongside our story. It would be great publicity for the newspaper and be great for its image,' argued Rafi.

As he paused to think, Rafi could see Kate visibly relax. 'If your paper were to start the ball rolling with, say, a £250,000 donation and top it up as more stories were rolled out, I reckon Kate and I would be very happy.'

Pete looked pensive. 'I reckon my editor would go with that if I got an exclusive.'

'Where else would we go?' asked Kate rhetorically with a huge smile.

They chatted for almost an hour and a half. For the photo shoot, the hotel proprietor arranged for them to be slipped out of the back of the hotel in a laundry van down to a nearby beach where the pictures could be taken in the morning sunshine. They returned using the same means of transport.

With the story and the photos in the bag, Pete made arrangements to meet with Neil, said his thanks and slipped off to

London with his scoop.

At Kate's request, the proprietor briefed the journalists and TV crews camped outside that a press conference would be held the following morning, at 11 o'clock, in the dining room.

Kate and Rafi spent the rest of the day chatting and discussing what he might do next and about her career ambitions in the police force. It was settled that he would move in with her for a couple of months before he made any decisions. It was a happy day. He had a future; one which filled him with great expectations.

They ate in their room that evening, turned in early and breakfasted early the next morning. Rafi tentatively tucked into a small English breakfast while reading the newspapers.

They couldn't miss Pete's article: it ran to twenty pages! On the front page were a smiling Kate and Rafi walking hand in hand, in the sun, on the golden sands by the sea. The trilby hat and the flowing scarf hid many of the scars and bruises, and all things considered he looked remarkably well. The headline under the photo was: *In good hands*. The article talked of Pete's breakthrough in tracking down the terrorists' getaway vessel, *Golden Sundancer*, in Iceland and explained Kate's and Rafi's roles in unravelling the terrorists' plots. The article revealed the work that Kate's team at the City of London police and MI5 had done in finding the locations of the terrorist attacks. It also described the role of the Air Chief Marshal, the Prime Minister, the Defence Secretary and the head of MI5 – and even mentioned Aidan's team working with the Chancellor of the Exchequer and the pulling of the financial rabbits out of the hat. There were photos of the hotel proprietor presenting the doctor and his wife with a large bouquet of flowers, as well as pictures of John, Emma, Giles and David.

The article included one new nugget of information. There was a picture of Miti Lakhani. Despite the best efforts of MI6 and the CIA, he had disappeared and the terrorist training camp run by him was deserted. Also, tucked away in the text, was a paragraph alluding to the fact that one of the terrorists had, at the end, tried to save their skin by doing a deal. Rafi smiled. It was another nice way of playing Maryam and the other terrorists off against each other.

The hotel's dining room was packed for the 11 o'clock press conference. Pete's story had whetted their appetites. Before the session Kate received a call from Neil, thanking her for getting Pete to talk to him before going to press. Basically, Neil told them that they could mention practically anything, except for the sleepers, but they should remember that the more they told, the more the journalists would want to know.

Kate and Rafi sat at a long table covered with a smart white tablecloth and flower arrangements at either end. Bright lights were trained on them.

The questions were like cannon fire. First they focused on the recent terrorist shooting and Rafi's wounds, then the questions backtracked to the lead-up to the Stratford disaster and, finally, they were asked their views on whether politicians, prior to the Stratford tragedy, had pushed the boundaries of spin too far.

'It takes two to tango,' Rafi replied. 'Irresponsible journalism goes hand in hand with spin. I applaud responsible investigative journalism which questions whether the full truth is being revealed by publicity-hungry politicians. More attention to the minutiae and not just to the big glossy picture would be welcomed.'

After a barrage of further questions, Kate stood up. 'Thank you, you should by now have more than enough! Rafi and I came here for a holiday to recharge our batteries. It's not turned out as we had hoped. We have only four days left before we go back to London and it would be *much* appreciated if we could have that time to ourselves.'

Despite calls for more answers to questions, Kate and Rafi had had enough and left through a side door, picking up their coats and heading for the fresh air and the solitude of the windswept beach.

★

The last four days of Rafi's convalescence went by far too fast. They chatted and laughed as if they didn't have a care in the world. It was a happy time. On Sunday, it was with sadness that they packed before their drive back to London. It felt like the end of the long holidays and the impending return to school.

Back in London, Monday morning felt strange. Kate set off

for work early and Rafi was left in her flat alone. It was the first time for ages that he hadn't been with her. He missed her.

It was a sunny day; spring was in the air. On the spur of the moment he decided to look at Stratford and the new wall around the exclusion zone. He took the underground straight through to Old Street station and walked east towards Hackney Road. After about half a mile Rafi came upon a sign by the roadside. He was entering a restricted area. This was, he assumed, the beginning of a buffer zone. Not far ahead of him he could see a military roadblock in front of a fifty-metre strip of cleared derelict ground. Past this were a three-metre high, heavy-duty steel mesh barrier and the beginnings of a brick wall. Beyond that he could see piles of rubble, empty properties and, incongruously, a number of newly planted trees.

As he stood taking in the enormity of the dispossessed area, a soldier came across.

'This is a restricted area, sir. You should turn around and make your way back to the other side of the buffer zone.'

'Sorry,' Rafi said. 'I was only trying to fathom out the true size of the exclusion zone.'

'I understand that if you take the underground to Belsize Park and walk to the top of Parliament Hill, on the south side of Hampstead Heath, you get a good overall view.'

'Thank you.'

Rafi returned to Old Street underground station and took the tube across to Hampstead. The journey brought back memories of the lead-up to his arrest; it all seemed eons ago.

He was soon back on his old home ground. It felt strange; he was revisiting a chapter of his life that had been closed. He had left the keys to his flat at Kate's. As he walked down Well Walk, past his building and on towards the Heath, he wondered what his redecorated flat looked like. He shrugged his shoulders – that was for another day, he told himself.

Twenty minutes later he was standing on the top of Parliament Hill, 100 metres above the exclusion zone, the scale of which beggared belief. It was a miracle that the relocation and decontamination process had passed off without any major incidents.

Rafi strolled down to Belsize Park tube station, past the Royal Free Hospital. The sign to the oncology department sent a shiver down his back as he fleetingly envisaged the many people suffering from radiation poisoning.

An hour later he was back in Kate's flat. Physically exhausted, he settled down, read the papers and had something to eat. Whilst he missed Kate's company, he had always enjoyed having time to himself.

*

Over the next couple of weeks he recharged his batteries and enjoyed the freedom of having nothing in particular to do. His hair grew sufficiently to cover the scar on his head and for him to stop wearing a hat in public. All his wounds had healed and he was beginning to wonder what he should do next. Of one thing he was certain: he would not be going back into fund management.

Yes, there had been several phone calls from prospective employers trying to entice him to work for them. The golden hellos on offer were mouth-wateringly large, but his heart was no longer in that line of work.

Rafi decided he was in no hurry and would give himself another month or two before starting to job hunt.

*

One evening, before Kate had returned from work, the phone rang. It was an ebullient Saara.

'Rafi, would you believe it? I've had a job offer I can't refuse.'

'Like what?'

'The Chancellor of the Exchequer invited me to Number 11 for a working lunch. It was just me, the Chancellor and four of his Treasury suits.'

'Sounds like fun,' replied Rafi.

'They want me to run a team which advises on research and development grants allocated to UK universities. Dealing with renewable energy, hydrogen fuel cells, energy efficiency, clean carbon technology, carbon sequestration, under sea storage and,'

Rafi interrupted her, as the list seemed endless. 'That sounds right up your street.'

'I know, isn't it great? I'd be involved with all the areas that could give the UK economy a competitive edge post nuclear power.' Saara chuckled. 'I liked the sound of the job but I told them I had loyalties: my existing research work and Steve. And that I was very happy in Birmingham. You know what? The Chancellor started smiling. He said I made an excellent negotiator. He then floored me. He said that Steve's research had caught the eye of those at University College London and that they'd be asking him to work with them on secondment. Plus, he can bring his research team with him! The Chancellor has sorted it out with my boss at the university. He thinks it's an excellent opportunity for us both! Basically, I was well and truly stitched up. But, Rafi, I wasn't pleased to find you were part of the fit up.'

'Pardon?'

'Well, they told me that Jeremy had spoken to you, and confirmed that Steve and I were most welcome to use your flat on a long-term basis, as you were now living with Kate.'

'Of course you are welcome to use it, and it explains why Jeremy asked me about you and my flat out of the blue.'

'Isn't it fantastic? I've talked it through with Steve and, if it's alright with you, the move is on.'

'I'm really happy for you. I'll send you a set of keys,' said Rafi.

'Thank you… And I'll be working at the Treasury. I'll have a workstation at Number 11. And they're practically tripling my salary. It's outrageous; I'm going to get a huge pay increase to do something I love.'

'It's about time,' remarked Rafi.

'Rafi, are you sure it's alright for me to use your flat?'

'Of course!'

'Steve says he's looking forward to living somewhere without rising damp. By the way, how much rent should we pay?'

'How about what you were paying in Birmingham?'

'Surely that can't possibly be enough?' said Saara.

Rafi heard Kate unlocking the front door.

'Sis, don't worry. Enjoy the flat and let's chat again soon. I've got to go now – Kate has just got home.'

'Bye and thanks,' replied a very happy Saara.

Chapter 10

They'd been back in London for almost four weeks. Thursday had been a quiet day. Rafi had cooked supper, which was being kept warm in the oven, and he was sitting with his feet up reading the evening newspaper. He looked up at the clock. It was almost 9.30 p.m. Kate had rung to say that she would be a bit late, so he was not worried.

There was a clatter downstairs as Kate opened the front door, bounced up the stairs and greeted him with a hug and a lingering kiss.

'Forgive me for being so late. Supper smells good. Thank you for waiting.'

'I hope it's still edible.'

He noticed Kate's cheerful demeanour. 'Did you have a good day then?'

'Yep, it was quite something. It seems I've been promoted. You now see before you Detective Chief Inspector Kate Adams!'

Rafi listened to her story of how she'd been dumbstruck when she'd been called into a meeting with the commissioner. 'Emma is being promoted into my job. Jack Fisher from John's team downstairs, who did all the work on the terrorist sleepers, is taking on Emma's role and Peter Ashby is to become their sidekick. According to the commissioner, that left him with a bit of a problem as to what he should do with his newest detective chief inspector! I didn't follow what he was saying until he said, "Yes, Kate, the appointments board has approved your promotion. It puts you as the youngest DCI in the City of London. Congratulations." I left feeling light-headed,' continued Kate. 'I was only promoted to detective inspector last year. I seem to have missed a large number of rungs on the ladder.'

Rafi leant across and kissed her. 'Fantastic! This calls for a celebration. It's what you deserve. I'd love to see your family's faces when you tell them the good news.'

'But that's not all. He asked if you and I would attend a

meeting with him, Ewan Thorn and the PM's permanent secretary tomorrow afternoon at 3 o'clock?'

"So we won't have to wait long to find out what they have in mind for you." Rafi gave her another kiss, got up and walked through to the kitchen. From the back of the fridge he pulled out a bottle of sparkling white wine, scooped up two glasses from a cupboard and walked back into the sitting room. Kate had kicked off her shoes and was sitting on the sofa with her feet curled up under her.

'Look what I found in the fridge.' He passed the bottle to Kate. 'You can do the honours.' There was a loud pop as the cork flew up and made a small dent in the ceiling.

Rafi put a glass out to catch the effervescent wine as it bubbled out of the top.

Kate filled her glass. Rafi stretched his arm out and she poured an inch of the liquid into his glass.

He raised it. 'A toast: to you, the most talented policewoman in the City!'

Rafi looked into the eyes he loved so much and, out of the ordinary, took a sip of the sparkling wine. It tasted different to what he'd expected. The little bubbles danced on his tongue.

Kate raised her glass and took a long swig. 'I've a confession to make: this isn't my first glass of champagne this evening.' There was a chuckle in her voice.

Rafi smiled. 'You deserve being made a fuss of. What exactly does your promotion mean?'

'Heaven only knows! I suppose they want me to move somewhere new, which is why they've asked for you to be there.'

They chatted over the well-cooked supper. Kate was buoyed up with the excitement of the news. As to what the future held, all would be revealed tomorrow. They left the dirty plates where they were and retired to bed.

Kate was up and out of the flat early the next morning. Rafi tidied up and spent a leisurely couple of hours reading the papers. He was feeling rested. The terrors of the previous month were a thing of the past. He left in good time, dropped into a florist on the way and headed off for the meeting at Wood Street. He arrived almost fifteen minutes early and went up to the fourth floor office to look for Kate. To his surprise, he found Emma sitting at Kate's desk and opposite her was Jack Fisher.

'Hi there, I came to have a last look at where I was imprisoned and to convey my congratulations to the two of you.' From behind his back Rafi produced a bouquet of spring flowers, which he handed to Emma. 'Congratulations and well done.'

Rafi turned to leave but Emma stopped him at the door. 'You can't get away that easily.' She placed her arms around his neck and gave him a kiss. 'You look after Kate, or else I'll come and sort you out. Got that? She's a very special girl.'

Rafi felt a firm tap on his shoulder. 'So this is what you get up to when my back is turned: making out with my best friend! I should have guessed that the two of you had a soft spot for each other!'

Kate winked at Emma. 'Come on, Rafi, we are meant to be elsewhere – if you can tear yourself away from those sexy lips.'

Rafi looked into Emma's eyes and sensed a real fondness. He kissed her on the cheek and followed Kate down the corridor.

'Nice to see Emma again?' asked Kate.

'Yep,' Rafi replied. 'You've a really good friend there. She left me in no doubt that I had to take good care of you, or else!'

Kate had a broad grin on her face as they entered Beverley's office. She waved them into her boss's meeting room.

The meeting room looked very neat and tidy. There, sitting at the table, was the commissioner, together with a dark-suited gentleman, who Rafi recalled as being the Prime Minister's permanent secretary, and Ewan from MI5. Kate and Rafi sat down opposite them.

The content of the meeting was a surprise. Rafi had gone along expecting Kate to be offered a posting far away from the south-east – somewhere like Manchester – and assumed he'd been invited along so he didn't feel left out of the process.

The meeting started with the PM's permanent secretary setting out his boss's stance. 'Following the recent terrorist attacks, the PM believes that the EU is missing a trick in the war on terror. Standards and ethics of what is acceptable and unacceptable, or what is legal or illegal, differ from country to country. Despite anti-money laundering legislation being enacted, there seems to be no let-up in the shady financial activities of terrorists and drug dealers. The PM believes that there is an urgent need for transparency. More information needs to be in the public domain as to who controls which company or business.'

He adjusted his cufflinks and continued. 'The Stratford terrorists built up large business interests and concealed them right under our noses. The concern is that with a growing number of public companies going private and the enormous wealth of a relatively small but significant number of individuals, the authorities are losing sight of who is controlling what, *and* what exactly the money is being used to finance in the shadier recesses of our countries. At one level, profits are being channelled out of Europe into tax havens and, at another, a growing number of private companies and individuals are operating as if they're beholden to no one. Giles, would you like to continue?'

'Yes, of course,' replied Giles. 'Before Stratford, being an immensely wealthy person entitled one to low levels of scrutiny. Key questions weren't asked for fear of driving business away. The richer someone was, the more a blind eye was turned. There's a dichotomy: on the one hand we have the politicians who have power to smooth people's paths, but rarely have much personal wealth, and on the other hand there are those with immense personal wealth and insatiable desires, but who need favours to pursue their ambitions. Too many people view greasing a palm or two as a legitimate cost of doing business. There are, across Europe, growing levels of corruption and a lack of transparency as to what is going on. This trend concerns the PM.'

'DCI Adams and Mr Khan,' interjected the permanent secretary, 'The President of the European Commission is also very concerned that the lack of financial transparency and the dubious financial practices are encouraging criminal activities and resulting in billions of Euros of tax slipping away. He is creating a new task force, led by the former head of a German State police force. His team will comprise four senior detectives, four special advisers and a small team of technical specialists who have a detailed knowledge of criminal practices and money matters. It will be based in Luxembourg. The remit is to report to the EU President on the practicalities of making European-wide financial affairs more transparent. DCI Adams, you are requested to apply for one of the four senior detective posts.'

Kate's mouth fell open.

'Obviously, as this is a European Union appointment, there will be an interview process to go through; a shortlist has been drawn up and unless you tell the interview panel to take a hike, I would submit that the post is yours. You would be seconded from the City of London police force and be able to come back here at a future date. Salary and terms and conditions will, we believe, be acceptable. There would be a modest flat in Luxembourg included in the package. The post in the first instance will be for three years.'

Before Kate had the opportunity to reply, the permanent secretary turned to Rafi. 'Mr Khan, you have shown yourself to be very enterprising in unravelling the web that the Stratford terrorists had spun. The President of the EU Commission and our Prime Minister have asked me to enquire whether you would be willing to have your name put forward to join the task force as a special adviser. You would suffer a significant reduction in remuneration, but it has been suggested to us that there may be other aspects of the job that would appeal to you, thereby making the salary less of an issue?'

There was a pause. Rafi looked at Kate. She had a big smile on her face, which he took to be a *Yes*.

'For whom would I be working?' enquired Rafi.

'Well, that depends to whom you're talking,' said Ewan. 'Officially, you would be employed by the European Commission, but in practice you'd be on secondment from MI5. I have it on good authority that Neil and his team are very impressed by you. Intelligence will be an important feature of your work, hence your inclusion with our security services.'

'Are you interested?' asked the permanent secretary.

Rafi looked at Kate again and then back at the permanent secretary.

'Would it be alright for Kate and me to discuss this by ourselves for a few minutes?'

'Of course; do use the room next door,' said the commissioner.

Kate sat down with Rafi in the adjoining office.

'What do you think?' asked Rafi.

'I have a few concerns: first of all, could you stand working *and* living with me? And how would you feel working *for*

370

me? And also, do you like the idea of living in Luxembourg and travelling around Europe, working out how the system is being manipulated?' asked Kate.

Rafi looked at her smiling face; there could only be one answer - 'Yes.'

'Excellent. Shall we give it a go? If we enjoy it, great, but if we've been sold a pup we can always come back to the UK and find something else to do.'

'I don't think we should be seen to be too hasty. Why not ask them a few more questions before saying yes?' suggested Rafi.

They walked back into the meeting room and sat down.

'Your proposals are intriguing and interesting,' Kate started. 'How much autonomy would there be?'

'It will be a small team and it will have autonomy.'

'If I'm operating overseas, why is MI5 and not MI6 involved?' asked Rafi.

'Good point,' commented Ewan. 'MI6 know nothing about what's going on. We thought that, as you know us and we know you, it would be simpler if you were seconded from MI5.'

Rafi nodded.

'Will other national intelligence services be involved?' asked Kate.

'Undoubtedly. It's likely that each special adviser will have an intelligence background. You, Mr Khan, are the so-called ace up one's sleeve. Whilst the Kates of this world know their way around accounts and corrupt businesses, and intelligence service people have their skills, you have the real market experience and a sixth sense for the extraordinary.'

'Is there a pecking order in the team?' enquired Kate.

'Yes. There's a boss, to whom you'll report, and, below you, you'll have a support team at your beck and call. As far as the four police officers and four special advisers are concerned, it's expected that you'll work as partners. The type of work you'll be doing doesn't go with structured hierarchies.'

Rafi looked across at Ewan. 'If I get the job, could I spend a few days with Neil's team to see what resources would be at my disposal?'

'Of course!' replied Ewan. 'If you accept this post you will become one of us and will have access to the full scope of our resources. And we might even throw in a spot of training as well! The PM is placing great importance on this specialist task force. There may only be a few of you, but what you might lack in numbers will more than be made up for by a combination of your individual skills and the resources behind you.'

'Why Luxembourg and not, say, Brussels?' enquired Kate.

'Luxembourg has become a major money and investment management centre. It's midway between the two European Parliaments – Brussels and Strasbourg – and it's within driving distance of Frankfurt, where the chief currently lives. Plus, it has a good little airport at Findel, five kilometres north-east of the city, which gives access to a large number of European cities. Also, there's a well-staffed British Embassy there. And I hear the standard of living is rather good,' came the reply.

'Last couple of questions,' said Kate. 'Are the identities of the other people known at this point in time and, if so, when do we meet them? And what's their English like?'

'Yes, I believe they are, and English will not be a problem. If you have no more questions then I can tell you that your interviews have been arranged for next week. They'll be at the EU's offices in Storey's Gate, St James's.'

Rafi raised an eyebrow indicating that the address meant nothing.

'Bottom of Horse Guards Parade.'

'Got it – thank you.'

'Assuming you decide to take up the offer of the jobs, we have arranged for you to meet the team for dinner next Friday evening in Luxembourg, as guests of our Embassy there. That way you can see how you get on. On the languages front, I have to stress again that your would-be colleagues have an excellent command of English as well as each being fluent in a handful of other languages. Your support team will provide you with the necessary translators, should they be required,' added Ewan, helpfully.

Kate looked at Rafi. He winked back. She slowly turned and looked at the commissioner, at Ewan and then across to the permanent secretary.

'Who buys the plane tickets and books the hotel room?'

'Funny you should mention that.' The commissioner turned

over several pages of the notebook he was using, pulled out a sheet of paper and passed it to Kate.

'In case you said yes, here are the details of your e-tickets and the hotel you'll be staying at. We've booked you on a flight from London City Airport; it takes off at 12.05 and lands at around 14.00 hours.'

Kate stood up, shook hands, said her thanks and goodbyes, and made for the door. Rafi stood up to leave after her.

'Mr Khan, would you stay with us a moment longer?'

Rafi sat back down. Ewan looked at him intently. 'Can you recall how you felt when you were at the Headland hotel and you knew that there was a person out there in the darkness who wanted to kill you and Kate?'

'Yes.' The memory sent a shudder through him.

'Please be under no illusion. We don't know what you and Kate may be getting into. There are powerful forces at work below the surface in Europe. These shadowy people have big vested interests and antiquated concepts of what are acceptable and unacceptable practices. Furthermore, the enlargement of the Union has brought into our midst both hard-working people keen to improve their quality of life and, unfortunately, a quagmire of organised crime. These criminals, like terrorists, operate freely throughout the EU. To put it bluntly, you'll be entering a very murky world – the world of sophisticated, ruthless criminals. We at MI5 and those at MI6 will do our utmost to protect you as and when things get difficult; the Prime Minister has made it clear that you will have our full support. But it's your decision as to whether you're willing to leave the comfort of the City and cross over to our world and its dangers.'

Rafi thought for a few moments. The Bishopsgate bombing had claimed four lives, Stratford would claim innumerably more. If there had been better financial transparency the terrorists would not have been able to operate so freely. Perhaps they would have gone elsewhere or have been caught in good time. It was a no-brainer and if it was what Kate wanted, then he wanted to be with her.

'Thank you for your warnings. I'd like to attend the interview next week and, interview permitting, I look forward to becoming part of the team.'

'That is good news,' said the dark-suited civil servant. 'The PM will be very pleased.'

Rafi got up and went to find Kate. His life was changing fast. Only a few months ago he had been a well-respected and very highly paid equities fund manager. He was now about to take a huge salary cut, work in Luxembourg and join MI5.

Kate was talking with Emma. 'I'm being posted to Luxembourg,' he heard her say.

'Congratulations! I'll really miss you though. You've got to promise to stay in touch,' replied Emma.

Rafi turned to Kate. 'What do you have planned for the rest of the afternoon?'

'Well, I need to tidy my desk. Then I can start planning the next chapter of my life with my new partner,' she quipped with a mischievous look on her face.

She spotted a pile of messages on her desk. 'Would you believe it? I've had a call from Jeremy and he's in Luxembourg! He says he will be there to meet us at the airport on Friday and show us some sights, before he takes us to our hotel, which is near the Embassy.'

Rafi looked at Kate. 'What, on earth, is Jeremy doing in Luxembourg?'

'Heaven only knows. But I hope he's been posted there; it would be great to have him as part of the team.' Kate hesitated. 'What time is it? I've just remembered a couple of things I need to finish off.'

Rafi looked at his watch. 'It's just after 4.15 p.m.'

'Could we meet back here at 6 o'clock? And could you find something to keep you occupied for about two hours?'

'No problem.' Rafi flicked open his mobile and rang Aidan. He felt slightly guilty that he hadn't made more of an effort to keep in touch since that day they'd given the presentation at Number 10.

Aidan answered the phone straight away. He definitely was not at the office; from the background noise Rafi guessed he was enjoying a glass or two of champagne at a local hostelry.

'Hi Aidan, Rafi here.'

'Great to hear from you. I thought you'd been avoiding me… Where are you?'

'Wood Street.'

'It's *POETS* day. Do come and join us; we're in the *Pavilion* at Finsbury Circus Gardens. It's been a rather good week; we're a bit over the top, but do join us.'

'See you in ten minutes.'

The *Pavilion* was a short walk away; it was a likeable wine bar in the middle of Finsbury Circus, overlooking a bowling green. Rafi grabbed his coat, hurried downstairs and headed down Chiswell Street towards the wine bar. On arrival he was greeted by a joyous Aidan. He had taken a few clients out for lunch and they were still going strong. As an equities man, Rafi's path tended not to cross with the derivatives specialists. They were high-octane people with a 'work hard, play hard' ethos.

'Let me introduce you to... Rafi,' Aidan said enthusiastically, and then suddenly stopped. 'On second thoughts, there's no need – I reckon everybody here will already know you from your pictures in the papers!' To general amusement, those that Rafi hadn't met before introduced themselves. Aidan ordered him a freshly squeezed orange juice and Rafi sat down and listened to their stories. Aidan was on cracking form. He'd picked up a whole host of new clients after all the publicity he'd received for his work for the Treasury.

'Rafi,' he said, 'have you heard the one about the managing director of a major international bank who one Monday morning turned up to the office to attend a video-conference meeting with a major client, only to find that all the equipment had been taken away for servicing?'

There were howls of laughter around the table.

'And he thought that I had something to do with it! He saw that the market was closed and decided it was an omen to go off and have an extended lunch.' This was greeted by more laughs.

'You know, every time I meet the MD, he asks me how I'm getting on in the second-hand electricals market – some cheek!' said Aidan.

The conversation went from pillar to post and time flew by all too quickly. Rafi said his goodbyes and left the ever-merrier group to their next bottle of champagne. He arrived back at Wood Street in a taxi, picking up a tired Kate before heading straight for Clapham. It had been quite a day.

The Tuesday interview at Storey's Gate was just a formality. Rafi sat at one end of a long table with two grey-suited individuals sitting at the other end.

The first twenty minutes were spent completing a detailed CV about Rafi: schooling, degrees, employment, work skills and competencies, leisure activities, and so on.

The first real question was: 'Do you think that your financial and analytical skills are appropriate for this position?'

'Yes,' Rafi answered, expecting a follow-up question.

'Thank you,' came the reply. 'We do not have any more questions. Do you want to ask us anything?'

Rafi shook his head.

'Good. On your way out, please pick up the envelope from the secretary next door. It contains your employment contract. Thank you for coming in.'

And that was it. Kate had a similar interview. Back at the flat, they went through the contents of their envelopes. Kate was bowled over by the hike in her salary. There was an accommodation allowance, a travelling to home allowance, even a clothing allowance. In her eyes the package was fantastic. Rafi's package was practically identical, other than his basic salary, which was a couple of thousand Euros less, but in the small print he saw that he would be getting a special allowance which brought him to a financial parity. He smiled. It was a nice touch.

Their flight out of London City airport on the Friday was uneventful. Luxembourg from the air looked smaller than they'd expected. Jeremy was waiting for them and was on great form. He had been posted to the Embassy a couple of weeks earlier as a commercial attaché. He showed them the sights and at Rafi's request they visited the spot where Callum and the Mercedes had been found. Standing there, Rafi felt a pang of guilt. Next time he was in England he would visit Callum's parents.

Kate and Rafi were eventually dropped at their hotel, with time to shower and dress for dinner.

'What do you think?' asked Kate. 'Do I look smart enough?'

The dark emerald, satin dress fitted her perfectly. Her matching high heel shoes lifted her almost to Rafi's height and accentuated her slim figure.

'Wow, you look stunning. Yep, you'll do very nicely!'

*

The dinner was held in a formal dining room. The Embassy had spared no expense. During the pre-dinner drinks Kate and Rafi were introduced to their prospective boss, Jörg Emcke. He was of average build and height, with receding hair - and introduced himself with great enthusiasm.

'I heard you wanted to know what my English was like. It's good, but I still find the English sense of humour impossible. But don't worry; I enjoy a good laugh, particularly when it's at the expense of those we catch!'

The individuals alongside whom they would be working looked genuinely unimpressive. They could have been having dinner with a team of auditors who were in the middle of a particularly dull company audit. However, Rafi soon found that appearances could be very deceptive.

The French police chief, Stephanie Doucet, looked incredibly businesslike. She was wearing a plain trouser suit and looked to be in her mid- to late forties. Rafi discovered that she had worked for the Parisian police force and then Europol and, like Kate, had specialised in criminal financial activities.

The Italian detective introduced himself as Celso Morassutti and his Polish counterpart was Ludomir Jablonkowski. Both, Rafi learned, had substantial experience of dealing with organised crime. The background of the three other men remained a mystery.

At dinner, Rafi's suspicions were confirmed. He had had a feeling that the group had met before and were sizing up the two newcomers. There was great interest in the jobs he had done, but he sensed that they had been fully briefed and were only filling in the gaps. On the other side of the table, Kate was also being discreetly quizzed.

After the main course had been cleared away, Jörg stood up. 'This will not be a long speech. A couple of hours should do!' He winked at Kate. 'Probably a lot less! As you know we've been tasked with advising the President of the Commission on what should be done to improve financial transparency. He wants there to be a level playing field, so that when EU tax harmonisation comes in, it will be harder for EU companies aviod paying their taxes. The sums involved are immense, as is the political will. Tens, if not hundreds, of billions of Euros per annum are involved. Our formal role is to be the data gatherers.Technically we will be part of the European Court of Auditors. Their offices are just around the corner in rue Alcide De Gasperi. We will therefore have excellent resources at our disposal.' He paused and then went on. 'This is the front under which we will be operating. Your real task is to understand how the criminal fraternity use the current opaqueness of the financial markets to assist them in their activities. While the ways of criminals and terrorists are not identical, the atrocity at Stratford has brought home the scale of the problems facing us. Our activities will remain covert - our aim is not to go out there and arrest people or close down bent corporations; it is to gather evidence that others will use to thwart the criminals and terrorists. I trust we shall all keep a low profile.'

Jörg studied Kate and then Rafi. 'Seven of us have met before on several occasions. This evening we are joined by the last two members of our team. They perhaps look on the young side to us. However, their track record speaks for itself. They bring to the table cutting edge experience of the lengths to which terrorists and criminals will go in order to get their way. Their knowledge will complement our skills-base. You're a team of equals – if there's to be any pulling of rank that is my prerogative and my prerogative alone. Unless I hear any dissenting comments, I shall assume that you are all willing and happy to work together as a team.'

He looked around and then continued. 'In that case, you will be expected to report for duty at our new offices a week on Monday. That, I trust, will give you sufficient time to sort out your affairs at home, to dust off your suitcases and to find suitable accommodation in Luxembourg.'

Jörg sat down, picked up a large cigar, chopped off the end, carefully lit it and started puffing as though he had no cares in the world – and smoking bans didn't exist.

After dinner things became more informal. They were ushered into a comfortable sitting room where they chatted and bounced ideas around. Rafi looked around the room: there was definitely an esprit de corps. The special task force was up and running.

At just after 1 a.m., Jörg said he was calling it a night and left with a simple parting remark: 'It has been a good evening. I look forward to seeing you all in our office on Monday week at 9 o'clock for a strategy meeting.'

It was almost 2 a.m. when Kate and Rafi walked back to their hotel.

The wind had a nip to it, but Rafi had a warm feeling inside him; it had been a fascinating and illuminating evening.

*

Back in the hotel room, Kate flipped off her shoes, sat suggestively on the corner of the bed and looked across at Rafi who had taken off his jacket.

'What do you think of this situation we've got ourselves into?' She sounded very excited. 'I am the luckiest girl in the world. My two wishes have come true: a fantastic job where I can do something worthwhile and a man at my side for whom I would do anything…'

'And what about my wish?' enquired Rafi.

She smiled and looked into his dark eyes. 'I wonder what that might be?' She turned her back to him and said, 'If you could help me with my zip…' but let her voice trail off.

Rafi sat next to her, ran his fingers provocatively down her back and felt a small shudder race through her.

Kate stood up; her satin dress slipped silently to the floor, revealing her breasts enticingly covered by a lacy black bra, just inches from Rafi's face.

Rafi sat still, taking in the sight before him. He was captivated. 'Do you like…?'

Rafi pulled her forward and kissed her. The question was left unfinished.

He felt his shirt being unbuttoned; as it went over his head, he stood up and moved closer to her. Her body was warm against his. Their lips met again - her tongue danced provocatively between his lips. He could taste a hint of Cointreau.

Rafi felt her hands effortlessly undress him. Her fingertips tenderly caressed his naked body.

Kate was enjoying the effect her teasing was having on him.

Rafi reached over and switched off the light. He lifted the sheet and slid under the crisp cotton, closely followed by Kate.

379

'Now where was I?' Kate asked playfully as she disappeared under the covers.

Rafi tingled all over as she slowly explored his body. She worked her way back up to his lips and kissed him lovingly.

'I meant what I said: I'd do anything for you,' she said as she moved on top on him. 'At the Headland hotel when I saw Dranoff's eyes latch on to mine and the sawn-off shotgun come out from under his coat, I was completely petrified. I froze. Out of the corner of my eye I glimpsed you flying down the stairs screaming at him, trying to draw his attention away from me. It all happened so fast: me thinking I was about to die, you screaming and firing and Dranoff blasting both barrels at you. I saw the wooden banister rail disintegrate into splinters only centimetres away from your body and when you landed in a gory mess at the bottom of the stairs.' Kate tenderly kissed his lips. 'In that split second, I realised how very much I loved you. You offered up your life to save mine. I was filled with amazement. I vowed there and then, I'd do absolutely anything for you.'

She snuggled closer. 'My fantasy is to make you blissfully happy.'

*

The next morning, when Rafi woke, Kate was sleeping soundly by his side. He lay still, not wishing to disturb her. He gazed at her elfin-like features and savoured the memories of the previous night.

They had a lazy breakfast, showered together and were several minutes late for their coffee with Jeremy in the hotel lobby.

'My, you're looking radiant this morning,' Jeremy said to Kate. 'I see that Luxembourg with a man in tow suits you.' He smiled at Rafi. 'Aren't you the lucky one?'

The question needed no answer.

'I hear that the dinner went well,' Jeremy continued. Rafi resisted asking whether they'd been bugged.

'Jeremy, how much do you know of what Rafi and I are doing?' asked Kate.

Jeremy smiled. 'Ewan has briefed me. I'm to be your liaison with MI5 and MI6. I'll be based at the Embassy and will have a desk next to yours in your offices.'

'That's great. Anything else I should know?'

'Don't tell Emma and Jack yet, but they'll be part of your support team.'

'Fantastic!' said Kate with a big smile. 'And is there anything more?'

'I understand last night you had lengthy conversations with the three police officers, but found their partners less than forthcoming.'

'Yes. They were rather secretive.'

'Probably best if they bring you up to speed once you start working with them. Basically, Pierre Simmon works for the DGSE, La Direction Générale de la Sécurité Extérieure, which is France's equivalent to MI6. Then there is Luca Duilio, who gained an impressive track record with the Italian Anti-mafia Investigative Directorate; he'll tell you in due course what he's been up to for the past couple of years. Bernhard Michalak is from Warsaw. And at one time he worked for the Stasi in East Germany and then had a stint with the FSB, the Russian Federal Security Service. He is a specialist on the whys and wherefores of organised crime in those former Russian states that are now part of the EU. Oh, and he's a close friend of Luca.'

Rafi looked carefully at Jeremy. 'They are a forbidding team, aren't they?'

'Yep, I'm glad that they are on our side. Heaven only knows what all of you will dig up!'

Their coffee was finished and they said their goodbyes. Kate and Rafi went off to explore the shops. After lunch, Jeremy had arranged for them to meet one of the Embassy staff.

The afternoon was spent looking at apartments. The first looked unremarkable from the outside, was comfortable and spacious on the inside, but had poor views. The second flat was smaller. However, it was only a short stroll from the office, overlooked a small square and was conveniently located for easy access to the airport. The main rooms were light and airy and the master bedroom was a good size with an impressive en suite bathroom. In the basement there was secure parking for two cars.

They both liked it. It would make an ideal and comfortable home for a couple doing a fair amount of travel. They decided not to look any further.

'Is it within our budget?' Kate enquired.

'Money will not be a problem,' came the reply. 'When you've settled in, do let me know if you need any changes and I'll happily organise them for you.'

*

Four hours later, Kate and Rafi were back in Clapham, sitting in front of her gas fire. They were tired, but elated by the prospects of their new lives.

Lying on the table amongst the post was a smart envelope with a crest on the back. It was addressed to both of them. Their company was requested at a reception and dinner at Windsor Castle, six weeks later, to celebrate a State visit by the President of the European Commission.

Rafi looked puzzled. 'I wonder why we have been invited?'

'It's probably to do with our new jobs,' replied Kate. 'Or perhaps we have gone up in the world following the capture of the terrorists?'

*

The day of the dinner at Windsor Castle arrived. Rafi and Kate had taken half a day off.

They arrived at Kate's flat in the early afternoon. She was dithering. 'It's alright for you; a dinner jacket is a dinner jacket, end of problem. What am I going to wear?'

'I thought you'd already bought an evening dress?'

'Well, that's the problem!'

'You've left it a bit late!'

'No, it's just that I have a couple of options and then there's what shoes and jewellery to put on.'

'How's about you put your choices on the bed and we go through them?'

'Would you be willing to sit through me changing in and out of things, dithering while trying to decide what to wear?'

Rafi nodded, trying to look enthusiastic.

'Give me a moment and I'll get everything out,' said Kate heading for the bedroom. What seemed like ages later, Rafi heard a call from the bedroom. He sauntered down the corridor, wondering what he'd let himself in for, and pushed open the door. There, standing in front of him was Kate with her hair up in a sophisticated fashion. Around her neck was a most exquisite gold necklace of blue gemstones with diamonds, pointing down to a lacy bra, panties, suspender belt and sheer silk stockings.

'Now watch this.' Kate smiled and walked into the evening sunshine. Rafi let out a quiet whistle. The blue gemstones in the necklace and the matching earrings had turned a fiery amber colour, setting off her hair perfectly.

'Magic, isn't it?' asked Kate with a grin.

'You look stunning… What are they?'

'Blue amber. I've always wanted to wear them but never had the occasion before. They've been hidden away since my granny died a few years back.'

'She had the same colour hair as you?'

Kate nodded.

'I can see why she gave them to you. They are fabulous. I love how the amber changes colours. You look ravishing.'

They walked back to the bed. Four long dresses were draped across the duvet cover.

Rafi picked up a pale gold dress which had an almost translucent quality. It shimmered as it moved in the light. He wasn't certain about the colour, but Kate seemed to like it. He suggested she try it on.

'Do you think the colour is too much with my hair? A little shop in Milan made it and some matching shoes especially for me. I paid them a visit while I was working there a couple of weeks ago.'

Rafi watched as she slipped it on. He was surprised at how much he liked it; it hugged her figure, enhancing her subtle curves, and the colour actually accentuated the beauty of her skin and hair.

'It's perfect. There's no need to look any further.'

'In which case we have a some time to kill,' said Kate suggestively, slipping off the silk dress. 'It's a bit cluttered in here. How's about we try the sitting room?'

★

The taxi arrived outside Kate's flat on time. The twenty-mile journey to Windsor Castle was good for the hour of day.

Emma and Aidan had also received official invitations to the dinner. Neither had expected the other to be there. The seating plan had them next to one another near the top table. Kate and Rafi sat opposite each other at the other end of the room, with a European Council member, two immensely wealthy Continental European industrialists and a French newspaper editor, Jean-Michel Coeurs.

Kate and Rafi noticed a lot of famous faces as they mingled during the pre-dinner drinks. The Royal family, senior politicians and the movers and shakers of the British economy were out in force.

At dinner, Rafi's conversation with those sitting around him ebbed and flowed. It turned to international businesses and whether too many were exploiting accounting and taxation loopholes. Surprisingly, it suddenly got interesting.

The industrialist on Rafi's left explained, 'As the chairman of a listed company, I have analysts crawling over practically everything we do. I've *got* to play by the rules.'

'That's your choice,' countered the other industrialist. 'I find life so much easier running a private business. I have a flexibility that gives me a distinct competitive edge.'

'What about the Commission and its approach to matters financial?' Rafi asked.

This sparked off a lively debate.

'Remind me how many millions - or was it billions? - of the Commission's budgets were unaccounted for last year?' asked Jean-Michel, the journalist.

'I can't answer that question as the accounts aren't due out for several months,' countered the bureaucrat defensively.

'OK, what was the figure for the year before, approximately?' asked Jean-Michel.

'Roughly, in percentage terms, around... one percent'

This seemed to rankle Jean-Michel. 'That's over €1 billion. It would be bad enough if that was the correct figure, but I believe the true figure is far, far greater. Didn't the European Court of Auditors raise serious concerns about where the €80 billion spent on agricultural and structural projects actually went?'

'Yes, there are undoubtedly a number of grey areas,' replied the bureaucrat without any hint of embarrassment.

The topic of conversation continued until the speeches, but the disputed figure still hadn't been resolved.

Rafi mentally missed most of the speeches. His mind was on the recent conversation. Two things struck him: first, the lack of concern that the bureaucrat had about the Commission's unbalanced books and the system's opaqueness, and, second, the opportunities to which the private industrialist had alluded, which enabled him to play the system, make easy money and enjoy being accountable to no one. Then there was the journalist, Jean-Michel; he seemed to know his stuff. Rafi made a mental note that he was a man worth talking to.

*

After the dinner, whilst Kate and Rafi were waiting for their taxi home, Jean-Michel came over and said his goodbyes. He too was on his way back to Central London.

'Why don't you join us? We practically go past the front door of your hotel,' suggested Kate.

'Thank you,' he said. 'That was a truly memorable evening. Your Royal family certainly know how to entertain and make guests feel special.'

During the forty-minute ride into London they chatted about various things. After a lull in the conversation Jean-Michel turned to Kate and said, 'I believe we have a mutual friend?'

'Who might that be?'

'Stephanie Doucet; she and I grew up together. I saw her for dinner a couple of nights ago. Our conversation touched on the terrorist attacks in London. She mentioned you, and that you reminded her of when she was younger. It seems you made quite an impression!'

The taxi came to a halt at the hotel and Jean-Michel climbed out. His parting remark was, 'Perhaps we could have dinner with Stephanie sometime and continue this evening's conversation?'

'That would be nice,' replied Rafi.

The taxi moved off. Kate playfully nudged Rafi in the ribs. 'Thinking about your dinner with Stephanie, are we?'

'No, I was thinking about our first night in Luxembourg and hoping you aren't feeling tired,' he said with a mischievous grin.

*

Early summer arrived; Kate and Rafi continued to travel around Europe. There had been a steep learning curve in understanding the intricacies of how the European Union, the Commission and big pan-European businesses operated.

Once every three or four weeks, they spent a weekend in London at Kate's flat. This Saturday, they had slept in, and were lying on the bed enjoying a breakfast of croissants and coffee while going through a pile of post.

There were two smart envelopes; their backs bore the Royal Coat of Arms.

Kate opened her envelope to find it was a formal invitation to a Garden Party at Buckingham Palace, to be held in five weeks' time. In the envelope there was a second gilt-edged card which requested the pleasure of her company at an audience with the Queen an hour and a half prior to the Garden Party.

Rafi opened his envelope. He, too, had two invitations. He recalled how, on his return from Newquay, he had liaised with an enthusiastic SJ at Number 10 regarding the idea of a Garden Party. He had thought nothing more of the conversation.

'First a dinner, and now a Garden Party *and* an audience with the Queen. Aren't we moving up in the world!' said Rafi.

'Wow, doesn't it look smart?' Kate exclaimed. 'What an excuse to buy another new dress!'

Rafi looked across at her beaming face.

'Would you believe it, I shall be in Milan again the week after next?'

Major Charlie Stavely and Saara phoned during the weekend to say that they, too, had received invitations to the Garden Party. They were very excited. After a flurry of phone calls, it was arranged that Kate and Rafi would see Saara and Steve for supper the night before the Garden Party and then meet up with family and friends the following morning.

*

Kate and Rafi had become accustomed to their European travels and over the past couple of weeks they had gone in opposite directions.

Their new boss, Jörg, and their paymasters were giving them the freedom to research and delve where they wished. Jörg was very good at keeping people off their backs and keeping the politicians happy.

To the unsuspecting outsider, the team remained a nondescript data-crunching organisation. However, in reality progress was being made on a number of fronts. The team was gaining an in-depth understanding of how pan-European players operated and the areas into which organised criminals had been drawn. It had not been the aim of their investigations, but links between corruption, wealth and certain well-connected individuals were becoming apparent. Rafi wondered how long it would be before they knew how dangerous a can of worms they were opening.

Kate and Rafi's cosy flat in Luxembourg remained a haven of tranquillity. In contrast, their office down the road was a different world. They had slotted into the team remarkably easily, and worked well with the other members, though they suspected that they were viewed as the junior partners. This had its benefits, though, as their colleagues seemed genuinely keen to help.

The date of the Summer Garden Party was fast approaching. The week leading up to it had been tiring. Rafi had been to Paris, Frankfurt and Amsterdam, whilst Kate had been to Prague and Milan.

They were looking forward to their supper with Steve and Saara on the evening before their outing to Buckingham Palace.

The hour's time difference meant that they could catch the 6.00 p.m. flight to London City Airport and be in Hampstead by 8.00 p.m., London time.

They chatted for much of the flight, enjoying one another's company. They had learned at an early stage not to talk about work in public places.

During a lull in the conversation, Rafi browsed through an English newspaper where one story in particular caught his eye. It was a follow-up on some of the families made homeless by the Stratford nuclear catastrophe. It described the public support that they had received and how they had been relocated and rehoused. The little girl whose teddy had become world-famous, and her family, had found a home in Norfolk. If the picture - which showed her with a broad smile clutching her teddy - was anything to go by, she was enjoying her new life. The article went on to report that she was one of the lucky ones; many of the dispossessed had still to find permanent new homes.

The journey from London City airport to Hampstead Heath was straightforward. The taxi pulled up in front of Rafi's old flat at 7.45 p.m. They stood in the passageway by the front door to the flats. It was the first time he'd been back since that fateful February morning. It seemed such a long time ago now, but he was still uneasy standing there; too many vivid and painful memories flooded through his mind. He had hoped that returning to his flat would help him to slay the ghosts of the past. It certainly gave him the creeps.

Rafi pressed the bell. Saara answered. 'Do come in.'

The door buzzed and opened. They entered. As they climbed the stairs, Rafi recalled his conversation with Kate, on their return from Cornwall, about where he might live. She had been surprised when he had asked if he could move in with her.

'But my flat is bound to be nothing like as nice as yours. Jeremy tells me that they've done a good job in putting it back together again!' she had said.

'Your flat has nice memories - mine has too many ghosts,' had been his reply.

They arrived outside the front door of his old apartment. Rafi knocked. It sounded different, very solid. The door opened and there in front of him was his little sister, looking very grown-up.

'Come in, come in. Sorry about the chaos. We only just beat you here! Steve is dying to meet you, Kate.'

'Hi there, I'm Steve,' he said, cheerily as he appeared from the kitchen. Great to meet you at last, Kate. Can I get you a drink? A cup of tea... or something stronger?'

'Tea would be nice,' replied Kate, as she and Rafi walked through to the sitting room-cum-dining room.

Rafi saw that his minimalist décor had been replaced by an eclectic mix of furniture and paintings. Saara and Steve's clutter was everywhere. Paperwork spread from the table, across the floor and on to the windowsill. It gave the place an untidy but lived-in feel.

Rafi looked at their faces. Their smiles said it all.

'We thought that, if it was fine by you, we would eat out at your favourite Chinese restaurant. Mr Cheung is looking forward to seeing you. He says his turnover has hit *wock bottom* since you moved away!'

'Sounds perfect,' grinned Rafi.

'Let me show you around,' offered Saara. 'The MI5 people arranged for the redecorating and the new steel front door. They said your old one had been sold for matchsticks!'

Rafi and Kate followed Saara into the spare bedroom. The pictures on the walls he recognised from her bedroom in their parents' house and the duvet cover from her house in Birmingham. The bed and curtains were new and very John Lewis.

'Kate, if you need anything when you're getting changed, please shout,' said Saara.

Rafi looked into the bathroom. He recalled the conversation with a man from MI5, apologising about all his furniture and personal effects. He now saw what he had meant. *Everything* had been replaced.

'Come on - come and see what Steve and I have done to our bedroom,' said Saara excitedly.

Kate and Rafi were ushered along the corridor and up the small staircase. Shambolic would have been a good word to describe the look of their room. Cluttered could have been an alternative.

'Isn't this great?' beamed Saara. 'So much floor space! Knocks our old house in Brum into a cocked hat!'

Rafi looked at Saara and noticed she looked a little apprehensive.

'It's been a hectic day. We prayed that your flight would be delayed, so we could have done a little tidying up.'

Rafi walked over to Saara and gave her a big hug. 'It's great. I'm pleased you enjoy living here. You should see Kate's flat,' he added with a wry smile. At which point he received a sharp dig in the ribs.

Saara looked at her watch. 'Mr Cheung is expecting us in half an hour. And Rafi, thank you - Steve and I love it here.'

Before leaving Saara's bedroom, Rafi walked over to the window and looked out. The Heath could be seen to the left and central London was in the distance. Rafi glanced down at the road. His heart missed a beat. There, in the evening shadows opposite, was the dark form of a large Mercedes car. Haunting memories rushed back. Kate, who was standing nearby, sensed his apprehension.

'Seen an old ghost?'

'Sort of,' he replied.

'We should be going soon,' came a shout from downstairs. 'We don't want to keep Mr Cheung waiting, do we?'

*

Thirty minutes later, after a quick wash and change, they were standing in front of the restaurant. Saara was at Rafi's side.

'You first, big Bro.'

He opened the door. The sight that met his eyes stopped him in his tracks. There, standing in front of him, were John and Jeremy. To their left were Aidan, Emma and the doctor and his wife from Newquay. He looked around the room. It seemed that everyone was there. The commissioner was in deep conversation with Ewan at a corner table. The brigadier and Colonels Turner and Gray were talking to an elderly gentleman whose back was to Rafi. Suddenly it dawned on him; it was his grandfather's back. He looked across to the other side of the room and saw Kate's brother. He glimpsed Kate's parents sitting down, looking very proper, with Air Chief Marshal Sir Nigel Hawser and the back of someone he couldn't quite place. Ah yes, it was Donald Hollingsworth, and next to him was Kate's former boss, David. He looked around again; to try and take in all the faces.

Rafi walked across the threshold and was greeted by a cheer. Mr Cheung, appeared as if out of thin air. 'Mr Khan, so pleased to see you this evening. No takeaway tonight, I think?' he said with a chuckle.

'I thought we were going out for a quiet supper,' Rafi said in amazement to Saara. 'How on earth did you manage to arrange something so big and keep it a secret?'

Saara grinned. 'It wasn't easy!'

Jeremy stuck out his hand which Rafi shook energetically.

'What a surprise meeting you here,' he said with a broad smile stretching almost from ear to ear. 'I had a devil of a problem travelling on the same plane as you without being spotted! Good training, eh? When Saara told me what she and her boss, the Chancellor, had planned for your party, I couldn't resist hopping on a plane. Oh, I forgot, the PM, the Defence Secretary and the Chancellor of the Exchequer send their apologies. They've got a meeting which is running late, but they should be here in half an hour.'

'You're joking. They are not really coming, are they?' asked Rafi.

''Fraid so. It seems the Chancellor reckons you deserved a proper thank you - it looks as if you're going to have yourself some party! Better be on your best behaviour!' said Jeremy with a grin.

'What can I get you?' asked John. 'Champagne?'

Rafi looked at Kate, who had started to shift into party mode. Her eyes sparkled and she looked fantastic in her summer dress.

'As this is a very special occasion, champagne would be great, please.'

As if by magic two glasses arrived.

Rafi gave Kate a kiss. 'Isn't this fantastic? Did you know anything about this?'

'Honestly, no. But I should have guessed something was in the wind given the strange phone calls I've been getting from Saara and Emma over the past few weeks!'

'How's about we circulate? See you in a bit,' said Rafi.

The evening went by far too fast - so many people to talk to and lots of news to take on board. As Rafi worked his way around the large room, he came across a few faces he didn't recognise. The retired commander and his wife, their two *daughters*, the SBS *boyfriends* and the two SAS soldiers were on good form recalling their escapade and their close call with the Moroccan Air Force.

Rafi was introduced to the crew of the first helicopter to carry concrete to the wrecked train, who by the end of the day had flown more sorties than any other crew. He then found himself talking to Roger and Steve from the Immigration team. They seemed awestruck by their fellow guests and were standing quietly to one side - conversation with them was an uphill battle.

'I'm so pleased you could come. Whilst you are here, you might like to make the most of it - where else can you meet the head of MI5?' Rafi surreptitiously pointed out Ewan. 'Next to him is the Chief of the Defence Staff and shortly we'll be joined by the Prime Minister. And, Roger, you might even pluck up the courage to tell the new Home Secretary what you think of the system you work under! You shouldn't feel out of place… please remember that without your help things would be far, far worse.'

They visibly grew in stature and headed off to mix with the other guests.

At that moment the PM and the Chancellor arrived with their entourage. Saara did the introductions, from which it became apparent she now had friends in high places.

The PM was apologetic. 'I hope you don't mind, but I've brought along a couple of gatecrashers. My last meeting overran and, as a *reward* for them talking too much, here they are!' he introduced the leaders of the two main opposition parties, who were now high-ranking cabinet ministers.

The PM moved off to work the room as only a top class politician can.

Meanwhile, the Chancellor was greeted by Steve and Saara. He was in an ebullient mood. The flak he had feared following the Stratford disaster had not happened. His initiatives had worked their way through Parliament and were having a rejuvenating effect on public sentiment.

'I've been meaning to ask you a question, if you don't mind?' asked Rafi. 'How close were we to joining the Euro?'

The Chancellor put his arm on Rafi's shoulder and ushered him to one side. 'Between you and me, it was close – very close! In the House, I was almost more worried waiting to receive the message from the Bank of England, which would tell me whether they'd done a deal with the Central Banks, than the messages telling me if the terrorists had been captured. When I stood up we only had a couple of smaller Central Banks offering to support Sterling, but it was at an unacceptably low exchange rate and contingent on others getting involved. The Governor of the Bank of England did a fantastic job.' His voice went quieter. 'I am told it is a senior individual at the Hong Kong Monetary Authority who we have to thank. He realised how intertwined Sterling, the City of London and the international financial markets were. Anyway, within forty-five minutes he had three of the top twenty countries with the highest foreign exchange reserves agreeing to support Sterling. Then Japan, the US and India came on board and the rest is history.'

The Chancellor smiled. 'I was jubilant when I read the message saying how much support Sterling had. I could scarcely believe my eyes. And I must tell you how much I appreciate all you have done. Your foresight into what was going on in the financial markets, and your team's proposals got me out of a really difficult situation. Thank you.'

Saara and Kate joined them. Rafi sensed that his conversation with the Chancellor had come to an end and he and Kate went off to mingle.

Food appeared. It was Mr Cheung at his best and Rafi told him so.

Plate in hand, Rafi stood in the middle of the room, enjoying the atmosphere and taking in the scene around him. He felt a soft squeeze around his waist from behind. 'If I'd known you were this well-connected perhaps I'd have taken you a bit more seriously!' said the seductive voice. 'And who would have guessed that so many of my friends are friends of yours?'

The sentence was interrupted by the restaurant door swinging open. There, filling a substantial portion of the frame, was a heavily-built man. Behind him, was a well-dressed man of indeterminate age and a stunning dark-haired young woman.

The deep voice rang out. 'Have I missed all the fun? Look who I met at the airport – a Dutch generaal! Someone should have told me that Heathrow is further away than your City Airport; and whoever put in those bloody bus lanes should be told they screw up the traffic when you're in a hurry!' This was followed by a booming laugh. 'They tell me this is where we can find DCI Adams and an air chief marshal,' rang out the deep voice, 'And if I'm lucky, a Mr., Khan might be hiding here, with some vodka – if he values his life!' The colonel paused. 'If not, I've brought some best Estonian Türi.'

Beaming, Rafi and Kate went over to meet Colonel Matlik and his two companions.

He stuck out his hand as Rafi approached. 'Rafi, it is great to meet you at last! I hope you don't mind, I've brought my daughter, Kristina, with me. She knows nothing of your English ways. I thought if Kate and Emma were here to keep an eye on possible suitors, she might just be safe,' he said with a chuckle.

'And we have an invitation to see your Queen for tea tomorrow afternoon – such a nice surprise. Kristina has been impossible for weeks, fretting about what to wear. Now, where did you say the vodka was?' And off he strode as if he were a man on a mission.

Rafi looked across towards Saara. She was smiling. He sensed that the guest list was complete. Standing behind Rafi was the Air Chief Marshal, and next to him was the PM.

'Prime Minister and Mr Khan,' said the Air Chief Marshal, 'it is my pleasure to introduce you to Generaal Wilm Van Dijk of the Royal Netherlands Air Force. Had Wilm not stuck his neck out for us and lent us almost all his fleet of helicopters and transport planes, we would have been in great trouble.' They shook hands and started talking.

Emma came over and introduced herself to Colonel Matlik's daughter, Kristina. The colonel reappeared with two glasses and passed one to his daughter. 'I told you they do things a bit differently here.' He pointed out some of the more illustrious guests. 'Where else in Europe can one go to a local Chinese restaurant and meet the Prime Minister, the heads of the armed forces and the intelligence service, and two police chiefs – and find them all mingling with the public? There must be an election coming up soon!' he boomed.

David appeared at the colonel's shoulder and suggested he might like to meet Ewan. Emma, meanwhile, took Kristina under her wing and together they went off to find Aidan.

Rafi walked over to chat to his grandfather, but saw he was in deep conversation with Colonel Gray. He stopped and moved over to be with Kate, who was standing watching the party. Within moments he and Kate were joined by the two commissioners.

'We are most grateful to you for all you've done,' said Len. 'I always knew Giles had a good team at Wood Street.'

'I understand that we'll be meeting you again tomorrow,' said Giles.

'At the Garden Party?' enquired Kate.

'No, before that,' said Giles.

Kate and Rafi looked puzzled.

'Has anyone told you why you're to see the Queen before-hand?'

'No,' said Kate blankly.

'Well, Kate, you're to be awarded the Queen's Police Medal and Rafi is to be given the Queen's Gallantry Medal. The police force is very proud of you.

They both looked at Giles in amazement and Rafi gave Kate a hug.

Ewan joined them. 'Thank you for the invite; Jeremy tells me that you're keeping him busy. Oh, by the way, did you see the photos of Maryam in the newspapers a couple of months ago?'

Rafi nodded. 'I recall reading an article which described her as: *Helping the police with their enquiries* and intimated that she had *done a deal* - is that true?' asked Rafi.

'You shouldn't believe everything you read,' said Ewan. 'In reality she's being totally uncooperative. The photo was a set-up. She'd thought she was about to be released on a technicality and was meeting a European human rights judge. The sheikh, Basel and Jameel, who are locked away in separate high security prisons, just happened to see the papers that day. They're furious! As the saying goes, *Divide and rule*.' Ewan gave Rafi a friendly pat on the shoulder. 'Great party; if you'll excuse me there are a couple more people I should like to chat to. Do keep in touch.'

'Time to mix with family?' suggested Kate.

'Good idea,' agreed Rafi.

They walked over to speak to Kate's parents. They were sitting with their backs to the wall, taking in all that was going on in the room. Kate sat down next to her mother and gave her a hug, then got up and did the same to her father.

'I'm so pleased that you could come.'

'We almost didn't. But Rafi's sister sounded so very charming on the phone and said how much it would mean to you,' said her father.

'We've been chumps haven't we?' said her mother. 'I'm sorry we didn't understand how important your job was to you and what you'd make of it. The commissioner tells us you're one of the – if not *the* – youngest chief inspector in Europe and are doing more good work in Luxembourg.'

'I think he's exaggerating a *bit*!' said Kate.

'He's not the only one who says that we should be very proud of you,' said her father. 'We are proud – very proud.' He paused then went on, 'With Marcus's help we have done up the attic studio in the main house. Do please use it as your home whenever you have time.'

Kate gave a beaming smile to her parents. 'That would be lovely, thank you.'

Out of the corner of his eye, Rafi noticed Saara talking with her grandfather. He smiled; they looked very happy together.

The conversation between Kate and her parents turned to small talk.

'Have I told you,' began Kate's mother, 'that we've got your postcards stuck all round our kitchen cupboards? It was so nice of you to start up that family tradition again.'

Kate gave Rafi's hand a squeeze.

'You do seem to get around a bit these days,' continued her mother. 'Some weeks we seem to get a card every other day!'

Rafi sensed that the hurts and wounds of previous years were forgotten.

The sound of a wine glass being tapped echoed across the room and was followed by the raised voice of Rafi's little sister. She was standing at the side of the restaurant next to the Prime Minister, the Air Chief Marshal and Commissioner Giles Meynell. She had a champagne glass in her hand and was tapping it with a spoon. Silence fell over the room.

'Thank you,' she said. 'I am so pleased you could all make it to Rafi's surprise party. I should like to thank the Chancellor, my boss, whose idea it was to convene such a gathering and I would ask you to raise your glasses, please, in a toast: *To Rafi and determination!*'

The Prime Minister moved to Saara's side. With a beaming face he looked around the room. 'For once I shall be brief.' He paused as he noticed a wry smile on many of the faces in front of him. 'If I were to pay my thanks to each of you here, who selflessly gave so much, it would take a very long time. I am tempted… But not tonight!'

The PM reached for his glass. 'I would ask you all to raise your glasses and toast: *To all those who lost their lives or their good health*.'

The PM waited for his audience to finish sipping their champagne and for their attention to focus back on him. 'I would especially like to thank two people who have travelled a long distance to be with us this evening. Generaal Wilm Van Dijk and Colonel Hendrik Matlik: thank you for your help in our hour of need. I would ask you to raise your glasses and toast: *To our distinguished foreign guests*.'

Silence returned. The PM raised his glass and looked around the room making eye contact with as many people as possible: '*To you all! You are a very special group of people and I praise you for all you have done.'*

He moved to one side during the applause that followed. His place was taken by the Air Chief Marshal. 'I, too, will follow the precedent set by the Prime Minister and keep my speech brief. I should like to convey my personal thanks to the team I had with me on that fateful night. Their response and clear headedness was beyond anything I could have reasonably expected. I would ask you to raise your glasses and toast: *To all those who risked everything in countering the recent terrorist attacks and to the Prime Minister, the Defence Secretary, Ewan Thorn, Brigadier Sparkman and Colonels Turner and Gray for their leadership.'*

There was further clapping and a shuffling around, as glasses were sipped and recharged. The Air Chief Marshal's place was taken by Commissioner Giles Meynell. He looked across at Kate and John. 'During the investigation leading up to the snaring of the terrorists, we were truly fortunate to have the unerring resolve and meticulous help of a large number of people. I should like to pay my sincere thanks to all of you who made it possible for us to latch on to the terrorists' plot. In particular: Steve and Roger from the Immigration team, Jeremy and Neil from MI5 and Rick and Phil from Manchester; they all deserve special mention. We salute you.'

Giles paused and turned to David. 'Your team did you proud. Thank you.' He paused and added, with a glint in his eye, 'But another time perhaps we shouldn't have to rely on someone locked up in a police cell and then get him to provide us with the services of his friends! Aidan, Bob, Alex, Donald, Matthew, Saara and, of course, Rafi – thank you. We owe you all a great debt of gratitude. I should like to ask you all to raise your glasses and toast: *To tenacity and all those who helped in our time of need.'*

Rafi caught sight of Kate's parents sitting holding hands. Beside them were Marcus and Susannah. He wished he could have captured their expressions and given the picture as a present to Kate. He looked round and saw Kate smiling at him; she too had spotted her family's proud faces.

Saara waited for silence to return. 'That is the end of the formalities; there's no closing time and Mr Cheung assures me that he has more than enough food and drink to satisfy your appetites and quench your thirst. Thank you all for making this the most memorable and enjoyable of evenings.'

Saara seemed taken aback by the spontaneous applause and for the first time in ages looked a little self-conscious.

She came over and gave Rafi a hug. 'So how's the party boy?'

'Very contented, it's been a wonderful evening. Thank you for everything.'

They were joined by Kate and made their way across to her parents, who looked extremely happy.

Her mother started the conversation. 'Kate, dear, this has been such fun, what an evening to remember! But now that we've had a chance to talk with you and have seen your friends perhaps we should be getting off; it's well past our bedtime.'

'Pardon?' interjected Kate's father. 'But we're having fun! Our hotel is not far, so why don't we stay for another drink or two and then head off?'

Kate's mother smiled. 'As you say, dear.'

'Rafi, might there be any Scotch on the premises?' asked Kate's father.

'I'll see what I can find,' replied Rafi. 'And then there is someone I'd like you to meet.'

Kate's father raised his eyebrows as if to say, 'Who could be more important than the PM?'

Rafi found Mr Cheung and asked for a bottle of his very best Scotch.

'Blended or single malt?'

'Would you bring both, please?'

Then Rafi went over and extracted his grandfather from the conversation he was having.

'Grandfather, do you like Scotch?'

He beamed. 'Is the Pope Catholic?'

'There are a couple of people I'd like you to meet.'

As they walked across to the table where Kate's parents were sitting, Rafi added Marcus, Susannah, Saara and Steve to his entourage.

Rafi approached the table. Kate's father was trying to decide which Scotch he preferred. He looked up and smiled.

'Major Sir Percy and Lady Yvonne,' Rafi said. 'It is my pleasure to introduce to you my long lost grandfather, Major Charlie Staveley, my little sister, Saara, and her partner Dr Steve

Morris.'

Introductions complete, their conversation started slowly, then the two majors found that they had several interests in common.

Rafi noticed Kate standing hand in hand with her brother, Marcus, who caught his eye and beckoned him over. 'Rafi, you're so elusive. I've been meaning to thank you all evening; I've never seen Kate look this happy. You're a real tonic for her.'

Rafi smiled. 'I think it is *I* who should be thanking her. Without her I'd be languishing in some grubby cell, whilst the country had next to no electricity!'

Marcus looked carefully at Rafi. 'I'm glad you're looking after each other. Make the most of the time when happiness is in abundance. It's such a precious gift, which few people ever get to fully appreciate. Please, for me, don't lose it.' The conversation changed as Saara, Steve and Susannah, came across to join them.

In a short time it was agreed that they would all meet for a Sunday lunch at Leverthorne Hall and inspect Kate's new studio flat in the attic.

To Rafi, the next forty-five minutes flew past as lots of people came over to say their hellos.

Roger from the Immigration team made Rafi smile. 'I did as you said, plucked up courage, and went over and talked to the Home Secretary. I apologised before I started telling him the system was run by data junkies. You know what? He's asked me to explain my concerns to one of his ministers next week!'

After saying goodbye to Roger, Rafi at last had a moment to himself. He took a step back to look around the room and see if he had missed someone he really should have talked to, and, in that moment, literally bumped into a stunning blonde. Rafi smiled weakly. His senses picked up her evocative perfume. Then it hit him: he knew this woman. What a transformation!

'Great party! It was so kind of your sister to invite me.'

It was the first time that Rafi had seen SJ outside her office environment.

She looked up at him from under her lashes and then casually said to Kristina, who was standing next to her, 'I'm sorry, have you been introduced to Rafi?'

'Yes, thank you,' replied Kristina. Then, smiling at Rafi, she added, 'My father tells me that you and your friends are very remarkable.'

At that moment the little group was joined by Kate.

'Hi, SJ,' said Kate. 'Hello again, Kristina. I've been talking to David and he tells me you're at university. Is that right?'

'Almost finished – I have my finals next month.'

'What are you reading?'

'Environmental sciences with biology.'

'Excellent - have you meet Rafi's sister, Saara?' enquired Kate. 'Her contacts are fantastic.'

Kristina shook her head.

'Let's find her, and I'll introduce you. We'll be back in a moment. Rafi you'll be OK with SJ, won't you?'

Kate and Kristina moved off. There was an embarrassed silence. 'You look very different…' stuttered Rafi, realising he'd been staring at her shapely body. He was starting to blush. 'What with your hair down and in that amazing dress.'

'You approve?' SJ asked with her head tipped slightly to one side.

'I'm surprised that all the red-blooded men in the room aren't queuing up to get your phone number. I still can't get over the transformation.' Rafi cast his approving eyes from head to toe. 'You look stunning.'

SJ felt the hairs on her bare arms stand up. The visit to her friend, who was a professional hairdresser and make-up artist, had been worth the hassle.

She hesitated. 'Forgive me if it's private, but is it true that you turned down a six or seven figure sum from the newspapers and gave it to charity?'

'Sort of – yes,' Rafi replied. He sensed she was hoping for more. 'It seemed that the money would be better used helping those suffering from radiation exposure. Hospices survive thanks to donations and at the moment they desperately need money.'

'Have you ever visited a hospice?'

Rafi shook his head.

'If you and Kate have a spare moment sometime, perhaps you should visit one? I'm sure we could get you good press coverage, which would help boost their donations. I could even see if the PM had a spare slot in his diary so he could be there with you.'

'Sounds like a good idea,' agreed Rafi. 'Unfortunately though,' he quickly added, 'Kate and I aren't in the UK very much these days.'

'No problem, I'm not going anywhere,' said SJ casually, hoping that this wasn't going to be the end of the conversation.

There was a pause. 'I'm sure I should know, but is Sandy Jane your Christian name or your full name?' enquired Rafi.

'Jane is my surname. I know, it sounds silly.'

'It's a nice name, better than Smith or Khan; there are hundreds of thousands of us,' said Rafi with a grin.

Kate returned to Rafi's side. 'Sorry, we had to wait a bit before I could introduce Kristina to Saara,' she said with a smile. 'What have you two been chatting about?'

'I was suggesting to Rafi that the PM might be able to help you in your efforts to raise money for the hospices.'

'That sounds like a great idea,' replied Kate enthusiastically. 'Rafi's sister works next door to you; she tends to know when we're over in London. If you come up with a plan perhaps you could liaise with Saara, so we can find a convenient time to meet up.'

SJ couldn't believe what she'd just heard. Surely Kate must sense that she was attracted to her boyfriend? It wasn't fair that the man she thought was gorgeous just happened to have a charming, self-assured girlfriend – who she even *liked*.

'I'll speak with Saara and line something up. Nice chatting to you both,' said SJ. She turned and made eye contact with Kate. 'I've been meaning to ask... Wherever did you find your dress? You look absolutely gorgeous. Rafi is very lucky.' Before Kate could reply, SJ had left and was on her way to the bar.

'SJ seemed particularly pleased to see you this evening,' commented Kate. Then she added, while smiling to herself, 'She's taken a fancy to you! She's stunning, isn't she?'

'Yes, but she isn't *you!*'

Kate lent forward and kissed him.

Over in a corner, Emma and Aidan were deep in conversation.

Kate squeezed Rafi's hand. He followed her look. 'They enjoy each other's company, don't they? From all Emma tells me, she's

401

having a great time being wooed by Aidan.'

'I can't say I'm surprised. Emma would be a great catch for any man with a half-decent IQ,' Rafi replied.

Kate was about to comment, when the last of the politicians came by to say thank you and goodnight. It was almost 1.30 a.m. Only a few guests remained.

A beaming Pete Lockyer came over to thank Kate and Rafi for the great party. 'It's been an exceptional evening. The boys at the office will never believe who I've met tonight!'

Kate grimaced.

'Don't worry! I know this was a social; the evening is all off the record. Thanks again. You know where to find me if there's anything I can do to help.' And with that Pete left with a broad grin.

Kate left Rafi's side to chat to Emma, who was preparing to leave.

It had been the best party Rafi could remember. Standing thinking to himself, he felt the presence of someone behind him. A deep, quiet voice started talking to him from behind, so that no one else could hear. It was the unmistakable voice of Colonel Matlik. 'Rafi, my friend, thank you for this evening; Kristina and I very much enjoyed ourselves. By the way, I'm keeping track of all the work you, Kate and Jörg's unit are doing in Luxembourg. You have an impressive team around you. I know your colleague Bernhard Michalak – he is a good Pole.'

The colonel's whisper became quieter. 'Some shadowy figures are coming out of the woodwork. My sources inform me that a number of racketeers and other undesirables from Russia and Central Europe were caught up in Maryam Vynckt's investments and suffered massive losses. Rafi, dear boy, a hornets' nest has been stirred up. Several of the large criminal organisations are seriously short of cash. They are furious, and intent not only on replenishing their coffers but also on revenge. To complicate matters, their competitors have noticed this weakness. A new playing field is being created. Former allegiances have been shattered and a war of attrition has started.'

He paused. 'Desperate people do desperate things. The stakes have been raised and they may have to think big to survive. Be careful not to cross their paths – they are in a dangerous mood.'

Rafi felt the colonel place his large hand on his shoulder. 'I have more bad news. Just before I left I was informed that the FSB have reopened their investigation into the death of Pinja Koit. They now think that the charred body in the plane crash was not his after all. Perhaps you could tell your people at MI5?'

The colonel's voice reverted to his normal deep growl. 'Great party, thank you, Rafi. Kristina has had a ball. She's very excited; it seems your sister has invited her over to shadow her for a couple of days' work experience; even offered to put her up. Say a big thank you to Saara for me. And, Rafi, remember, let me know if I can be of any help. You know where to find me.'

Rafi hesitated before replying; he was still taking in what the colonel had just said. Jörg Emcke's team were only in the preliminary stages of researching the financial grey areas and piecing together the web of cross-border crime syndicates. Colonel Matlik had given him another whole angle to consider.

Rafi turned around to ask him a question, but he had vanished into thin air.

Kate was standing nearby.

'Have you seen Matlik?' he enquired.

'Yes, he left a moment ago, just after chatting to you,' replied Kate. 'You look as if you've seen another ghost.'

Rafi took a deep breath. A sense of foreboding came over him. If Matlik was right and the criminal classes were about to flex their muscles, Jörg's team had two groups to worry about. On the one hand there were those whose finances had been crippled by their losses in the derivatives markets – they needed to make money fast. On the other hand, there were those champing at the bit to grab market share, intent on eliminating their weakened competitors. *And* on top of this, Kate and he possibly had two rogue bulls to contend with: Pinja Koit with his Chechen contacts, and Miti Lakhani about whom they still knew practically nothing. They would have to watch their backs. Unwanted memories of the Headland Hotel crept back into his mind. A cold shiver ran down his back.

Kate squeezed his hand. 'Are you alright?'

Rafi pulled his overactive imagination back to the present. 'Sorry, I was just mulling over something Colonel Matlik said. Oh, by the way, Saara has offered Kristina a couple of days' work experience and invited her to stay after she has finished her finals. Your introduction seemed to do the trick!'

'I'm pleased for her.'

'Have you seen Jeremy?'

Kate pointed to the back of the restaurant.

'I won't be long – there is something I need to ask him.'

Jeremy was sitting at a corner table talking quietly with Ewan.

'Am I interrupting you?' Rafi asked them. 'As it's work-related, would you prefer we chat when we're back in Luxembourg?'

'Not at all,' replied Jeremy. 'We were just catching up on a few matters relating to Maryam and her bank.'

Rafi sat down with his back to the room.

'We have managed to get into the bank accounts Maryam was using to fund the terrorist activities,' added Ewan. 'In some cases the payments go back over three years. She was using numbered accounts so at this stage we have not been able to put precise names to them. However, what has caught our attention is the series of large payments which first went to an Estonian bank account, but stopped and then started again a week or so later, but this time they went into bank accounts in Pakistan and Iran. We were speculating as to whether these accounts were linked to Pinja Koit.'

'Could I add something?' asked Rafi butting in. 'I have just been chatting to Colonel Matlik and he was telling me that the Russians – the FSB – have been looking into Pinja Koit's death. There seems to be considerable doubt as to whether he was on the plane that crashed.'

'When was that?' enquired Ewan.

'About fourteen months ago,' answered Jeremy. 'He makes a good addition to our team, doesn't he, sir?' added a beaming Jeremy. 'It seems Colonel Matlik trusts him more than you or me!'

Ewan nodded, deep in thought. 'Fourteen months ago… That ties in with the switch in the bank payments. So we can assume Mr Koit is still out there.'

'That makes sense,' added Jeremy. 'And when Radu Dranoff arrived to help Aslan Popovskaya, I bet it was Pinja Koit who arranged it. He must have been involved behind the scenes coordinating all the dirty work. As I see it, he was so incensed by you, Rafi, that he sent Dranoff to take you out. Unfortunately, I don't see why he shouldn't still be pissed off.'

Rafi looked shocked. He thought for a moment. 'How do you think Jameel Furud and Basel Talal's charity, the suicide bombers and Kaleem Shah fitted in?'

'I am not sure,' said Ewan. 'The attack on the atomic weapons establishment at Aldermaston and the style of Kaleem Shah's operation have had me thinking. I am wondering whether it was the terrorists' insurance policy to get the Iranians on their side.'

'Pardon?' said Rafi.

'Well, let us assume for one moment that the terrorists' plans had been successful; Maryam, the sheikh, Jameel and Talal would have become pariahs in the Western world and would have needed somewhere to go to escape the reach of our laws.'

'Hence Iran?' asked Jeremy.

'That is my thinking,' said Ewan. 'Especially as they are prevented from having any nuclear capabilities. Iran doesn't like being excluded from the nuclear club and they can't have been happy with the UK's decision to upgrade Trident. One set of rules for us and another for them.'

'So do you reckon Pinja Koit is in Pakistan or Iran regrouping?' asked Rafi.

'Yes; probably Pakistan,' replied Ewan.

'But they have one serious problem,' interjected Rafi. 'They will have lost their source of funding!'

'Good point,' said Ewan, 'but we shouldn't underestimate Koit's capabilities. I will bring MI6 up to speed and make tracking him down a priority.'

'In the meantime,' added Jeremy, 'if I was you, Rafi, I'd try and avoid dark alleyways – and that applies to Kate as well.'

'On the bright side, after Newquay, we at MI5 and the SAS owe you one, so we will do our best to keep an eye on you,' promised Ewan.

Rafi was about to reply, when Saara ambled over. 'So this is where you have got to!' She was beaming. 'Steve is making a real night of it. I doubt whether I'll get him home for hours. I've given Kate my set of keys, in case you want to leave before us. Last I saw of her she was looking for you.'

Jeremy smiled at Rafi. 'Let's chat some more back in the office.'

Rafi spotted Kate in the distance. He got up and shook hands with Ewan. 'Thank you for bringing me up to speed. If you will excuse me, I should go and see why Kate wanted me.'

'It has been a pleasure talking to you... And Rafi, please, remember to keep Jeremy in the loop with all your thinking. I sense that these are still treacherous times,' added Ewan.

Rafi, with Saara beside him, went off to find Kate.

Kate greeted him with a hug and a lingering kiss, and then jangled Saara's keys in front of his nose. 'How's about we say our remaining few goodbyes and then try out the new bed in your flat?' she asked.

'Great idea,' Rafi replied.

He looked at her smiling face and realised that she made him feel alive. He had traded the comfy and highly paid world of the City for the adrenaline-filled world of counterterrorism, and to his surprise he wondered what he had ever seen in his previous existence.

Then he saw in Kate's eyes the same fire that had burned that first night they were in Luxembourg and with a flutter of her eyelashes, any worries he had about the jeopardy that lay ahead vanished.